ELLIE IS AN IRISH AUSTRALIAN AUTHOR BASED IN Geelong, Victoria. She is the author of four novels, the first of which, *Reluctantly Charmed*, was a top ten Australian debut and a bestseller. Her most recent novel, *Family Matters*, was published in 2022. Ellie's writing has been described as charming, whimsical, funny and touching. To date, all of her books have been set in Ireland and she's not entirely sure why. Australia has been home for over ten years but her storytelling blooms from the streets of Dublin.

Family
Matters

Ellie O'Neill

ALLEN&UNWIN
SYDNEY • MELBOURNE • AUCKLAND • LONDON

First published in 2022

Allen & Unwin
83 Alexander Street
Crows Nest NSW 2065
Australia
Phone: (61 2) 8425 0100
Email: info@allenandunwin.com
Web: www.allenandunwin.com

A catalogue record for this book is available from the National Library of Australia

ISBN 978 1 76106 630 6

Set in 12/17.8 pt Sabon LT Std by Bookhouse, Sydney
Printed and bound in Australia by Griffin Press, part of Ovato

10 9 8 7 6 5 4 3 2 1

The paper in this book is FSC® certified. FSC® promotes environmentally responsible, socially beneficial and economically viable management of the world's forests.

For Hughie

1

Evie

EVIE MCCARTHY WOULDN'T SAY SHE WAS SURPRISED WHEN she came face to face with the Grim Reaper. A little shocked, definitely, but not surprised. The signs had been there, nudging her for months now, demanding that she pay attention. But she didn't want to, she wasn't ready. Who'd be ready for that?

Instead, Evie decided to stop draining her teacup a few weeks back when the tea leaves started to form a very clear pattern. She threw stones at that bloody magpie perching on the gate of her cottage, as brazen as you like, eyeballing her every morning. She ignored it when the painting of Kilmore Beach toppled off the mantelpiece one evening as she was watching *Coronation Street*. What a clatter it made when it fell onto the hearth, and how the glass glistened as it smashed into smithereens and mingled with the ocean spray on the shore of the beach. She had made love hidden in those sand dunes fifty-something years ago, huddled under a picnic rug when herself and Michael were newly engaged, fumbling and reaching for each other. It had been a little bit of a disappointment, the sex, Evie remembered, not Michael—being that close to Michael was always glorious—but the deed itself wasn't quite how the novels had made it out to be. They got much, much better at it as the years went on.

Evie had also turned a blind eye to the single snowdrop that peeped up under the oak tree in the back garden. A snowdrop in autumn only meant one thing. But it was proving more difficult to ignore the scent of roses that followed her everywhere: down the aisles of Tesco, into the changing room at aqua aerobics, it even lingered at choir class when she stood next to Sean Roche, the mushroom farmer, who hadn't changed his clothes in over a decade. Deliciously sweet, she could close her eyes and allow herself to drift into the magnificent aroma, to fall deeply under its heavenly spell. But that's what it wanted, wasn't it? It wanted you to just drift away into its comforting arms.

But Evie McCarthy had never been passive; she had never floated into anything. She was a woman who had always confronted her life head on. Wasn't it Evie who had rallied the women of her hometown Ballyhay to march on the streets of Dublin for divorce in the nineties? And wasn't it her who'd thrown a full glass of whiskey over John O'Brien and punched him square in the eye after he'd accused her of trying to fix a race? (He had been right, but that's beside the point.) And wasn't it Evie herself who called door to door to get donations for the Syrian refugees? She was a woman of action. So, she knew she needed to face up to what had been poking and prodding her for the last few months.

Evie slung her forest-green cardigan with a real fur trim that tickled her neck over her shoulders, fastened the top button across her chest, checked her bright red lipstick in the hall mirror, smoothed out her auburn curls and headed into the kitchen on a mission.

She'd found the tarot cards a few years back at St Columcille's school fair. They were on a bric-a-brac table with brightly coloured plastic toys missing pieces, and some of that awful chutney that Brigid Mahoney who ran the stall insisted everyone buy. Evie didn't remember picking them up but there they were in her hand as Brigid bagged up her chutney and called out for fifty cents.

They were beautiful, heavy cards, and when she clasped them Evie could feel the many hands that had held them before, hands like hers—knowing hands, seeing hands. The intricate designs wove their way around pictures, showing stories of journeys and golden chalices. She hadn't known what she was doing at first, how to lay them out, but she let the cards guide her, and over time they found their own pattern.

She gazed at the deck lying on the Formica-topped kitchen table, took a deep breath and laid her hands down.

'Are you watching, Michael? I just hope there's enough time to sort out our girls.' She shuffled the cards slowly, carefully, her mind and her heart focused on her daughter Yvonne and two granddaughters Molly and Rosie. Evie spoke into thin air, her words bouncing across the burnt-orange tiled floor of the kitchen. The sunniest room in her three-bedroom cottage, where her children had squished carrots into the floor, her grandchildren had streaked naked, where herself and Michael had drunk icy gin and tonics and mulled over the everyday.

She knew every corner of this room, the ghosts that walked it, the secrets it harboured, the memories.

Evie fingers stopped and she spread the cards face down in a half-moon shape. She paused for a moment, closed her eyes and allowed her fingertips to hover and slowly descend, sliding six cards out and away from the pack.

As each card turned over, there he was, in one form after another. Death was coming for her and he was coming soon.

2

Rosie

Rosie had been plucked, contoured and preened since 5.30 this morning for her two minutes of glory on *Sonya's Sofa*. Her dark hair was tumbling down to her shoulders in the manner of a fairytale princess. Her blue eyes were now hooded with false lashes, and while normally she had freckles popping up all over her face (years of riding horses), Rosie had been delighted to see that they had been painted magically away. She was suffocating in head-to-toe Spanx, lightly covered by a very expensive luscious cerise dress, which she had lovingly admired in her wardrobe since the spring. To wear it she'd dropped five kilos in six weeks and was now a size 12, thanks to a collection of rotten tasting strawberry shakes and a good old diet of apples and air. Simon had declared her to be utterly shaggable, which was great—obviously totally great—and would have remained great if she hadn't caught him leering over underwear models in g-strings on his phone, all vacant eyes and ribs poking at you. They literally looked like a different female species, one that she suspected ranked much higher on the shag-o-meter than her. But pink dress on, hair blown out and tummy sucked in, she looked great. Maybe even the best she was ever going to look, which quite frankly was a little bit deflating sitting next to the glorious Sonya.

'Just relax.' Sonya stretched across the deep, cushioned sofa and patted Rosie's knee reassuringly. She was so breathtakingly beautiful in person that Rosie felt an uncomfortable urge to reach out and touch her face, which would be wholly inappropriate and creepy. Rosie sat on her hands, not quite trusting herself, and wondered if Sonya's eyes would be described as jade. They weren't just green, they were leagues fancier than that. She was, however, very thin, Rosie mused, which maybe made her eyes look a little bug-eyed. Still, bug-eyes and all, it was working for her.

The producer she'd met earlier stepped between them, her face directly in Rosie's. 'Okay, remember camera two.'

She was wearing a headset, so Rosie wasn't one hundred per cent sure that she was talking to her, but she smiled and nodded because it seemed likely that she was. This was her moment after all; it may have been *Sonya's Sofa*, but the next two minutes and twenty-four seconds were all about Rosie. She checked her position on a nearby screen, legs crossed at the ankles like she was riding the couch side-saddle, her hands folded on her lap as if they belonged to a well-mannered nineteenth-century mannequin.

'Great name.' Sonya beamed at her. 'The app?' She raised her eyebrows in a question but no lines appeared. *Pumped with Botox*. Rosie sighed victoriously and then instantly felt annoyed with herself for being happy that a beautiful woman wasn't perfect. *We're all sisters together*, she reminded herself. Still, though, Sonya must be fifty but managed to look thirty. She had been Miss Ireland in the days when the host smoked cigarettes on stage and patted the girls on their bottoms in the swimsuit section. She was a fixture in gossip columns in Sunday newspapers when Rosie was growing up: married and divorced to a rock star, briefly a game-show host, a celebrity stylist and a Weight Watchers ambassador, which was clearly a ruse when you saw the skinny legged cut of her. You just knew she'd never worried about how many points were in a packet of Maltesers. More recently, Sonya had launched a hugely successful chat show on her own YouTube channel; the platform, her profile, her age shouldn't have worked, but in the current digital landscape of authenticity and incessant shoulder shrugging—why wouldn't it?

'The Love Guru?' Sonya strained across the couch to get Rosie's attention and slowly bring her back to YouTube-land.

'Yes, it's good isn't it? Pretty crap spelling, though—DeLuvGuru. But everything close was gone. It's amazing the way all these names get snapped up. I really didn't want a number in it or an emoji. You have to have some standards you know? Literature has really gone to the dogs, don't you think, Sonya?'

Sonya nodded but Rosie wondered if she really, truly shared her enthusiasm for the demise of literary standards. Rosie was babbling. She knew she was babbling. It was one of her least endearing traits, along with flicking her fingernails and an unbridled passion for *Dancing with the Stars*. No one had ever called her babbling endearing, at least to her face. Maybe behind her back people commented on how cute her incessant nonsensical stream of talking was, but she doubted it. It was particularly babbly when she was nervous, like now. The words just shot out of her. *That'll get you in trouble one day,* her mam always warned her. But sure, when did talking ever get anyone in trouble? Anyone who wasn't a politician or on TV anyway. Rosie eyed the camera lens peering at her, swallowed loudly and decided to clamp her mouth shut.

The producer's face appeared again, and she pointed aggressively to a screen. This was to be a live stream and one of the reasons *Sonya's Sofa* was so popular, popular enough anyway to have a producer and two actual cameras, which was two more than most phone-hugging vloggers.

'That's yours, camera two.' She started to walk backwards crouched down, like she was in the jungle camouflaging herself in the long grass from a herd of hungry lions. She adjusted her headpiece. 'We're on in five, four, three, two . . .'

Sonya grew about five elegant inches and purred into a lens. 'My next guest Rosie O'Shea is the founder of DeLuvGuru a matchmaking app with a difference that has dating apps quaking in their virtual boots. Is it true, Rosie? Are you about to change the dating scene?'

Rosie's answer was so rehearsed that she didn't even realise she was speaking. Her brain caught up to her voice a few seconds in. She was relieved to hear that she sounded good, and there was no sign of the squeaky, nervous choirboy who had made a few shocking appearances at the kitchen countertop during some late-night practice sessions. Rosie had the spiel down pat.

'I think we are, Sonya. We're offering services that the online dating industry hasn't even considered. We are the new wave. Our algorithms are incredible. Most dating apps out there, not naming any names—' smug smile, eyebrow raised '—just skim the surface. They're only interested in a tiny slice of who you are. They want to know your height, your hair colour, your bank balance, your location. But how on earth are you going to find your perfect match based on that sparse information? And anyway, let's be honest, most people bend their answers a little bit, stretch their height, slim down, try to make themselves sound more exciting. We're all guilty of that, aren't we?' Rosie paused briefly and looked to the camera, not to Sonya who surely wouldn't need to lie on her *I'm an ex-beauty queen* dating profile. 'But you know when you fall in love with the right person, they love you for you—the real you, the warts and all you, not the photoshopped version of you. So, at DeLuvGuru we need to know all of you, not just the information on a form you fill out with a few white lies, and the curated photos you send us. No, we want your online history, we want your data, we want your social media package. You literally can't hide anything from us. You might say that you like six-foot-tall blondes, but we will know from face mapping and your online searches that you actually prefer short statured men.'

Sonya interrupted her, eyes narrowed accusingly. 'It sounds a little bit invasive?'

It did. Rosie knew it did. And truthfully, she didn't fully understand how it worked. Your data, his data, her data, their data and magic. She preferred the glitter, the fireworks and the heart palpitations. But it worked, Simon said it worked, he had explained it to Rosie many, many times, and many, many times she had nodded in agreement and behind her agreeable half-smiling demeanour was utter confusion, white noise, and some type of scientist in a white coat throwing numbers at her. She didn't get it.

Rosie took a deep breath and rolled out the rehearsed answer. 'Not at all. It's your data so you have to agree to sign it over to us. We're just using what's already out there—with your permission. And when we have it, we spin it all together and boom!' She splayed her fingers out, just like she'd practised for dramatic effect. 'We find you your soul mate.'

'You think everyone has a soul mate?'

'I wouldn't do this if I didn't believe in it. I absolutely believe that before we came into this world we were split in two, and it's our life's work to find our other half.' This was true. She did believe this. Rosie was an incurable romantic. She teared up at coffee ads when the Italian waiter made 'come to the funfair' eyes over a creamy cappuccino at the dark-haired single mum who'd had a terrible morning and a bike puncture. Sometimes when she was feeling sad about life Rosie googled love letters just to be reassured that they were out there. That love was out there. A love that would make someone pour their feelings onto a page, or maybe write, *I don't ever want to imagine a world without you*, on a post-it note stuck on a fridge door. That was one of her favourites. It was perfect in every way. Rosie believed in love more than anything and had been in love more times than she could remember. She couldn't help herself. It was just so beautifully addictive. She dove in head first and didn't come up for air. Every time the opportunity arose, she chased those butterflies down. The heart-racing moment when you realise he likes you, the full-toothed smiles, the very first time you touch his hand. The glorious goosebumps of it all. Rosie was proud to say that since her first head-over-heels romance (literally, she met Paddy Stewart at the roller disco age fourteen and he'd held her hand around two wobbly circuits and asked her to go steady as she'd tumbled to the ground) she has never been single. There've been long-term and short-term flings, but there's always been a boyfriend. Rosie was happy about that because she firmly believed you had to trust in love and you never knew if one of those guys was going to be 'the one'. She'd had some near misses, too; there were always going to be a few bumps on the road. She'd thought she could have been on a path to being in love in college with Richie Fox during second year. But then he stole her laptop and the toasted sandwich-maker from her house-share to feed his greyhound racing addiction. Her flatmates literally didn't eat for days until Rosie's grant came in and she could replace it. Rosie bounced back very quickly, so she knew she couldn't have loved him, although unfortunately all these years later he was still omnipresent in the form of a tattoo of an Irish harp with Richie emblazoned across it on her lower back. It had faded and blurred and now looked like a dirty thumb print. She'd have to get it removed at some point. It was on her to-do list.

She paused, smiled and looked into camera two, hopeful and optimistic. 'There is so much noise in our lives that it can be difficult to find that person reaching out to you, and that's why at DeLuvGuru we're using technology to help get us there. What's the purpose of life if it isn't about love, huh?' Rosie felt like an old pro, she was loving it. The adrenaline was pumping around her body and her skin was tingling. She might even be good at this.

Sonya snuggled into the couch, seeming relaxed. 'Well, it all sounds nearly too good to be true.' Then she changed direction. 'Can you tell us a little bit about your grandmother? Isn't she a matchmaker? A traditional Irish matchmaker?'

Oh good, this question. Rosie was prepared.

'My grandmother is a matchmaker in Ballyhay—she's very well known, Evie McCarthy. Ballyhay is a small town in the midlands.' She pinched the air with her fingers to show just how titchy Ballyhay is. 'About eighteen thousand people live there. Two crossroads, one post office, two pubs, four churches.' She saw the neon light of Fresh Catch, the fish and chip shop, the milky tea in Elizabeth's Café, the bingo games in the town hall, the holy well of St Brigid that kept a stream of Holy Joes clutching rosary beads in olive-green anoraks frequenting Fresh Catch and Elizabeth's Café all year long. 'Traditionally, a lot of towns in Ireland had matchmakers to help people navigate marriage. I guess you couldn't travel around to meet someone, so a matchmaker would be brought in to help make introductions.' Rosie paused, knowing what she was supposed to say next but still found it odd and a bit witchy. 'It's considered a gift.' She wondered if the mysticism might snap, crackle and pop with Sonya. She seemed receptive, so she continued. 'My granny has always said she has a second sight and that's how she makes perfect matches. She meets people in the snug of the local pub, her pub—actually, well, now my mam's—and asks them to touch a book of names she has and then true love will find them.'

Rosie laughed at the silliness of Granny's little tradition and how quaint it sounded next to her algorithms and scientific explanations. She didn't mention that Granny charges a princely sum for her services—about double what you pay for a subscription to DeLuvGuru—and also ran a small betting operation on the side with Tommy Malone, a horse trainer who may or may not be known to fix races.

Sonya smiled, her eyes dancing with excitement. 'Do you have this gift?'

'Who knows?' Rosie shrugged modestly. 'Traditionally, this matchmaking gift is handed down from one generation to the next, along with the very well-worn leather book, but I think it's safe to say I'm more of a modern matchmaker. I'm bringing it into the twenty-first century and using a much more scientific approach than a handwritten book and second sight.'

'Well, I would like to meet your granny; she sounds like an interesting lady.'

You don't know the half of it, Rosie thinks.

'She really is. And she's a big fan of DeLuvGuru. She's given me all kinds of tips on matchmaking.' Rosie lied flawlessly, remembering their Skype call.

You're telling me people will pay for this? Ah no. It doesn't work like that? Ah no. Are you still with that Simon? Can he not talk any sense into you? That's not how you find love.

'So, you offer a true love guarantee?' Sonya smiled and somewhere behind her the shadow of a producer appeared, circling her finger in the air.

'We do. That's how confident we are in our algorithms. We *will* find your true love.'

'And if you don't, money back?'

Rosie shook her head determinedly. 'It won't happen.' She really hopes she's not lying. She really hopes this is true. Simon said it was. He said the algorithms have it worked out to a tee. We can do this. Imagine how great that would be to summon up your perfect match at the touch of a button? It was like something out of a sci fi movie. It would be incredible. It *was* incredible she reminded herself. This was happening.

Sonya piped up, 'Well, I wish you the very best of luck. The app launches today?'

'Tomorrow at twelve o'clock, midnight, but you can sign up now and be live tomorrow. We're so excited about this.' Her neck swung wildly, looking for a camera to gaze lovingly into.

Sonya and Rosie beamed at each other.

'True love awaits,' Sonya purred.

Rosie crossed her fingers behind her back for luck and said a silent prayer, *Please, God. Let it work.*

3

Molly

'RORY, STOP PLAYING WITH YOUR WILLY!' MOLLY ROARED across the playground, her words catching in the wind and falling flat somewhere around the slides. Rory didn't even look up from the sandpit, one hand busily digging a crater for his dinosaur and the other wrapped firmly around his willy.

I should never have called it a willy, Molly thought. It was always supposed to be penis, like a good mature mother would do. A sensible woman of the world would just name it; it's a body part—an arm, a leg, a penis. But she couldn't. Penis belonged to a big hairy man, a man with muscles and opinions, who could talk and drive and cook. Not this squishy little love-ball who was handed to her by a midwife, who smelt like heaven and had the softest kissable cheeks. He had a willy, occasionally a pecker, a todger, a wee wee, a pee pee. A myriad of names that will probably land them both in therapy at some stage.

'Rory!' She exhaled through gritted teeth. His two hands were now down the front of his pants. He was two weeks out of nappies, and two weeks into the discovery of his new excellent plaything at perfect arm's length. She really didn't want to get off her bench and walk over there. It was *her* bench. Molly deliberately got here five minutes before the town hall 'Mummy and Me' yoga session broke up. She moved her two children at hurricane speed to get out the door on time—*odd socks*, didn't matter; *wrong hats*, let's go; *forgot the snacks*, no problem. They'd swing into Andre's for a large latte with an extra shot and grab a muesli slice en-route. She was not going to give up this bench, she had earned it. It had a full three-hundred-and-sixty-degree view of the playground. You could even see under the slide where the kids set up shop and ate woodchips.

The yoga mums were circling in their floral lycra pants, pretending to stretch out like they didn't really want to sit. But she knew they had all clocked her, and the second she moved one tired butt cheek off her bench they'd pounce. She repositioned herself, took a sip of her latte and jostled Andy's buggy absentmindedly. At least he was asleep, she thought, that's good. Well, hang on, of course he's asleep; he'd been up half the night with her rocking him, patting him, shushing him, wiping away his little tears and then dosing him with Panadol because what else do you do with an eighteen-month-old who hasn't slept in eighteen months. Keep drinking coffee. Molly wasn't even tired anymore. She'd passed tired about a year ago; now it was just a haze of heaviness, like the air was a deep sticky mud and everything ran in slow motion.

'Sleep when they sleep,' the nurse had said kindly, patting her knee and pushing a box of tissues across the table when Molly had taken Andy for his twelve-month check-up four months ago, late, of course.

'But they don't,' she'd pleaded. 'They don't sleep.'

'Have you tried the shushing method?'

'Shush the fuck up?' Molly had blurted out, pausing through her tears to laugh at her own joke and then noticed the shocked look that appeared on the very young nurse's face and apologised immediately. 'I'm just so tired,' she said by way of explanation for her poor humour.

'You might want to take a look at some of these leaflets?' The nurse fanned out an assortment of advice on postnatal depression, eating well and reading to your baby, and pushed the postnatal leaflet to the fore.

'I'm not depressed, I'm not postnatal. I'm just tired.' Molly wiped back the tears and blew her nose. 'I'm fine. Honestly, I'm fine.'

'Do you have any help, family support?' the nurse asked.

'I do, I do. I just need to ask for it.' Dommo's mother was the obvious one, she knew this—her own mother was too far away in Ballyhay—but Angela was tricky. It had made sense at the time, buying a house four doors down from her mother-in-law. It was a lovely suburb in south county Dublin: well established with 'good types' already living there, lots of green areas, close to the sea and good schools. She had been pregnant at the time and this had been something herself and Dommo had emphatically agreed on—that their children, their many, well-behaved, beautiful children would attend excellent schools, they would be natural scholars, brimming with academic potential. It was still early days she knew, but the fact that Rory couldn't tell the difference between an apple and an orange and Andy called her DaDa did not bode well in the genius department.

There had been some bribery involved, too. Angela had *helped* them with the deposit. Well, actually, she had given them ninety per cent of it, the other ten per cent coming from a redundancy package Molly received from the Gas Board, where she had worked for five years. She had always planned on leaving when she got pregnant anyway, what with the cost of childcare being so outrageous—twelve gold bars and a mountain goat a day according to some reports—so the extra money was a windfall. And then it was all so disappointing. She had to spend it, all of it, *every last cent,* on a house deposit. She didn't get to buy those skinny jeans that she would fit into after the pregnancy when the baby weight had magically disappeared, or a pair of sexy high heels that would show off her newly slimmed-down feet, or all those organic soft baby gros, because her baby would only be dressed in organic cotton, or so she thought until she saw the price of it. It seemed like such a waste to put all that money into a house, when she had nothing really to show for it (except a house obviously, Molly knew this, but still).

Dommo had felt emasculated and guilty at the same time. He had always been terrible with money. He'd blown ten grand the previous year on tickets to the World Cup in Russia. Ireland had never had a chance of getting through, but Dommo and his mate Rich had talked about going since their school days. It was their dream, their childhood fantasy. Molly hadn't cared. It was his money. But when it was her redundancy, she really did care. Dommo knew this. They'd always been very good at knowing each other; he'd order an extra spring roll for her in the Chinese takeaway even though she said she didn't want one, because she always did. He knew when to make her a cup of tea in the evenings and when wine was needed instead. When her blonde hair looked frizzier than normal and two little red circles appeared on her cheeks and a hardness set in on her jaw, he knew he'd probably done something wrong. He knew when her chin wobbled, and she didn't talk to him for a few hours that she was going to have a meltdown as soon as the kids went to bed because she was so overwhelmed. When her hand fell on his thigh and she might raise an eyebrow there was a distinct possibility they'd have sex later, although that didn't happen very much lately.

Dommo promised her hand-on-heart that he'd get better with money. They'd smash through that mortgage and repay Angela. They were full of optimism about bringing the figure down, but it never happened. He tried desperately to get a promotion at work but that didn't happen either. He got a miniscule bonus for bringing a project in on time, and to celebrate he'd bought her the skinny jeans she'd wanted, but it was after Andy had been born and the baby books had lied and she felt destined to remain the size of a small hippopotamus for the rest of her life. So, she had thrown them at him and burst into tears. He returned the jeans and settled on a pair of opal earrings, which brought a smile to her face and much relief to him.

It had made sense. Angela was on her own and this would be her first grandchild. The woman had been a school principal, she said she loved children. There'd been a mixed response from Molly's friends who had commented that 'You'll be very close to your mother-in-law.' The obvious had been stated, 'Would that be okay?' Molly supposed it would; she didn't really know Angela, not really. Herself and Dommo called in most Sundays for a lunch of coleslaw and cold meats that looked a bit pink and sweaty, and sometimes a shrivelled-up quiche with the head of a broccoli stem peeping out of it. It was all very forced friendly, all a bit, *Excuse me, Thanking you, I'll clean up, No, you sit down*, clinking china cups and lace doilies.

Dommo remained solidly mute during these hours, folding his large frame into an armchair and tucking his chin into his chest, his eyes downcast like a naughty schoolboy. Molly never wanted her boys to be like that with her. She wanted them to be themselves. She didn't want to smother them but she planned to still hug them tightly even when they were six-feet tall, to tousle their hair when it was soaked in styling gel and to continue to kiss their cheeks after stubble appeared. She would always be part of their lives. Not on the periphery offering awkward lunches but in life with them whatever way it unfolded. She would be a Safe Place for them. Molly knew this, and she also knew that trust and love was built in the everyday—every knee scraped, nose blown, socks pulled on and off, stories read, all mattered.

'You're all weird when you're with your mam,' she said when they were lying in bed one Sunday evening, the city lights just starting to flick on around their titchy one-bedroom apartment. They always seemed to have great, vigorous and enthusiastic sex after the lunch. Whatever it was about those quiches they turned into pent up hormonal teenagers just dying to rip one another's clothes off. 'Angela acts like you're still eight years old. I can't believe she won't even let you clean up. I'd say if you dropped your dirty washing off, she'd do it.'

'You're right. I don't know what to say to her sometimes. She's always just fussing and telling me what to do, like I'm a child.'

'Dominic,' Molly put on a shrill voice pretending to be Angela, 'more coleslaw for my growing boy? Some ham? Some fruitcake? You'd need at least three slices of fruit cake.'

'Ah, would you stop. She's just Mam. It's just how she is.'

'You could tell her that you're a fully grown man?'

'She wouldn't believe me,' he'd laughed. 'That's just the roles we're stuck in—I'm the boy she's the mam. It is what it is.'

'You might get on better if she saw you for who you actually are.'

Dommo had sighed. 'Maybe. I don't know, I'm sure our relationship would be different if Dad was still around, he was great. She wasn't so uptight then.'

Molly felt her eyes prickle with tears, and she shifted up in his arms and buried her nose into his neck, inhaling him, somehow trying to breathe in the stinging heartache of losing his dad. She hated the world sometimes for making her husband sad, this good, honest, beautiful man. Why couldn't his dad still be here? She wrapped her arms around Dommo shoulders and squeezed him as hard as she could.

'She's alright, though, Mam. Just a pretty shit cook.'

'She means well,' Molly said.

And they settled on that, nodding in agreement in the dusky light, and then more kissing, and then more sex, which led them inevitably to ravenously dialling a pizza at ten o'clock at night.

Four years later, Molly wasn't so sure Angela meant well at all. In fact, she worried that borrowing the money from her was the biggest mistake they'd ever made. And if she wasn't so exhausted, she just might have to think about doing something about it.

'Those bitches can get lost if they think they're getting your bench.' Anna, Molly's favourite mum friend plonked down beside her. She had on her staple swish of bright red lipstick and a white woollen coat, a throwback to her days of working as a lawyer, despite the warmth of the early morning summer sun. It was the least mum-friendly coat any playground had ever seen, ever. She wore it with pride that screamed, *Yes, I am a mother pushing a buggy, but look at my coat—I used to be somebody that chaired meetings for million-euro companies before I spent my days stewing organic pumpkin and listening to True Crime podcasts.* Anna unclipped her daughter, Bev, from her City Jogger buggy and watched her toddle off. She fished into her handbag and produced a bag of rice crackers, offering one to Molly.

'I hate these things.'

'Me too.' Molly batted the bag away. 'They're rotten. No wonder the kids don't eat them.'

'They're like cardboard.'

'Organic cardboard.'

'Andy's asleep, that's good.' Anna gestured towards the cherubic-like angel dreaming deeply.

'If you're up all night, you're going to sleep all day,' Molly said, draining the end of her latte.

'Oh darling, what about a sleep nanny? Or that mother-in-law? Or Dommo? You know it's his sperm that did this?' Anna crumpled up the rice crackers and threw them into the bottom of the buggy.

'I can't even think about Angela right now, and Dommo is away for the next few days at some staff thing in Athlone. I don't even know what; I didn't ask him and I don't care.' Molly shook her head in dismay. 'Is that terrible? Am I a dreadful wife not to even care what he's at?'

'You're a mother of two babies. Of course you don't care what your husband is up to.'

'We couldn't afford the sleep nanny.' Money was so excruciatingly tight. There were no extras. No second car, no nights out, no holidays in the Canaries with salty chips and frothy beers. Just a mortgage on a house on the southside of Dublin.

'What about your mam? Yvonne could come down to help for a few days? While Dommo is away.' Anna was dealing with Molly's problem with corporate efficiency; there would be a solution.

'Well, Mam's so busy with the pub that she doesn't get much free time, but I do wonder if I could ask her for money. She's always very flash with the cash. Just a bit maybe for a sleep nanny, would that be . . . ?' Molly heard herself trail off. She didn't even know if she could make a clear decision with this deep fog enveloping her. Would that be a good idea? Or a terrible idea? She just might close her eyes for a minute to think.

'Oh dear, Molly, *Molly!*' Anna shouted, 'Molly, wake up! Oh, you poor darling. Right, let's gather up these terrible children and I'll watch them at your house and you, my dear, are going to bed.'

Molly woke with a jolt.

'This can't go on, Molly,' Anna said. 'Something has to change.'

4

Yvonne

YVONNE WAS EXACTLY EIGHT MINUTES INTO A FORTY-FIVE-minute spin class. A minute had never felt so long, and thirty-seven more was an eternity. She had her gears down to zero, and was essentially freewheeling, but it didn't feel like that. Her lungs were burning. How can they even do that? Surely, they're not built to burn? Where had all the air gone? She'd drunk half her water. When? In the last eight minutes? How was that possible? She'd have to save the rest of it, but God her mouth was dry. Her teeth felt dry and her tongue somehow bigger. *UP? She was getting up?* Yvonne watched as the instructor, Maria Manifold, rose up in her stirrups, and like a flower awakening into full bloom, exploded, her legs whirling in a torpedo-like frenzy as if she were powering the electricity for a small nation. Jesus, she wasn't human.

'Come on, team. Let's speed it up.' All that whizzing around, and she could still speak. 'If it's your first class, feel free to stay seated.' Maria Manifold looked towards Yvonne and winked at her. 'This is your class so go at your own pace.'

Yvonne wasn't sure whether she should feel insulted or relieved. She settled on relieved because quite frankly her bum wouldn't have been able to get up off the seat. Standing was not an option. And, smugly, she thought she had teacher's permission to sit, so she'd sit. But should she sit, really? This was all ALDI's fault. She never shopped there, and had no need for their German pickled gherkins or whatever it was they sold. She'd heard they had inflatable mattresses going for fifty euro that were like sleeping on a cloud, and she needed an extra bed in the house for when Molly came down with the kids. Rory was in a big bed now. So, in she popped. Five minutes was all it was supposed to be so she didn't even bother with a trolley; all she was getting was the one item, she was popping in. *Pop, pop, in, out.* But lo and behold, the middle aisle caught her eye and before she could say *gut buster, leaf blower and three-step ladder*, she had grabbed and loaded up a trolley and got into a polite ladies-who-lunch style tug of war with another woman over a wooden train-track set on special. Yvonne had won, flashed a smile, mouthed a thank you, and balanced the box precariously on top of an indoor herb garden as she pushed the wobbly trolley towards the check-out. She probably shouldn't be buying so much as she didn't need any of it except for the mattress, which she hadn't been able to find. But sure, it was for half nothing, she could put it on the credit card.

'Yvonne McCarthy, I don't believe it.'

'Maria Manifold.' Her name was there. It spilled out of her, even though it must have been forty years since she'd seen her last.

'You look exactly the same.'

Yvonne immediately shook her head in denial. 'No, no, no. But you—' she felt herself squinting '—do.' Now to be fair, Maria Manifold looked like a much older version of her eighteen-year-old self, deeply tanned and with more lines. There were angles to her face that Yvonne didn't remember. But her rather wiry hair was still a chestnut brown, and her smile just as broad. 'You still look exactly like Maria Manifold.'

'Well, I've been Manifold, Clerkin, O'Sullivan, almost a Murray and now I'm back to Manifold.' She squeezed Yvonne's arm. 'I should have just kept my maiden name. I won't be making that mistake again.' She threw her head back and her laugh reached right up to the fluorescent lightbulbs. 'God, it's been years. How are you?'

And this time it was Yvonne who laughed. How was she nearly forty years later? She had swum through oceans and was still out of her depth. 'Well, I'm not smoking rollies round the back of the chippers anymore, and I haven't drunk a can of Ritz since 1980.' Yvonne had a wonderful flashback of them as schoolgirls: white shirts, ties askew, lipstick applied at the school gate where the nuns couldn't see them.

'Oh, we were terrors, weren't we? Our poor mothers.'

'We couldn't wait to grow up. All that hairspray.'

They both smiled fondly, and Yvonne was sure she could smell Impulse body spray, the toxic rose-tinted fumes of her adolescence.

'I never went to any of the old school reunions, did you?' Maria asked.

'A few, at the beginning, and then I moved to Dublin and you know how it is. I kept in touch with some of the girls for a while—it's easier now with Facebook.'

'I know, I used to have to get the town gossip from Mam, now I can get it online.'

'How is your mam?' Yvonne had a flash of Mrs Manifold at school events a hundred years ago, looking like a much more overweight grumpier version of the woman standing in front of her.

'Dead. Passed away eight months ago.' Maria instantly shushed away the sympathetic look Yvonne was giving her. 'Honestly, it was a relief. She'd had Alzheimer's for years and we were living with a shell. It was horrible and sad but, you know, life.' She'd blinked back the tears that rimmed her eyes, took a shaky breath and then broke out into that same smile again. 'That's what brought me back to Ballyhay. I never thought I'd return here, sure all I wanted to do as a teenager was run away from the place. I inherited the house. I was going to sell it, but I couldn't bring myself to put it on the market, and before I knew it, a few weeks ago I'd a moving van come from Dublin and I'd unpacked.'

'Back on Johnstone Street?' Yvonne marvelled that she remembered the house, but then she did used to cycle past it regularly in the hope of spying Tommy Manifold, Maria's older brother.

'That's it. And you? Are you back living here? Weren't you . . . ?' She was actively searching the cogs in her brain, desperately looking for what Yvonne had once been—a model, a Dublin socialite, a doctor's wife . . .

Yvonne stopped her. 'I took over the family pub, McCarthy's, about three years ago.' In truth, I came back with my tail between my legs, looking for a new life in an old one and making a mess of it all, driving the family business into the ground. 'Now I'm back behind the bar, pouring the pints. It's in the blood, I suppose, you can't escape it.' She forced a wide smile.

The town felt so different to the town of her childhood and it looked different too. The main street still curved along the river bend; the town square still housed a monument to the 1897 uprising; the flour mill which had once upon a time employed over half the town, and had been converted to a hotel twenty years ago, still loomed large on top of the hill. But shopfronts had changed, different languages were bouncing down the aisles of Tesco's, far-flung nationalities weren't just passing through, they'd settled. There was money, too. It had never been a wealthy place but now BMWs parked next to Land Rovers were blocking up Main Street. Yvonne could see a charm to Ballyhay that had been invisible to her when she was younger. The parochial town that she'd found so stifling as a teenager was welcome to her now. She liked that she knew her neighbours. And the town was quaint, something that the locals were proud of. They hung flower baskets from lampposts; buildings on Main Street were freshly painted in bright colours every year; there was a pride in the community and its modest achievements. Ballyhay was a lovely place to live.

Maria paused and her eyes widened. 'You had that husband? Brandon was it? A doctor? Remember, I met you both—it must have been twenty years ago—at a drinks party in Dublin?'

Yvonne shook her head, she couldn't remember that night. There had been so many cocktail parties and events herself and Brendan had to attend. They all blurred into each other.

'I could have talked to him all night. He was a delight. And I remember afterwards saying to my friend that I needed to find a man who looked at me like he looked at you. Has he opened a practice in town? Small towns always need more doctors, if you ask me.'

Yvonne felt her colour rise. It was three years later and she was still unbearably uncomfortable describing herself as single. 'We're, eh . . . not together anymore. We're separated.' Although Brandon wouldn't be separated for much longer. He was re-marrying. Was that the right word or was it just marrying? Did people conveniently drop the 're' out of respect for the new bride? Patricia, that was her name, her ex-husband's fiancée.

Rosie had handed her the heavy cream invitation card a week back. *They'd really like you there, Mam.* Her daughter had looked so young and naïve. Yvonne had accepted the invitation with a head shake. Not a chance.

Maria nodded knowingly and raised her eyebrows to the ceiling. 'Life, hey?' She sighed. 'You're the very same, Yvonne.'

'No, I'm not.' Yvonne tugged on her light summer jacket, which had taken a beating in the rain outside but stood up well, grateful that she could zip it up to the neck, hopefully disguising her double chins. She was glad, too, that she'd had her hair done recently. The roots were blonde and not the silvery blonde she insisted to herself were a type of blonde and not a type of grey when she couldn't summon up the energy for hairdresser chitchat. 'I feel like a very different person.' She sounded so sad, she heard it herself. She never spoke like that, never in the darkest moments, into her deepest self, had she heard herself sound so sad. Where had that come from? She was completely thrown off guard, but Maria reached out and caught her.

'Nonsense, she's still in there. We all are. Us Lady of Mercy girls need to stick together.' She rummaged into her handbag and thrust a flyer into Yvonne's pocket of her padded jacket. 'Come to my spin class on Thursday and we'll get a coffee after.'

It was the kindness in her eyes that caused Yvonne to nod. The genuine empathy that was almost unsettling. 'I will. I promise.'

Yvonne hadn't been in a gym in years. She'd never had to exercise when she was younger. Way back when, exercise wasn't good for you, it was just about not being fat. Fat was the only reason to work up a sweat. There were none of these endorphins, nobody spoke about the benefits for mental health or the general business of staying alive—it was just about fat or not fat. And Yvonne had never been fat.

That long lean body had served her well. She thinks of it fondly, like an old friend who had died too young. She remembers turning up for a Dunnes Stores underwear shoot at a posh hotel in Dublin, and being the only model that laid into the buffet table, heaping the ham sandwiches and lemon drizzle slices onto her plate. The other models had looked at her in horror, but Yvonne hadn't even known she wasn't supposed to eat, that as a model it was her duty to be in a constant state of starvation. So, she ate, and she continued to eat right through her career. She laughs to herself. Career? Would she really call it a career? It was five years at most. The summer she finished school, before the leaving certificate results, before her epic exam failures were common knowledge and her father would either kill her or force her to repeat another year (he may as well kill her). She had taken the bus to Dublin and marched into a modelling agency, brimming with bravado and naivete and smelling of at least a can of Impulse. If she had a job her dad couldn't make her repeat; she'd be bringing in money and there was no arguing with that.

Yvonne thought maybe she was good-looking. People had always told her she should model, but they also said it to Johanna Feely and she looked like the backside of a horse. To be fair, in a tiny town there wasn't that much competition.

The well-manicured fearsome-looking booking agent told her with a swift appraisal that she had *commercial appeal*, whatever that was. What it meant in reality was that the phone in the house didn't stop ringing with bookings. Within nine months she was making enough money to rent a room in a flat in Dublin with two other models and they never once exercised. Never did so much as take a walk around the block.

She did do aerobics classes after Rosie was born, that was when the weight started piling on. Was that really twenty-four years ago? Had she not exercised in twenty-four years? Was that even possible? No, surely not. There must have been brisk walks and sit-ups somewhere along the line. There were definitely chips, lattes and buttery croissants. Just keep on pedalling and stop thinking of croissants. Pedal, pedal, pedal, and try to remember, she thought, that woman up there winning the Tour de France is the same age as you.

Keep up, keep up. She should be able to keep up at the very least. She knew this. She would not be adding spin classes to her very long list of failures. No. No. She wouldn't give in, not yet, anyway. There were more serious battles ahead to test her.

5

Evie

WIGS HAD REALLY BEEN EVIE MCCARTHY'S SAVIOUR. THAT sounds shallow and silly, and yes, she believed she was a little bit of both those things. She had found it soul-destroying watching her hair thin out as she got older. She didn't have the aches and pains that she heard other people her age moan about—she was in good health, never better really—but her hair, it was so . . . disappointing. Evie had stormed out of Klassic Kutz, the local hairdressers on the main street of Ballyhay, ten years ago when Carmel, her hairdresser of two decades, had suggested a perm, *a perm, like an old lady perm?* The rage had inflamed her and Carmel had witnessed Evie's blind anger. How dare she? Her mother had had a perm. Evie was not an old lady, her hair was just failing her. Clearly Carmel needed to upskill if she couldn't see this. Evie took matters into her own hands, and with the help of her granddaughter Rosie, found a very fancy website in America that sent her Lucille

Ball–style wigs. As far as she was concerned, it took twenty-five years off her. Evie had built up quite a collection over the last decade. What she liked best, she supposed, was the consistency in the colour—a vibrant, luminescent titian and shades of auburn. She had been a natural red head, and then a bottled one, and now without her wig a balding one, but nobody needed to know that.

She hadn't gone back to Klassic Kutz, but heard from her friend Maura that they'd opened a nail salon at the back. Maura's nails were painted lilac with a shimmering silver, and they were breathtaking. Evie knew she wouldn't be able to do that herself even with a YouTube tutorial. She just adored the practical advice those videos gave, but no, she may have to consider swallowing her pride and visiting the salon. Maura had assured her that Carmel didn't do the nails, it was a young Brazilian girl who was very professional. She could just snub Carmel at the desk and storm on through. She'd have to think about it.

Tonight, Evie was wearing a loosely curled bob, with a medium bounce. As always, her lipstick was red, and she had applied pink blusher. Her nails were painted coral and every finger wore a jewelled ring. Her mother had taught Evie never to leave jewellery in a box, always wear it. What use was it in a box where you couldn't show it off? Her charm bracelet hung off her wrist, and her neck was adorned with a collection of gold chains of various thickness. She was ten minutes early to the pub, McCarthy's. She was always ten minutes early. It gave her time to relax, set the scene and most importantly be in control. The bar next door sounded quiet. She could hear the dull chat of some customers, the occasional clink of a glass hitting the counter—eight or nine people she reckoned. Occupational hazard. When you'd spent a lifetime behind the bar, it was hard not to tally the takings in your head. You didn't even need to count, it was just there. McCarthy's had been Michael's father's pub. It had stood in the town for over a hundred years, on a side road off the top of Main Street beside the supermarket. The building was painted white with *McCarthy's* in bright red letters over the door. The sign had always been in red, as far back as Evie could remember anyway. There were flower boxes on the front wall just beneath the windows, which were shades of amber and sea-blue stained glass so no one could see in. Michael had to buy out his two brothers once his father had passed. It had caused no end of disagreement, but it would have always been his. He'd been serving pints, collecting glasses, charming the customers since he was knee high. It was fitting, she supposed, that her daughter Yvonne was back behind that same bar. It was her pub now. Evie had signed it all over, lock, stock and Guinness barrel for the princely sum of one euro. She was happy to, and there was no argument with her son in Singapore—he'd never shown a bit of interest in running the pub. She was a little surprised that Yvonne had wanted to take over McCarthy's. Her life had been away from Ballyhay for so long, but of course Evie was glad to have her back.

Evie had done the hard yards behind the bar, too; and back in the day she'd also looked after the books. That was where she had really sparkled, keeping the figures in line, weighing them up and watching how they soared when she opened up a little sideline business—taking bets on the greyhound races initially, and then the horses. It wasn't strictly legal but back then an awful lot of business was done with a wink and a nod and a handshake full of cash. The locals were delighted; it saved them taking a trip down Main Street to the bookies where they might have been spotted by their wives. This way they never had to leave the comfort of their pint and Evie was a model of discretion, especially as her side business grew more and more profitable.

Evie loved the snug. It was her favourite part of McCarthy's pub. A little cosy section that played host to multi-coloured, stained-glass windows and pine partitions. The tiny room was completely secluded from the rest of the pub in a discreet corner and could fit eight people on its two wooden benches at a push. It still had access to the bar. Traditionally, snugs were only for women to keep them sheltered from rowdy menfolk, she supposed, or more likely to stop wives spying on husbands or vice versa. McCarthy's snug had its own entrance onto the side street, so the wives could slip in and out unseen. It served as the perfect spot for Evie's business where discretion was once again everything. She poured some tea from the pot in front of her into a delicate china teacup, enjoying the noise of the pub and soaking in the atmosphere. There was a small plate of biscuits laid out, Jaffa Cakes and Fig Rolls. She'd told Yvonne not to bother, that she wouldn't touch one, but now she wasn't so sure. She did love a Jaffa Cake and knowing what she now knew, there was very little point in worrying about her diet. Her blood pressure and her cholesterol could go to hell. She might as well die happy. If she couldn't eat a biscuit now, when could she? Evie grabbed one, rammed it wholly into her mouth and bit down hard, enjoying the sugary explosion and sticky and sharp textures. There would be some perks to the next few months after all.

'Mrs McCarthy?' A pink-faced man hurriedly removed his flat cap and bowed his head reverentially.

Evie had seen this before, sometimes people thought she was hallowed, or saintly or priestly even. She'd had women kiss her fingers and touch her feet. It depended on her mood really how she'd respond; occasionally it was nice to be treated extra specially. Tonight wasn't one of those nights, though, and she felt matter of fact about the business at hand. 'The very one. Paul, isn't it?'

'Aye, Paul Glynn, but people around here know me as Paul the pig farmer.' He pulled at the edges of his ancient tweed jacket and shifted his large frame uneasily from side to side.

'Take a seat, Paul the pig farmer.' Evie gestured to the bench opposite her and smiled trying to put his nerves at ease. He was in his fifties, she guessed, never married. He had the ruddy complexion of a man who worked outdoors. His wide hands resembled a pair of shovels and were scrubbed clean, but the calling card of farm work left a dark sliver of dirt under his nails. He hadn't needed to mention the pigs because she could smell the livestock on him. She'd try and keep this meeting brief.

'It's fifty euro up front for the first consultation, and one hundred and fifty when I match you.' Evie clamped her lips shut. She wouldn't utter another word until the fifty euro was in her purse. She'd been in this business long enough to have learned more than a few tricks.

'Of course, of course.' Paul rammed his hand into his trouser pocket and removed a wad of cash, folded fifties that almost made Evie speak. Almost. He slid a note across the table, nodding as if it were the fatted calf. 'I've just come from the market, and well, we sold well, always do in the month of August for some reason.'

Evie shook her head dismissively, pretending not to be impressed by the money, and slid the note with great speed into her purse. 'Now, Paul, tell me about yourself,' she asked, but she already knew all about him. Or rather she knew all she needed to know. Evie had, what her mother had always called *The Knowing*. There was no voice speaking into her ear, telling secrets about the person in front of her, she just knew. She knew their essence. She knew who that person really was inside of that body they'd been put in. Underneath the layers and layers of labels they'd given themselves and the world had thrown at them, Evie knew their soul. Some were buried so deeply they were harder to find; people who lost themselves in trappings—too rich, too poor, too unhappy. The soul was always there, it could be a flickering ember or a roaring fire; regardless, Evie would find it. Like this man in front of her, Paul Glynn, he was easy to see. She knew he was a good man, a gentle, kind-hearted soul and that he was ravenous for love. He wanted to give his love to someone. He was brimming over with a pure, beautiful heart. Evie sighed happily, sometimes she loved what she did. She let Paul speak.

'I suppose I always thought, I mean everyone always said, you know, the right woman will snap you up, she'll be along in no time. And, I dunno, I believed them. I thought maybe she'd just knock on the door one day, or something. But I'm fifty-four, Mrs McCarthy, and she didn't come along, and now I've no wife, never had one. And I'm too old now. I won't be wanting children. I'd just like to have someone at home for me.' He slapped a meaty hand to his forehead. 'Oh no, not home waiting for me, I don't mean that. She can work all she wants. I mean someone who cares if I come home, and I care that she does, and I'm happy if she's happy. And maybe we could go to Rosslare for a weekend, if she'd like that.' He never shifted his eyes from a spot on the table, the line of his mouth was downcast and serious. 'I've plenty of money. I've seventy-five acres all me own, and no one's coming to take it. After mammy died two years ago, I inherited the lot.' He brushed at his cheek and Evie could see he was crying. It was hard for him to talk about himself. 'Mammy took care of me my whole life. I minded her in the end, it was the least I could do, I didn't want her in a home. But maybe, you know, maybe she minded me too well, you know, that I never had a wife.'

Bingo! thought Evie. Well, at least he can see it. Good that Mammy's out of the picture, too, because Mammy is often the problem.

'So, I like women with dark hair, and you know slim figures.'

'I'll stop you there,' Evie interrupted in the manner of a strict schoolteacher. 'That's not how I work. You don't give me physical attributes. You love the person for who they are, not for their hair colour.'

'Oh yes, of course. I'm sorry about that.' Suitably reprimanded Paul shrank at least three inches back into his seat.

'Now, I'll get you to put your name in the book.' Slowly and with a certain degree of ceremony, Evie unzipped an oversized tote bag on the chair to her left. She placed two hands around a large leather-bound tome and heaved it onto the table. The dark brown leather was worn at the sides with a shiny smooth cover where bumps and ridges had been faded away by caressing fingers. The pages inched out unevenly, jutting forward through the edges of the front, showcasing their heavy cream colour and thick texture. The book must have been one hundred and fifty years old. It had been handed down from Evie McCarthy's grandmother, an original town matchmaker. The first few pages of names were barely legible, some signed with Xs, as a lot of people wouldn't have been able to write back then.

'Just here.' Evie pointed to an empty space and watched as Paul excitedly lifted his biro and scrawled his signature. She closed the book. 'If you can just place your two hands on the cover for a few seconds, please.'

Paul took a deep breath, closed his eyes and hovered his hands over the battered old book as if he were preparing for a séance. 'Like this?' He peeped at Evie through one narrowly open eye.

'On the cover.' She let maybe thirty seconds pass. 'That'll do.' Evie slid the book into her tote.

Paul looked brighter, happier somehow than when he'd walked through the doors of McCarthy's. This often happened, people were so delighted to unleash their heart's desire. 'So, how does this work? Do you set up a few dates?'

'No, there'll be one date, one woman. I'll get her for you. And I'll keep you informed.'

He looked confused. 'Will it be this Saturday? The sooner the better.'

'It won't be that quick. Be patient. Paul, you've waited fifty-four years for the right woman, so give me a bit of time.' Evie knew you always had to set parameters for people. 'And I'll call you, don't call me.'

'Right so.' He stood to leave, adjusting his cap back onto his wiry-haired head.

Evie crossed her arms and leaned further onto the table. 'And Paul, with that money in your pocket, get down to the leisure centre in town. Use the steam room and the showers in there and then go to Fallons menswear tomorrow and buy yourself some new clothes, top to toe, shoes, socks, underwear—the works.'

'For my date, like?'

She nodded.

'Hang on a minute, you said she's to love the real me, not the physical attributes.'

'True, but women have certain expectations.'

'I can't say that I like girls with dark hair, but I have to get new clothes.' He looked genuinely confused.

Evie sighed. 'It's very hard to find the real you to fall in love with, Paul, underneath the smell of pig shite.'

His faced crumpled, and he released a soft noise and nodded slowly. His mouth rose to a half smile. 'You're some woman, Mrs McCarthy, that's for sure.'

She smiled back and waved him off, laughing quietly to herself as the door shut behind him.

Her phone buzzed in her bag. She pulled it out and saw it was a message from Rosie.

I'm a YouTube sensation Gran.

Evie clicked on the link which took her to YouTube. She could see her gorgeous granddaughter sitting on a couch with a blonde-haired woman with big lips.

'Yvonne.' Evie knocked on the bar counter and shouted into the bar, 'Come have a look at this!'

Yvonne turned at her name, her blonde hair tied up in a loose bun at the top of her head, her make-up applied perfectly around her large almond-shaped blue eyes. Hearing her mam calling, a warm smile spread across her face to reveal straight white teeth. She marched up the long counter, pulling at the denim shirt that stretched across her middle. Evie knew her daughter was beautiful, but she wished Yvonne could see it for herself and understand that carrying a bit of extra weight didn't suddenly take that beauty away.

'Come on, let's watch this. It's Rosie.'

Yvonne clapped her hands together with excitement and held them up to her face. 'This is the sofa thing, Mam, that I was telling you about. She's launching the app on this.' She grabbed the phone from Evie and held it up to her nose. 'Doesn't she look amazing? Oh, she's a beautiful girl, I'm so proud.' The tears welled up in Yvonne's eyes.

'Would you stop with the tears. She might fall off that sofa, for all we know. Play the damn thing.'

And for two minutes and twenty-four seconds they watched in awe as Rosie O'Shea knocked their socks off. They stared at the screen in stunned silence.

'Well, she's a natural,' Evie said resolutely.

Yvonne's eyes had fully misted over. 'You got a mention, Mam.' They both laughed. 'Sure, I'm famous, too.'

'She gets it from me. I'm sure of it,' Yvonne giggled.

'And me. Don't be selling me short.'

Evie leaned across the counter and grabbed her daughter's hand, squeezing tightly. 'Our Rosie's a wonder.'

'Isn't she?'

'Now hook that thing up to the TV and play it in the bar. Let's tell the world about our girl.' Evie heard a catch in her voice.

'Are you okay, Mam? You've gone all teary.'

'Have I?' Evie patted her cheeks and lifted her eyes to heaven. 'It's wonderful for Rosie, I'm thrilled to bits for her.' And she was, she absolutely was, but she also had a horrible realisation that she wasn't going to be around to see what happened next. Time was passing far too fast and she did not feel one bit ready for what lay ahead.

6

Rosie

ROSIE SLID INTO HER DESK LIKE A STEALTH BOMBER, ARTFULLY tapped her laptop keyboard and activated the screen. Her eyes darted around the office; had she been spotted? She was only ten minutes late, but Serious Steve was onto her, especially after she took the day off yesterday.

During her third interview of five at CRUSH a year ago to enter their graduate program with Steve and Amanda (who is currently off on stress leave primarily caused by being in such close proximity to Steve), they harped on and on about what a great work environment there was at CRUSH. They were all about balance, lifestyle design and flexible working hours. Rosie had nodded with such enthusiasm she thought she'd put her neck out. There was yoga, a meditation room, foosball tables, bake-a-cake Friday, every employee was entitled to sessions with a personal trainer and use of the company gym. This sent Rosie's brain into a spin. It was true that she had never set foot in a gym before, they were too expensive and, you know, sweaty, but this new job would potentially create a new her. She had visions in that interview of how her life would play out. Power suits, many of them, in a rainbow of different colours to choose from, and with her new gym-honed body she would wear them with sleeveless blouses and she'd also have a light tan. Shoes, high ones, in which she would clop fiercely around the building, with bouncy hair, real leather handbags and a dewy complexion from all of her zen meditation and a balanced emotional self.

What they failed to mention in that meeting was that the work never stopped. There was no time for all the yoga. The foosball tables gathered dust, the gym was frequented sporadically at daybreak, the meditation room was occasionally used for nervous breakdowns and a quiet little cry. The only free hours in the day for the essential 'me time' that the company encouraged was left for non-productive things like sleeping. There were emails after midnight, there was weekend work, there were crumbs on laptops from eating a quick lunch, there were deadlines on top of deadlines and projects that Rosie found suffocating. Stick that on top of launching a sideline matchmaking app business, and Rosie didn't have to wonder where the dark circles under her eyes had come from.

CRUSH is an online retail megastore. It employs four hundred people in its Dublin office, which is its European headquarters. You name it, CRUSH sells it. Rosie works as a content writer for the fashion division. She was originally writing for household items, but there are only so many ways you can describe a shiny new kettle before your brain freezes. Now she writes blogs with keywords that Google will find. She also invents names for women's fashion items. Bizarrely, giving a dress a name sees an increase in traffic. Old fashioned girls' names were going well this season, The Emily, The Addison, The Niamh. Rosie searched names and slapped them onto designs that seemed to fit. She wrote product descriptions for them that all seemed similar but just different enough: The Alannah, *floral patterned, flouncy chiffon dress with delicate buttons and a sharp v neck, perfect for summer bbqs when paired with a wedge heel and boater hat.*

She loved CRUSH. She loved working there in spite of the pound of flesh they demanded from her. CRUSH had been more educational for Rosie than the five years she'd spent at college propping up the bar and photocopying small forest-loads of paper. Besides, she had grown very fond of most of her overstretched and exhausted co-workers and loved their occasional karaoke nights out.

Rosie looked down at her runners and white blouse. Her hair was pulled back into a tight ponytail and she had on no make-up. She was wearing mum jeans. She knew she couldn't really carry them off with her strong and sturdy child-bearing hips, but still, they were comfy. Not a power suit or flouncy chiffon dress in sight. Her marvellous work wife, Catriona, was currently waving discreetly at her from the other side of the desk, beaming happily. Holding a notepad in her hand, she got up, shook out the braided dark hair that fell loosely onto her shoulders and walked purposefully towards Rosie.

'Rosie, I need to have a word about the spring/summer collection!' she shouted across the office just in case Serious Steve was within earshot.

'Sure, pull up a chair,' Rosie replied at equal volume, and straightening up her screen, she locked eyes with Catriona and stifled a giggle. 'I'm delighted you brought it to my attention.'

Catriona sidled up to her and murmured, 'I think Serious is in a meeting. Haven't seen him in about twenty minutes.'

'Relief.' Rosie visibly relaxed and she sat back on her chair.

'Can we talk about your YouTube success? You were amazing.' Catriona's big, dark eyes were dancing with excitement. She was always a supportive friend, the kind of friend who didn't forget sugar in your coffee and would send a pic of an outfit/handbag/shoes she thought would be perfect for you.

'Would you stop?' Rosie never could take compliments. She knew you were supposed to say 'thank you' and smile politely, but God wouldn't you look awfully big-headed if you just said that? Anyway, she didn't think she was a natural, at best she was probably okay. She had done what she was supposed to do, what they'd practised, so that was the important thing. 'I haven't even watched it. I don't want to hear my own voice. I know I'd sound like a newsreader, trying to be all posh but with a cold and a stuffed-up nose. I mean I can't even listen back to my voicemail message. I will never watch that clip.'

'Mam watched it, too. She thought you were ace.'

'Tell Phil I said thanks.' Catriona was one of a growing trend in Dublin of twenty-somethings who can't afford to leave home. The media dubbed them boomerang kids, but that implied they'd actually left home at some point and maybe gone somewhere sunny before returning of their own free will with inappropriate piercings and a phone full of photos. It was a lot less exciting in Catriona's case—college debts and insane

Dublin rents made it impossible to break free. She got on great with her mam so that helped. Rosie doubted herself and her mother would go so well. Not that it was an option, what with her mam living in Ballyhay. They were polar opposites: Rosie was decisive and organised, a list-maker who did her Christmas shopping in September and never ever bought at full price; while her mam had been known to max her credit card on getting her chakras realigned and would spend days trying to decide what colour to paint her nails.

'Coffee? I'm going to be here until midnight anyway to make up for yesterday, so what's another fifteen minutes?' Rosie said, feeling a mixture of defeat and rebellion. 'Love this dress combo, Catriona. Is that The Sarah?'

Catriona did a little shoulder shuffle as she stood to her full height, a willowy six foot. The Sarah was a pale blue, high-necked fitted dress, which popped against Catriona's brown skin. She'd paired it with dark leggings and runners, giving a streamlined effect that showed off her slim waist.

'It'd be up my arse if I didn't wear it with leggings.'

'Am I supposed to feel sorry for you having Amazonian legs?'

Rosie turned to Mark, her desk co-pilot and another graduate hire. 'Coffee?'

He wobbled his head and they both watched his tight curls dance. It was mesmerising.

'I've just got to . . .' Mark pointed to his screen. He had a habit of letting sentences just hang in the air and drift off on a summer breeze. It was infuriating. As was his inability to collect coffee mugs from his desk. He also had difficulty chewing on an apple like a normal human being. Rosie tried to be the bigger person but sharing a desk with Mark had many challenges.

She glanced at his screen and nodded, ignoring the Excel tab at the foot, which she knew was what he was really planning to work on. Mark was organising a gamers' convention in a field in Louth in four years' time—Gamerz Ink. It promised to be a super geekfest, complete with installations and celebrities from the gaming world, whoever they were, and probably people dressed in costumes. To be fair, Rosie was in absolute admiration for Mark's meticulous planning. His spreadsheets, which he had taken her through, ran for forty-seven tabs. Literally, there wasn't a stone in the county that he hadn't upturned, examined and put into play.

'I'll get you a white coffee, yeah?'

She didn't wait for a response. Herself and Catriona walked towards the kitchen area across the light-filled, open-plan office that overlooked the lazy flowing River Liffey. The floor was decorated with bright red and green graphics and motivational quotes from what looked like a random Instagram feed. The tip-tap sound of fingertips on keyboards followed them, no eyes flickered in their direction as they moved past, all heads bobbed down in fierce concentration.

Catriona whispered to her, 'Friday's deadline got moved back to Thursday yesterday, on top of next week's deadline which was pushed back to Wednesday.'

'Eugh,' Rosie murmured, understanding the intense pressure her colleagues must be under. 'They'll have to cancel the ping-pong tournament again so.'

They both smirked in acknowledgement of the fake playground the company projected.

Catriona found some cups in the kitchen and started banging the coffee machine. 'Hooray, the beans are already ground. I always mess it up. Latte?'

Rosie had started opening and closing cupboard doors, searching for some biscuits. There were energy balls, sugar-free nut bars, protein snacks, but not a straightforward biscuit laced with evil sugar to dunk in her coffee anywhere. A Thai green curry last night had seen her officially throw the towel in on her diet, she'd reached a size 12 and couldn't see what all the fuss was about. She looked the same as when she was a 14 only with a distinct glint of starvation to her eyes. Dieting was not for her. As she popped her third spring roll into her mouth, she'd told Simon she'd just buy bigger clothes and that would be the end of that. Predictably he'd raised an eyebrow and mumbled something about the gym, which she ignored. Sometimes it was hard dating someone with a six pack. She'd discovered extensive cultural differences.

Rosie grabbed two nut bars, resigned to the best of a bad lot. And made a mental note to start bringing in her own biscuits again.

'I got an email this morning from DeLuvGuru saying it's live at midnight tonight.' Catriona grinned, she was one of the four hundred and thirty-six people who had pre-registered for the app. Rosie had been shameless about promoting DeLuvGuru— she'd relentlessly battered social media and spammed herself into oblivion. People from primary school were invited, friends of her sisters, ex-boyfriends' families, the women who work in the local Tesco's. If at some point in her life Rosie had breathed the same air as them or knew someone who did, an invite was sent.

'There'll be another email this afternoon with a link to download it. And then we're off.' Rosie touched her hand to her chest in disbelief.

'Seriously, you've no idea how excited I am to get going on the app.' Catriona handed her a mug and lowered her voice. 'I am so sick of dick pics and these idiot men who think it's okay to send them. You think you're having a normal chat with someone and then boom! There's a penis on your phone. Like, who thinks that's okay? Who?'

'Ah, come on, it's not that bad out there?' Rosie loved Catriona's dating stories, which were fuelled by drama and only loosely based on actual facts.

'You've no idea, Rosie. You don't know how lucky you are with perfect Simon and his Prince Charming hair. He literally ticked off your entire list. Do you know how impossible that is?'

Many moons ago, a brief weekend in-between boyfriends and concerned that Cupid may overshoot his arrow, she compiled a detailed list of her perfect man. And while Simon didn't read feminist literature or wear beige woollen cardigans on Sundays, he did check off a surprising number of essential criteria.

'But he is old, though. Like he's *old* old—thirty-six. He's the oldest boyfriend I've ever had. And there's the app, which is kind of weird, considering we've only known each other three months. Like it's definitely unusual to be in a business with your new boyf, you know?' Rosie always downplayed her relationship for Catriona as she didn't want to come across as settled. Which she wasn't, like they hardly even knew each other, like *knew* each other. She'd fail a Mastermind quiz on him, definitely.

Catriona unwrapped an energy ball and inhaled it while looking decidedly unsatisfied. 'You're like some power couple— you're the yin to his yang.'

'The app is mainly his business. I'm just the mouthpiece because of the matchmaking stuff and Granny. And he's kind of out of it, it must be his age, like he doesn't know how to use social media properly. He asked me what a meme was. I just didn't have the heart to go into it. And in a weird way he's kind of shy.' That was an understatement, Rosie remembered the fight when she had said she would not be the face of DeLuvGuru. For all her mouthiness, Rosie hated the thought of exposing herself to the evil trolls of this world. Simon had assumed she'd want to be the spokesperson. Well, that was a bit of a jump—it was more of a case of how much he really, really, ashen-faced, sweaty palms, voice quivering did not want to be the mouthpiece. Rosie had been puzzled by his shut down. It was his company, although 7000 euro (her entire life savings, which may not be a lot of money for some people, but for Rosie O'Shea, who'd been squirreling away her babysitting money since time began, it was everything) had bought her ten per cent of DeLuvGuru. It made sense, Simon explained, because neither of them could draw a salary from it for the first year. This way, having company equity meant that Rosie wasn't working for free.

To be fair, Simon was doing ninety per cent of the work, because it was his baby. Honestly, Rosie didn't even under-stand how the back-end worked, so by rights it should be him promoting the app. But with the matchmaking family link and her natural ability to talk the hind legs off a donkey, Simon had persuaded her. It took ten days, four bottles of red wine, three takeaways, and a promise of a weekend break as soon as things died down to finally get her to sign on.

And she was enjoying her momentary dance in the spotlight. Her phone had experienced a mini-earthquake trembling with congratulatory messages since yesterday. She was amazed by some of the names that had crawled out from the past, most of them were friendly and supportive. It was social media that had the potential to bruise, so she stayed glued to that with one eye open, tweeting back, smiling and high fiving, doing her very best to stay positive and so far, so good. Twenty-four hours into her spin under the disco lights and things were going well. There seemed to be enough pissed off singles out there, like Catriona, who were looking to try something new. They had swiped, and grinded and were tired of putting their best face forward. The prospect of someone matching them up, the real them, was appealing. And how romantic? Rosie was a dewy-eyed mess over what it might mean for lonely and lovely singles.

'Do you think you'll get rich?' Catriona drained her cup. 'I think you will. Maybe you can be my boss and hire me to make coffees, because this one is pretty good.'

Rosie shook her head. 'It'd be great, I suppose.'

'Well, if this takes off, you could go global, we can all move out to Silicon Valley together, and you know, do whatever people do there in the sun. So, that would be nice.' She smiled, gathered up their cups and popped them in the dishwasher. 'In the meantime, I can't wait for you to sprinkle some of that magic matchmaking dust all over and find me a man!'

Rosie nodded. 'Honestly, Catriona, and I'm not even joking, you are the app's number one priority.'

'Good.' Catriona looped their elbows together and they started walking back towards their desks. 'You're not allowed to be getting all up yourself now.'

'What do you mean?'

'Well, perfect boyfriend, amazing best friend, business entrepreneur. It's a lot to handle.'

Rosie nodded. It was a lot. She knew it. Things were working out for her. 'It's like my life is a movie.'

'A horror!' Catriona joked.

'A romance.'

'With a twist in the tail?'

'God, I hope not. I really hope everything stays as it is and we all live happily ever after.'

Catriona's shoulder bumped her. 'Dream on, sister. In the real world there's always a villain around the corner.'

7

Molly

MOLLY WAS AT THE KITCHEN TABLE NEGOTIATING A WEETABIX deal with Rory that would vex even the most skilled politician.

'Where are the nappies?'

She heard a faint call-out from Dommo, like an eagle's cry lost on the wind. She chose to ignore him. Well, not quite—she whispered to Rory, 'Silly Daddy.'

'Mols.' A louder, more irate shout came from the bedroom.

'The nappies are where they always are,' she said in a sing-song voice, 'in the easy-to-find pouch on the side of the nappy table. Daddy knows this.'

'Mols.' Third time's a charm, except for when it's not. She heard his footsteps hoofing down the corridor. He appeared in the kitchen, a naked Andy cradled in his arms. Dommo was already dressed for work in a pale blue shirt and navy pants, his dark curly hair was still a little wet from the shower, and he had a shadow of stubble across his jaw line. He hadn't had a chance to shave yet. His soft brown eyes darted around the room furiously searching. 'Are they in here?'

'What?' Molly looked up doe-eyed and innocent.

'The nappies? I've been shouting for the last twenty minutes for them.'

'Oh, and I didn't jump to your request?' She splayed her hands out in front of her indicating her current Weetabix-based battle.

'That's not . . . oh Jesus.' They both watched as Andy spouted wee magnificently like a fire hose on a mission all over Dommo's work shirt. He held him outwards and a pool formed under Dommo's legs.

Molly sighed. 'It's all over the floor now.'

'And you know, *me*.' Dommo handed Andy to her like he was a live grenade. 'I'll have to get changed. I'm going to be late.'

'You're fine. You've still time.' Molly blew kisses onto Andy's round cheeks. He squealed in delight. She hooshed him onto her hip and sauntered into the boys' bedroom while Dommo stomped around the house now looking for a clean shirt. 'The wee will dry out in the car—it's not that bad,' she shouted, while taping Andy into his nappy and sliding him into leggings and a t-shirt.

'I can't go to work with wee on my shirt.'

'Of course you can. You work in IT, no one's looking at you.'

'This'll do.' Dommo was in a wrinkly, pale yellow shirt, which looked to be missing a button. 'It's a bit creased.' He bent in for a kiss.

'It's perfect.'

'I'll shave in the car.' Dommo grabbed a bag sitting at the foot of the hall door like an unloved dog on his way out. 'I told you I'd be late back, meeting on this new project. They're squeezing the delivery dates.'

Molly nodded and ushered him to the door, propping herself against it she watched him slip on his shoes and absentmindedly tuck his very crumpled shirt into his belt. He kissed her again, and she smiled at him.

'Bye, lads,' Dommo cried into the empty hallway. 'Love you, baby.'

She nodded and closed the door after him, answering, 'Love you, too,' to the door latch.

Good sense of humour was her number one desire in a partner, so her dating profile had read all those years ago. They'd met on match.com, a precursor to Tinder. She'd quite liked dating and the conveyor belt of men the site threw at her. She was a discerning shopper. And then Dommo came along with his dark curly eyelashes and a smile that would stop traffic. She remembers being dazzled by him—his charm, his humour. They'd sat across a rickety table in a pub on seats that had yellow stuffing poking out of its cushions and ordered pints of cider and salt and vinegar crisps until closing time. As the barman shuffled by putting chairs on tables and flicking lights, Dommo asked her straight out if she'd see him again. She was the cat who ate the canary—a gorgeous, straight-shooting guy liked her. And that's how she always felt when Dommo was around. He was a loving partner, kind and generous, an adoring father who may not be able to find the nappies in the morning but would spend Saturday crouched on all fours as a dinosaur that gave dino rides all over the garden.

She heard some tinkling sounds coming from the living room. Rory had somehow managed to turn the TV on, which she was impressed with, as previously he'd used the remote control only as a boat for his monster trucks. Delighted with himself he was jumping up and down in front of the well-spoken pigs.

Molly couldn't stop herself smiling. 'You are a clever boy, Rory. Maybe we'll watch a bit.' She snuggled down onto the couch with Andy on her lap, who was bum-wriggling to the music. 'TV at this hour of the morning probably stunts your growth or something but we'll buy you shoe lifts for your eighteenth.'

An hour, maybe two, passed in a Peppa Pig daze with square-eyed contented children. Molly even got to scroll through social media uninterrupted. She wondered why she didn't invite TV into their early morning lives more often. It was on most afternoons. She knew she should probably turn it off, but then what?

The door clicked and a 'Yoo-hoo, only me' shattered their peace. Angela. Molly had completely forgotten about Angela. Angela never forgot, and Angela much to Molly's regret, had her own key.

'You've the TV on? At this hour?' Angela was in the living room before Molly could wrestle the remote off Rory.

'Literally on two seconds, one second even.' Molly was up, wiping the sleep from her eyes.

Angela bounced across the room to the TV set in her lilac floral leggings and pink zip-up top, her blonde ponytail swishing from side to side. She leaned across and switched the off button, to Andy and Rory's wails of utter consternation.

'We don't want our boys turning into couch potatoes, do we? I've just come from the gym.' She shook her shoulders and rubbed the front of her thighs showcasing what was indeed a rocking sixty-two-year-old body. Her eyes landed on Molly's loose black t-shirt hanging over her yoga pants. They were her good yoga pants in spite of the fact that they were maternity yoga pants and had never once seen the inside of a yoga class.

'You're not ready? I would have done an extra class if I thought there was time.'

'No. No. I'm ready.' Yes. She was bringing Andy for vaccinations. No. She was not ready.

Angela stared at her stony-faced, then slowly turned her gaze to the boys. 'Come on, let's go play outside, get some fresh air into those lungs while your mum gets herself ready.'

'Yes, thank you, Angela, thanks for being here. Five minutes.' She quickly checked her watch.

'More like two.' Angela smiled tightly and spun around to look at the kitchen. 'Maybe I'll just get the breakfast things first, I suppose you haven't had a minute.' She peered at the Weetabix debacle on the kitchen table. 'And is that a spillage?'

Eugh, Andy's wee. That was still sitting in a puddle two hours later.

'I'll get it, not to worry. I'll be two shakes of a lamb's tail.' She hurried herself around with forced speed.

Molly couldn't bring Rory with them to the doctor because he went hysterical when they even drove past the entrance to the clinic. It was not worth the drama, so she had called in her mother-in-law. Angela with a spring in her step, who'd raced into early retirement to enjoy Pilates five times a week, cycling with the Over 50s Back Wheelers on a Saturday, and rigorous hill walking on a Sunday with a singles group. Although who would ever find love racing up the Wicklow Mountains in Gore-Tex and sensible boots with ruddy complexions and a flask of tea was beyond Molly. Dommo's ex-girlfriend was in the walking group. Herself and Angela had remained friends after the relationship fell apart. She was also a teacher, a *real career woman* as Angela would say, apparently nothing at all like stay-at-home Molly. *Ruth has a marvellous figure from all the hill walking. She just bounces up the mountain, it's no bother to her. Still single you know, up for assistant principal role at her school.* And she'd throw a wistful look at Dommo.

'Any thoughts of going back into the workforce, Molly? I'm sure you could pick something up here and there now the boys are bigger.'

'I work in the home, Angela.' Molly sighed.

'It's good for a woman to work.'

Stop it. Molly wanted to shout but didn't. *Stop. It.*

In the early days, herself and Dommo would have laughed about the put-downs, but these days the niggles grated on her. It was tiresome. Judgy Angela was exhausting.

Molly was sure that Angela had never in her life turned the TV on in the morning or lounged in maternity pants eighteen months after it was acceptable to do such a thing. But she was reliable, and she was free. And a bitch, an absolute bitch.

Andy sucked happily on a lolly in his buggy. He was, Molly thought, decidedly brave for a one-and-a-half-year-old. He hadn't flinched and had kept his eyes fixated on the lolly when the smiley nurse had jabbed a long needle into his chunky thigh. Molly, on the other hand, had held her breath and bit the inside of her mouth to stop herself from crying. She was meeting Anna for a quick walk around the park that was in between their two housing estates.

After Andy was born, Molly joined a breastfeeding support club. She had the feeding down but wanted to meet more mums in the neighbourhood. As it turned out so did Anna. And as every mum in the group whipped out a boob and attached their little one, Anna had produced a bottle, expertly sprinkled in powdered formula and given it a shake. Molly remembers the jaws dropping like dominoes. Unperturbed, Anna had announced to no one in particular, 'I hated it, I hated breastfeeding. It just felt like another assault after the birth. No thank you. Not for me.'

Molly exploded in giggles. She shouted across the room, 'You know this is a breastfeeding club, right?'

Anna replied, 'I used to go to raves and never do drugs, what's the difference? A club is a club. I brought my own baby.'

'You did, and she's very cute.'

'And the formula hasn't poisoned her, imagine that?'

And with that a friendship was born. An honest one where everything was on the table from haemorrhoids to mothers-in-law.

'I can't win with Angela,' Molly moaned to Anna.

'You'll never win. You took her precious son.' Anna moved at full speed around the leafy park. Her legs taking long, powerful strides as she pushed the buggy in front of her, she was a woman on an exercise mission. The sun had broken through the clouds and the daffodils leapt to greet it, raising their shiny heads to the sky in adoration. The trees clung to their summer greenery even though the end of summer was looming and autumn was knocking.

'It's true, I won't like it when my boys' partner up. No one will be good enough.' Molly was wheezing slightly, struggling to keep up. Either Andy had packed on the kilos or she was a lot more unfit than she thought.

'That's the spirit. At least you can see things from her perspective.'

'She's so judgy. The way she looks at the state of the house, like she's appalled that it's a mess.'

'She had Dommo. She knows what kids are like.'

'Yeah, but Angela worked the whole time . . . She doesn't get what I'm doing.'

'You're different people. She needs to respect that.' It was obvious what Anna was saying, Molly knew this, but she could never imagine asking Angela to respect her choices. That was how people in movies spoke with lighting filters and false eyelashes; not real people, especially not daughters-in-law like her who tried hard to walk the careful family line. She was fairly confident that conversation wouldn't end in a Hollywood hug.

'The boys love her, all that energy from hill walking. And she's always sharing photos of them with her friends. I get stopped by women in the neighbourhood telling me what a proud grandmother Angela is. But then I ask her to babysit and you'd think I was looking for a kidney.'

'She likes the job title, but not the job. You could confront her but you'd upset the apple cart?'

'It's family, it's all complicated. She's Dommo's mam. I can't tell her to go to hell, and she's on her own.'

'So, you put up with Angela for him?'

'Isn't that what you do in a marriage?'

'I suppose so, that and the sporadic free babysitting,' Anna said, sounding decisive. 'You can't underestimate that.'

'Do you want to call around for a wine this afternoon?' They had started a Mums' Afternoon Wine Club a few months previously with a view to meeting other like-minded mums in the neighbourhood. Initially, they approached a few likely candidates from kindergarten, and a few who had seemed like jolly, friendly types from the playground. But it had been a mistake. While many mums liked to joke on social media about drinking wine—they posted funny memes about wine o'clock, and martinis at breakfast—they didn't actually want to join a Mums' Afternoon Wine Club. In fact, many were quite horrified at the prospect. Molly and Anna were not to be deterred, however, and continued to fly the flag with at least one afternoon a week spent in the other's house, draining a bottle of chardonnay. The club, they insisted, was open to other members as soon as they could find them.

Anna shook her head. 'Can't, sorry. I'm going to that women in business lunch in the St Stephen's Green Club. Even though I'm not officially a woman in business at the moment, I will hopefully be one again someday, so it's a good networking opportunity.' She brought the buggy to a complete stop and spoke into the wind. 'Listen to me, networking opportunity, what am I like?'

Molly couldn't help but feel a pang of jealousy, which she immediately tried to suppress. Molly suspected that Anna had always been a high-powered type. She was a lawyer and child rearing was just a blip on her radar; she'd be back in the workforce at some point, Molly knew this. It just felt like Anna had somewhere else to go, another life waiting for her, whereas this *was* Molly's life: endless walks around the park and hunting for rice crackers in the bottom of buggies. It's not as if Molly had ever even liked working in an office; she had been bored witless most of the time. She had spent her mornings planning her lunch (mentally debating a tuna roll versus a toasted bacon sandwich) and her afternoons dreaming of her dinner (Chinese or Thai takeaway with Dommo), only to be interrupted by sending emails, answering phones and some filing. But still she did wonder if she had taken it seriously, even for a nanosecond, would she be climbing a corporate ladder now? Probably not. A degree in fine art had been a lovely, pleasurable couple of years, but it didn't allow for much in terms of real-world experience. Still, she thought it would be nice to swing in to a café for a latte on your commute, to have a whole twenty minutes to yourself on a bus listening to a podcast, to wear smart-looking clothes, shirts and lipstick, even a pair of heels. Her feet had grown half a size in her last pregnancy, who knew that that could even happen? That a baby in your belly could cause your feet to grow. Molly had felt so betrayed by her body. She had drawn a curtain on her high-heeled shoe collection after that, like a coffin slipping through the velvet drapes at a crematorium. It was over. She would never wobble a night away in her size 8s again.

'That sounds good, you should go. We can drink wine tomorrow and you can fill me in.' Molly hoped she sounded like a supportive friend, because she wanted to be one. It wasn't Anna's fault that Molly had never got her career off the ground, and besides, herself and Dommo had always agreed that she'd stay at home and raise the kids. That was of course before they'd had kids and it seemed like a laugh.

'Oh, it'll just be full of power women pretending they're doing it all and nailing it. Although, I do think some of them are, if I'm honest.'

'Kids?'

'Yes, but they'll have nannies and au pairs; they'll have worked out some balance.' Anna looked to be mulling something over.

'Well, good for them.' Molly caught up with her and power-walked side by side. 'I've got that number for the sleep nanny by the way, I'm going to call her later. It's all change, Anna, all change.' She laughed.

The sleep nanny cost three hundred and fifty euro for a consultation and two visits, and Molly had decided to ask her mam for it. Just for some help. She always seemed to have plenty of money. Gifts arrived regularly for the boys, often impractical outfits with velvet trims and detachable fur collars that would make Little Lord Fauntleroy blush. Molly was sent dresses as well—wildly expensive ones that she had nowhere to go in. Her mam was a shopper, she liked to spend, so hopefully she'd like to loan, too. Molly could also try her dad, although he was often tighter with the purse strings. She knew it wasn't that much money to anyone else but herself, and Dommo just didn't have any spare cash.

'Check you out, power woman.' Anna picked up the speed as if that was even possible, and the two of them motored their way up the hill.

Molly would put the wine in the fridge when she got home. She'd put the boys down this evening and lounge on the couch.

She'd open some of those peppery crackers and blue cheese that Dommo loved. She'd surprise him by still being up when he got in late from work. Even if they just stayed up for an hour, they could pull some chairs out into the back garden, and enjoy the bright evenings while they still had them. She'd be able to tell him the good news about the nanny. Molly felt cautiously optimistic that with some sleep, some snacks and some time together, they could reconnect and get back on track. She knew their wheels had come off a little, but surely they were easy to reattach?

8

Yvonne

YVONNE WIPED A TOWEL OVER THE BAR COUNTER AGAIN. IT ran the length of the pub's two rooms and it shone back at her. She was over halfway through her morning routine: she still had to do a quick vacuum, water the flower baskets and dust the lounge. She spritzed the mirrors with Windex and ran a cloth over the ornaments behind the bar: the battered old teapot, the map of Ireland, the tiles with Irish witticisms. *Be yourself, everyone else is taken. Oscar Wilde.* She'd liked that one so much she got it printed up and framed in her own house. All the patchwork pub memorabilia that was familiar and interesting, that gave cause for pause and conversation from the many people who approached the bar. She'd already decided to skip the bottle polishing, that only needed to be done once a week anyway. Kegs of Guinness and Heineken were being dropped into the cellar by a very nice young German man called Hendrick or Helmut. She'd asked him to repeat himself and still didn't catch it second time around, so she'd smiled politely, muttered something about it being a lovely name and directed him to the cellar. As the door sprung open a smell of hops fizzed in the back of her nose. It was always on her, the scent of the pub. Even during all those years that she was in Dublin, she could still conjure up the air of her childhood: the musty, heady smell with the lingering effects of cigarette smoke that never left the furniture. She'd catch a waft of a memory and it felt like home. Her dad propped on his elbows, cigarette dangling from his lip, white shirt sleeves rolled up, discussing the football and allowing his voice to rise and fall as the ball had. Mam in the snug reading cards or talking horses, herself and her brother on high bar stools with colouring books and then later behind the bar pulling pints.

Yvonne had hung the chalkboard out the front, admiring the sunny day and looking out at the hustle on Main Street. The tourists were in. They'd be staying in the caravan park on the river, wearing their summer clothes and getting Irish tans, t-shirt marks firmly in place for the last of the summer sun. The board announced today's lunchtime special: chicken and leek pie and chips. There were five pies left in the freezer, they would probably all go, but if not, she could have one for dinner. They weren't great: soggy pastry, springy chicken with a grey mulch sauce. She had to admit the chips saved the pie. It was her own recipe. They were treble fried—oh, the badness of them was delightful, crispy and delicious—and served with lashings of chicken salt. Yvonne was proud of the chips. She'd inherited the pies and had to get rid of them. The previous manager had stocked the pub freezer with bulk buy pub food and pre-paid food orders with an iron clad agreement that Yvonne had tried and failed to get out of, so every few months the food turned up: rubbery lamb shanks, indecipherable pies, curdled chowder. Nothing that Yvonne would ever normally serve up. She liked to think of herself as an amateur chef. She even once considered applying for a bake-off style program, but by the time she'd figured out how to position the camera on her phone to a flattering angle, the desire had left her. Regardless, she had to sell these Michelin flat tyre pies. Tomorrow it would be their even poorer cousin, the frozen beef burgers, and the day after a freeze-dried stir fry. She couldn't afford to cook the food she'd like to and she knew she had to sell out the freezer first, but she could see the bottom of it now so that was good. Maybe then she could start a new menu, if the pub was still going. Yvonne felt the parasitic knot in her stomach that had arrived six weeks prior as a letter from the tax office had landed on the doormat. *How had she been so stupid? Why did she ever think she could run a pub? She'd only ever been a housewife, or a model, fat lot of use that was to her now.*

Yvonne thought she'd be up for it. Her dad had always said that the pub was about the people and the atmosphere they created, and that the tone of the pub was lost and found in the publican. It was as simple as that.

Except it wasn't as simple as that, was it? It wasn't just happy chat and bubbling pints and bacon fries. It was spreadsheets and invoices and bills and borrowing money to pay off someone else and taking out another loan and begging the tight-lipped bank manager with a pole up his arse for an increase to her overdraft. It was falling deeper and deeper and deeper into a black hole until a giant tax bill landed on the floor. Yvonne had managed to dodge the tax man for three years. It wasn't much of a victory. She'd only been running the pub for three and a half and now there was nowhere to run. *FINAL WARNING* shrieked at her in big, bold, red print and so did the amount of 22,643.00 euro. It was so far out of her reach it might as well have been a million euro. She knew only too well that selling some chicken and leek pies at lunchtime wasn't going to make a bit of difference. Still, she had to do something, didn't she? Other than what she had done, which was to rip the letter up into tiny pieces of confetti and throw it in the bin. *Take that, you bunch of robbers.* They wouldn't be hearing from her anytime soon.

The pub had practically landed in her lap just as her marriage was ending. Her mam's latest pub manager had once again failed to meet her expectations. *He wasn't a McCarthy*, she'd explained. Yvonne had listened and found that she was slowly concocting a plan of her own and it involved the pub. She had been leading a long and painfully silent war. She had decided to leave Brandon. It had been a slow realisation. No dramatic moments, no broken dishes, or illicit affairs. Just sad, tear-stained and gut-wrenchingly painful emotions when she finally understood how utterly miserable she was in the marriage.

'I'm tired of living your life.' That's what she told him that fateful night.

'What?' His face had paled, she remembers that. He went as white as the wall behind him. 'Can we . . . What are you . . . I'm exhausted, Yvonne. I've had surgery all day, and this . . .' He looked at her suitcase in the hallway where she had stood waiting, frozen to the spot for the past two hours, the camel-coloured coat buttoned up to her neck. 'I don't know what this is.'

'This is exactly what I'm talking about—you're exhausted, you've had surgery all day. It's always about you. I'm always making your life easier, but what about my life? What about me?'

She'd watched as he'd had to steady himself against the hall table. His breathing got so heavy she worried he'd keel over.

'Can we talk about this, Yvonne?'

'No. You'll just persuade me to stay, and I don't want to. I want to be me. I don't want to be part of you, of this.' She'd had a whole speech rehearsed with lots of wise words and strong feminist references, but no, in the moment *I want to be me* was all she could muster.

He had wobbled again and bent his shoulders forward like he'd been hit in the stomach. It took every inch of her resolve not to rush to him, gather him up and settle them both on the couch, saying it was all a mistake.

'But you never said ... I had no idea you were unhappy. Yvonne, I don't understand.' He genuinely looked perplexed, which amazed her, and somehow gave her the strength to go.

'It's been years, Brandon. You've never listened to me. You've been so caught up in you, and I can't do you anymore.' She was proud she managed that sentence, she thought it sounded like it was out of a movie. She doubted Brandon even heard her, though. He seemed in shock as she gathered her bag and headed for the door. No tears from either of them. She was surprised at that.

'I'm sorry and you should be sorry, too.' That was her parting shot as she fumbled for the latch.

Leaving a marriage that was one person's decision, after a lifetime of compromise, was a singular blow, she knew this. She was ending a game when the other player was only halfway through, cruelly closing a door on all their memories and experiences and colouring their past. She was leaving. She was saying that this moment was finished and another awaited. Yvonne wanted another life. She didn't want to be someone's wife anymore, not Brandon's wife, not anyone's wife. She didn't want a joint bank account, she didn't want to consult someone about the little things. She didn't want to be married. She wanted her own money that she had made herself. She wanted to paint the walls of her house red and not have to discuss it with anyone (well, she didn't really want to paint them red; she wanted white, plain simple white walls and white floorboards and white couches). She wanted to order Chinese and leave the takeaway boxes out overnight (she did it once and admitted to herself immediately it was a mistake, the house reeked of black bean sauce). She wanted to do things on her own, not as a couple, or a family, she wanted to be Yvonne McCarthy again. She couldn't remember who *she* was, she hadn't been *her* in thirty years. Back then she'd been gorgeous. Oh, she still had the pictures—she was feisty, confident, funny, she had her own money in her pocket and a wardrobe full of stylish clothes. And then along had come Brandon O'Shea in his yellow Toyota. An earnest medical student with bright blue eyes and a tweed jacket. He asked her to dance at a party and then devotedly didn't leave her side for thirty years. They'd been too young, she'd decided as she waited in the hallway on that fateful night, they'd married too young. She felt she'd never had a chance to develop into a grown woman on her own. Or at least that's what she'd landed on. That's what she'd been happy telling herself for the last few months. That Brandon had suffocated her. It was his style of loving to control. He did love her she'd never doubted that, but she didn't want to be under his protection anymore. She wanted to be on her own, open to opportunities. She wanted to be herself.

With her suitcase and her camel-coloured coat, Yvonne had gone straight to Ballyhay and resumed her position behind the bar of McCarthy's, happy and contented. She was home. She was choosing her own life and had never been more certain that she had done the right thing.

And how life laughed, because right now with that tax bill screaming at her Brandon was the one person she wanted to talk to. She knew exactly how it would play out, how it had played out the times before when Yvonne had maxed her credit card, had forgotten to pay the car tax or house insurance, had let the money slip through her fingers as it was wont to do. They would sit down over a cup of tea as they had done a thousand times during their marriage and she would probably start to cry and his voice would get softer and gentler, which would make her cry even more. And eventually he would crack a joke and make her laugh and tell her it was only money and they would do something to figure it out. Then he would take the tax bill away into his office and make some phone calls and the bill would vanish, and Yvonne would never know what had happened to it. He would tell her it was all under control and not to worry anymore. And she knew she would feel like a complete failure. And yet even knowing how it would play out she still wanted to talk to him. She started to wonder if Brandon managed Patricia's finances as tightly as he'd managed hers, and then she stopped herself. She couldn't think about her and him together. It stung. Unbearably. And it shouldn't. She had left him.

'Enough maudlin, Yvonne,' she spoke to herself. These little pep talks infiltrated her day. She was her own mini life coach bouncing around her head, shedding positive vibes. She'd clean the windows, just the inside to give them a spruce up. No point standing still thinking about tax bills when there was work to be done. She grabbed some furniture polish and a fresh cloth from under the bar counter. Her phone vibrated in her pocket, Molly.

'Darling, how are you? How are the kids?'

'Good, Mam. How are you?'

'Great, love, I'm in great form. I did a walk this morning with Mam. The weather was beautiful so we went down to the river. She's thinking of heading to Dublin soon to see you and the boys.'

'That would be brilliant. I love it when Gran comes to stay.'

'She'll be in later so I'll tell her I mentioned it. Have you seen Rosie?'

'She popped in yesterday for two seconds for a cup of tea. She's got so much going on that she's hard to pin down.'

'It'll settle in a bit when this launch is over. Any mention of Simon?' Yvonne heard the judgemental tone creep into her voice. She couldn't help it. Here was this man, this older man, dating her daughter, starting a business with her and she'd yet to put a face to him. Quite frankly, she was put out not to have met this Simon who was dominating her daughter's time.

'No, and, Mam, I only met him briefly. You're not the only one that thinks it's strange.'

'I know I've said it before but I can't understand why she's hiding him, or us . . . Could she be hiding us? Are we that embarrassing? I'm sure I've only ever been very nice to Rosie's boyfriends.'

'Ah, I don't think that's it. I don't know . . . umm . . . Mam I wanted to ask you something . . .'

'I can hear it in your voice, love, what's wrong?' Yvonne dropped the spray bottle onto the counter and rested her elbows across it, ready to hear her daughter out. Whatever it was. Her girls were everything to her. A croak in a voice, a longer sigh than normal and she was ready, like a finely tuned athlete, to run to their aid.

'Mam, would you stop?'

'No, there it is again. I know you're trying not to cry. Talk to me, darling. Is it Dommo?'

'No. Why would you ask that?'

'Oh just . . . no, no, no, you tell me.' Yvonne immediately regretted mentioning Dommo. He was a good, honest, stable man, a doting father, that was all true, but sometimes she wondered.

'It's the boys, mam, they're not sleeping.'

'Well, they haven't ever slept, have they? Not really?' Yvonne did her best not to sound critical, but it was hard. Rory was three and a half now and Yvonne thought it was ridiculous that he didn't sleep through the night. And as for the baby, they let him rule the roost. It was madness to be beholden to children this way. She had never let her girls dictate like this, why did Molly think it was okay? 'Have you tried that Dr Spock book? That was our bible when you were small.'

'Yeah but, Mam, he says just let the babies cry and you know Dommo has to get up for work . . .' she trailed off, her voice croaky.

Yvonne took a deep breath, a million thoughts buzzing through her head but she held her tongue. 'Parenting is very hard, Molly.' Yvonne congratulated herself on being a model of restraint.

'God, I know. But, Mam, there's this sleep nanny I've heard about who can sort them out. She can do it in three visits.'

'A sleep nanny? I've never heard of anything so ridiculous. Babies haven't been sleeping since the beginning of time and these people are laughing all the way to the bank, preying on exhausted mothers.'

'Oh, I thought it sounded good.' The disappointment in Molly's voice was palpable.

'Just let them cry for a few nights.' Yvonne knew she was being particularly unhelpful.

'Well, Dommo . . .' Yes, indeed, *Dommo*, Yvonne thought. 'Well, I was going to ask you for three hundred and fifty euro to help me hire her, but it doesn't sound . . .' And with that Molly burst into tears. Her wails were echoing down the line and reverberating into Yvonne's heart.

'Oh hun,' Yvonne backtracked immediately, 'of course I'll help you hire her, you poor thing.'

In between sobs, Molly managed to blubber, 'I'm just so tired, Mam, I need help.' And all of a sudden there she was. The little girl with mousey, stringy hair and a face full of freckles, stomping her feet in a wild protest that *Mammy was not listening to her when she has something important to say that she can't remember right now.* Yvonne would crouch down, make eye contact and tell her, *I'm right here love, talk to me.* And then they might have some biscuits. Yvonne loved when they were little people and it was so easy to fix their problems: the ripped teddy, the scraped elbow, the hungry tummy. A few kisses, a chocolate bickie and all was well. She loved them older, too, even though the problems were harder to help solve. They were such beautiful women and she was endlessly proud of them.

'Take a few deep breaths, darling.' And with those words the two of them sucked in the air and exhaled in unison. 'Of course I'll help, of course I'll send the money to you.' She had posted those two lamps on eBay just three nights ago and she could increase the reserve. She'd bought them for seven hundred euro, after all.

'I mean I could ring Dad, I just thought you'd probably understand better. I didn't want to have to explain.' She sounded flustered.

'Of course, your dad would help you, too, of course he would.' Yvonne never doubted her ex-husband's kindness or love for his girls. 'I'll get the money to you, does that sound good? And when will you and the boys come and visit?'

'Oh yes, I'd love to. It's just because they haven't been sleeping. I don't even know how the kids would cope in another house after two hours in a car, you know.'

Two hours is nothing, thought Yvonne. It's well under two when the traffic is with you. It had been four hours to Dublin when the girls were small, before the motorway by-passed towns all over the county. They used to pack the girls into the back of the Ford and take off with tomato sandwiches drowned in mayonnaise and crisps for the journey. Sometimes

Yvonne wanted to shake Molly and tell her just to get on with it, stop letting the kids prevent you from living your life. Yvonne used to go and stay with her mam all the time, and Brandon would visit for a few days and head back to Dublin. She had loved those trips, showing off her beautiful girls, and things were always easier with your mam around, they just were. That was a fact of life.

'Well, let's get this sleep nanny sorted and maybe you can come then? I just bought a little train set for them in ALDI, which I've set up in the spare room. I am ready. Now, after my spin class last week with Maria Manifold—'

Molly interrupted. 'Seriously? You did a spin class?'

'Maria was teaching it.'

'Is that Maria who you were in school with?'

'The very one. Don't sound so shocked, she's a great teacher altogether. We went for coffee afterwards, and it was like we were seventeen again. The giggles out of us. Anyway, she's talked me into going to a singles' night in Arklow next week, sure I might as well.' Yvonne had protested, she had no interest in meeting a man; she didn't want a boyfriend, a husband, an anything. *What about sex?* Maria had asked her straight out. *Wouldn't you like to have sex?* And yes, Yvonne had agreed, it would be very nice to have sex, but really she couldn't even imagine how that would work with someone other than Brandon. *Well, let's just go and flirt a little and have a few drinks.* And Yvonne had settled on that, because that sounded exactly like what seventeen-year-old Yvonne McCarthy and Maria Manifold would have done.

'Okay, Mam, I mean do you really think you're ready to date? Wait, are you dating already?' The quiver in Molly's voice was palpable. Her children were adults, they were not supposed to be affected by their parents splitting up and moving on, not really anyway.

'No, I'm not. I just thought it might be fun. Can't I have fun?'

'Of course, I mean Dad's getting married. Maybe you could bring a date to the wedding?'

'Oh, I'm not . . . I'm . . .'

There was a long pause. 'You should come, Mam. Rosie and I will be there, Rory might be the ring bearer. It's going to be lovely.'

Another pause.

'He's happy, Mam. She's . . .'

Yvonne interrupted, shouting loudly, 'I don't care!' She lowered her voice, attempting to control herself. 'I don't want to hear about this wedding. I'm not going and that's final.'

Yvonne could hear Molly trying to restrain herself and failing.

'I think you should come, so does Rosie.'

'This is not up for discussion. You don't get to tell me what to do.' She sounded undeniably cross. 'Just come visit soon, and I'll sort out that sleep nanny for you. And let's not talk about the other stuff again. Okay?'

'Of course.'

And of course, Yvonne would send her the money. Of course she would. It was only money, and yes, there was a tax bill but that would have to wait. Sure, what could they do to her anyway?

9

Evie

EVIE SAT IN DOCTOR FLYNN'S OFFICE. AS SHE ALWAYS DID, she studied the photographs of his smiley wife and curly-haired children on his desk and his medical degrees proudly positioned on the walls.

'Blood pressure is a little high but nothing to worry about.' He loosened the black velcro strap from her arm.

'Give my heart another listen, would you?'

Doctor Flynn narrowed his gaze and readjusted the stethoscope around his neck. 'Is there something you're not telling me, Mrs McCarthy?'

Evie shook her head.

'No shortness of breath, no dizzy spells. You're sleeping well?' He looked down at the manila folder on his desk and leafed through the pages one more time.

'I feel fine, great, in fact.'

'For seventy-nine years of age, Mrs McCarthy, you are in fact in great health. There's the mild arthritis in your hip and a slightly elevated blood pressure, but really you are remarkable.' The doctor smiled at her, hoping to ease whatever it was that had her anxiously wringing her hands together.

'Check my heart one more time?' She nodded at him.

Dutifully he bent down and held the stethoscope to her chest, marvelling once again at her strong heartbeat. What he didn't know was that his patient was mentally checking off fatalities, trying to determine her own cause of death. Evie had assumed it would be the heart, that finally it would give out on her. It was broken anyway; it had cracked irreparably the day Michael had died. She didn't care what the well-meaning Doctor Flynn said about a steady rhythm. She had insisted that he take her bloods too, although she felt it was unlikely to be cancer. An accident seemed a possibility but she was sure the cards would have given a warning. No, she was confident that it would be her body giving up on her somehow. And she would just like to know how she was going to go so she could make arrangements. If she was to be in hospital for a long time, well, she wouldn't like that with nurses fussing over her, insisting on fluffing up her pillows and watering her with milky tea. It would give her less time to sort things out with her girls, too. She needed to be on the ground, trying to find out what the problems were that the cards were warning her about. She was desperate to help them.

Like how Yvonne's marriage had collapsed. She hadn't uttered a word to Evie until the night she arrived on her doorstep, suitcase in hand. Evie had welcomed her with open arms and nursed her with countless cups of tea. *It was time to go,*

Mam. It's time for me to have a second act. Yvonne had repeated this on a loop and Evie had listened into the pauses and heard Yvonne's uncertainty. Over the coming months she watched Yvonne keep herself busy to stay away from herself. Always cleaning, countless trips to the supermarket, always running around—she was in perpetual motion. Evie loved having her around. Every Saturday morning without fail they pulled on their runners, zipped up their jackets and walked the river path. This was followed by tea and scones at Elizabeth's Café, getting in early before she ran out of their favourite blueberry scones. They knew how to talk and there wasn't a sneeze in the town they didn't hear, but when Evie broached the subject of Brandon, Yvonne seized up.

'Have you thought any more about the wedding?'

'Of course I think about it.'

'And . . . ?' she clinked the spoon around the edges of the teacup.

'It's not like I feel happy for him, Mam. I feel sad for me, I mean . . .' She'd shaken her head and started to chew on her thumbnail. There it was, the pause again. A novel could be written in that silence.

'Do you want to marry him again? Is that . . .' Evie whispered, being ever so careful not to upset her daughter.

'No, no. I mean I left him.' Eyes wide, Yvonne nodded emphatically, reinforcing her own actions of three years prior.

'I know you did, love.' We all make mistakes, Evie wanted to say, but swallowed the words. 'Would you like to meet somebody else maybe? Go on a few dates?'

'No, I don't want a man. I just want to be me.'

And are you? Evie wondered. Were all these rash decisions and life-changing swings and roundabouts bringing her back to herself, Evie worried. Almost eighty years of age and she still carried the weight and wonder of motherhood.

Evie knew all about the choices people made to let the light of love blow out. Yvonne had let it go and now Brandon was on another journey. His soul had connected with someone else as it is wont to do. Patricia her name was. Evie felt sure he was happy and she was sure Yvonne wasn't. Except for when she was behind the bar, she glowed then. Maybe that was enough for her, Evie mused.

Evie had seen it so many times with her clients—couples who she had matched, couples who had an undeniable chemistry. Soul mates had sat in front of her as the years had passed with pinched faces and insisted she had got it wrong. They weren't soul mates at all. She remembers George and Mia Ray, she had matched them ten years previously. She hadn't had much of a hand to play in it, those two were always going to find each other. There was a powerful pull between them from whatever had gone in lifetimes before. She directed them both to the Annual Tidy Towns Winner Night (Ballyhay had won for the third year in a row thanks to Brid Connolly's devotion to hanging baskets) in the August at Martins Bar and Grill. She had watched as Mia arrived in a blue dress with red roses speckled on the front, a giddy twirl to her step and her dark hair curled into the nape of her neck. With an expectant air she moved around the lounge, which was stuffed to the brim with weather-beaten farmers inhaling pints. Evie had seen her shoulders drop and posture freeze as the door blew open and in had walked George Ray. His checked shirt sleeves were rolled up just past his elbow and his fair hair was slicked back. He had a prominent nose but luckily large blue eyes that prevented his nose from taking over his face. Evie saw it instantly—this only happened with a handful of couples—a blinding white light grew out of his chest and shot, like a magnificent arcing arrow, towards Mia. Over the pint-wielding farmers perched at the bar, the sticky carpet and scattered tables, their souls were reaching out to one another. George moved, danced and skirted five, six, seven steps until he stood by Mia's side, and then she turned to him and their eyes locked. It wasn't magic; it was love. It was two soul mates reconnecting after a lifetime of searching. And ten years later they had sat in front of her in the snug of McCarthy's and told her it was a mistake.

Evie had shook her head, trying desperately to suppress the rage she felt at both of them for letting it get to this. 'It was never a mistake. I can still see your connection here. It's just your light has dimmed. You've stopped working on it, haven't you?'

'Well, if she'd just stop nagging . . .' George's face creased into an ugly frown.

Evie raised her hand in protest. 'Stop this. This is your fault, and your fault.' She swung a pointed finger wildly between their bewildered faces. 'You don't just get to skip off into the sunset for eternity. You've got to be there for one another, day in day out. Do the boring stuff together, that's what makes up a life. When's the last time you emptied the dishwasher, George?'

'Well, now that's not fair . . .' George's mouth pulled tight.

'Or you, Mia. When was the last time you hopped into the shower when George was in there?'

'Mrs McCarthy!' Mia did her best to look shocked, but she couldn't hide the corner of her lips that curled into a smile.

'Live your life. Love together. Make each other happy. Always put the other first. Always. You two are old souls, you have crossed many paths before, your destinies are mapped out. Don't alter that because of petty disagreements.'

'Well, her sister . . .' George narrowed his eyes looking for understanding.

'Who cares about her sister? It's about the two of you. Once you both get that into your thick skulls, you have the makings for great happiness.' Evie was tired of holding back. 'I didn't make a mistake ten years ago and neither did you.'

They'd left with hangdog expressions, a heavy silence following them. They were still together as they should be. Sometimes people clung onto the drama and they layered and layered it up between them until it became very difficult to see the light of love. Evie had often thought about writing a relationship book. She was going to call it, *Get On With It*. Love had peaks and troughs and you had to stay around in the shallows to ride the high of the waves. It was all worth it.

For thirteen years she had endured Michael's insistence on clipping his toenails in the TV room. For thirteen years she watched the clippings ricochet off the fireplace.

'You'll be doing that every Tuesday evening, will you?' Evie had asked a few weeks into the occurrence.

'S'pose so.'

She watched as he wedged his ankle over his knee and with great heaving and hawing bent down to examine his unshod foot. The opening bars of *Eastenders* strained in the background annoying her even more.

'Oh Michael, for God's sake, wouldn't the bathroom be the place to do that?'

He never stirred from staring at his foot with forensic intensity. 'No chairs in there.'

'Outside then. Go sit on the garden bench.'

'It's raining cats and dogs out there.'

'It's unhygienic, for crying out loud. I don't want to look at your foot.' She heard her voice raise and knew she was losing her cool, which never worked with Michael, it just made him move slower.

'Only me and you in the house, and you've seen this foot many times before.' He was getting smug now.

'Right, so I get *Eastenders* and toenails, do I? That's what I get to look forward to on a Tuesday, is it?'

'I'll tell you what, I'll run the vacuum around afterwards and I'll make you a cup of tea?' And Michael raised an eyebrow and smiled at her.

'There better be biscuits, too.'

'No promises.'

And that was that. For thirteen more years, every Tuesday while *Eastenders* streamed into the TV room, his big white feet were on show. That was marriage. Compromise with a side of toenail clippings.

Doctor Flynn removed the stethoscope from her chest and shook his head. 'Remarkably strong, Mrs McCarthy. Now, please, tell me what's really bothering you?'

'The price of turnips.' She smiled her million-dollar smile at the good doctor.

'Please, Mrs McCarthy.'

'I'm old, Doctor, everything and nothing bothers me. I want to make sure I'm as good as I can be for the time I've got left.'

He seemed happy with that answer. 'Rest assured that you are. Let's schedule in another check-up in three months' time, early November, to make sure you're still as good as I think you'll be, okay?'

Three months felt optimistic to Evie.

'Well, you never know,' she said cryptically, 'I'll have a word with Siobhan on the desk.' She rose to her feet with great ease, limber as ever thanks to her regular aqua aerobics class.

'How's your wife, Doctor?' She looked at the photo of the happy family smiling on a beach, sun-kissed skin and knotted hair. She didn't wait for a response. 'Take her out for dinner.'

'Oh, did you? Have you . . . ?' Confused, Doctor Flynn looked from the photo to Mrs McCarthy. He knew as everyone in town did that she seemed to see things about people, things that nobody spoke openly about. As a man of science he really didn't hold much heed with it, but Mrs McCarthy was a lovely woman underneath the hocus pocus, if not a bit mad, but definitely lovely.

'Every woman wants to have a nice dinner with her husband, Doctor. Set it up.' Evie shook her head at his stupidity, what was wrong with people these days? Maybe she would write that book and hand deliver it to all the married people in town.

'See you now,' she called over her shoulder. Evie made her way through the waiting room, scanning as always for familiar faces. In a small town the doctor's waiting room was where front-page headlines were created. Sure enough, there was Mad Joan wrapped in a coat four sizes too big for her. In to get some more pills no doubt and tell the doctor the sky was falling down. She nodded hello to Sean Weston, hypochondriac if ever you'd met one. Convinced he'd had cancer ten times over, was regularly running up to A&E in Dublin with heart attacks or brain haemorrhages or strange tropical diseases. The worst thing that ever happened to him was the internet. Every week a new disease with that one. And there . . . Evie stopped, frozen. She felt her hand come to her mouth. Was it? Could it be? Karl?

'Evelyn as I live and breathe.' The man rose to his feet.

'Karl, it is you, isn't it?'

'Almost sixty years and I would know you anywhere.'

So tall, he'd always been so tall. He was almost better looking in his old age. His face had been thin and angular as a young man, but now it seemed distinguished. And those eyes were the same, the warm woodland colour, the very same.

Karl held her gaze. 'I often wondered if I'd ever see you again.'

Evie had wondered the same thing.

'Isn't life strange?' She heard a short laugh come from her. 'What brings you to Ballyhay?'

'Just a small construction project and I decided to stay . . . Do you remember my aunt's house?' He leaned towards her looking into her eyes.

The big house out of town. She remembered it well.

'There. I'm staying there. I wondered if I'd see you.' Karl shook his head, a dreamy look washed across his face as if he couldn't quite believe what he was seeing.

'So, you said.'

'How are you? How have you been?' Such a loaded question when it had been so long.

'Well, I've been well.'

'And Michael?'

'I lost him a while back. Thank you for asking after him. I'd heard you married?'

'Pauline, yes, I lost her, too.' His face fell. Evie understood completely. 'A few years ago, I miss her all the time.'

'I'm sorry.' What an empty sounding sentiment those words were. I'm sorry that the person who gave meaning to your world isn't here to hold your hand anymore. I'm sorry that they didn't get to live a long life. I'm sorry that life is such a mystery.

'Do you think . . . ? Would you . . . ?' He blinked and cleared his throat. 'I find myself tongue-tied.'

They both laughed. Evie was feeling a little awkward.

'Would you maybe like to come out to the house and see it before it's knocked down?' Karl asked.

'Knocked down?'

'Yes, the estate is being turned into townhouses.'

'I'd love to see it, yes.' Evie didn't hesitate. She wondered if he remembered running through the gardens with her? Did he remember holding her hand almost sixty years before?

'We had some special times there.'

Oh, he does, he does. Evie felt herself blushing.

'Marvellous. Lunch, one o'clock? Thursday?'

'Thursday.' Evie nodded and turned to leave. She straightened her jacket and pulled her handbag under her arm. Karl. Of all the people to meet, he was a surprise. A pleasant one at that. She couldn't hide the smile that crept across her face. Karl. All too aware that she was now the waiting-room headline news and her conversation had been earwigged by those twitching magazine holders, Evie still couldn't help herself. She'd come to the doctor for bad news and now she had a lightness to her step. She turned around and announced to the straining ears in the room, 'I am very much looking forward to lunch, Karl.'

10

Rosie

ROSIE STRETCHED HER ARMS OUT, LUXURIATING IN THE RICH Egyptian cotton sheets. The bed was massive, in full starfish sprawl she couldn't touch the sides. She felt like she was in a movie, waking up in this sun-drenched apartment that overlooked Dublin's oldest city centre gardens, St Stephen's Green. There were empty closets in the two spare rooms. Two. It was like finding a unicorn. Space. The hallway was the size of Rosie's entire apartment, which was really just four walls of shelving and a sink. Even having a hallway felt like the height of decadence. Here, there were fluffy rugs, sunlight bouncing off the stripped wooden floorboards, floor-to-ceiling windows that opened onto a small—yes, small but perfectly formed—balcony overlooking the leafy green. Rosie felt like this life belonged to someone else. And technically it did. It was Simon's apartment; well, actually, it had been Simon's ex-wife's apartment. He'd acquired it in the divorce settlement in which he claimed he had been fleeced. The ex must be dressed in gold on a throne somewhere in the Maldives, because from what Rosie could see Simon had done pretty well. She'd only been here twice as they spent more time in Rosie's poky place. Her studio flat, which was effectively an over-priced wardrobe, was seriously lacking in basic living human requirements, like air. She'd moved in two years ago, having grown world-weary of flat shares and washing up other people's day-old Weetabix bowls and never sitting on the toilet seat because of her flatmate's crusty friend who came for a night and stayed for a month. The rent had seemed extortionate at the time, but just doable with her well-paid job at CRUSH, and she was happy to pay the extra to be home alone. Amazingly, as rents had steadily risen in the city, in some kind of upside-down world she had snagged a bargain. Her wall-to-wall shelving unit with bed would probably be another five hundred euro a month on today's market, but her landlord hadn't mentioned it so neither would she.

Obviously, Simon had a need for privacy, which was why they weren't in his bachelor pad often. Although his need for privacy hadn't stopped Rosie doing a full Hercule Poirot sneak around the place looking for clues after their second date. Well, you never know what she might find that he wouldn't reveal in person: unusual fetish, photos of an ex, pharmaceutical habits, passion for eighties rock bands, unhygienic living standards. It was best to build up a full picture of who she was sleeping with. But the place was devoid of any interesting quirks: there were no photos on the walls, there was nothing in the drawers, a few boxes of cereal and protein shakes in the kitchen and a sparse wardrobe of sports clothes. *Minimalist,* he called it. *Boring,* she'd said with an eyeroll.

Rosie fiddled with her phone and turned the music up. Surround speakers in the bedroom. Nice. She closed her eyes preparing for the Phil Collins drumbeat solo to kick in when her bliss was interrupted by Simon with a big smile, and from what she could feel, a big erection.

'What twenty-four-year-old listens to Phil Collins?' Simon whispered in her ear.

Rosie didn't open her eyes. 'Shh, I'm not talking to you, old man. Phil's about to get personal.'

'So am I.' He kissed her cheek and slowly moved his hand underneath the cotton sheets caressing her stomach and tracing circles around her belly button. 'Should I go higher or lower? Higher or lower? Rosie?'

Rosie chewed her lip and half opened her eyes, giggling, she said, 'Lower, I think you should go lower.'

Simon slipped his hand between Rosie's legs and waited for her body to respond to his, which it always did. And before Phil had belted out the chorus they were wrapped around each other, sheets askew, knocking the headboard loudly against the wall.

Rosie often wondered if Simon was trying to prove something in bed because of his height. He was relentless with her orgasms. Multiple orgasms. She never left the bed without a half a dozen. She wouldn't have believed it either if someone had told her. And while he was very handsome—spiky slightly greying blonde hair, blue eyes, beaming smile with perfectly tiled white teeth, and a lean toned body from all those hours in the gym—he was short. And he seemed to have a complex about it, which is why Rosie reasoned they spent a lot of their time together lying down. They rarely went out, they hadn't met each other's friends or family, and yet it was still by far the most grown-up relationship she'd ever been in. There was so much sex. She was a regular sex-on-tap diva: *sex for breakfast, sex for tea.* She was sure there would have been sex for lunch too if she wasn't at work.

'The natural order is intimacy, then love and then lovemaking.' Rosie had cringed when her granny had said *lovemaking,* she was straight out of a G-rated Mills & Boon novel. But Rosie had been young when she started turning to her for relationship advice, and Granny's vocabulary had never really changed in that regard. Rosie adored her gran, who was always up for something new. They'd taken a weekend-long intense make-up class together last year. They'd loved it and were now equally obsessed with primers, highlighters and the benefits of contouring. Her granny never judged, she listened and she only gave relationship advice when asked, even though Rosie knew she had buckets of it. She had literally seen it all. She had been fairly adamant about the lovemaking (eugh) though. 'When you shuffle things around it's very difficult to get the other two right. Particularly when lovemaking comes first.'

Well, for once she hadn't been right about that. Two weeks into seeing each other, lying in bed drinking tea and eating buttery toast, Simon announced, 'I love you, Rosie.'

Now, this wasn't the first time Rosie had had a man proclaim his love while the sun was still rising in their relationship. She'd had a declaration two hours into a first date once. So, true to form and absolutely delighted with herself, Rosie had placed her tea on the nightstand and looked at Simon with new eyes and decided that, yes, she loved him, too. And what could be more wonderful? To celebrate their love, Simon bought her flowers and took her to a restaurant for lunch where waiters put the napkin on her lap and she drank prosecco that bubbled up her nose.

Simon was an entrepreneur from Norwich in the United Kingdom. Rosie had to Google map it. He had a northern English accent and said things like *cuppa tae,* and *bloke oft telly.* He'd moved to Dublin with his now ex-wife (who from his stories definitely seemed a bit on the bunny boiler side of things) and had been involved in a few tech start-ups. He knew his way around getting funding and investors. When Simon met Rosie he had fully developed the software for a dating app, but just couldn't get it off the ground. What he'd been looking for was the front end, the idea. And really, he would say, it came from Rosie—DeLuvGuru was her idea. Before she could say, *Pour us another vino there,* they were off. Rosie invested her money and DeLuvGuru was born.

Rosie would never have done this on her own, but now she was in it, why wouldn't she do it? Steve Jobs had started a company; he was just a man, a human being. People had to start somewhere. She wasn't going to give up her job or do anything silly; it was just like a hobby with an attractive man at the helm. She'd be crazy not to get involved when she saw Simon's projections and the figures he aimed to bring in by year five, in fact she knew she had to jump fast. Very quickly Rosie was walking a little bit taller, practising imaginary conversations with people on the street who might casually ask, 'So, what do you do with yourself?'

Rosie would toss her hair back and confidently reply (in these imaginary scenarios she was always wearing a bold lipstick), 'I have an app in development. I'm planning on shaking up modern dating.'

And they'd look at her filled with awe and admiration, a mere human being revolutionising dating.

Of course, nobody actually asked her, and what really happened was that she felt terribly tired from working one crazy-houred job that paid money, and another app development role that paid nothing and was kind of annoying when you didn't really know what you were supposed to do most of the time.

The whole thing had snowballed very quickly. Within weeks there were mock interfaces and Rosie was hammering through social media.

'I'm a celebrity now in Ballyhay, they played the YouTube clip in the pub. Me and that guy from the chip shop in town, with the cat in the tutu who got booted off *The X Factor* in the first round, we'll probably get the keys to the town.' Rosie, still in bed, scrolled idly through her phone.

'Oh yeah. What'll that mean?'

'Big stuff like we'll be able to graze our sheep in Main Street. Free cocoa from Elizabeth's Café. I might even swing a bingo card.'

Simon wasn't listening to her, his head deeply bowed over his phone.

She ignored him and kept scrolling through her Instagram feed, marvelling at how and why people posted what they did. Rosie had once watched an influencer in a shopping centre exit a lift five times as her patient and well-moisturised boyfriend captured the moment on his phone. Five times she gave an excited and slightly startled look as the doors slid open.

'You've got that—' Simon peeped up from his screen.

'I know, I know, interview in five minutes. I'll do it from the bed if you go make me some coffee.'

He got up, throwing on a t-shirt and a pair of shorts as he sauntered towards the kitchen.

The phone interview was with a singles-in-the-city style influencer, which should be straightforward. Unlike the one she had later this evening, which was with a tech site that would focus more on usability and how the app was so simply designed. Rosie hoped she'd be able to handle it.

She grabbed her t-shirt from the floor, pulled it over her head and opened her laptop. The app looked amazing and this was only phase one. The bright green colour popped on screen, and the font which had taken about one hundred years to get right was clean and elegant.

'Rosie,' Simon shouted from the kitchen, 'have you heard of Isabelle Love?'

'Yeah, she's an influencer—skinny, fashionable, has a massive following.' *She's regularly in her underwear, lounging around her apartment while posting about suffering from anxiety.* Rosie wasn't a fan.

'Did we . . . ? Have you paid her off?' Still shouting, Simon was starting to sound annoyed.

'No!' Rosie screamed across the room, equally irate. Rosie would always rise to a fight. It was as if she had some invisible code of honour to protect. She used to get into regular brawls, hair pulling and nails in the school yard. She had a track worn to the principal's office much to her mam's despair. 'I've contacted influencers but I'm not paying anyone until phase two.'

Laptop in hand he appeared in the doorway looking flushed. 'She's just given us a glowing post. Jesus, Rosie, she has a hundred thousand followers.'

Rosie threw her own laptop on the bed and crossed the room to take a look at Simon's screen.

There she was—beach-tousled hair in silk pyjamas, Bambi eyes staring at the camera. Underneath the image they read:

> Guys I am so excited, finally a dating app that makes sense #DeLuvGuru doesn't want me to fill out some bs form. They want my online history. They want to find the real me, and this way I will find my real love. I will expose my genuine self to find genuine love. Let's see what crazy adventures this brings #crazyoptimist #lovelove #icanthide #lovemyself #therealme

'She posted that five hours ago.'

Simon quickly flicked screens onto the registration data— two thousand two hundred and sixty registrations. The colour slipped from his face. 'We've only been live twenty-four hours. This is way beyond . . .'

Clutching the laptop he started walking back towards the kitchen just as Rosie's phone was ringing. The interview. She propped herself on the edge of the bed and for the next ten minutes delivered an upbeat optimistic speech that was very similar to the conversation she'd had on *Sonya's Sofa*. Rosie was learning that she was very good at putting on a show. After she hung up, Rosie scrambled into the kitchen to find Simon bent over his laptop, talking into his phone, every muscle in his face seizing up.

'There's a flight at 2 p.m., I'll be on it.' He hung up. 'That was Ruth the developer in London. The infrastructure we have in place can't handle a number this high this early.' He looked at Rosie accusingly. 'It was supposed to be a slow build.'

She felt her hackles rise. 'Hey, don't go all mansplaining to me. It's good news—we need more numbers to build matches.'

He stood up, chest out. 'You shouldn't have gone out to the big influencers so early.'

'The chances of someone of Isabelle Love's calibre actually even reading a DM I sent was so slim. She must get paid tens of thousands for a post. We just struck gold.' She crossed her arms defiantly. 'I did great. Thank you.'

The look Simon threw her was not one of gratitude, it was dismissive. 'You don't get it, Rosie.' He marched into the bedroom and threw a bag on the bed.

She followed, stamping her feet. 'Well, explain it to me if you're so smart then.'

He was throwing a collection of t-shirts and jeans into the case. 'What's the point? You'll just put your fingers in your ears and pretend you can't hear me.'

'I did that once.' For crying out loud, what was his problem? 'How long are you going for? That's a lot of t-shirts.'

'It'll be a while as I have to sort this mess out.'

She watched as he zipped up the case and slid it onto the floor.

'Can you just shut the door on your way out?' he said.

Rosie felt her mouth drop open in surprise.

'I'm going to be out of town for a while.' He looked at her like she was the most stupid person on the planet. 'You've really messed this one up, Rosie.'

'Oh, you know what? You're some asshole.' She picked up some papers on the table and threw them on the floor in a rage.

'Real mature, Rosie.' Simon's eyes flashed at her, he grabbed his keys, wheeled his bag after him, and with a click and a slam of the front door, he was gone.

Rosie was left reeling. What the hell had just happened?

11

Molly

'YOU'RE A MAN.' MOLLY HEARD THE WORDS FALL OUT OF HER faster than she could catch them.

'Last time I looked.'

'And you're . . .' Gorgeous, smiley, young, divine. 'Eurghhhhh.' A strange noise came from her innards as she exhaled while trying to compose herself. 'Here, you're here.' Molly settled on sounding strong and definite while feeling decidedly weak-kneed. 'I just thought Charlie was a woman, like Charlotte the princess—although she's probably only called Charlie behind closed doors.'

'No, short for Charles. Pleased to meet you.' The tall, handsome stranger with a touch of the Mediterranean about him—olive skin, jet black hair, deep-dark magnetic eyes—thrust his hand forward for a handshake. His head bowed slightly as he attempted to shelter from the rain and wind whipping wildly around the south Dublin suburb, and he offered a smile that would melt the coldest of hearts.

Molly shook his strong hand with a limp wrist and quickly tried again to gather herself. 'You probably get that a bit do you? The man part?'

'Well, not in the supermarket per se, but it has happened now and again on the job. It's not a big deal.' A slow, comforting smile crept across his perfectly sculpted face, and as Molly watched in awe, a dimple imploded on his left cheek.

'Right.' She recognised that this was probably her cue to laugh, but couldn't quite muster up the giddiness. She was absolutely in a state of shock.

After a long pause, Charlie spoke. 'So, there's a Rory and an Andy? Is that right?'

'My children, yes.'

'Are they here?' He raised an eyebrow and edged a little closer across the threshold while leaning against the wind.

Molly got a blast of cold air in her face, which startled her back to reality. 'Come in, I'm so sorry I've left you standing here on the doorstep. Where are my manners? I haven't a brain in my head. Come in, come in. The weather's desperate, isn't it? You wouldn't even know it's still summer.' She ushered him in the door with a madness known only to shepherds herding sheep before a storm. Practically pushing him into the kitchen, Molly flicked the kettle on and started bustling and banging cups and a milk jug onto the countertop.

'I've no biscuits,' Molly howled at her guest as if this were the utmost tragic news and surely the ruination of their day. 'Sit yourself down,' she said, glancing at him already seated comfortably at the kitchen table.

Simon was taking a number of files and folders out of a bag across the crayon-scribbled surface. 'Just a cup of tea is fine, thank you.' Charlie smiled up at her.

Molly looked at the floor, the ceiling and finally positioned a fixed glare on the kettle. *Get it together, Molly, for crying out loud, it's just an attractive man. You assumed he'd be a she, because you are, at your very core, a sexist. You've just had a little shock, calm down. Yes, he's gorgeous, and yes, I agree it is very strange to feel those butterflies leaping in your stomach. It's been a while. But you are also his client who is paying him—well, your mother is—for his service . . . He is not a gigolo, he is not a gigolo, no, no, no . . . He is going to get your babies to sleep. Focus.*

She slapped two steaming cups of tea onto the kitchen table and filled a milk jug shaped like a cow dancing joyously.

'I've just remembered where I hid some chocolate last week when I started a diet. I'll be right back.' Molly sped off down the hall, grabbed her phone and with lightning speed fired a text to Anna:

WTF, sleep nanny is a HE and a ridey ridey ride.

Whenever she started a diet, which was at least twice a month, the entire house had to be purged of all sweets, biscuits and chocolates, and depending on the diet, all carbs, dairy or proteins. That was except for the emergency stash, which stayed in one tin, high up, which was tricky to open and held a maximum of four chocolate biscuits. She'd already visited them this morning right after Andy had almost blinded his brother with a Thomas the Tank engine. And then there was the emergency emergency stash—dotted around the house in innocuous and often very difficult to remember spots—to be used in the event of no sleep, tears (hers or the kids') or period cramps. This was the hardcore chocolate: Cadbury's dairy milk, Snickers bars, fun-sized full packs of Smarties and Aeros (not of the mint variety—which doesn't even deserve to be called chocolate). Molly rummaged in the back of the coat cupboard, diving deep into the pocket of a long-disused rain jacket, and plucked out a Cadbury's dairy milk chocolate with hazelnuts and raisins from the emergency emergency stash. Phew.

Anna responded:

GET A PHOTO

Molly tutted, as if that was going to happen? Hmm, could she? How would that work?

'We're on.' She laughed, walking back into the kitchen and waving the chocolate in the air, suddenly noticing the disarray surrounding her. There were toys strewn everywhere, dirty bibs at the sink, her one pot plant shrivelled and thirsty, and the view from the kitchen window was an equally unkempt garden. 'Sorry about the mess of the place.'

Charlie shook his head calmly as if he had all the time in the world and hadn't even noticed the green-painted handprints smeared on the wall. 'Please sit down and thanks for the tea. Are the children around?'

'Rory is watching TV and Andy is mercifully asleep which never happens, by the way. Obviously.' Molly sat down opposite Charlie and started to break up the Cadbury's.

'I guess, just to give you some background about me.' Molly watched as Charlie pushed paperwork towards her. 'I'm a registered paediatric nurse and I've been working with The Sleep Nanny for two years now. I effectively work two part-time jobs that roll into one full-time job.'

'A paediatric nurse, you work with sick kids.' Molly could hear it in her voice, the mooning as her mam would call it. The absolute awe she felt in the presence of kindness mixed with handsomeness.

A smile broke across his face. 'Sick kids are just kids. I have the best job in the world. I spend half the day playing.'

'Of course.' She had to stop herself staring. 'Here, have some chocolate.' Molly rammed two pieces at once into her mouth.

'So, what I do is conduct an initial chat with you and your husband to find out how your daily and evening routines work with the kids and then I'll meet the children. I'll shadow you this evening as you put them to bed, if that's okay with you? Following that, I'll come back on Tuesday with a complete plan and schedule that should fit into your day and will hopefully lead to full night's sleep for everyone.'

'I might hug you.' Molly laughed as much as her chocolate-filled mouth would allow her. 'I can't even imagine what it would be like to have a full night's sleep.'

'It's not just about the bedtime routine. It'll be about their day: how they eat, how they nap and play and how you and your husband parent—'

She interrupted. 'How we parent? I don't know that we "parent".' She made air quotes when she said parent. She hated people who did air quotes. 'I mean really I think we just get through, you know? There's no real "parenting".' Air quotes again. She'd have to sit on her hands. 'Just you know, existing.' She sipped her tea. 'And screen time. There's plenty of that, for all of us. So, you should know from the outset that I'm not a great mother. They haven't had organic food in weeks and they're being raised by the Disney Channel.' She was only half joking. Maybe she wasn't joking at all. Charlie listened. She suspected immediately that that was one of the things people said about him with knowing nods, *That Charlie nanny/nurse is a great listener. And a ride.* Those knowing nodders would definitely agree on that.

'Will your husband be joining us?'

'Dommo?' Saying his name shattered her brief infatuation with Charlie; her husband, her life partner, her lover, the father of her children, oh yeah, him. 'Let me . . . actually, yes, he should be here.' She slid her hand onto the kitchen countertop and found her phone, quickly scrolling through messages. 'Ah, there you go, I missed one from him earlier. He can't make it, he's working late.'

'No problems, so is it normally you who puts the children to bed?' Charlie's voice was soothing in the manner of a counsellor or an easy listening DJ.

'No, we do it together, nine times out of ten. He's just very busy at the moment.' Molly wondered why she was lying. She knew it was her every night: cooking every meal, changing every nappy, every pair of pyjamas, kissing every tear away and wiping countless snotty noses. Dommo had been busy at work for months now, fading into the family like a ghostly weekend presence. He wasn't fitting with them. The boys were irritated that he didn't know how to spin the Hotwheels cars the way they wanted. He had even dressed Rory in a PJ Masks t-shirt, not realising that Rory was now scared witless of the PJ Mask ninja fighting trio. Of course, Rory had thrown an almighty tantrum at the thought of wearing a shirt that, granted, had been his favourite two months before. And herself and Dommo weren't right either. He irritated her, too. Herself and the boys had a routine going on. He didn't fit it.

Things had started to go off a few weeks back, when Molly had fallen asleep on the couch waiting for Dommo to get home from work. They hadn't talked or seen each other in so long. She just wanted a chat with an adult—not just any adult, her lovely husband. She wanted to snuggle up to him and tell him funny stories about the kids, and then he'd laugh, kiss her and tell her how much he loved her. They would agree that this was a hard period in their lives, but also fantastic because they had each other. That's it, that's all she wanted. So, she'd stayed up after the kids had gone down, turned on a Swedish detective story that she couldn't understand on Netflix and fell asleep ten minutes into the first murder.

Dommo gently nudged her shoulder awake. 'You should have just gone to bed.' His eyes were bloodshot. He shifted her sprawled body up the couch slightly so he could balance on the edge. He rubbed her arm gently.

'I wanted to see you. I haven't seen you.' Molly shifted up the couch, patting her face down and smooshing back her hair, half dazed. 'What time is it? Are you only in now?' She rummaged for her phone under the couch. 'Nine-fifteen. God, it's late. You must be exhausted. You've been working all this time?'

'Boys in bed?' His eyes danced slightly.

'Of course, there's at least another twenty minutes before the night-time shift kicks in.' Molly half laughed, and scooted down the couch slightly, rubbing her sports-sock-clad foot up against Dommo's hunched back. She raised her eyebrows. 'Twenty whole minutes.' She hooked her other leg around him. 'You're trapped.'

A look of confusion and excitement passed over Dommo's face. 'Seriously?'

'You know it, baby, and I've no bra on.' And she flung her arms over her head and jiggled her boobs. 'Time saver.'

Without a moment's hesitation he leaned over her. 'Oh baby', he uttered as he moved his lips to hers and dove in for a long soft kiss.

Almost instantly she pulled back, her arms pushed against his shoulders and she sat up, suddenly very awake. 'What? Were you drinking? I can taste it.' Her fingers pressed her lips in shock. He shrank away, towards the end of the couch.

'I just went for one with Paul.'

'Where?' Her chest froze.

'Brogans.'

'You went for a drink?' She didn't know if she felt hurt or angry, sad or mad. 'I sat up waiting for you and you were in the pub.' The tears arrived, they fell instantly. They streamed down her face.

'Ah, don't be like that. It was just one drink with Paul. All we do is talk about work. It's not a big deal. It's just like being in the office.' Flustered, Dommo's face had turned pink as the excuses tumbled out of him.

'I thought you were working late. I felt sorry for you.' Molly spat the words at him.

'I was. Twenty minutes, Mols, that's all it was.' His eyes were pleading with her to understand.

'You didn't tell me.'

'It just happened. I was leaving and Paul said, "Come on let's get a quick one in before home." He made it sound so simple.'

'It's not the same. Paul doesn't have kids. He doesn't have a wife, a family. You do.' Molly was surprised at how calm she sounded.

'You think I don't know that. You think I don't know how lucky I am.' There was a defensiveness to Dommo's voice. 'That's why I'm working like this, for us, for all of us. To pay this bloody mortgage that has us strung up.'

There was a long pause as a million thoughts drifted through Molly's head, each one arguing with each other. *It was just one drink, it's no big deal. There's no need to be* that *wife. Of course he can go for a beer.* Versus, *He's your husband. He needs to support you, you're drowning and you don't think he's going to catch you. The kids need their dad. Why would he rather be in the pub than with you?*

Andy broke the deadlock by roaring his little head off upstairs, waking at full throttle.

Dommo jumped up, saved by the bell. 'I'll go.'

'Yeah, you do that, husband of the year.' She heard it: nasty, bitter and angry. She watched him deflate.

He turned his head over his shoulder, his eyes crestfallen. 'I'm sorry, Mols. It was just one beer.'

Molly rubbed the heels of her hands into her stinging eyes and waited for him to leave.

They'd danced around one another for a while after that night, Dommo got home for dinner a few nights in a row, gave the boys their bath once or twice, but then a deadline was missed and a project expanded and they returned to being ships in the night missing each other's SOS calls.

And a few weeks later Molly sat in her kitchen asking another man to help her with their children.

'Look, I'm the primary caregiver, so it'll probably just be me,' Molly said matter-of-factly to the handsome stranger who was going to help sort her life out.

'And me,' Charlie added. 'We'll tackle this together.'

12

Yvonne

IT WAS LUKAS'S NIGHT OFF AND YVONNE WAS HOLDING COURT, front and centre. Lukas had been at McCarthy's for seven years and could have run the place blindfolded if he was let, but his ethereally beautiful Brazilian wife, Esmerelda, had other ideas for him that did not involve such a lowly trade as running a bar. So, Lukas was a reluctant accountancy student by day and an enthusiastic barman by night, which helped fund his wife's little splurges. She'd recently taken a holiday to Lithuania and returned with a mouthful of veneers and butt implants. In all fairness, Yvonne had to admit she did have a lovely shapely bottom. Horses for courses and all that. And Lukas was only delighted with his wife's new assets and he'd probably make a great accountant one day if he put his mind to it. Herself and Evie were very fond of Lukas, he was like extended family now, a lovely fella altogether, very kind with a smile for everyone. There was a thriving Polish community in Ballyhay, spawning two Polish shops on Main Street selling much the same stuff as far as Yvonne could see, but still, busy out. Little Viktors and Ludmillas competed at the Irish Dancing in the national school, able to speak three languages: Polish, English and Irish, sounding marvellous altogether. It gave the town a lovely cosmopolitan feel. There had been a short-lived Polish café, round the back of the church, but the Poles weren't bothered spending their money there and the Irish weren't ready for boiled sausages. She supposed integration took time.

Yvonne watched as John Henderson heaved a shoulder bag through the pub, the weight of which caused him to almost topple over. He was also known as Gianni Versace on account of having once worn a bright yellow t-shirt. He dropped the bag on the floor as quietly as the loud thud permitted, shook his jacket off and propped himself up on his usual stool, readjusting into his familiar stoop.

'That better not be what I think it is, John?' Yvonne faced him dead-pan and pulled a clean pint glass from under the counter. Automatically, not waiting for confirmation, she flicked the Guinness tap.

'Well, sure I wouldn't be knowing what you'd be thinking, Yvonne. A fine woman like yourself could have all manner of thoughts running through your head.'

'Flattery will get you nowhere, John.' She left the Guinness to settle on the tray, and pointed to the bag on the floor. 'I mean it, that is not coming out.'

Every so often John chanced his arm and brought his accordion into the pub, in the hope that there would be a sing-song, which there was occasionally, and in the even greater hope that Yvonne would let him play. She couldn't abide it, the mournful whinge out of it. It was abysmal. Couple that with some song about a long-dead Finian rebel, which were the only tunes John knew, and it was a recipe for headaches and hangovers.

'Well, you never know, we'll see how the evening plays out anyway.' John deliberately looked over her head and down the long bar with an air of expectancy for the world's greatest trad session about to kick off in the lounge.

'If U2 walk in here later and say they're looking for someone to play the squeezebox, I'll send ye all off to Finnegan's. I mean it.' Finnegan's was the other pub in town; smaller than McCarthy's, it plied a regular trade.

John stroked his beard nonchalantly. The pint had settled.

Yvonne topped up the finishing inch and watched the creamy head rise. She slid it across the counter to him.

'We've been practising.'

She cocked an eyebrow at him.

'The lads.' He made an all-encompassing gesture around the fairly empty pub.

Yvonne bit back a smile. Her regular clientele could be called many things, but lads? That conjured up cajoling and back patting, hijinks and good-natured ear twists. Not the white-haired brigade that slid off stools after six pints.

'We've called ourselves The Ballyhay Trad Band . . .' He paused dramatically waiting for rapturous applause, she presumed.

'Well, I'm glad to hear you've been practising.'

'You'll have to book us in soon before we take off. We're going to put a video on YouTube.' John's chest swelled proudly. 'After that it's up, up, up.' His arm flew towards the sky like an airplane in full flight.

'Good on ye.' And Yvonne meant it. Why shouldn't they post videos and play their little hearts out?

Billy Byrne was sitting two stools down. He'd been nursing a pint for an hour now. Clearly hard up and wondering where his next one would come from, he'd tried to get his first of the night on the house.

'I'll pay you Tuesday. I get me pension on Tuesday.'

Yvonne had shaken her head. 'I'd be broke, Billy, if I let you drink here for free, we both know it. And you'll be straight into the bookies Tuesday, I'd be last on your list.'

That stopped him in his tracks. 'Oh, you're always first on my list, Yvonne. As soon as you're ready to marry me, I'll be here, with my hat in my hand.'

'What good is a hat to me, Billy?' And they'd laughed, good humoured as always but he paid up for his first drink. She offered him dinner on the house, but he passed it up. She'd never let him or any of them miss a meal; she looked after them all in her own way. Yvonne knew he'd move down the bar shortly and strike up a conversation with John, who'd more than likely buy the next round. Billy could sing. He'd been a tenor in his youth, sang at the National Concert Hall. Yvonne didn't mind when he let loose, he could still raise a tear for 'The Rose of Tralee'. John was itching to play, and if Billy got enough pints down him he'd sing along. They were like some ancient boy band, if they busted a move they'd crack a hip. 'Are you part of this band, Billy?'

'The Ballyhay Trad Band. I am indeed. We're fierce good, Yvonne.'

Maybe she'd let them play, see how the pub filled out. It was a little busier than normal for a Wednesday, that was good. There were some tourists down the back, a bit late in the summer for them. The season was normally petering out by the end of August. They might be religious ones, after coming to see the well and say a few prayers. There were fewer and fewer of them every year. The Catholic Church had really lost its shine. Elizabeth in Elizabeth's Café used to make a mint selling rosary beads and holy water. She had a little shelf on the left-hand side as you came into the café that you had to walk by to give your order and pay, stacked to the brim with Holy Joe stuff: mini sacred hearts, Virgin Marys, crosses on keyrings. It sold so well it nearly paid her mortgage one year. But not anymore. There probably wouldn't even be a queue if the Pope turned up for a cup of tea and some banana bread.

Here came Phillip Toomey in the door. Right on time every evening, 6.30 p.m. His son dropped him off and his daughter picked him up at 9 p.m. after he'd had his two pints. He was dressed as always as a dapper gentleman: white shirt, tie, waistcoat and jacket, hair Brylcreemed back. Phillip's wife had passed away two years ago and this nightly ritual kept his foothold firmly in the community. From his high stool perch he spread more gossip than he heard, and knew the business and history of every family from here to Galway.

Yvonne poured another Guinness and smiled to herself. She was never shy of marriage proposals behind the bar, never had been. There's something about a woman in control of the pints that drives them wild—the gatekeeper to all that joy, she assumed.

'How's the young wan in Dublin?' Phillip sat upright, immediately fishing for information.

'Good.' Yvonne waited for him to pursue his line of enquiry which she knew he would have been mulling over on the drive in.

'Bit of a star now, I suppose, after YouTube.' He raised his eyebrows knowledgeably.

'S'pose.' Yvonne left his pint to settle, deliberately giving him nothing and wondering where he was going.

Phillip slowly removed his jacket and placed it on the hook under the bar counter, running his hands over it to shake out the creases.

'Will she be taking after the mother?' Bingo. He didn't make eye contact.

'In what way?' Yvonne poured the remainder of his pint out, the creamy Guinness whirling like foam on the beach. She plopped a beermat down in front of him and positioned the pint accordingly.

'You know.' He stared down at the glass.

'If I knew why would I ask?' Yvonne took a step back from the counter and leaned herself against the shelf.

He sighed heavily. 'The magic and all that hocus pocus.' He made his shoulders do a little dance and Yvonne smiled. 'Just like the mother.'

'I think Mam is in that business all on her own.'

'But she's matchmaking, too? Same as her granny and isn't all that stuff—' another shoulder dance '—handed down the generations?'

'Well, then sure wouldn't I have it as well? Wouldn't I be in next door telling fortunes and not serving pints to you?' Yvonne had been asked this many times before. Where was her gift? As if she were lacking in something fundamental like a common sense, or the ability to drive.

Her mother had watched her and her brother closely for any signs of a second sight. She asked them questions that her friends were never asked by their parents: about their dreams and how they felt walking into a new place. She studied their early drawings and she waited patiently. But there was nothing. They never knew who was on the other end of the phone. They couldn't remember their dreams, nor did they get 'feelings' off people. Evie declared it a 'Blessing in disguise' and a 'Relief that it had ended'. Yvonne supposed it was. She didn't know. She couldn't miss what she'd never had. But she suspected by her mam's hopeful gaze and disappointed face that she desperately tried to hide from them that she was missing out on *something*. These days her mam seemed to have everything under control, and the matchmaking and card reading was a gentler escape for her. It had been many years since Yvonne had watched her endure an episode. As a child they'd been more frequent, or that could just be her memory; you always remember the bad things.

Yvonne had learned to spot the signs, little things at first: her mam's blouse would be buttoned incorrectly, she'd forget to put her lipstick on, her nail polish would be chipped. Yvonne would instantly start to feel uneasy, her senses heightening as she looked and listened for clues. She overheard hushed conversations between her parents. She wedged herself at the hinge of the door to the sitting room, peering through the slimmest of cracks.

'Now, love, maybe it's time to see the doctor. Get something to ease your nerves.' Her dad would say in a calm voice, he might put an arm around her mam or pat her knee.

'Nonsense, that just quietens the voices. They're trying to tell me something, Michael, and you're trying to drug me.' Mam agitated, her voice clipped. 'It's not my bloody nerves and you know it.'

'You haven't slept in weeks.'

'And I won't until I know what they want. They're coming at me from all angles, Michael. There are important messages coming. They're just not clear yet.' She'd be up, pacing the room, gesticulating. She'd start moving furniture around; Yvonne could hear the squeak of the chairs across the tiles.

'You've stopped taking care of yourself again. I'm worried. It's a sign that it's time for the doctor.'

'Ah Jesus, Michael, how many times do I have to tell you? I'm not taking the pills.' Back and forth, again and again. *Take the pills, I'm not taking the pills.*

Yvonne knew the fight inside out. It was followed by family life becoming disjointed. Chaos would creep in as dinners went uncooked and school uniforms unwashed.

As a teenager, Yvonne remembers feeling embarrassed by her mam at these times: catching her muttering to herself, staring into far-away places and going for long walks to look for something only to return with nothing but leaves in her hair. She seemed mad, there were no two ways about it. Yvonne heard the whispers around town, too, the thin-lipped sympathy: *Poor Evie McCarthy. Poor Michael McCarthy. She'll end up in the mad house.* Yvonne had heard stories of people being taken to institutions, snatched away from their families. And so, she tried very hard to keep things normal. She learned to cook for the family, to work behind the bar when Evie was on one of her walks. Dad would always step in. He would

take some time off from the pub to straighten things out until
the episode passed. After a while Evie would reappear in her
packaged form: lipstick on, gold bracelets jangling, hair up
and smelling of vanilla again. 'They're gone,' she would say
to much relief. Sometimes, she may have taken a trip somewhere to deliver a message. Sometimes, a letter or a phone call,
but once, Yvonne remembered because she was in her teens
and old enough to know what was going on, the guards were
called because Evie had gone and knocked on a front door in
a housing estate in Cork City at two in the morning. When
no one had answered she'd delivered the message at the top
of her lungs to the family inside.

Those events had been unusual or Yvonne had been shielded
from them and there hadn't been anything like that in over
twenty years. Yvonne wondered if her mam had finally taken
the pills to calm down the voices. She never discussed it with
her. Those days were not open for discussion. These days the
gift seemed more of a blessing than a curse.

Her mother particularly still watched Rosie. She had heard
her asking the same questions Yvonne had been asked moons
before, waiting patiently for something to happen, but as it
hadn't in twenty-four years, she should probably relax a little.
It was Rosie's birth that had peaked her mam's interest. An
excruciating sixteen hours of labour followed finally with the
blinding relief of pushing the baby out and the end, the glorious
end of contractions. Yvonne had waited to feel the warm weight
of her baby on her chest. She waited to feel the heavenly beat of
her baby's heart next to her and to wrap her in her arms. But
there was a pause, a momentary breath taken by the doctor
and the many nurses in the room. Something was wrong and

to Yvonne's heightened senses, every moment, every pulse and heartbeat that that baby was not on her chest was a lifetime. She watched as a nurse placed her hand to her mouth, eyes wide.

Yvonne roared at them as fierce as a lion. 'What's wrong? What's going on with my baby?'

They clicked to their senses and a gentle speaking nurse whispered to her, 'She's a beautiful baby, it's just that she's still in the sac. We haven't had a birth like this in a long time. It's very rare. She's a caul baby. She's blessed, your little one, a real good luck charm. She'll be one of the great ones.'

Yvonne had been reluctant to tell her mother about it. She did eventually and they agreed that if Rosie ever showed any signs of magic, Yvonne would direct her straight to her mam for guidance. Over the years, Rosie had thrilled her with wild enthusiasm about anything and everything: from horse-riding, to tennis to Pokémon and science projects. Rosie grabbed life with both hands and ran every which way. At school sports days, Rosie was never the medal winner; she was always the cheerleader, hair in bunches jumping and roaring until her voice gave in. She was a delight, Yvonne always felt that about her, but magical? No. There was no magic there.

'Two more, John. No bother.' John tapped the bar with two fingers, deep in conversation with Billy who was earning his free pint.

'You're a great man, John. Thanks very much. I'll get you back, mind.' Billy clapped him on the back as John shook off the gratitude.

Yvonne knew John would probably buy Billy another four before the night was out. Sure, what harm, they were enjoying one another's company. She didn't mind a slow evening now and again, but nothing made her heart soar like a busy night: shouts coming in over the bar, the walls pulsing with chat, the noise, the bustle. She'd play the taps like a piano, one hand on the till, one grabbing packets of cheese and onion crisps, and totting up the total for the next four vodka and tonics. She never felt more alert, eyes darting, never missing a customer or serving one out of order. It was a gift, a raw talent and Yvonne loved it. Some weekend nights she'd get a taste of it again, there'd be a rush and she'd be flying on adrenaline, her legs dancing and mind pulsing. Every pub needed regulars to keep the till ticking over and she had hers, they were a family of sorts; dysfunctional and argumentative, but good humoured and on friendly terms most of the time. They weren't enough, though, Yvonne needed a steadier stream, or a lotto win.

She had a plan, or she thought she had a plan. She'd mentioned it in passing to Maria Manifold. Well, now, she didn't mention that she was in dire straits and the tax man was positioning a noose around her neck, but she'd made a throw-away comment about how it would be nice to have more access to money for a holiday or a new car—two things which couldn't be further from her mind. *A second mortgage*, Maria had announced triumphantly; she had done it after her second marriage had collapsed. *Easiest thing I ever did, had the money in a few days. Took a trip to San Francisco.* Yvonne felt it was worth a shot. She really had nothing to lose.

'I might have some pies in the back, Phillip, if you'd like one?' Yvonne was never sure how well Phillip coped with the cooking since his wife was gone so she always offered him dinner.

'One of the steak and kidneys? Did you make 'em?'

'Not this lot, no.'

'I won't, so, I only like the ones you make.'

'Sure, I haven't time to be cooking for you.'

'G'wan you do. You'd love to cook for me all day and you will when we're married.' He grinned at her and took a long sip of his pint.

'A proposal that has me chained to the stove all day and behind the bar all night. Well, sure, I'd be a mad woman to say no.' Yvonne shook her head and laughed.

'Ah, it won't be like that. We'll be fierce happy and I'll be fat as a fool.' He patted his shirt down at the waist.

'Will there be a song tonight?' He had spotted John's accordion hiding under the bar.

'I'm in a good mood tonight, there might,' Yvonne said loud enough to be heard by the rest of the bar.

And with that John practically fell off his high stool and into the accordion with happiness. 'You're fierce good, Yvonne. Sure what would I do without you?' he roared, straightening himself up.

'We'd all be long dead and buried in the ground if it wasn't for Yvonne,' Billy Byrne piped up from the chorus line.

'G'wan with you.' Yvonne waved them away. She turned her back on the bar and made a fuss of some scampi fries spilling out of a cardboard box. She had to make this work. Somehow. She had to keep McCarthy's doors open for all of them. It was more than just a pub, it was family. She couldn't fail family.

13

Evie

EVIE HAD SECURED A WINDOW SEAT. THE MINIBUS SPED ALONG the motorway, and they'd just passed through Ballygarrett, so it was under an hour now until they got to Dublin. The laughter on the bus had quietened down a little. Two members of the senior aqua aerobics class had nodded off and the other eight were chatting happily or watching the fields speed by while draining the last of the prosecco from plastic glasses. Mary Moloney had produced a bottle from her handbag to shrieks of delight as they reversed out of the leisure centre car park in Ballyhay. They organised an excursion a couple of times a year. The last one, a trip to the Titanic museum in Belfast, had ended badly when they had to call in security to find Shane Ferguson. The one and only male of the group, to all intents and purposes, had disappeared. It caused a terrible flurry, with everyone racing around trying to retrace their steps; of course he'd told Mary that he had to FaceTime his grandson so had retreated to a café across the road for some peace and quiet, only Mary had forgotten. They were moments from calling the guards when he strolled happily across the road waving a bag of chocolate croissants to share on the bus back. They set up a WhatsApp group after that, Swim Patrol, and all agreed to check in every fifteen minutes if they got separated, but hopefully they wouldn't have to test it out. They were off to see a matinee musical at the Gaiety, *Falling Slowly,* followed by an earlybird supper in Dublin Castle and then home again. It was all organised and paid for. The sun was shining, everyone had an itinerary and a few glasses of bubbles on board; it promised to be a great day.

Evie was wearing a green silk dress, emerald green. It had a full, pleated skirt and delicate, gold buttons formed an orderly shimmering line down the front. Her black woollen coat with a leather trim was in the overhead compartment along with her handbag. She didn't like carrying much money in her bag, especially not in Dublin, so strapped onto her bra in a special pocket she made herself was five hundred and fifty euro in case of an emergency. Well, you never knew, did you? It was always better to be prepared. Molly was going to collect her from Dublin Castle. She'd decided not to return on the bus but instead spend a few nights with her granddaughter. She didn't see enough of her or those two beautiful boys. She remembers how hard it was with small children to do anything, let alone traipse across the country to see your grandmother, so she would make the effort and come to her. She had new books for the boys packed into her overnight bag, bouncing around somewhere underneath the bus. She felt weak with happiness at the very thought of having them sit on her lap and point out the trucks and ducks pictured. There was such exquisite pleasure in having a sweet little boy snuggle into you and delight in the very stillness and comfort of having a story read to him. Evie knew that life was littered with these happy, peaceful moments; there was so much joy in the everyday. Tonight, she would breathe in the top of her breathtaking great-grandsons' heads and savour their silky smell and laugh when they rummaged in her bag for chocolates. Of course, she had chocolate for them, what kind of a great-granny was she if she didn't have chocolates? She had found racing-car-shaped chocolates, football ones, a chocolate train that was as long as her arm and a large box of handmade truffles for Molly, who'd always had a sweet tooth. Molly had popped up twice in the cards this week—nothing sinister, just indicating a change of some sort. Evie knew that the cards were guiding her and had been for the last month. What may seem innocent this week could quickly escalate. She knew that something was heading her way, something was coming down the line for all the McCarthy girls, she just wished she knew what. The cards frustrated her. They could be too vague, too easy to misinterpret. They were just another tool for her to use, but she wished they could be clearer. All these chalices and coins presenting themselves for her to decipher were all very well, but a text message, a few emojis, now that would be easier.

Evie had always been more than a matchmaker; over the years she'd also broken up couples. She wasn't particularly proud of it but sometimes that's what was needed. When Susan and Tony Smith had come to her, years ago, she knew it was over by the way he sat down in a chair with a heavy sigh and a sadness lingering in his eyes. He pulled his check shirt tight across his chest and folded his arms. Evie had matched them years previously.

'I think you got us wrong!' Susan had shouted accusingly with a tight mouth and anger tensing her shoulders, barely able to sit still.

'I didn't get you wrong then, but you're wrong now.' Evie didn't hold back. What was the point?

'So, we're not a match made in heaven then?' Tony's voice was heavy with sarcasm.

Susan threw her arms up in the air in a gesture of defiance and disbelief, finally agreeing with Tony.

'Well, you were. You had everything you needed to make it work, but you blew it.'

'That doesn't make any sense. If we're a match we're always a match. You don't know what you're talking about.' Susan was choking on the words.

Evie leaned forward and spoke clearly. She had no intention of repeating herself. 'You let the lights go out. You let the love fade away. You only have yourselves to blame. If you lost your car keys you'd go looking for them, wouldn't you? But you didn't look for your lost love, you let it disappear.' There was no point sugar-coating it for some people.

'Well . . .' Susan suddenly sat quietly.

Evie tapped her fingers on the table. 'Sometimes you can work very hard and stoke the embers and fire up the light of love again, but other times it just burns out. And that's what it's meant to do and even after trying to fire it up again you find you can't. And that's the journey, and if you've tried, if you've really tried and it hasn't worked, then it might be time to move on.'

They'd looked from one to the other.

'So, what you're saying is—' Tony lowered his voice '—that you got us wrong, that we're finished now.'

Evie didn't need a spotlight to see their unhappiness. 'I'm saying what was there is now gone and you'll both be happier away from each other.'

Their shoulders dropped as they exhaled.

Evie could feel their relief. 'You don't have to listen to me, but listen to yourselves, bickering and arguing with one another. Why? The love burned out. It's no one's fault, sometimes it just happens. And now it's time to move on. I'm in the match-making business, not breaking people up, but God almighty you two are miserable. Life is good you know. Enjoy it.'

Evie became a counsellor and a confidant, too. She knew she could understand people and she often made unpopular decisions. She'd found herself in trouble with a lot of the Ballyhay mammies over the years. The town was too small for their children. They needed to get out and spread their wings, to find adventure and romance overseas. To bloom in the world and not be trodden down in a place they didn't fit. Maura Phillips sprung to mind. She'd turned as mad as a *Bachelor* finalist who didn't get the rose. She'd sent her only son to Evie to be matched, she wanted him married, settled and getting ready to take over the family dairy farm. Any idiot could see he'd no interest in cows. Numbers came flying at her the minute Evie met this shy, unassuming young man. He'd chewed on his thumb, shrugged his shoulders and said, 'I suppose it would be okay to get married.'

No interest. 'Is there an offer? A university?'

He practically sprung out of his seat. 'How'd you know that?'

Evie stopped herself from rolling her eyes.

'Yes. A Masters degree at Trinity in Dublin, pure maths.' His face hung down defeated. 'It won't be much use to me on the farm.'

'Take it. Go. And then you're going to go further. This is just the beginning for you. You'll be in the far east for years, with work, very successful.' She could see his vocation clearly.

His face lit up. 'I've always wanted to work in aeronautics. I'm fascinated by it.'

Evie nodded.

'But Mammy, oh lord, what'll I do about her?'

'She has her life to lead and you have yours. No one should stand in the way of a soul's purpose. She'll be fine, eventually.'

Well, she wasn't fine as it turned out. She still crossed the road when she saw Evie McCarthy coming towards her and turned her shoulder to her in the frozen foods aisle of the supermarket. She wasn't one to forgive all these years later, because even though her son was very successful, he was still unmarried and that drove her wild. Evie had a few enemies in the town, if you'd call them that, *people scorned* might be a better turn of phrase. The problem was that she couldn't keep her mouth shut when she saw wrong decisions being made. She'd even broken up a wedding ceremony or two and that had not gone down well, what with the cost of the big day. But it was for the best, it was always for the best. Young people can't live the lives their parents have mapped out for them, life doesn't work like that.

She'd been young herself when she'd first met Karl, nineteen years of age, that summer before she knew Michael. And how that chance meeting in the doctor's office just recently had made her suddenly feel that rush of youth again. He still looked young to her, although he wasn't. His wrinkles told another story as did hers. But still, there was the memory. It had all been so fleeting. A blink really. A deep breath in a lifetime of a billion breaths. And yet sitting across from him the day before over a tuna salad and a white wine in the grounds of his aunt's house, it felt like they had known each other their whole lives. Which they had, of course. Karl was funny. Evie hadn't remembered him being funny. Maybe it was the confidence of age that somehow had allowed his humour to grow. He was distinguished, his blue shirt pressed, his tie a deep red, his shoes polished but it could also have been the surroundings that lead to an air of assurance. Karl had moved into the cottage in the grounds of the big house, bringing with him a lot of grand old artefacts which had been cleaned out before demolition began. They were dining with Waterford crystal glasses and real silver cutlery under the eyes of a Jack B Yeats painting. There was a chandelier in the kitchen and an antique French armoire in the bathroom. He had thrown his arms to heaven at that one. 'I don't think we can call it the pauper's cottage anymore.'

And Evie had laughed. She heard a girlish giggle escape from her and wondered where it had come from. 'Why did you hold onto it for all this time?' she asked.

'Nostalgia maybe. My aunt's memory. And it was rented out so it just ticked over. I bought my brother out a while ago, and honestly, I didn't know what to do with the place.'

'It's such a beautiful old house.' Evie felt wistful at the memory of it. 'Your aunt and her diamonds and furs. She was so very grand, especially for a place like Ballyhay.'

'She thought she was better than this town. I think that's why she lived here, to feel superior.' He pushed the tip of his finger to his nose. 'She was an unadulterated snob.'

'Well, living with chandeliers would give anyone notions.' Evie sipped the cool wine from her glass. 'Not to mention the antique crystal.'

'It was one of the chandeliers that brought it all to a head, almost came down on the tenant, huge tonne of a thing in the dining room. Then we found out the house was falling in, completely rotten, been held together by woodworm and some of Aunt Freidman's diamonds.' He looked happily across the table at her. 'I'm so glad we can still talk.'

She knew exactly what he meant.

'Would you like to have a little stroll around the gardens? While there still are gardens,' he explained. 'It'll be a building site next week. The house will be demolished. The gardens flattened.'

'Progress, I suppose,' Evie had said. 'It'll be a shame to see it go.'

'It will. But I've held on to it for long enough. It's time. And it's a great construction project for my son. We'll work on this one together but it's the handover, my swan song, after this the business is all his. I'm stepping away or more like shuffling away now in my old age.'

Again, Evie heard that giggle. 'No, we're not old. We've still got it.' She smiled and kept beaming as they moved outside and enjoyed the fresh air, the wealth of greenery and the crunch of stones beneath their feet.

'You've definitely still got it, Evelyn. You never lost it. May I?' Karl held his open hand out towards her, and surprising herself, without pausing for breath she took it in hers. And like they were nineteen all over again, they walked hand in hand around his aunt's garden, admiring the towering ferns and stopping to smell the lavender. And it was marvellous, and Evie felt a flicker inside her that she had not known could reignite.

'You're making me giddy, Karl.'

'Well, that's a good thing, isn't it?' He smiled back at her. 'Evelyn, at our stage of life we know what matters.'

'Oh, you've gone all serious.' And he had, he'd stopped straight as a soldier frozen in action. His eyes, those woodland-coloured eyes, flashed with sincerity. 'Maybe, but the truth is we don't know what's around the corner or how much time we have left, and I know I'm planning on enjoying every minute.'

Evie smiled, conscious now of the knot that had formed in her stomach. The difference was she knew how much time she had left and it wasn't long at all.

14

Rosie

'I'M SORRY TO SAY THIS, ROSIE, BUT YOU'VE BEEN DUMPED.' Catriona looked mournfully into their shared plate of loaded nachos. They were lunching at a tiny Mexican restaurant with plastic cacti swinging from the ceiling that managed to bop her on the head if she even so much as hovered off the seat.

'No offence, but I think that's a little extreme, like you've just jumped off the end of the pier here.' Rosie nodded sharply at her. She knew Catriona had good intentions but always with the drama. There was no way Rosie had been dumped.

Catriona took a deep breath. 'Okay, let's look at the facts. You haven't seen him in six days, there have been no texts, no calls, no social media interaction. You're assuming he went to another country almost a week ago but . . .'

'You make it sound so . . .' Rosie stared at her pointedly.

'Prior to this fight what was the longest period without contact?'

'I mean a couple of hours, but that doesn't mean . . .' Rosie grabbed a nacho and munched sulkily. 'He's busy, there's a crisis, he needs to sort it out.'

Catriona placed a hand over hers. 'I'm so sorry, Rosie, but I've seen this a million times, you're being ghosted.'

The poncho-wearing mariachi band suddenly livened up and started to belt out a Madonna medley. Rosie fought hard not to chair dance to it.

'It's not that I don't believe you, Catriona. It's just that Simon loves me. We're in love. Besides I've never been dumped before or ghosted.'

'Have you ghosted people?'

'Absolutely, I am queen of the number blockers and I've dumped people. It's horrible, but you know, it's good manners in a weird way—the rules are understood and I'm a stickler for the rules. It's just never happened to me and it definitely hasn't happened with Simon.' Rosie shook her head in disbelief. She had *not* been dumped. He was busy and fully immersed in work. He didn't have time to text.

Catriona's phone shimmied a little dance on the table, she glanced down at it. Eyes wide, she spoke slowly, 'I realise this might be wholly inappropriate at such a delicate time, but OMGeeeee look what's just come in on my phone.'

She flashed her screen hosting a smiling, slightly stubble-faced man at her with a message from DeLuvGuru. 'Hooray, you've found each other.'

'Oh my God. He's gorgeous.' Rosie snatched the phone from her and quickly swiped through his profile. 'He's tall, too. And—' Rosie zoomed in '—he has exceptionally kind eyes. He'd bring you chicken soup when you had a cold-eyes, soup he'd make himself not just from a packet. You can tell by those eyes, he's not a packet soup kind of guy.'

'This is weird. He's my one, right? I mean is this the moment I'll be telling my grandchildren about, how I met Grandpa Barry? His name is Barry, isn't it?' Catriona looked back at the screen.

'Maybe.' Rosie started to laugh, a nervous giggle rumbled from her belly. 'Your grandchildren will be holograms anyway. It'll be normal for them.'

'Or they'll be living in a cave by candlelight in a dystopian future, huddled around one copy of the only book that survived the war, *The Handmaid's Tale*, waiting for the battle cry to revolt against the Empire from the rebels?'

Rosie threw her a sideways glance. 'Okay, seriously lay off the YA books for a while.'

Catriona shrugged in a *don't say I didn't tell you the future is bleak* way.

'He looks nice.' Rosie couldn't help but smile at the charming array of pictures Barry had posted, including one with a golden retriever. 'Sorry, he looks perfect. Did you know he volunteers at a homeless shelter? For God's sake, did you write this profile? Ahhh . . .' She screamed and dropped the phone with a clatter as a text popped in.

Barry: Hi, good afternoon, how are you?

'Sweet mother of God.' Catriona stared.
'Text him back!' Rosie ordered.
'What?'

'I don't know. He's your husband not mine, but I already love him a bit for not using predictive text and not one emoji. Not one. He's a bloody miracle. Just say hi.'

'Okay and then what?' Catriona started texting.

'How are you?' Rosie watched as Catriona's fingers flew across the screen. She peered up at her. 'And . . . ?'

'No. This isn't *Cyrano de Bergerac*. It's you and him remember? Not me, third wheel.' Rosie made shooing gestures at her.

'You're better at this than me. You're so good at talking.'

'And you're good at texting. Text him. And while you're doing that, I'm going to text my boyfriend for the umpteenth time and ask him how he is? Or maybe I'll ask him if his phone has fallen down the loo? Or maybe he's dead? I'm thinking death is probably the most logical explanation now,' Rosie joked, but inside she was beginning to wonder. Was it possible? Was he ghosting her? More than likely it was the silent treatment, a fight followed by a cooling-off period. They loved each other after all, people in love didn't ghost each other. Maybe he *was* dead.

'Barry wants to meet.' Catriona stared across the nachos.

'Meet him. You're going to marry him after all, so you'll have to meet eventually.'

Catriona gasped. 'Tonight. Hang on a minute, he's still typing . . . The Spiral Stairs Book Café. He loves books as much as me.' Her mouth fell open in shock. 'It's just, I mean seriously . . . look at me.' They both gazed down at her arm held proudly on display. 'Goosebumps.'

'This is what DeLuvGuru is all about. It's supposed to be this weird. Love is crazy.' Rosie felt she was putting up a good game, saying what she was supposed to say, but honestly, she felt more than a bit wobbly, too. It was bizarre. Was it really going to be this simple? Was everyone going to live happily ever after? She knew she'd said that; she'd rattled off the sales spiel in interviews, and Simon had told her that the technology worked, but had she actually believed it? Could finding love really be as easy as signing up to an app?

It was the earliest Rosie had ever made it into the office the following morning. She hadn't heard a peep from Catriona, who had promised to at least fire an emoji at her after the date. But nothing. Instead, she'd received four texts in a row from her mam.

> Are you awake?
>
> Are you watching the Masterchef rerun?
>
> Can you believe the paella?
>
> Remember the one I made with a lime and the difference it made?

While Rosie was no amateur chef, she did consider herself a professional eater and was very passionate about her mam's cooking. As always, the many texts led to a long FaceTime call with the two of them in their beds propped up on pillows and chatting about the important things in life.

'Mam, you're too far gone. You can't just jump into season two of *Killing Eve*, you've no context.'

'I watched the recap. I get the gist, mad Russian killer on the loose.'

'But why skip? Why not watch and enjoy it?'

'But I know what's going to happen now. I'll keep going. Call me in the morning and let me know how Catriona got on. They might have eloped; hopped on a plane to Scotland and straight to Gretna Green. People still get married there, don't they?'

'Ask Gran.' Rosie laughed. 'If she was going off to get married, I'd be a bridesmaid, I know it. No, something else is going on.'

'Maybe they want some privacy.' Rosie watched her mam's eyes enlarge and mouth form a pout.

'Maaaaaaam. Stop it.' She wriggled uncomfortably.

'Take it as a good thing that she's not texting you, her hands are too busy.'

'That's it, Mam, I'm hanging up.'

'Lovemaking, isn't that what Mam calls it?' Yvonne was laughing hard.

'Goodnight.'

For the rest of the night Rosie had stared at her phone willing it to buzz with news from Catriona, and also maybe hoping for a text from Simon. After a fitful night's sleep she'd decided to throw in the towel at first light and was up, showered and powdered by 6.30 a.m., prowling the office floors like an alley cat looking for scraps by 7.30 a.m. An excruciating hour later, Catriona strolled in, braided hair tightly pulled back in a neat bun, fresh-faced, in a baby pink shirt, white jeans and loafers that made her look like a member of the royal family spotted off-duty buying goats cheese and champagne at the local organic grocery. Serious Steve clicked down the hallway after her, putting a freeze to Rosie's spring, so to get Catriona's attention instead she coughed like a one-hundred-and-four-year-old asthmatic on the verge of convulsions.

'Rosie, you should get that seen to,' Serious shouted across the open-plan office. 'Don't want you spreading germs around here.' He hopped back nervously and moved as quick as lightning on a golf course to the furthest possible point from Rosie.

Rosie patted down the air around her. 'It's nothing, just something caught in my throat.' She wiped away the surprising amount of spit that had found its way to her chin and decided to sit quietly for a moment watching Catriona as she moved towards her desk and flicked on her computer. Not once did she look her way. Why not?

Rosie typed a message.

> Rosie: Ehhhhh hello?
>
> Catriona: Morning
>
> Rosie: Well?
>
> Catriona: Let's grab a coffee

Rosie leapt out of her seat as Catriona reluctantly rose, head hanging low, eyes downcast and wrapping her arms around herself. She joined Rosie on the walkway. Rosie knew, she knew by her stooped posture and the fact that she couldn't look her straight in the eye that something was wrong.

'Are you okay?' she whispered, picking up her pace, grateful that Catriona mimicked accordingly.

'I'm so sorry, Rosie.' Her voice caught.

'What? What are you sorry for? What happened?'

As they reached the kitchen, Rosie grabbed Catriona's elbow and pulled her into a corner.

'Are you okay?' Rosie repeated herself, this time positioning her nose forcefully as close as she could to Catriona's in spite of her towering height.

'Yes, I'm fine, I just . . .' She stopped, her dark eyes narrowed. 'I don't know how to tell you this.'

'Just tell me!' Rosie's whisper shouted at her.

Catriona took a deep breath. Rosie watched her nostrils flare and her chest rise and fall. 'I didn't like him.'

'What?'

'Yeah, I mean he was fine. Niceish, a bit up his own arse, but fine. But I didn't like him and I definitely didn't fancy him.'

'Oh.' Rosie felt herself shrink with the weight of disappointment. 'But that's not possible.'

'I mean he was polite and everything, but he was just so dull. I don't think he cracked a smile once. He didn't ask me anything about myself, nothing. I could be a cattle-farming cowboy for all he knows. And he did that really annoying talking over me thing; anytime I opened my mouth, which wasn't often, he just talked straight through it.' Catriona shook her head apologetically.

'Was he cute?' Rosie asked, dry-mouthed.

'Again, fine, he was fine looking and he did look like his pictures. He's probably handsome, but he might have looked better if he'd smiled.' Disappointment was oozing out of her friend. 'Honestly, Rosie, it was a pretty terrible date.'

'I don't understand.' Rosie knew how the first world explorers must have felt when they learned the world was round and not flat. 'It doesn't make sense.'

'I know.'

'He was supposed to be it.' There was a tightness developing across her chest.

'He's definitely not.' Catriona clamped her mouth shut in defiance.

'Are you sure?' Rosie raised her eyes and her hopes slightly.

'Not a chance.' Catriona crossed her arms in a battle pose.

'Could this just be, you know, another good story that you want to tell but really you fancied him?'

'Come on, Rosie, you know me better than that,' Catriona sighed and her chin wobbled slightly. 'I wanted this to work so much. I want to meet that guy. I want to fight with someone over Netflix and watch sports I'm not interested in. I want to have a horrible mother-in-law and fall over giant size 12 shoes in the hallway because you know they're his and it's him and all the shit is worth it.'

Rosie took a deep breath and heard her voice meekly asking, 'Would you go on a second date? What if he's a slow burner?'

'And waste flames on damp fuel? I don't think so, Rosie. I'm so sorry.' Catriona reached across and gave her a tight hug, wrapping her arms right around her.

Can you please squeeze me harder?' Rosie needed to feel something other than the shock that was coursing through her. 'Harder again, please.'

Catriona caught her wrist behind Rosie's back and rocked her gently from side to side in a comforting dance. 'It'll be ok. You'll figure this out,' she said in soothing tones.

'Will I? What will I figure out? Does it not work?' The words were coming out in a series of panicked clicks.

'I don't know.' Catriona squeezed the last bit of air out of her lungs and held Rosie in an iron-clad grip.

'Shitbags.' Rosie eloquently responded.

Back at her desk a few hours later, Rosie made an executive decision—she was still going to revolutionise dating. Every company had bumps and bruises at the beginning, and this was just the kick-off point. There was clearly some kind of a computing error somewhere in the system. Something at the back end, she decided. Everything would be fine with a little bit of jiggery-pokery to the program. There was no need to get upset. Steve Jobs didn't just roll over one morning and find an iPhone underneath his pillow, a gift from a misguided tooth fairy. No, he would have had lots of different versions; Rosie herself had already had five different iPhones, imagine how many Steve Jobs had had. DeLuvGuru was on version 1.0 and it needed to get to 6.0. In a mature business-like moment, putting all emotions and arguments aside, while Serious Steve was not patrolling the halls of her real job, Rosie sent an email to Simon at her other job.

Simon,

I know you're not talking to me and I'm not talking to you either, hence the email. But I think DeLuvGuru has a problem. I suspect it's on your end. I'm not blaming you but I'm just saying it looks like you completely messed up on the programming somewhere so maybe I am blaming you. Catriona got matched with a guy called Barry, went on a date with him last night and didn't like him. I repeat, SHE DID NOT FALL IN LOVE WITH HIM. There is something wrong with the programming. Can you look at those algorithms and change them? I'm serious Simon. I know it's only the beginning, I know we've only been live a week, but this app should work. You said it would work. We promised people, I promised Catriona. Can you take a look at it and tell me what happened?

Rosie

She hit send. He would have to respond. She deliberately hadn't asked how he was or where he was, and there was no romantic or even *mildly fond of you* sign off. That would show him.

Rosie had a mountain of work to get through: she had four emails to write for a mid-season sale (that had some genuine bargains she'd be snapping up herself), three landing pages and a stack of new product descriptions that had found their way into her inbox late last night. She wouldn't have time to breathe all day, let alone worry about DeLuvGuru. She had a wage to earn and floral fit and flare dresses to write about. And then something most unexpected happened—Simon's email bounced back.

15

Molly

Trim the meat and chop into one-inch-cube size
pieces. Coat with two tablespoons of flour.

Molly took a deep breath. Her sleeves were rolled and an
apron was neatly tied around her waist as she held a giant
butcher's carving knife threateningly over six striploin steaks.
Trim means cut the fat, she reminded herself, one inch means
bite size. Right, she could do this.

'I mean how in this day and age could he not be on social
media?' Anna threw her phone down in disgust. She was
perched at the island in Molly's kitchen, cradling a cup of tea
and making her way through some Jaffa Cakes. Anna had
come over for moral support—batten down the hatches and
call in the army—Molly was cooking.

'It just seems, you know . . . suspicious somehow. And I've
gone deep—very deep—into the internet and I can't find him.

You know how good I am at finding someone?' Detective Inspector Anna's nose was most definitely out of joint. She had spent precious time frantically googling and trawling through social media for Charlie, the phantom Mary Poppins. And in spite of keeping a tight surveillance of Molly's front door via many drive-bys and countless buggy push-bys, she had not caught sight of the drop-dead gorgeous sleep nanny.

'Maybe I've made him up.' Molly cocked her head over her shoulder, laughing.

'At this point it's the only explanation.' Anna sounded genuinely annoyed. 'I bet if I go up to your bedroom right now, I'd find a blow-up male nurse in your wardrobe that you drag around the house and talk to when no one is here.'

'My secret. Ahhh—' Molly turned the knife towards her own chest and pointed it down '—there's no other way out.'

'Just get a picture of him, that will keep me happy.' Anna pushed the plate of Jaffa Cakes to the edge of the island. 'Take these away, would you?'

'I'm going to have to call Mam. I don't understand half of this recipe.' Molly ignored Anna, grabbed her phone and FaceTimed her mam.

Yvonne picked up immediately. 'Your hair! Hold the phone back a little bit to give me a full three-sixty.'

Dutifully, Molly spun herself and her phone around, angling the camera at her head. She was still getting used to her new pixie look—platinum blonde with a long side-swept fringe that nipped in at the nape of her neck. It had been a last-minute decision; the kind of impetuous move Molly used to make. She came across the voucher tucked away in a rarely opened kitchen drawer under the potato masher and next to an unused whisk. Someone, she can't remember who, had gifted her a salon voucher after Andy was born. It was out of date by eight months, but one quick call, and hey presto, they promised to honour it. Angela arrived to babysit with a grimace.

'Great for you popping out to the hairdressers mid-week. I've always worked so it was weekends for me with the hairdressers, a real treat for you. I'm due a cut, too, but I just can't find the time.'

Molly plopped her handbag back down, her heart sinking. 'Angela, if this doesn't suit, I'm sorry.'

'I'm here now.'

'It's just that they told me to come in quickly as they had a spot. It's an out-of-date voucher . . .'

'Go. Enjoy,' Angela responded, devoid of any enjoyment.

And Molly had zipped up her light-weight jacket and left with a stomach lined with guilt. All the joy of a pampering session sucked out of her.

She sunk into the smooth leather seats, flicking through a magazine and something overtook her: guilt, anger and an overwhelming desire to do something unexpected.

'That. I want that.' She firmly planted her finger on a picture of Gwyneth Paltrow fashioning her nineties' hair-do, which was exactly the same as Brad Pitt's, her boyfriend at the time.

'I want Brad and Gwyneth's haircut combined, please.'

The hairdresser paused, surveying her client. 'Divorce? Are you going through a divorce?'

'No. I have young children.'

And solemnly the hairdresser confided that she too was a mother and offered her twenty per cent off any deep conditioning products.

Molly gave Angela a hair mask on her return which went down like a cheap cocktail.

'You're not to spend your money on me. Take it back, I don't want it.'

Molly had already broken the seal to have a sniff so there was no returning it in any case.

'Sorry, I just wanted to say thank you.'

'Not by spending money, no. That's why I help out so you don't have to pay a babysitter and you can save. I don't want this.' She wagged an admonishing finger, making Molly feel two-inches high.

'Thank you,' she said meekly. She would have to talk to Dommo. This was not working. She hated asking Angela for anything. But on the plus side Molly did love her new hair. It was such a dramatic change but it suited her. Even she could admit that she looked younger and more vibrant somehow, her eyes looked bluer. It helped that she had taken two minutes in the morning to spread some primer on her skin, layer on a fine coating of mascara and a brush of blusher. And of course, it helped a lot that she'd slept for the last four nights. Every particle in her body felt bouncy.

'It's just gorgeous,' Yvonne cooed down the line.

'Charlie thinks so, too,' Anna sung in the background.

'Anna!' Molly scolded her. 'I'm talking to Mam.'

Anna waved behind her, showing her presence to Yvonne.

'Hi, Anna. Can neither of you cook?' Yvonne laughed.

'Toast and chicken nuggets are my speciality!' Anna shouted.

Yvonne, patiently and for the third time that morning, started to go through the boeuf bourguignon recipe, slowly explaining how to braise the meat, the importance of red wine and shallot onions. Once again, Molly listened like a good student and took notes where needed, while thinking that she may have lost the run of herself. Surely a few chicken kievs thrown in the oven would fill hungry bellies just as well. Two weeks after Charlie had turned up on her doorstep to start the sleep routine, it was finally working. There had now been four nights of full sleep, in a row, and Molly's world had turned upside down; she felt like herself again or a jacked-up version of herself. It was as if she'd spent the last eighteen months locked in parent jail quietly creating bucket lists of what she'd do on release, and now here she was checking them off with military precision. Yesterday, she had brought the boys to the pool, something she hadn't done in the six months since Andy had shut the toddler pool down when a giant poo snuck out of his nappy like a toxic submarine coming up for air. With great defiance, they had slipped into their togs, repeatedly visited the toilet, and splashed happily for approximately fourteen minutes. She brought the boys to the library and took a Cathy Kelly book out for herself. She had downloaded the 'Couch to 5k' beginners' jogging app and may even consider starting it. And tonight, in honour of her grandmother extending her stay a few days, she was cooking a fancypants meal for her family. Her sister Rosie was coming, Dommo had promised to be on time, and in a show of unmistakable kindness and goodwill, the new and improved Molly had invited Angela. That gesture should earn her some kind of medal in heaven or a fast-track pass through the pearly gates. She had also decided to wear a pre-pregnancy dress that was a little snug, but just about passable if she popped a few buttons when she sat down and wore a cardigan to hide the fact that the zip was only pulled up halfway.

She hung up from her mam and methodically started to carve away at the meat.

'You're a brat, Anna. You shouldn't have said that about Charlie. What if Mam had heard?' Molly giggled.

'Well, it's true, isn't it?' Anna opened and closed the fridge looking for something, but not quite knowing what.

Molly didn't respond. It was true that Charlie had said he liked it. Well, actually he'd said, 'You're lovely.' Then he'd looked suddenly away and apologised, 'Sorry, I mean your hair is lovely.' Charlie's third visit had fallen on the day after her hair appointment and his mouth had fallen open slightly as she'd answered the door with Andy on her hip, his pudgy little hand slapping her cheek repeatedly. She watched in amazement as Charlie stammered and fumbled his way into the house. Was she having an effect on him? Was this something she could possibly do? Still? Back in the day, when her skirts were dangerously short and her tops were circulation-stopping tight she'd had plenty of offers, but it had been a while. And now this previously polished man was sneaking sideways glances as if he didn't quite recognise her.

'Tea?' She had thrown her standard greeting out at him.

'Go on. I will, I'll just . . .' He had unpacked, swung his bag off his shoulder, stripped off his jacket, popped his shoes at the door and was crouched on the ground playing racing cars with Rory before the kettle had boiled.

She slipped the mug of tea into his hand and found herself humming as she straightened the kitchen. 'Dommo's working late!' she shouted into thin air, not sure why she was marking his absenteeism. Dommo was never there, he never made bedtime anymore. He hadn't even met Charlie. He'd spent last weekend on emergency conference calls. And his absence was exhausting.

'The red one has turbo jets.' She heard Rory excitedly revving up his cars, knowing how delighted he was to show off his collection.

She watched Charlie crash and zoom his non-turbo jet car into second place.

'Loser. You're the loser.'

'Looks like it.' Charlie feigned devastation. 'Come on, let's go again. I'll win this time.'

Molly heard more zooming, whirring, smashing and delighted yelps from Rory.

'Again, Charlie lose again!' Rory howled in happiness.

'Okay, losers, let's get this show on the road.' Molly was breaking up the car party. Immediately, at the sniff of bedtime, Andy threw himself on the ground in full meltdown, kicking tiny feet and thumping fists.

Charlie and Molly caught each other's eyes and she gave a knowing smile. They'd been through this. He had given her coping mechanisms that did not involve a quick look at videos on her phone. And so, under his watchful gaze she started putting them in place. She turned her attention to Rory, took his hand and moved towards the stairs.

'Rory, you're going to have a lovely bath,' she sung to him.

Andy continued to roar, but by the time they'd reached the first step, his cries were dimming to a whimper. He peeped up to see why no one was looking at him. Charlie's peaceful presence hovered in the background as Molly went through the night-time routine. Right through the bubble bath, the nappy refusal, the great pyjama chase and the never-ending toothbrushing nightmare, Charlie offered calm, helpful advice and encouraging words, praising Molly and her efforts not to lose her shit.

Rory had recently become a night walker; small blessings that Andy couldn't climb out of his cot yet. Within five minutes of being put down, Rory sprung like a jack-in-the-box out of his room to roam the house looking for mischief. Tonight, Molly and Charlie positioned themselves at his doorway. Molly was going to redirect him back to bed. They sat side by side on the floor, their backs resting against the wall of the dimly lit hallway.

'Thanks, Charlie.' Her fist gently bumped the side of his knee. 'They're hard work.'

'Not at all. They are fantastic little guys with a lot of energy.' He said quietly, 'You're doing a great job, you know.'

Molly felt a lump catch in her throat. She had never been sure she wanted children. Some women were just so sure—they knew, or they pretended they knew. Molly couldn't understand how you could know *that*. How you could be so certain that having a child was the thing to do. But herself and Dommo had decided to go for it because that seemed to be what you did. She got pregnant so easily. Now she knows how lucky they were, but at the time she felt shocked. Pregnant. Wow. They were really doing this. But all of it: the bloating, the sleeplessness, the all-day sickness and exhaustion. Every second was worth it when she met Rory. She had howled and sobbed with the outpouring of joy at his very existence. *He's here, he's here.* She had waited her whole life for him and she hadn't realised until that very moment when his soft, warm little self weighed down on her chest. The glory of him. She inhaled him. Consumed him with kisses. This insanely precious being. This was an abundance of love. This was sunshine.

'They're as great as they are because they have a mum like you.'

'Stop it.' Molly tried to speak but felt the emotion well up in her, so she just made a hissing sound like a puncture in an inflatable pool. Charlie turned his head to look at her, his eyes holding hers, seeing her. It was so hard. She loved her boys so much her chest ached when she thought about them. But at every step she worried she failed them: too much TV, too much meat in their diet, not enough books, not enough outside time. She knew she had emptied herself caring for them. She had been tipped over and poured out. She had given everything and it still wasn't enough. She wasn't enough. Perfect mums haunted her, posting hilarious #mumfails on Instagram, that looked nothing like her actual mum fails. Adorable kids smothered in chocolate sauce didn't compare to yet another drive-through McDonald's Happy Meal for the third time in a week because Mum couldn't get it together to cook. Or sleeping in their clothes because the pyjama battle was just too hard. Or realising she'd forgotten to brush their teeth for ten days, maybe longer. Not quite Insta perfect moments.

'What you're doing is amazing. You have the hardest job in the world. Well done.'

Molly would have crumbled. She felt her shoulders shaking and stomach knot. She was close to splintering, but then Rory appeared. He burst through the door in the nip, pyjamas thrown asunder and a nappy on his head. They'd started laughing and got on with the task at hand.

She had said goodbye to Charlie that night feeling lighter, more capable somehow. And the boys had slept through.

And he liked her hair. She bit back a smile. *He liked her hair.*

'Let's have a drink?' Anna, not waiting for a response had started to pour two glasses of chardonnay. 'The kids are happy watching TV, your granny is napping, you're a confirmed domestic goddess—let's have a glass to celebrate winning at life right now.'

Gladly accepting the chilled wine, Molly said, 'I love you. Have I ever told you that?'

'I love you, too. Cheers to that.' They dutifully clinked.

'I have news.' Anna looked warily at her.

Molly clasped her hand to her mouth. 'Pregnant?'

'God no.' She stared into her glass. 'I've got a job. I'm going back to nine to five. McCanns headhunted me, if you can believe it? I'm going to be a corporate lawyer again and I can't wait.'

'Congratulations.' Molly heard her own voice, weak and shaky.

Anna rushed to her and pulled her into a hug. 'Oh, come here, you big loon. I'll miss you so much. All this time we've been mums together. You've just been the best friend I could ever ask for.'

'You too. It's great, I really am pleased for you,' Molly spoke into Anna's neck, her words catching, the sniffles starting. 'What'll happen now?' *To me?* Molly meant but didn't ask. *What about me? What will I do without my friend? Who will be a mum with me?*

'We'll get an au pair, probably someone French and skinny who I'll hate and love in equal measures. I'll feel guilty I don't get to spend time with Bev so I'll spoil her rotten and ruin her sense of self for the twenty minutes I do get with her. And we'll see how it goes.' Anna's worried eyes flitted around.

Finally, Molly knew what to say. 'This will work. Lots of people do this. It works out great for everyone.'

Anna nodded her brow creased in concern. 'It'll work, and if it doesn't, I'll leave.'

'Of course, and come back to pushing buggies around the green with me.'

Molly swirled her wine and focused hard on smiling. She tried and failed to stop the screaming inside, *But what about me? What will I do now?*

Molly watched Rosie's cheeks bloom as she got deeper and deeper into her story, holding the table spellbound with her natural charm. It was something about her boss and someone bringing their dog to work. Rosie's dark hair was swept up into a loose bun, highlighting her long chandelier earrings, a smattering of freckles tickled her nose. She waved her hands around and picked up and replaced her wine glass repeatedly without ever taking a sip. Molly felt nothing but love for her little sister as she watched her eyes moisten with laughter and her red lips never dipping from a happy smile. After their mam and dad had split, Molly had been overwhelmed with the need to protect Rosie from the upset. There were six years between them, but she'd never felt such an overpowering urge to be the big sister and tell the world to get lost. Their parents had invited them to afternoon tea in The Merrion Hotel, a posh city centre hotel, where everyone speaks in hushed voices and pretends they're not trying to spot a celebrity. She smelled a rat immediately, but assumed her parents were about to reveal an illness. She gripped herself for cancer, mentally rejigging her life to bring whichever parent it was to exhausting chemo sessions and planning a family holiday for everyone in Florida as soon as they were out of the woods. She could see them all waving to Mickey Mouse and slurping down ice-creams at Sea World. They'd get through it because that's what families did. Families did not separate. Her parents would slide into retirement, golf trips and rum and cokes on the Costa del Sol. They'd held hands when they told them. Her mother had just popped half a scone slathered in strawberry jam into her mouth. Her dad wearing a canary yellow jumper reached for her mam's hand and held it on her knee.

He spoke up. 'Your mother and I have decided to go our separate ways. We'll always love each other, very, very deeply, but sometimes people just grow apart.' A lonely solitary tear trickled down his cheek.

'You're not dying!' Rosie had shouted at him.

'Lord, no. Whatever gave you that impression?' Yvonne had looked shocked.

'We're in the bloody Merrion eating cucumber sandwiches. I thought you were dying, at least one of you. Are you sure?' Rosie asked suspiciously.

Beside her Molly was quietly weeping, ladylike sobbing like an aristocrat in *Downton Abbey* who's been caught having it off with the stable boy. 'Me too, I thought you had cancer,' she managed to splutter. 'But this is worse, so much worse.'

In her defence, Molly was heavily pregnant. Her brain had ceased all rational functioning weeks before and she was now running on ninety per cent hormones and ten per cent muscle memory of who she used to be pre-pregnancy.

'I'm not happy about this one bit.' Rosie stood up and gallantly threw down her linen table napkin right onto the petit fours. 'I think you're bastards. You're both bastards. What are we now, orphans? Or something like that. How could you do that to us? We're only children.'

'It's just incredibly selfish,' Molly agreed.

Yvonne interrupted her, looking flustered. 'We're people too, you know. We're entitled to choose our own lives. We're more than just your parents.'

'How could you say that?' Rosie was clearly affronted.

'Because it's true. I'm not just Mam, you know?'

'Oh, so this was your doing, was it?' Molly clambered up beside her sister.

'Hang on a minute.' Their dad put his hand in the air defensively. 'This is no one's doing. It just happened.'

'So, it was you?' Rosie pointed a finger.

'It was no one, there's no blame, and would you two calm down. You're both adults.' Yvonne had sounded very cross.

'No, no,' Rosie was practically shouting, 'you're the ones acting like children here, just running away from the problem, not even trying to stick it out. What's wrong with you? Come on, Molly, let's go. Let's go find an orphanage.'

They had stumbled out of the tea rooms and straight into the bar.

'Bit dramatic with the orphan thing.' Molly watched Rosie down a brandy for the shock.

'They are bastards, though. I was right about that.'

'What'll become of us?' It was as if the roof had come off Molly's house.

'I wish you could drink. I'd like us to get roaring drunk,' Rosie announced.

'I'm sure this is just shock. We're in shock.'

'You don't think one of them is having an affair, do you?'

'Oh Jesus, no. What if Dad has a younger woman?'

'And we have to call her Mam and she's younger and skinnier than us.'

'Everyone is skinnier than me.' Molly rubbed her giant belly.

'Why did they tell us here, with all the richy-rich shit in The Merrion?'

'Because they have good scones?' They started to laugh at the insanity of it all. And the tears rolled down their cheeks as they slapped their hands on the bar counter and ordered another drink for Rosie and a sparkling water for Molly.

It was unsettling. That's what Molly had told the therapist who Dommo had made her see when her tears had not stopped six weeks later. It had surprised her how deeply she'd been affected by it. She thought only kids got damaged by divorce, not adult children, especially not twenty-seven-year-old married adult children. Her therapist had stroked his moustache, and through soothing *ooohs* and *ahhhs*, quoted studies to her and recommended self-help books. There was an entire shelf at the bookshop for adult children of divorce. Who knew? Molly started to pick them off and began to understand her cascading emotions a bit more. She was angry with her parents for a long time, and now, when pressed on it, she admitted to being very sad.

Bizarrely, it had brought herself and Rosie closer. They were united in their grief, their laughter at the whole situation and their resolve to help their parents not to be lonely. Although, really, that only applied to Mam now since Dad had Patricia.

Rosie seemed well, Molly thought, she seemed happy.

'More boeuf bourguignon?' Molly played up her French accent with a pout.

'Ooh la la, mon chérie.' Dommo grinned and held up his licked clean plate. 'You bet I do.'

'Does she cook like this every night, Dommo? I'll be round if so.' Rosie spooned some sauce on her plate. 'This is delicious.'

'Nah, just since she's got her new foxy haircut.' And he winked across the table at her. Molly self-consciously ran her hand up her neck and looked away, quickly squeezing a tight grin from the corner of her mouth that didn't reach her eyes. Herself and Dommo were struggling to get their rhythm. He was annoying her. Right now, winking across the table at her like some jack-the-lad, that was annoying. Like it's all alright with a wink. He'd hurtled into the kitchen earlier after work, like some kind of star football player about to save the day. Like he expected some rapturous applause that, yes, hooray, he'd made it home from work on time. He threw his bag onto the middle of the floor exactly where everyone would trip over it and dramatically started to roll up his shirt sleeves. Dommo grabbed a dishcloth and screamed like he'd scored a goal, 'Right, what are we cooking?'

Coolly unimpressed, Molly responded, 'I have cooked, the boys are bathed and in their pyjamas. Why don't you go into the sitting room and have a gin and tonic with Granny?'

'You sure? I can put some garlic bread in the oven?'

'We're not having garlic bread. I've got the meal sorted. Go. Gin and tonic.' She pointed to the sitting room. 'Granny's dying for a drink.'

Molly didn't know if this was true, but it was easier to have Dommo out of the kitchen than running around sabotaging her dinner.

'Gran? Some more?' Molly smiled expectantly.

Evie shook her head, and then changed her mind. 'A smidgen maybe, with a few potatoes?'

'Angela?'

'No, no, I never do seconds.' Angela paused and caught the end of a sigh from Molly. 'But it was delicious, thank you so much.'

Molly relaxed and dished out the remainder of the meal with a smile. The evening was going so well. She had dominated the cooking, and the kitchen buzzed with laughter. Rosie had taken out her phone and was demonstrating DeLuvGuru to the table. It was her sales pitch and very effective.

'So, in just two swipes, you can find love. Look . . .' With great aplomb and an overextended finger she swiped across her screen.

Mesmerised, her audience marvelled at her genius.

Angela had put her glasses on and leaned across the table for a better look.

'It's really that easy?'

Rosie nodded. 'It's the technology, the algorithms behind the programming.'

'English, Rosie, please?' Granny raised her eyebrows at her.

'Your online history matches you. You can't lie about it, you see? People lie on dating application forms all the time, but if we've got all your information how can you lie about it?' Rosie was happily swiping through photographs and interfaces.

'I dunno, Rosie. I might spend half my day on celebrity gossip sites or Instagram but I don't really care about it, I'm just flicking through. I'd never want to be partnered up with someone who actually did care about that stuff?' Molly piped up.

'But maybe you'd like them to be mildly interested?' Rosie asked, eyebrows raised.

'Well, I'm out. I couldn't give a stuff about celebrity gossip, I'm a straight-up sports guy.' Dommo took a satisfying swig from his glass.

'And I don't care about sports.' Molly felt her jaw jut out. 'I'm not even mildly interested.' She sang the words but there was an edge to her voice, a hardness that had crept in. She shook it off and tried to sound lighter somehow. 'Besides that stuff doesn't matter when you're married with kids. You don't even have time to go online then.'

'Well, I don't really understand it, darling.' Evie sat back from staring at the screen. 'It's definitely not how I've worked at matchmaking people over the years. I hope there's good money in it. There's always money in matchmaking, mark my words.'

'I know it's different, Gran, but instead of just doing one-on-one the way you do it, this can be matching hundreds of people at once.' Rosie's eyes glistened with excitement.

'By a computer?' Evie shook her head sceptically. 'There's so much a computer will never know about people and their ways.' She looked off into the distance. 'But I'm sure you could charge like a wounded bull.'

Rosie shrugged.

'Simon has developed the back end of this?' Dommo spooned the last of the beef into his mouth. 'What program has he used?'

'I dunno. I don't know anything about the techy stuff.'

'I'll be honest with you, it sounds pretty amazing that you're getting people to hand over all of their data. I mean data is king out there, it's practically our most valuable currency as human beings at this point. That data you're collecting would be worth a lot of money.' Molly could see the cogs and wheels in Dommo's brain clicking over. 'That's the real business there, not the matchmaking. Targeted advertising, audience projections, that kind of consumer information is gold. What software are you using for security?'

'I don't know. I forget you work in IT, Dommo. You sounded vaguely knowledgeable there. I thought you just switched computers off and on and gave the photocopier a kick.' Rosie attempted to dodge the techy questions and resume her comfortable slagging relationship with Dommo.

Dommo didn't take the bait, in fact he sat up a few inches taller, and nibbled the edge of his thumb pensively. 'What kinds of terms and conditions do you have people agreeing to? Did you get a compliance lawyer familiar with EU regulations, because these laws change every day?' Dommo was concentrating on Rosie now, his eyes clear with focus and a look of concern creasing his brow.

'Simon handled all of that.' Rosie was starting to look uncomfortable; she twiddled self-consciously at her earrings.

'Where is he?' Dommo looked around as if hoping to find Simon hiding under the table.

'He's, um . . .' Rosie looked to Molly for support even though she hadn't quite brought her up to speed. Molly had only met

Simon once and had been decidedly mute afterwards, which was never a good sign from her opinionated and always vocal sister. 'He's in London, with the developer, sorting out a few glitches.'

'Well, I'm very proud that you're following in my footsteps as a matchmaker, darling,' Evie interjected, while beaming at her granddaughter. 'And the most important question of all is does it work? Are you helping people fall in love?'

There was a long pause as Rosie considered lying to her family but then decided against it. 'No. It's not working. Yet.'

'No?' Molly, who had started to clean off the table, abruptly sat back down. 'Shit. But you're live, it's out there?'

Rosie batted away Molly's words, attempting to downplay the situation which she somehow successfully had done in her own head. But now, looking at the reactions from across the table, she saw deep concern flashing across their faces and slack jaws that needed to be slammed shut and she wondered if she had been just a little bit laissez faire about it all.

'It's fine. Yes, there seems to be a little bit of a problem with the matching, but Simon is going to fix it.' Did she still believe that? His emails had bounced back and there had been nothing but radio silence for days. Did she honestly still believe it? A few heads slowly nodded in agreement, but their faces showed how worried they were for her. Rosie couldn't help her blabbermouth self, she threw fuel on the fire. 'Remember my friend Catriona from work?'

'Gorgeous, tall, dark-haired girl,' Dommo answered straight out of the traps and way too fast for Molly's liking.

'Yes, so she got matched up and went on a date, and didn't even like the guy, let alone want to jump his bones.' She looked around the table. 'Oh gosh, sorry, Granny.'

Evie patted Rosie's wrist, and with her typical good sense of humour, replied, 'Don't you worry, I know all about jumping someone's bones.'

'It's clearly a glitch in the programming, mistakes like this happen all the time,' Molly added hopefully.

'In testing,' Dommo said quietly, but still managed to be heard.

'A lot of people signed up very quickly and we weren't ready for it.' Rosie sounded apprehensive.

Evie patted her wrist again in a rhythmic tap. 'You know, sometimes it's wisest just to look after your own corner and not worry about everyone else. Start small and watch happiness ripple out. It always does.'

Molly thought that Rosie wasn't listening to Granny, but she had.

'I'm going to crochet that on a cushion as soon as I learn how to crochet,' Rose said.

Everyone laughed, even Angela cracked a smile. She had only met Molly's granny on a handful of occasions and every time she had looked slightly uncomfortable in her presence. She shifted around her uneasily. Evie had that effect on some people, they wanted to avoid being seen by her. But tonight Angela had embraced Evie and chatted away about the boys and the weather; she had to all intents and purposes been a delightful dinner guest. All of which just reinforced Molly's theory that Angela hated her, and not everybody.

'Who's for dessert?' Molly jumped up from the table, remembering the chocolate cake that looked like a heart attack under plastic she'd bought from Tesco's.

'You sit down, love. I'll get it.' Dommo sprung to her side, and quickly swiped the dinner plates out of her hand. 'You've done enough, you've really done an amazing job.'

His eyes caught Molly off guard, brimming with adoration for her, hopeful and loving. It felt equal parts nice and unexpected. She sat back down.

'Dominic, you've been working all day. You must be exhausted. I'll get dessert, you sit down.' Angela rose from the table, throwing a side eye at Molly.

'It's fine, Mam.'

'No, no, you work so hard. You shouldn't have to do all the work at home, too.'

Molly groaned loud enough so the whole room heard her. 'He doesn't Angela, he doesn't do anything at home. He doesn't even know where the bloody nappies are.'

Angela neatly pushed her chair into the table. 'Well, that's between you two, but you know he is working so . . .'

'And I'm not? Is that what you're saying?'

Dommo leapt across the kitchen and in between the two women in his life. 'What about some ice-cream?' he said, all jolly, like he was at a children's party.

'Just use the chocolate cake that's in the fridge,' Molly said.

'I'll run to the shops to get ice-cream. I fancy ice-cream.'

'What?' Molly pushed her chair back and heard it screech across the floor. She stood up, hands on hips and snapped, 'Sit down, Dommo. There's cream with the cake. I've got this.' She felt a burning fury inside her. It had all being going so well and now he was going to blow it up.

'A bit of ice-cream would be nice. It'll only take me ten minutes.'

'No. You don't get to change everything. There's no garlic bread. There's no ice-cream.'

'Literally five minutes in the car.'

'No!'

'Jeez, Molly, calm down. I'm just trying to help.'

'Never tell a woman to calm down!' Molly hollered.

'Lads,' Rosie interrupted them with a warning tone. Standing at the top of the kitchen was Rory, face wet with tears, looking from one parent to another, settling on Molly before erupting in an earth-shattering roar.

Molly swung back. 'Well played, Dommo. You've woken him. Probably thrown out his whole sleep schedule. But you wouldn't know anything about that, would you, because you're never here. You're always at the pub.'

'I'll put him to bed,' Angela piped up.

'No!' Molly roared. She scooped Rory up, cradling him like he was a baby once again, shushing and kissing his hot sticky cheeks. She marched up the stairs, listening to the sounds of Dommo apologising to the table and feeling utterly shattered that they could come apart so publicly and so easily.

16

Yvonne

YVONNE MUST HAVE BEEN MOMENTARILY POSSESSED BY A demon. That was the only explanation. If she had been her usual self, she would have fled the scene: handbag bumping her hip, cheeks flushed, hair flapping in the wind outside on that grey blustery day, maintaining a strong, steady stride towards her car. Instead, that demon pushed the door open and Yvonne entered the bank. Dry-mouthed and a little bit startled, she felt her breathing quicken and she nervously reached for her handbag strap like a child's security blanket. She was wearing a flattering, tailored blue dress, with a large leather belt with an even larger gold buckle at her waist. Happy, smiling families of various ethnic backgrounds standing outside well-built, semi-detached homes smiled down at her from posters on the wall. Large, bold fonts shouted optimistic slogans at her: *We help your dreams come true, Need money fast—no problem, Small business big future.*

Gone were the bank tellers peering out of glass-fronted compartments, in the days where you'd choose the longest queue because that teller was obviously a soft touch. Now it felt like a hairdressing salon, with two puffed and primed girls hovering at a high table tapping their well-manicured nails, more used to scrolling their phones than counting money.

'Can I help you?' one of the girls asked, studying her screen.

Yvonne cleared her throat. 'I've an appointment with Paul Mercer about a mortgage.' A second mortgage. Her heart rattled in her chest.

'He's just with someone at the moment, if you want to take a seat and wait? Please help yourself to tea and coffee.'

Clutching her handbag as if her life depended on it, Yvonne perched herself on a bright-red couch that looked directly into a number of glass offices. What was it with transparency these days? She didn't need to see everything that was going on? Surely people were allowed some privacy and messy desks? The painted smiles peering down at her were off-putting and not comforting. Anyone with half a brain in their head knew it was all lies. Banks didn't give out money to young families trying to buy a small house, in spite of what the TV ads told you. And you could forget it if you were a start-up business struggling to get off the ground. They didn't want to hear your new ideas about dog cafés or sushi bars or apps to bring dancing communities together. They liked rich people and big, fat-cat companies that were already full to the brim of gold bars and caviar. They threw money at them, they called them up and offered them more money, while the rest of us whirled like restless dervishes never free of financial worry.

'Yvonne, sorry to keep you waiting.' A fetus in chinos and a button-down shirt purposefully extended a hand. 'Paul Mercer, lovely to meet you.'

Well, at least he has good manners she thought, while at the same time registering that it was such a pity that men didn't wear suits anymore. Paul Mercer could age himself up a good five years in a suit. That's what she'd tell him if she was his mother, just a little advice that he probably wouldn't take anyway. Kids never listen. She'd lost her voice trying to impart some life skills to her girls only to watch them do the exact opposite. They succumbed to every fad diet as teenager: cabbage diets, keto, protein shakes. Pale-faced and cranky, they never listened. Paul Mercer shuffled her into a glass office, one with two armchairs on full display to anyone who walked into the bank or peeked in from the street. She sighed as she sat down, and quickly tried to turn it into an apologetic cough. She would remain upbeat.

'I understand you dealt with my colleague in the town branch previously in relation to McCarthy's pub.' Paul poured them both a glass of water and dutifully nudged a glass towards her. The town branch was too close to home for what Yvonne needed now. She couldn't just march in the door where the world and his wife would see her. No, she couldn't risk her financial woes getting around town or back to her mam. She didn't need to be worrying her or her girls for that matter. She'd be so terribly embarrassed if they found out what a mess she was in. She liked to think they saw her as responsible and steady and safe, like a Volvo. Isn't that what mums were?

Yvonne sipped on the water. 'Yes, but I'm not here about the pub. I'm here on a personal matter.'

He nodded encouragingly.

'Well, as I said on that form I was made to fill out on the internet . . .' She paused as the memory of the frustration of box clicking and 'quick survey' pop-ups cluttered her screen and mind. 'I want to get a second mortgage on my house. I currently have a very small, practically miniscule mortgage on the house and I wanted to bump it up. You know?' To get rid of the Revenue who were breathing down her neck, so she could sleep again, so she could stop thinking about twenty-three thousand euro at every waking moment, so maybe her heart rate might calm down back to something normal, so she could run away from the black clouds circling her.

It had felt like a strange payout when Brandon had given her money. She had left him, and yet he gave her money. She hadn't wanted to sell the family home. She'd wanted the girls to still have a home—silly as it seems when they were both grown up—but just because she wanted to leave the marriage, it didn't have to mean that their family life would be upturned, too. So, no, she had insisted that Brandon keep the house. She would be gone to Ballyhay anyway, she didn't need it. He had emptied out their savings, their nest egg and literally spilled it into her purse, pleading for her to buy a house. 'Somewhere safe and nice, put the money into a home,' he'd said. 'You'll make it lovely like you always do.' His blue eyes had pleaded with her. *Too late*, she'd wanted to scream at him. *This is all too late.*

He was broken after she left him, or so he said. He was devastated. He spent months and months pleading with her to attend marriage counselling with him. To give it one more go. Yvonne wasn't broken. She had emerged powerful, brimming with enthusiasm for her own life. She refused to do counselling and doubly refused to see the financial planner he'd kept *helpfully* suggesting. She recognised it immediately—he was still trying to control her even though she was out of the marriage. Still tugging on the purse strings. Yvonne bought her house and admittedly went a bit wild spending on the décor. But it was understandable given it was her first true liberation, and she had money in her pocket to spend. Why wouldn't she? He went to the counselling sessions. The girls filled her in on that. They said he was reading self-help books, that they'd found him taking notes from *Men are from Mars, Women are from Venus*. That was new. Then the letters started from him, beautiful beseeching letters. He had always had a lovely way with words. He asked for forgiveness for all his mistakes, he was focused on being a better man, and he hoped she would take him back one day. No, no, no. Words, empty words. Too late. And then after about eighteen months, they stopped. And he stopped pleading, and she didn't hear from him so much anymore. And then about a year ago, there were whispers of Patricia. And it stung. Which made no sense, it shouldn't sting. She had let it go, she didn't want to be married to him anymore, but still, the sting.

Buying her house was the first thing she had done as a newly single woman, and it had felt glorious. She knew exactly what she wanted, a new build, where nothing reeked of the past and previous family's dramas hadn't soaked into the walls. She'd wanted a shiny kitchen with a double sink and an island where she could roll out pastry during the day and decorate with vanilla-scented candles at night. A bright, airy front room that she'd line with bookshelves and happy photographs of her grandchildren, a comfortable bedroom, a small backyard where she'd grow vegetables: sweet tasting carrots and bright purple beetroot.

When she found the two up, two down newly built town house at Craanford, on the edge of town, it was as if she had dreamed it into being. She moved in right away. It had been her best decision, and she *had* made it lovely. There were brightly coloured peonies cascading out of window boxes, a tiny rockery was shadowed by a rose bush on her postage-stamp sized, front garden which she tended to with a religious fervour. She'd never gardened in her life before. They'd had a third of an acre in Dublin that she'd paid a gardener to mow and sweep the leaves once a fortnight, but here at Craanford she got such pleasure watching the flowers bloom and fade. She enjoyed the delicious ache in her bones after a day of weeding and working outdoors, a hot bath in her own home had never felt more satisfying or deserved.

'So, I'm looking for a second mortgage on the house for twenty-three thousand euro.' She nodded her head resolutely and watched as Paul Mercer took a deep breath and smiled.

'Unfortunately, we won't be able to give you that amount,' he beamed across at her. 'While the property is sound and your own mortgage is, as you said yourself, miniscule, your income as a business owner is not. Quite frankly, McCarthy's pub is operating at a loss. You're barely breaking even most weeks; in fact, you're in the red. But you know this, Yvonne.'

'Of course, I know this. That's why I'm here.' She sat up straight and fixed a cold stare on this opinionated young man.

'The pub was in profit, it was doing fine up until three years ago, until you took over, Yvonne. My advice here, Yvonne, is not to throw good money after bad.' He spoke firmly, more like a school principal than a pupil. Why did he keep repeating her name? Had he learned that at some bankers' course?

'I didn't ask you for advice, I asked you for money,' she snapped back at him, heckles raised as a clenching dread settled inside her.

He pensively stroked his chin, where one day when he was old enough, stubble would grow. 'There's also the issue of your personal credit rating . . .' He paused, eyeballing her.

'That was a misunderstanding. I paid off that credit card.' Well, Brandon had.

'And you now have another four. All of which are not having minimum payments made.'

Yvonne felt her breathing quicken. She raised her chin to the air. 'That's all under control, and quite frankly I don't see why that has anything to do with me getting a second mortgage. It's a second entity.'

'The best I can do is give you five thousand euro, which I don't recommend you take. I think a wiser option here is to sell the pub and get out while you still can.'

She found she was standing up, and her voice was raised. 'I don't tell you how to run your business. Why should I listen to you?'

'I understand.' Paul Mercer was not for budging.

'No, you don't, you have no idea. That pub is in my DNA. I was raised there, my dad is in every breath, my seventy-nine-year-old mam sits in the snug sipping brandies most evenings. Sell it and then what? Turn it into a shop, a house, a car park, knock it down? McCarthy's is part of the community, a dwindling community, do you want to end that, Paul? Where will the auld fellas go who prop themselves up at the bar like roosting hens every night and spark the only conversation they've had all day? McCarthy's is all they've got. It's all I've got.'

She walked towards the office door and fumbled aimlessly for a handle. She glanced back at Paul who signalled to a button on her left.

'What's wrong with handles?' she muttered. 'And you can keep your five grand. I'd choke on it.'

It wasn't a spectacular exit, but it had been noted by every straining neck and curious passer-by as they peered through the glass windows desperate to spot a fight, to see someone scrabbling, to see someone worse off than them.

'Piss off the lot of you!' Yvonne hollered to the smiling families on the walls with their newly acquired mortgages as she stormed out. There you go, that felt better. There'd be another solution. Something else would come up. It had to. She wouldn't lose it all.

17

Evie

EVIE HAD GONE TO BED WITH A HEADACHE AND WOKEN UP
with a worse one. The light peeping through the curtains in
Molly's guest bedroom was too bright, the bed covers felt
heavy, the walls seemed to pulsate. The room was spinning.
She closed her eyes and took a few deep breaths to centre
herself. A gentle knock sounded on the door. Evie wanted to
shout, go away, but couldn't muster the energy. Molly snuck in
quietly carrying a tray with tea and toast on it. She placed it
on the bedside table as Evie braved a peep under her eyelashes.

'I just thought I'd see how you were, Gran. It's gone ten,'
Molly whispered delicately.

'I've a bit of a headache, love. Thanks for the tea,' Evie
managed to mumble.

'There's some headache tablets there, too. They might
help. I shouldn't have let Dommo pour you that gin, he has
a heavy hand.'

'Shush.' She traced her fingers blindly along the bed sheets until she found Molly's arm and patted it gently. 'It was a lovely night. It's not the drink, it's my head. I'll have a little nap now.'

She heard Molly leave, her slippered feet shuffling quietly out. It definitely wasn't the gin, the one drink she'd had would never cause this. The searing pain was behind her eyes, it seemed to come from her legs, if that was possible. She'd try to sleep and see if that would help, often her body just needed to shut itself down and reset. Although the shut-downs got longer with age. She tried not to let her mind wander and she reined in the thoughts as they jumped and scurried down dark alleyways. This was the start of it—she was going to slip away much quicker than she'd thought and what use would she be to anyone if she had a headache that felt like her head had split open like a cracked egg. No, this was not how it was supposed to go. But she couldn't stop the wandering, her life was playing out before her, running like a scene from a film or one of her visions. Evie was feeling nostalgic, remembering. Ever since she was a little girl, her visions, or whatever you want to call them, were as clear as day. She'd always found it difficult to understand how other people didn't know what she knew.

She must have been seven years of age when she first knew something that mattered. 'Mammy, the bull's stuck in the ditch.'

'Shush, child. No, he's not.'

'He is, he can't get out. He's shouting and roaring.' She could see him clear as she could see her mammy standing in front of her. 'He wants to get out, but he can't.'

'Your daddy was just there.' Her mammy looked at her cross now, Evie was wasting her time.

'After daddy left he broke free of the field and wandered onto the road, he fell into the ditch.'

'You've been playing here in front of the fire this whole time and you're telling me the bull, two mile down the road, is in a ditch. For God's sake, you couldn't be knowing that.'

'I do, Mammy, I can see him, like a dream in my head. His leg's awful sore.'

Her mammy had stared at her a little too long and said, 'If you're lying to me, Evelyn, I'll give you a hiding when I get back.' Then she had blessed herself and pulled her coat tight around her as she took off into the fields. It was too late, the bull had broken his leg when he fell.

Mammy and Daddy looked at her differently after that. *How had she known? Who told her? Had she snuck out?* They shook their heads in disbelief that she *just knew.*

But they listened to her six months later when she just knew that Old Paddy Grogan had gone looking for a fight with Sean Ward, which ended with him throwing him clean out of a window. A year after that she had just known that Father Murphy had a sickness in his lungs that wouldn't ever clear up. She had told her teacher in school who gave her that same frozen look her mammy had given her, blessed herself and told her to *Shush now, that's the devil talking.*

After that, Daddy had taken her aside and kissed the top of her head and held her hand with great tenderness and softly explained, 'Sometimes, love, it's best not to tell people about these things. They might not understand and they might think badly of you. Sometimes people get scared of things they don't understand, and that can make them mad. My mammy,' he'd said, 'was just like you. She knew things like you do, and seeing as you're the seventh child of a seventh child, well, that's why you have this gift, too. And you'll be just fine, pet, if you let me lead you.'

So, Evie learned to confide in her daddy when 'the knowing' came to her, and he always believed her, and when it was needed he would intervene.

Years later, when she was seventeen, Evie occasionally saw colours around people; sometimes just a faint glow, a hint of a rainbow that almost bounced off their shape, sometimes nothing at all. It didn't mean anything to her and she wondered what the light was.

It was at the Bog Dance after the village had cut, dried and removed the turf from the bog. It was always a great celebration, the last hoolie of the summer, and once the turf was brought home, the village could rest easy that houses would be warm over winter. That evening was when The Knowing started to make sense. Evie had been excited to go, it was the first dance that she was allowed to go to without her parents. Her friends had spent the week planning what to wear and who they'd dance with. She wore her favourite blue dress that had gold buttons at the cuffs, she'd cycled her bike there, floating with excitement. She spotted Mary Muldooney within minutes of arriving. Mary was sipping tea from a china cup on the far side of the town hall, her back turned to the door. Her dark hair was styled in a loose bun with soft curls. She wore a plum red dress. She swayed from side to side moving to the band who were playing a slightly out of tune 'Danny Boy'. Evie's eyes were locked on her. She didn't know why. In walked some of the lads from Tinnock, the town five miles over. They were jostling at the door all laughs and excitement for the night ahead. Nearly every head in the room turned to them with the noise they were making, except Mary Muldooney's. She kept moving back and forth from one foot to another, dancing gently on her own. That was when Evie saw the light, it shot out of Mary like a cannon ball racing for a target. This brilliant white light catapulted across the room. It abruptly stopped and hovered over one of the Tinnock lads. He had his brown hair greased back, and the shirt cuffs rolled up to reveal pale white arms. He scratched his head, and Evie watched as his eyes darted across the room and rested on Mary Muldooney's dancing figure. Evie knew without any doubt that he would cross the hall towards her as she watched a similar white light soar from his chest and follow Mary's light. Mary turned to greet him with a glowing smile and Evie had to look away. Their lights fused. It was blinding. It was, she imagined, what staring into a star might look like: burning, infectious, beautiful and dangerous.

Now, decades later, Evie realises that that was the start of her journey as a matchmaker. Now she knows that that light is the soul's torch looking for its match. Now she knows that some souls have a desperate need to find their connection with the one it was united with before it came to this earth. Now she knows how those souls cannot rest until they come in contact with their match. But back then, Evie's seventeen-year-old self, who had been to Dublin once and didn't like it, who had never tasted an orange, or read a newspaper from cover to cover, who went to mass every Sunday and confession every month, who was at her first dance wearing her best blue dress, and whose life started and ended in the small town of Ballyhay, was terrified. She ran straight home without taking a breath and dove under the bedcovers shaking with fear.

It was the matchmaking that brought the townspeople of Ballyhay around. Nobody liked the visions, or The Knowings that Evie seemed to have, they couldn't be God-like, that was for sure. But matchmaking, now that was different. Sure, wasn't that a bit of fun? Evie's daddy produced a large leather book and told her to tell people that it had belonged to her grandmother who had also been a matchmaker from the island of Hy-Brasil off the West Coast. Years later, Evie learned that that wasn't true, her grandmother had had visions and maybe even visitations but she had never been a matchmaker. Her daddy had invented the leather book which didn't hold any special powers whatsoever. He had been clever enough to realise that people were comfortable with tradition and he needed to give Evie a tool for her trade.

And it had worked.

As a young woman, Evie started to meet with townspeople initially, and then they came from further afield. People came looking for love, couples came wanting to know if they were suited—widows, widowers, lonely people, warring spouses.

She was so young and so inexperienced in the ways of life and yet they listened to her. These people decades older than her sought her advice. At first, she didn't have the language to explain what she could see and what she just knew. Her daddy came with her and interpreted her childish words. She grew confident under his watchful eye. Slowly, she learned her trade, and more importantly, learned how to talk to people to say what needed to be said without causing tears or breakdowns. And to have people trust her.

Evie wished her girls trusted her more. Then she wouldn't have to second guess what was going on with them. Although the last few days had been revealing. Molly was floating on high energy, but there was an underlying feeling of nervous unhappiness about her that made Evie uneasy. And then she had met the cause of the high energy, the morning after she arrived.

'Gran, meet Charlie. The godsend I've been telling you about.'

Handsome wouldn't cover it. He was a modern-day Omar Sharif: dark hair, broad shoulders and a smile that would look at home in Hollywood. He was a dish, there was no two ways about it. Evie felt her own hand automatically go to her hair to fix it, she scrunched up her curls and pressed her lips together to smooth out her lipstick. She couldn't stop herself, the very sight of a handsome man caused her to preen.

'Lovely to meet you, Charlie. I've heard nothing but good things.'

He smiled and if she'd been a younger woman her knees would have given way.

'He's a wonder, Gran. He's made such a difference. We're all sleeping, it's a miracle.' Molly orbited him like a lost satellite. Giddy. She'd brushed back her hair and straightened her clothes, posturing and posing.

Evie understood, of course she understood, but this felt different, dangerous somehow. Evie watched in despair as Molly touched him on the shoulder. 'Will you have a cup of tea?'

'No, no, I'm not stopping. I was just passing and wondered how the last few nights had gone. I hope you don't mind me calling in.'

'Mind?' Molly's laugh verged on hysterical. 'I'm only thrilled to see you.' She started to peacock around him, shoulders and hips wriggling in opposite directions. 'It'll take two seconds to boil the kettle.'

'No, no, I won't, Molly, thanks. But I take it everything is going well and the boys are sleeping?' Charlie Handsome—as he would forever be known now by Evie—seemed genuinely concerned about the boys. Another plus in her book.

'Much improving. Still a few tricks being pulled by Rory . . .'

'Hiding his books?' Charlie grinned.

'Yes.' Molly nodded. 'And that thing with his cars.'

'Easy fix. I'll be back Thursday night, so.'

'Looking forward to it.'

Evie ticked off the signs—this was trouble.

Later that evening, Dommo came home, head hung low he sheepishly slunk through the hall door after eight o'clock. His eyes carried large suitcases underneath, his hair looked thinner than the last time she'd seen him and his waistline fatter. He had hugged Evie hello and received a chaste kiss from Molly, who directed him to the microwave to reheat his dinner. The heavy shoulders, the twisted mouth, the bodies angled away from each other—oh no, these two were not in a good way at all. This was not a joyful home, in spite of those beautiful boys. Molly would have to be careful because she was gambling with the most precious thing in the world—her family. They needed to talk, always talk, she told her couples endlessly, talk until your throat is hoarse, talk about the everyday, the happy moments and the sad moments. Talk until you're blue in the face and sick of talking and then talk about how you're sick of talking. And listen. Listen to what's really being said, to the pauses and the breaths between them. Years ago, maybe thirty years ago, Orla Flynn's mother had come to her in the snug, wringing her handkerchief into pieces, her fingernails chewed and her face wretched with worry. She was as far as Evie knew a happily married woman, she didn't know why she'd need to visit her. After she'd passed the money across the table she began.

'It's my daughter, Orla. Works in the post office.' She bit the words back, talking so quietly that Evie had to lean across the table to hear her. 'Now, I know you didn't match her and Gerry, but the thing is, they need help.'

'I know her, and Gerry Flynn the school teacher.' Evie pictured them in her mind's eye, a tall handsome couple.

'Well, they're not speaking.'

'It happens.'

'No. At all. It's been ten months and they haven't said a word to each other. Not one word. And the thing is Christmas is coming and how is that going to work? And it's no family, and it's no marriage at all if you live under the same roof and don't speak a word to each other.' A flush of anger rose up and reddened her cheeks.

'And you're here because . . . ?'

'I'm her mammy and I can't bear to see it. And I don't know what to do.' She took a deep breath. 'She's here with me, she's outside the snug. I had to drag her, thirty years of age and I have to drag her here to save her marriage.'

Evie had a flash in that moment. She doesn't want to save her marriage. 'Bring her in.'

Orla Flynn strode in, confident, self-assured, her jaw set in a determined stance, she sat abruptly and crossed her arms. 'Mrs McCarthy, my mammy insisted I come, but there's really no need.'

'There's every need. Your marriage is falling apart.' Her mother rubbed the handkerchief to her eyes.

'So, Orla, you haven't spoken to your husband for ten months?'

She shrugged her shoulders. 'We had a fight, and I was giving him the cold shoulder and it just didn't stop. I mean he's not talking to me either.'

'I'm sure there's plenty of talking in your head. Plenty of imaginary conversations going back and forth. Ten months is a long time to keep an argument going.' Evie eyeballed her, curious about her lack of emotion.

'Suits me fine.' She turned to her mother and said, 'Mammy, I don't know why we're here. Seriously. I think we should go.'

There's someone else. Evie saw him, a playboy type, fun, nothing serious. 'You won't fix the marriage you're in by looking over your shoulder at someone else.'

Orla's neck practically snapped she turned so quickly.

'He's not a keeper, he's not going to whisk you out of this marriage and save you by bringing something exciting to your life. Stay where you are, work with what you've got, make excitement in the marriage. Don't keep chasing the first thrills. They're just fleeting moments. Real love is different and a lot more rewarding.'

Evie knew Orla wouldn't listen to her. She'd already made up her mind. Her poor mammy could plead all she wanted.

She heard later that Orla left the marriage, took up with some other guy and that fell apart pretty quickly. She left Ballyhay shortly after, gone to England apparently, chasing some other man, some more excitement. Not talking to one another was a sign, a bad sign.

Evie rolled over in the bed and snuggled down deeper into the covers. She heard her phone buzz with a text on the bedside locker. She didn't have the energy to look. She wondered if it was from Karl. They'd been texting. He sent very long wordy texts. More like letters than anything else in beautifully composed English. He wrote about the goings-on with his aunt's house, the difficulties with the builders, the weather. And she replied, surprising herself with the breadth of honesty she poured onto the screen. She told him about Molly and how worried she was for her marriage. And she shared stories of the boys and how Rory would race from one end of the garden to the other with his batman cape on, trying to fly, and how Andy would only eat avocado for dinner. It was nice to talk with someone who knew her when she was young and beautiful and who remembered the things she remembered. And even though Evie had extended her stay in Dublin by another week because she knew she was needed here, Evie looked forward to seeing Karl on her return. Rosie had caught her on her phone.

'Who are you texting, Gran? You're always checking it?'

And Evie had shaken her head and made a noise hopeful of dismissing the conversation.

But ever determined Rosie was not one to be deterred. 'If I didn't know better, I'd say you had someone on the go.'

Evie raised her eyebrows and found it difficult not to smile.

'Well, spill. I'm all ears.' Rosie had sat herself down, crossed her legs and raised her arms to heaven waiting to accept all that might grace her.

Evie had mentioned Karl to Yvonne. She'd tried to be nonchalant about him, but Yvonne knew her too well. Still, she tried the same approach with Rosie. 'Someone I knew a long time ago has walked back into my life and he's a real gentleman and easy to talk to.'

'And . . .' Exactly the same as Yvonne, those two were peas in a pod. Rosie wasn't content with broad strokes. 'Is he a boyfriend? A gentleman friend?'

'Do we have to name it? Can't we just be what we are?'

Rosie had narrowed her eyes suspiciously. 'I know you don't want my advice, Gran, but don't let him string you along. What if he's a player?'

Evie had laughed out loud. 'Well, then I get played, and you know, it might be a bit of fun.'

'There's nothing wrong with putting a name on it, Gran. Take it from me. I always get a guy to officially ask me out. Lock it down, no grey area.'

Evie loved her forthrightness. Rosie was adamant that love followed procedures and rules. Evie knew that love either was or it wasn't.

'We're just getting to know each other again and that's nice. You don't need to worry about me, love.' Evie was doing enough worrying for both of them. She worried that she was enjoying talking to Karl too much. She worried that he felt the same and she wasn't being fair embarking on something new, when she had no time left for a new relationship. Her time was up. Evie worried she was being cruel to someone who she could care about deeply. And what if Karl cared about her, too? Reluctantly, it seemed there was every possibility that she might be the player in this game.

18

Rosie

'ROSIE, I THINK YOU NEED TO GET DOWN HERE IMMEDIATELY.' Lorraine on reception at CRUSH was whispering with a furious intensity down the line. 'Seriously. Now.'

'Really? Why? Oh my God, is the Muffin Man here again?' Rosie was already hovering out of her seat, happy to run away from the morning's work to find the Muffin Man and his most excellent apple and cinnamon offerings.

'No. Way more trouble than him. Two uniformed guards are here. They asked for you, but Serious happened to be passing and has started talking to them.'

'What the hell?' Rosie felt like someone had shoulder-slammed into her, knocking her down. 'Why do they want me? Oh God, is someone dead, oh Jesus?' She grabbed the edge of her desk, the wind sucked out of her.

'No,' Lorraine said immediately. 'I don't think it's anything like that, because they've kept their hats on. Wouldn't they remove them if the news was bad? They seemed more suspicious than anything.'

'Suspicious of what? Me?'

Rosie heard the phone drop and started to half walk, half run towards reception. Catching a fleeting thought that maybe someone had called a strip-a-gram and there'd be a half-naked muscled cop waving hand cuffs at her from the lobby. She'd act surprised and be all, 'You guys, it's not even my birthday. How did you know I love a near-naked law enforcer?'

There they were. Two navy uniformed guards, not particularly looking like they'd take tips in their g-strings, were standing with their backs to the office in deep conversation with Serious Steve. Lorraine's eyes had popped out of her head and she shook her hair wildly in the direction of the guards as if Rosie couldn't see them for herself, the only people standing in reception. Serious looked up and caught her eye, Rosie heard him speak.

'You can ask her yourself, guards. Let's just move into a meeting room, shall we?' With surprising dexterity, Serious managed to manoeuvre the guards into a nearby room, sit them down and quickly scurry out, shutting the door behind him. 'Lorraine, can you make sure no one goes in there? Rosie, a word.' He gestured to the side of the reception, a white leather couch that was too low to sit on, so purely existed for hovering or tripping over, and a glass coffee table. He spoke in a hushed tone. 'They want to talk to you.'

'About what?' Rosie forgot to whisper, her hands automatically went to her waist in a stance of defiance.

'Simon Fitzpatrick.'

'What? Seriously? Simon? What about Simon? Is *he* dead?' Rosie didn't want to say I told you so but . . .

'No, it's nothing like that . . . Do you have a lawyer, Rosie?' Serious had narrowed his eyes.

'No. Why would I need a lawyer?' Rosie felt appalled at the very suggestion. A lawyer might mean that she'd done something wrong. She was a law-abiding citizen. She broke out in a cold sweat if she thought she forgot to fully weigh her fruit and veg on the self-checkout at the supermarket. Save underage drinking on two occasions before she turned eighteen—one glass of champagne at a wedding, and the other a toe-curling vodka, rum and cider mixture at Joe Simpson's seventeenth birthday party—she had never veered into anything even remotely illegal. The mere thought of it made her skin crawl with guilt; she'd never sleep again, she'd be hopping every time the doorbell went.

'They look like they mean business—they're from the internet fraud squad.' Serious Steve spoke slowly, which was probably wise given the information overload that was now cramming Rosie's brain.

She gulped hard, momentarily speechless.

'They want to ask you some questions about Simon.'

Rosie focused on the shine on his bald head to try to stop the room from spinning.

'I can see if I can get someone down here from the fifth floor, from legal, if you want?'

Rosie shook her head, surprised she managed to speak in spite of the sawdust in her mouth. 'I haven't done anything wrong.' She wondered how this could be about Simon, it must be about something else, but what? Every possible variation of every possible crime raced through her mind; she always wrote down what she took from the stationery cupboard, especially the Sharpies, unlike many of her colleagues who seemed to think it was a free-for-all. She paid her TV licence bill, a ridiculous, money-swindling scam by the way, but she believed firmly in the stern voiced-adverts that shouted, *You will be prosecuted!* She hand-on-heart had never downloaded an illegal movie, she was far too scared of bugs and who knows what level of porn would appear on her laptop if she just clicked *Okay.* She never drove over the speed limit, her credit card was paid off like clockwork. No, Rosie was sure she was very close to being a model citizen.

Steve nodded. 'Okay, look, legal will just say to you what I'm going to say to you. You don't have to answer any of their questions, it doesn't make you look guilty. Just say I'd rather not answer that. And don't, don't dig a hole for yourself. Do you understand?'

Rosie felt her head involuntarily nod.

'You'd better go in.' He gently pushed her lower back and guided her to the meeting room. 'Guards, this is Rosie O'Shea. Can I get anyone a cup of tea or coffee?'

The two guards pushed back from the circular glass table and stood up in unison, both in navy v-necked jumpers with blue-collared shirts peeping through. They had removed their hats, one older woman with greying temples, one younger man. Both simultaneously stretched their arms across the table to shake her hand. The younger one pulled back, and Rosie found herself offering a limp wrist to the older one. She sat down then, moving like gravity had been pulled away from her. She found she was wearing her shoulders as earrings, took a deep breath and tried to remember some Instagram quote about not letting troubles into your head. Although Rosie was pretty sure that that particular quote was about getting stressed in the supermarket and didn't quite cover being face-to-face with guards.

'Hi.' She exhaled.

'A tea would be great, thanks,' the older guard said to Steve. 'Tea all round, yes? She nodded for the room, making the decision for all of them. Rosie watched as her eyes quickly flashed to the door, waiting for her boss to exit. Which he dutifully did with a worried expression on his face.

'Hi,' the younger guard smiled gently, inching slightly closer to the table. He had red hair combed neatly to one side at the front and standing up in tufts like a loose hay bale at the back.

'Rosie O'Shea, thank you so much for talking to us. We appreciate you taking the time.' The older guard, a fit-looking woman in her late forties, short hair and a ruddy complexion, took the lead. 'I'm Garda Shauna Lonnergan, and this is Garda Aidan Lalor.'

Focus, Rosie, remember the Instagram quotes, something about life, being in the moment, these are all just foothills and we need to climb the mountain, or something. Try and stay calm.

'We're from the internet fraud squad. We understand you're a director of DeLuvGuru, the online dating app.'

Rosie nodded her head in agreement.

'We'd like to ask you some questions about it.'

'Am I under arrest or something? Like, what do you want to question me about? I haven't done anything.' Her eyes darted from one guard to another. 'Have I? Why would you possibly want to talk to me about anything? Am I in trouble, seriously? Am I?' Rosie babbled instantly forgetting Serious Steve's advice about remaining silent. The older guard, Lonnergan (was that her name?) opened her mouth to speak, but Rosie didn't give her a chance.

'And, like, how do you even know I'm here? How do you even know my name? And how could this be about Simon or DeLuvGuru, it's only been live for what like ten days, sure that's nothing?' She paused took a deep breath and continued, 'I just don't know what you want from me? It's weird isn't it? A little bit?'

Aidan Lalor was taking notes on a lined A4 foolscap notebook.

'You're writing? What are you writing? I haven't said anything.' Rosie fired over at him accusingly.

'Oh, I know, it's just the date, I just wrote the date, here look, on the top of the page.' He started to slide his notes across the table, until the older guard's hand intercepted the page and pushed it back towards him, frowning and tutting at Aidan Lalor.

'Okay, Rosie, I understand that this is unusual, and we may be causing you some upset by being here, but I assure you we just have some questions and hopefully that's the last you'll hear of us.' The older guard decided to take hold of the situation.

'Well, I've seen *Orange is the New Black*, and I've no interest in a boiler suit. I know they're all the rage and I've tried adding a headband, retro style, but my hips just can't carry it off. So, I can't go to prison, okay?' Remembering Serious Steve's words, she asked, 'Do I have to answer you? Like, can I plead the fifth?'

'That's in America where you do that, not Ireland. And it's mainly in films.' The older guard wasn't smiling. 'You're not under investigation and you are not obliged to answer any of these questions, but we would very much like your assistance.'

'Oh, okay. Right, that seems fine, I guess.' She nodded and sat up a little straighter, absentmindedly flicking her dark hair off her shoulder and pulling down her blue shirt dress. Rosie could feel the sweat pooling under her arms; this dress was a demon for not hiding sweat patches. Of all the days to wear it.

'DeLuvGuru was set up by yourself and Simon Fitzpatrick?' The older guard had opened up a manila folder with a number of printed pages inside. She seemed to be reading through them as she spoke. 'You are a ten per cent shareholder, is that correct?'

'Yes.' Rosie smiled weakly.

'When did you first meet Simon?' The older guard was not smiling.

'Around three months ago, we met in Hogans.' Not too tricky, Rosie thought.

'Know it well,' the younger guard piped in cheerfully and was quickly shut down with a withering look by Lonnergan, who Rosie was establishing as the boss.

'That's a very quick timeline, to be working together, and have an app live, all in the space of three months, isn't it?'

'Well, when you know, you know, don't you? Simon had all the back end already done from a previous app he'd worked on, so it was really just a matter of doing up new interfaces. If you're wanting technical answers to stuff, you'd be better off speaking to him.'

Serious Steve appeared at the door carrying a noisily clinking tea tray with him. He wobbled to the table and slid the tray down, his ears cocked to catch anything.

'Thank you,' they all muttered and Serious took it as his key to exit, throwing earnest looks at Rosie as he walked backwards to the door.

'So, what has been your role in DeLuvGuru?'

'I suppose you'd say anything that's not technical. I wrote the copy for the site and I'm doing the marketing, which is pretty much just some socials and contacting influencers. Anything we can get for free really . . .' Rosie paused and wondered why they were listening so intently to her. Was she saying something wrong? 'I mean this is my real job here at CRUSH, the app is just kind of fun, or you could call it a hobby that takes up way too much of my time.' She attempted a half smile. 'I work here about sixty hours a week and spend maybe twenty on the app. Do you need to know that kind of stuff?'

The paperwork was spilling out of the manila folder, the older guard was flicking through some pages, looking for something. She found it, turned and slid a page towards Rosie. 'Do you recognise this?'

She nodded. 'That's the company registration form, they put it in both our names. Yeah?' She looked up for approval, remembering how very grown up and excited she felt signing that form.

'And this?' A photo of Simon came across the table. 'Who is this?'

'That's Simon. Why do you have his picture?' It was a grainy picture of Simon getting out of a car, a blue Ford, in some car park. 'Has something happened to Simon?'

'Do you know where Simon is right now?'

'He went to London about ten days ago, to meet with the developer.' Rosie's voice hung in the air, embarrassed. She didn't want to go into details especially not with guards. Did she have to, she wondered? Like where would she start, *Well, guard, we just had sex and he was being an asshole.* She wondered if Garda Aidan Lalor would scribble it down. God, the mortification of it all.

'Where exactly in London?'

'I don't know. He just said London. I never asked.'

'What's the nature of your relationship?'

'Um . . . he's my boyfriend.' Or maybe he's not, maybe she had been ghosted.

'Have you been in touch?'

'Well, no, actually. I haven't heard from him. He's in a snot, I think. We'd had a bit of a fight.'

'So, you haven't heard from him in approximately ten days?' Lonnergan asked deadpan. This was more of an emotional grilling than lunch with Catriona.

'Why are you asking me about Simon?' Rosie was beginning to wonder if the guard wasn't particularly bright.

There was a long pause, as if she were considering whether or not to tell her something, then she said, 'The man you know as Simon Fitzpatrick has a number of aliases. He's also known as Paul Wetherby, Simon Fitzgerald, Johnny Lukeman. He is wanted for questioning by police in four countries in relation to identity theft.'

'Um . . . what?' Rosie heard the words spin around the room, the different names, the *wanted in four countries*. She heard it all. 'What?'

The guard didn't answer her. Instead, she pushed across a number of pages, all with Simon's picture on them but with different names: a driving licence, a passport, a mug shot.

Rosie grabbed hold of the edge of the table to steady herself. 'Oh my God.' The words started spilling out of her on a loop: 'Oh my God.' A stream of white noise filled her ears. 'Oh my God.' She wrapped her arms around her waist and started rocking back and forth. 'This isn't a joke, is it? Don't answer that.'

It was all there—clear evidence piled up in front of her, which a guard had handed to her.

Garda Aidan Lalor nodded in agreement, looking somewhat downcast.

'Who is he, Jason Bourne? Like, who the hell has two passports?' She picked up the different pieces of paper and stared at them. 'This is bad, isn't it?'

'It is serious, yes. We've been chasing him for a while.'

'Why didn't you get here sooner? Like last week?' Rosie tut-tutted at them, deadly serious about their clear incompetence. She took a deep breath and said, 'So, what does this mean? I hope you don't think I had anything to do with this? I am Rosie O'Shea, there are no other passports.' Rosie folded her arms across her chest in disgust. 'Because I'll have you know that I would never, ever, ever get involved in anything dodgy. I had no idea he was a spy or whatever the hell he is. What is he?'

'Simon, or Johnny, or whatever you want to call him, runs internet scams. He has executed similar scams previously with unsuspecting female victims.' The older guard looked to be choosing her words carefully.

Rosie suddenly felt self-righteous here. 'I'm not a victim. He didn't do anything to me.'

'Rosie, if you're not a victim, you're involved. You own ten per cent of DeLuvGuru.' There wasn't a flicker of emotion on her face.

'Hang on a minute, that's a legitimate company. I . . .'

'Rosie did you ever give Simon any money?'

She shook her head. Lying. She was lying to the police. The shame.

'Any large gifts?'

'No. Nothing. What do you take me for?' She could hear the outrage in her voice.

'Anyway, he has money. From the divorce, he's an entrepreneur, his apartment?'

'The apartment at St Stephen's Green?'

She nodded.

'It's an Airbnb. He only paid for two weeks and there's a dispute.'

That really hit a nerve with Rosie. 'It wasn't his. An Airbnb?'

The guard took a long breath and said, 'Simon Fitzpatrick attaches himself to a female—young, probably mid-twenties with some digital expertise—and lets them know he's about to start an app and asks if they are interested in getting involved. Some women have given him large amounts of money to get it off the ground, others like yourself and DeLuvGuru have been a gateway for his secondary business, which is in data theft. He has been on our radar for a while. He started with online romance scams and has progressed. He has set up other dating sites in the past, along with a weight loss app, a travel company—there's a long list.' She gestured to a sheet of paper.

'The app? It's not real?' Suddenly Rosie was blinking back tears. It struck her this might be the thing that would upset her the most, that DeLuvGuru the magic matchmaking app might not be the real deal.

'Well, it's real in the sense that people are handing over an awful lot of their data, which was Simon's goal.'

'No, not that. The magic algorithm that brought people together to fall in love?' Rosie felt a terrible weight hit her chest.

'The app is a tool to get people's personal information, which he then sells on the black market. There's no magic algorithm. It's written in very simple code, any matching is random selection.'

Rosie's head collapsed into her hands. Her fingers dug into the roof of her skull. 'I can't believe it's not real. I never understood the technical stuff, but I believed him about it. I really thought that we were going to make people fall in love.' She took a deep breath, and then looked up, eyeballing the two guards. 'I'll be honest with you, I'm devastated.' She took a long look around the room. 'I knew there was a problem when Catriona's date didn't go well, but now you're here, and you're saying it doesn't work, that it never worked. That's hard to hear.'

'I understand.'

'I don't know if you do. I really believed in it. I was revolutionising dating, like Steve Jobs but for dating, and now you're telling me I wasn't doing anything like that, I was actually involved in data fraud. Like BOOM! Seriously, my head just exploded.' Rosie held her hands up in the air and waved them around. 'I'm devastated, genuinely devastated.'

The younger guard hastily started pushing a cup of tea over to her. 'Ah God, here, have some biscuits, too. It's not your fault.'

'Thanks,' she said, 'but maybe it is. I should have been more aware of what was going on. I just accepted everything. I didn't ask enough questions, did I? I was just so excited.'

'You were dealing with a skilled manipulator. He has done this many, many times before.'

Rosie appreciated the kind words, but they didn't really go far enough. 'What happens now? What about all those people who have signed on? People have put their trust in me?' Her hand was clawing her neck.

'You'll need to close down the app, refund everyone. Aidan can help you with the logistics.'

Aidan nodded enthusiastically, but still managed to keep a hangdog look on his face, as if he truly understood Rosie's situation.

'Really? Just like that?' Rosie heard the disbelief in her voice.

'DeLuvGuru is not offering a matchmaking service, it's mining for data. It's operating illegally and under false pretences. Now that you have this information, you would be in serious trouble if you did not take action based on our advice.' The older guard sounded stern now.

'But they haven't found love,' Rosie pleaded, picturing Catriona. 'What am I going to do about that?'

'I can't help you with that, I'm afraid.'

'No, I don't suppose you could. God, I've made such a fool of myself, haven't I?' Rosie tapped her fingers on the table. 'Don't answer that. I was a YouTube hit, you know?' She sighed heavily, her shoulders hanging in defeat. 'So, what happens now? I'm not in trouble, am I? It's just Simon or whatever his name is?' What was his name? What had just happened? Had she been a victim of a scam? Was she in trouble?

'We'd like you to come down to the station with us for further questioning. You're not under arrest; however, the fact that you're a ten per cent shareholder of a company stealing data means we have further questions in order to understand exactly what your involvement is. We hope to avoid an arrest. We will ask that you fully cooperate with us and do not leave the country during the course of our investigation.'

Rosie's blood ran cold. She swallowed hard, nodded and blinked back tears. Was she going to jail?

19

Molly

'YOO-HOO, IT'S ONLY US.' THE CLATTER OF LITTLE FEET SCUR-rying down the hallway made Molly's heart soar. She hunkered down administering kisses and inhaling the scent of the boys' hair, giving them the fleetest momentary hugs until she was slapped away as they ran for their toys.

'I can't compete with monster trucks.'

Angela hovered in tight, pink sports gear.

'Thank you so much for watching them. I needed to give Rosie some space to work, her own flat is too small. The guard was here earlier, Garda Aidan Lalor.' Molly gave him his full title to convey the seriousness of the day and her dire need for childminding. He had stayed for three cups of tea, some paperwork and a few chats with Rosie and Gran. Lovely guy. Molly had been devastated for Rosie. DeLuvGuru was a scam, Simon was a . . . well, she didn't know exactly what Simon was but definitely an undeniable shithead. Rosie looked like she'd been pulled from the trenches after a battle; pale, startled and jumping out of her skin at the slightest noise. Molly had needed to get rid of the boys.

Like the human tornado she was, Angela bounced across the kitchen tiles scanning the chaotically untidy room.

'The boys had dinner, some organic chicken and veggies. Andy is a marvel with broccoli. He just loves it.'

Molly nodded in agreement knowing that Andy, when presented with broccoli from her, enjoyed it purely to demonstrate trees coming out of his ears and absolutely never, under any circumstances, to eat it.

Angela in a singular fluid motion glided to the sink, started to run the tap and rinse off the breakfast dishes.

Molly protested. 'No, no, Angela, please don't. I'll get to them. I just wanted to give Rosie some space.' Molly gestured towards Rosie who was hunched over her laptop at the kitchen table.

'I'll be as quiet as a church mouse. It'll take two minutes. I'd rather do it than Dominic have to face it after a long day. No one wants to come home to dirty dishes.'

And it did, it took two long, excruciatingly painful minutes, as Angela hummed to herself a number of aphorisms, all feeling like sling shots in Molly's direction. 'A clean house, a clean heart. It only takes a minute to organise yourself. Life looks better clean and tidy.' Having finished the dishes, Angela scanned the kitchen for what else needed her attention as Molly's hands hung to her sides defeatedly.

'Dominic not home?' Angela started to fold a dish cloth. 'On a Friday evening?'

'He's working late. He normally does on a Friday, the office is quieter.'

'Oh, is that what he said?' Angela was polishing a glass with an intensity it didn't deserve for a one-and-a-half euro Ikea number.

'What do you mean? What he said?' Molly's hackles rose.

'Oh, nothing.'

'Well—' Molly took a step closer towards her, feeling attacked in her own kitchen '—you can't say that! Why . . . what do you mean?'

'It's none of my business, but I thought he'd said there was a party after work, drinks or something. I must have misheard.' Angela stopped polishing and peered up at her through her eyelash extensions.

Molly prayed her face wasn't betraying her.

Angela raised her eyebrows and looked directly at Molly. 'It's important to keep your ship in order and look after your captain.' She waved her hands around the bombsite kitchen, her eyes trailing over Molly's baggy leggings and oversized t-shirt. 'Well, I hope you had a nice leisurely day, Molly, and caught up with some things.' Molly looked to Rosie for support who grimaced at Angela's remarks.

'Thanks for looking after me all day, Molly,' Rosie piped up dutifully.

'Well, I was just telling Angela that you needed peace and quiet today, that you've had a lot on your plate.'

'And I needed my big sister and tea and biscuits.' Rosie bit into a custard cream.

Molly raised her hand to rub her forehead. She'd have to talk to Rosie about being just a tad more supportive of her. 'Thanks for doing the washing up, Angela, and for watching the boys.'

'I'll be off, book club tonight. Busy, busy.' Angela padded through the kitchen, calling out over her shoulder, 'Good to see you, Rosie. Good luck with it all.' And she was gone. Door clicking exit.

Molly felt winded and uncomfortable and vulnerable. She needed to talk to Dommo, to check in and feel anchored.

She settled down on the couch in the sitting room with her phone, falling deep into the cushions and rearranging herself around a dinosaur cluster. Rory was happily playing with some trucks on the floor.

Dommo picked up after a few rings.

'Hey, I just wanted to talk to you,' Molly blurted down the line.

'What? Sorry, I can't hear. Hang on a second, I'll just go outside.'

Molly heard the distinct sound of chat and laughter. 'No. Wait a minute, stay exactly where you are. Where are you?' She felt herself on high alert and pressed the phone as close as she could to her ear. She heard a long groan down the line.

'Dommo? Seriously?'

'Brogan's,' he responded heavily.

Molly couldn't speak, it was as if a virtual tumbleweed encircled them. And then in the background she heard a voice, high, shrill and distinctly female.

'Another pint, Dommo?'

Keeping her voice level, Molly managed to ask, 'Who's that, Dommo?'

'Ah Jesus, don't be like that, Mols. It's just Tansey. You know Tansey?'

Molly's brain started to scan frantically for a Tansey, desperately trying to recall nights out with Dommo's work crew, searching hard for a face. Bingo. Blonde, pretty, infinitely perky.

'Tansey, is this . . . like, what?' She couldn't compose a thought.

'There's a whole gang of us. Come on, Molly.' He sounded angry. She didn't open her mouth. 'I didn't tell you because I knew you'd just start at me. It's Tansey's birthday and the whole department has come down for a drink. I couldn't not come, it would look so bad.'

God forbid you'd disappoint your work colleagues. Oh no, you could never let them down. But as for your wife and family, who cares about their disappointment, hey, Dommo? That's what she wanted to say, it burned on the tip of her tongue. *Let me be the scorned wife, the angry nag at home, the pain in the arse, but you go and be Jack the Lad and enjoy your pints.*

'Well, you'd better not miss out on the party then, had you? Go on, Dommo, Tansey's waiting for you.' There it was, cool-headed, calm and an internal boiling point that had just been reached and bubbled over. She hung up. Never in all their years had she hung up on him without a bye-bye-bye-love-you. But God, if he didn't deserve a hang-up now, he never would.

She could feel hot prickles behind her eyes, angry tears were going to slide down her cheeks any second now. Her phone started to vibrate, Dommo was calling her back. She let it ring.

What was wrong with them? What had happened? Was she really *like that*? Had she turned into some fish wife who wouldn't let her husband go out for a few pints? Would she really have said no if he'd asked? Did he have to ask? She could have arranged to have met him tonight, squeezed into something black and crippled herself in high heels, she'd love to go wild and hit the town. Back in the day, she'd have met him for after-work drinks, they would have gone onto a night-club, bought rounds of shots and she would have ended up bellowing some cheesy tune sliding across the dance floor on her knees, hair flying everywhere followed by a feed of curry chips. But that was before, before, before. It was before for her, was it not before for him? Does he not get it? Everything has to change when kids come. Had he even been working late all these days? Had he been in the pub? He'd been lying to her. That hurt, a red flaming-poker kind of hurt. They had never lied to each other. What else was Dommo lying about? Was he having an affair with Tansey? No, she immediately dismissed that thought, he would never do that to her. But she would have said that he would never have lied to her, and yet ... Molly was up, pacing around the sitting room, circling the couch. Tansey? What was that work trip he went on a few weeks back? Was it even a work trip? What had happened to them?

They were best friends, they were building a family, they were happy. Were they happy? She loved Dommo. Absolutely hands down, he was a good, kind man. But was she deliriously happy? No, but who walked around like that? Other than people in pop videos skipping through life in poodle skirts and swishy ponytails, singing songs about lemon drops. Real people just got on with it. There were ups and downs and sucker punches and sometimes lemon drops and sunshine. So, herself and Dommo had been a little off with each other but that was marriage, wasn't it? You muddle through and know that eventually the sun will come out, and pop music on the radio will have you up and dancing in the kitchen again. You don't run to the pub for Tansey's birthday and lie about it.

She felt sick, but more angry than sick. Furious in fact.

She typed an SOS on her phone screen.

Anna, can you call in? Some crisis management advice needed at number 54!

Five minutes later, Molly had positioned the iPad, Rory and Andy alongside Rosie at the kitchen table and Anna arrived in a gust of Dior Addict with a clinking handbag swinging wildly on her shoulder.

'I grabbed what I could, it sounded urgent, but I've drunk most of the supplies in the house. I've got a bit of gin, a half bottle of Baileys and some kind of lemon liqueur that I got in Greece about ten years ago. That'll do until Uber Eats gets here. Don't you think? What's going on?' Anna threw her coat on the rack and eyed the scene in the kitchen curiously. 'What's . . . ?'

'I'll fill you in,' Molly started. 'Let's go in there first, we have a few situations here that need your input. I'll get some glasses. You really are a wonder in a crisis.'

'I should work in the UN, I'd be a marvel. Ancient lemon liqueurs could solve all kinds of conflicts.'

One quick gin, four chocolate-dipped wafer biscuits and an agreement on a Thai food delivery if and only if it included prawn crackers, which are not a Thai speciality but some are known to do it, and Anna was fully up to speed on Rosie and Dommo. Both scenarios had induced looks of shock and worry to Anna's face.

'I think you and Dommo need a date,' she concluded. 'I think you need to be on your own and have some fun. I'll babysit.'

'But what if it's too late?' Molly asked despairingly.

'Don't be ridiculous, he's in the pub with the work crew. He hasn't flown off into the sun on a mini-break to somewhere with soft towels and coconut-scented hand cream with some twenty-year-old.' Anna sounded a little angry.

'He's lying to me.'

'Let's try and keep perspective here. I'm not going to call Dommo a shit. He's not.'

'Isn't he?'

They sat in silence and swirled the remainder of their gin in the bottom of their glasses.

'I'll probably be more help with next door's problem.' She nodded her head towards the kitchen. 'I'll try to get a handle on what's going on, and work with Rosie on her statement— make sure she doesn't say anything incriminating. It's hard to know if she's in trouble until I get the full facts of the case.'

'Thank God you're here. I've missed you.' Molly sounded relieved. 'Do you do divorces?'

'Stop it.' Anna reached across the couch and slapped her friend's thigh. 'He's just in the pub. It's not the end of the world.'

Molly shrugged, and felt those nasty tears threatening to spill over again. *Isn't it?* she thought. They sat bolt upright at the sound of a key turning in the hall door.

'Dommo!' they whispered to each other. Molly didn't know why she felt so nervous, but she did, she absolutely did.

Anna jumped to her feet. 'I'm going into the kitchen. I'll send your husband in here.'

'Hey.' Softly spoken, Dommo positioned himself in front of the fireplace, legs astride and hands placed on his hips, like a superhero preparing for flight.

Molly knew if she looked at him she'd cry. So, instead, she studied the empty glass in her hands. She pursed her lips, swallowed hard and willed the bitterness to seep out of her. 'Good night?'

He slowly deflated in front of her, and half-heartedly raised his arms to the sky. 'I thought maybe we could talk.'

She did want to talk, she wanted him to hug her and to make everything okay, but she also wanted to shake him and scream at him, and maybe smash something. She was mad and battle ready, prepared to go to war, but she also felt like she'd already lost. She crossed her arms, bulling for a fight as she practically spat at him, 'Well, talk then.'

'What's the point when you're like this? Jesus Christ, Molly, why are you like this?'

'Oh, I dunno, maybe because my husband is a liar.'

He stared at her, his jaw clenched and his shoulders tight. Dommo shook his head with slow resignation and walked out of the room.

20

Yvonne

YVONNE DIDN'T HAVE THE HEART FOR THE PUB TODAY. IT WAS as if she couldn't look it in the eyes, which was stupid what with it being a building and all. To her, though, the pub felt like a living, breathing thing; her family, her past, her future. And she was failing it. The weight of disappointment was a terrible thing, such a heavy burden to shoulder. Last night she had sat at her kitchen island and photographed candle sticks, mixing bowls and a linen tablecloth—lovely things she'd bought for her house—and posted them on eBay. Scolding herself as she went along for being so flash with the cash when she had moved in. She'd filled up two trollies, two, in Dunne's Stores homewares! The expensive part at the front. She hadn't even thrown an eye to the bargain bin. She had hotel quality sheets on her bed, throw rugs and fluffy mats in a neutral palette as far as the eye could see. She had four glass vases, surely she only needed one? Click, eBay.

She was being strict tonight as sometimes she'd find herself on eBay selling and bidding at the same time. *A false economy*, her rational voice screeched at her. But eBay *was* an economy, she reminded that little voice, she wasn't paying full price. Besides, sometimes she just needed to shop, she needed the newness in her hands, she needed to feel the transaction and enjoy her purchase. Shopping made her feel powerful. She used to love popping into Grafton Street, racing around high-end shops. She could spend one thousand euro before lunch and then saunter across the red cobblestoned road to her favourite store for a summer dress, and without blinking, there'd be a few hundred more euro gone on two pairs of the same sandals in slightly different colours. It was all so easy. She had been a regular in the expensive boutique La Crème in Foxrock village in Dublin. She had loved living in Foxrock, where big rambling houses with mature gardens sprawled and urban foxes made their homes. Yvonne's friends seemed to possess ninety per cent of the money in that small village. They were the ladies who lunched and drank at the nineteenth hole at the golf club, who had their kids in private schools and took lengthy skiing trips in winter, who moaned constantly about the size of their tiny villas in the south of France and took weekend shopping trips to New York. It had been a lot of fun, and there had been a certain standard to maintain. Not that anything would be said out loud, but it was understood that you would always have your hair styled, you'd carry a matching handbag to your heels and your house would shine when it needed to. And so, Yvonne would pop into La Crème once a week. They stocked top European labels, and everything was exquisitely made by nimble-fingered Italian tailors. She adored the thrill of walking through that door; hearing the gentle tinkle of the bell, the smell of sandalwood and feeling the lush softness of the carpet underfoot.

'Yvonne, so nice to see you.' The shop assistant always greeted her like a long-lost friend and not a major shareholder, which she could have been.

'I'm not buying. I just thought I'd look at that green necklace you have in the window. It would go so well with my . . .' Yvonne's eyes scoured the shop, her mouth dry as she felt an excitement bubble from her stomach up. 'You have new stock.'

'I actually put a few bits aside for you. There's a beautiful pink silk blouse, which would go with the cream palazzo pants you had last season. A real statement piece.' Professional and polite as always. 'Would you like me to show them to you?'

Yvonne recognised the naughty schoolgirl in herself. 'Oh, I really shouldn't. No, no, I said I wouldn't. I went a bit wild on the credit card last week and told Brandon I'd rein it in. I'll just look.' She traced her fingers along the padded hangers, swishing her hands gently down the length of the clothes, feeling the texture. Absorbing the lusciousness of the fabrics, the endless possibilities of what it might feel like to wear them. 'Oh, go on, I could just try them on. It won't hurt.'

Fifteen minutes later, she was trying them on, twirling and giddy, and loving the new her in bright, vivid colours. The pink did suit her. And it worked even better with a gold buckled belt and wedge heels with a metallic bow at the back. Oh, it was heavenly. The infinite potential of who she was in these clothes and who she could be. And the bags—the delicious weight of those carry bags; beautiful, heavy paper with knotted string and gold thread running through it. Yvonne loved those bags.

She'd skip out of the shop every time delighted with herself, but as she'd get closer to home, the pep in her step would dampen, her brain a flurry. Where could she hide her bags? She couldn't let Brandon see, she'd promised him she'd stop. The pounding in her chest, the worry. She'd hidden bags in the front garden before and in the boot of her car; there were nooks and crannies all over their house, it was full of hidey holes. But it always made her nervous that she'd be caught. Sometimes hours after the adrenaline high of shopping, she'd find herself collapsed in tears, devastated by her loss of control. But not all the time, most of the time if she could get away with it, she felt fine. Yvonne found that online shopping was much easier to hide. She took a box at the post office. The freedom to shop was glorious, and opening packages was just as exciting as being in a shop. Brandon never knew about the post office. And now she didn't have to conceal anything, she could shop all she wanted, except she couldn't afford to anymore. It had all caught up with her, and she knew that she had to stop. She knew it. That's why she was on eBay, selling items. She wasn't going to bid on anything and she might make a couple of hundred euro from all the bits and bobs. Then what, she wondered? What would happen next?

The Tax Office had been calling. A stern-sounding woman, Breid Murphy, had informed her that she had two weeks to make a full payment or start a payment plan, incurring interest before they would be forced to take legal action. *Forced!* Yvonne had practically snorted down the line at her. No one was forcing Breid Murphy to do anything, she sounded like she'd enjoy a day in court. How could you make a payment plan when there was no money coming in? Yvonne wondered, but most definitely didn't ask Ms Murphy with her heavy breathing and judgemental sighs.

Are you coming to the wedding, Mam? The girls' texts were relentless. *Help us choose outfits?* She didn't want to think about the wedding. *He's happy, Mam, you should be happy for him, too.*

If life was a movie, maybe she would be happy for Brandon. She'd sashay into that ceremony, lightly tanned, in a stunning pale-red dress, with glossy hair and muted lip (no overkill). She'd be gracious and smile cheerfully. She'd peck the joyful couple on the cheek and wish them a lifetime of happiness. And she'd mean it. But she was not a one-dimensional character. She was complicated and layered and she found it very hard to feel gracious towards Brandon and his new bride. She didn't quite know why, but suspected that if she was making a roaring success of her life it would be a lot easier to be generous-natured.

Right now, Yvonne's brain was a muddy sea of debilitating thoughts and no lightbulb ideas were going to be able to shine through that.

The internet told her that exercise would help clear her head, so once again she wrangled herself into her lycra and off she went to Maria Manifold's spin class at the leisure centre. She deserved a medal for turning up, she really did. She slipped her feet into the pedals and off she whizzed, her legs pumping. When she could, Yvonne looked up and smiled at Maria who didn't even break a sweat unlike Yvonne who knew her face was as red as a boiled ham. But in all fairness, people were definitely onto something when they talked about endorphins. It wasn't like she bounced off the bike when the class was finished, she didn't; she wobbled with sea legs and held onto the bike for dear life, but by God she was delighted it was over, and that she had done it. Not all the tricky up and down bits, but you know most of it, and she felt good. She felt positively bouncy.

'Do you want milk?' Maria pushed the tiny milk jug towards her. Still in their lycra and now wearing a pink glow, they were enjoying an early lunch at Yvonne's. She watched as Maria cut into the flaky pastry and brought a forkful of chicken to her mouth, chewing pensively and swallowing it back with a sip of water. She released a groan of delight.

'Oh Yvonne. That's heavenly.'

'Would you stop, it's just a chicken pie.'

'No, it's not. There are all kinds of tastes there, and it's so fresh. I'm mad for it.' Greedily, she tucked in, piling more chicken and pastry onto her fork.

Yvonne thought she might burst with pride. She'd always liked feeding people and felt real joy seeing people with full bellies and round cheeks fully satiated after a meal that she'd prepared. She felt giddy about Maria's praise, and a little bit floaty, high almost. Maybe this is what drugs felt like, picking up clean plates and people complimenting you on your cooking.

Four more bites and Maria had cleaned her plate. She traced her fingertip around it, licking off any remaining pastry flakes and pools of sauce. 'Why haven't you been cooking this food in the pub the whole time? It's delicious.'

'I inherited a freezer full of meals and the orders had been paid in advance. I have to get rid of them before doing anything new. It didn't make financial sense.' She felt her chest tighten slightly at the mention of finances. 'I couldn't afford to buy in new food and leave all of that going to waste.' She drummed her fingers on the table, anxiously weighing up whether or not to speak. 'The pub's not going well, Maria. Between you, me and the wall, I'm in trouble.' Yvonne hadn't intended to blurt it out, but she supposed it was all that was in her head, she wouldn't be capable of talking about anything else. There wasn't room in there for chit-chat.

'Oh dear.' Maria reached across the table and squeezed her hand. 'I knew something was up with you, but I didn't want to pry.' She paused, her brow furrowed in deep concern. 'Thank you for telling me. A problem shared is—'

'Still a problem,' Yvonne cut her off.

'Yes, I suppose it is.' She tapped her fork pensively on the corner of her glass. 'How bad is it?'

Yvonne released a short laugh that caught itself a cry. 'I'm at the end of the line.'

'Does your mam know? The girls?'

'No. Just you. Mam's in Dublin with them at the moment. I don't want them to know.'

'What do you need?'

'A big lump sum and a steady revenue stream. A miracle.'

'That can happen.'

'In two weeks? In Ballyhay?' Yvonne blinked back tears and rammed half a bread roll into her mouth, swallowing back a sob.

'Will we go down to the holy well and have a pray?' Maria laughed. 'It worked for my exam results.'

'Your mother lit candles and did the pilgrimage up Croagh Patrick for your exams.' Yvonne laughed right back at her. It felt good.

'True, true, it's the only reason I passed maths. Divine intervention stopped the theorems coming up in the exam.'

'Do you remember the theorems? Fat lot of use they were to us. And Sister Mary going red in the face trying to explain them.' Yvonne was smiling now.

'I can stick some posters up in here?' She swung her head around the leisure centre café. 'You could do a bingo night, or karaoke? Speed dating? Beauty pageant? What'll get bums on seats?' Maria leaned forward, her eyes questioning.

'I'm not sure. They used to just be there, you know.' Yvonne sounded defeated.

'People have changed so much. My son's a vegan, he's twenty-nine and has never even tasted alcohol. That generation don't drink; they're nothing like we were.'

'We couldn't raid the parents' drinks cabinet fast enough. We thought it was a sign of growing up if we got plastered in a field. I think being a vegan sounds a lot more grown up. You can still eat fish, can't you? As a vegan?'

Maria shook her head. 'Just beans, as far as I can tell.'

'Shame. You're right, though, maybe I should try an event or something, an occasion? Try to fill the place out.'

'We could nick one of those holy statues from the church and prop it up behind the bar, tell people it's moving. That always used to draw a big crowd in the eighties.' Maria was laughing her head off now.

'You've lost it, you have. Did someone slip whiskey in your tea?'

'That's our miracle, bring the moving statues back to Ballyhay.' She made a grand gesture of slapping the table as confirmation of the deal.

'Or maybe we'll try and find a local band to play?' Yvonne shook her head. 'Or maybe I'll put the place on the market and sell it?'

Maria's face dropped.

'I've made an appointment with the real estate agency, Warren Estates, before Mam gets back from Dublin, I don't want to worry her. Just to have a preliminary chat, just to see.' Yvonne sighed heavily. 'Maybe someone else can run it better, maybe I was just made to pull the pints but not run the place. I thought it was in my blood . . .' She bit down hard on her cheek to stop herself from crying and took a deep breath. 'Look, I have my health, my mam, my girls, my grandsons, that's what's important.' And she knew that, of course she knew that. But the pub was important, too. Being a success on her own was also important. Being able to stand on her own two feet, that was all she'd wanted really. That was why she'd left her marriage, to forge her own life with her own money, and now look at her, and look at the royal mess she was making of it. She had been so sure. She had left Brandon with absolute certainty, and now, well . . . now she wonders.

Maria grabbed Yvonne's hand again and said, 'And you have friends. I'll do whatever I can to help.'

A few flyers and a beauty pageant won't raise twenty-three grand, Yvonne thought. But she had to start looking forward and thinking of new ideas, surely; she had to exhaust all possibilities. There were always solutions, except to Sister Mary's theorems; they never made a bit of sense.

'You're sure you couldn't cook more? Have a gastro pub? Stick up a chalk board; this food is something else.' Maria's eyebrows raised. 'What's the phrase, *We are all lying in the ditch but some of us are looking at the stars.* Wilde, was it?' Maria asked. not looking for an answer. 'You're in the ditch now, no doubt about it, but this, this chicken pie, that's the stars.'

'What are you talking about?'

'Your cooking—that'll turn your place around. Your hopes and dreams are in a chicken pie.'

'It was gutter. *We are all in the gutter but some of us are looking at the stars.* I don't think Oscar Wilde was talking about a few burgers and a chicken pie.'

'You're wrong. Dream big, even when you're in shite. That's what he meant. And with cooking like this, Yvonne, that's what you can do.' She waved her hands around excitedly. 'You've a full kitchen in the pub, a full licence to produce your own food and you cook like a goddess. I'm telling you, when word gets out, you'll be beating them off with a stick.'

Yvonne chewed her lip pensively. Could she have a go?

'Business will boom.' Maria was lost in her own world. 'You'll have the local community on side, sure. Where do they have to go for good food? The hotel is too expensive, the chip shop or some dried out buns from Elizabeth's Café. It's a no-brainer.'

Yvonne's phone buzzed on the table interrupting them— Lukas. She looked apologetically at Maria as she put her phone to her ear.

'Yvonne, there's a disaster here,' Lukas shouted, his accent a blur of Polish clipped vowels and Irish slurs. 'The freezer is on the blink. It's just pouring out water.'

'Oh no. It was fine yesterday . . . or was it?' Her mind raced back, was it fine yesterday? She had defrosted a lamb shank and chicken korma or was that the day before. It was, it was the Wednesday. 'I never checked it yesterday.'

'I've called Padraig, the electrician, but Yvonne, I'm so sorry, it's like mush. It's too late for the food. I'm going to have to throw it out before it starts to stink.'

'All of it? Can none of it be saved? There's hundreds of euros of food.'

'No, it's totally defrosted. You could only give this to the dog.'

Yvonne hung up. Every bit of life drained from her. She noticed a tremor in her hand. Shock, she presumed.

'Well?' Maria asked, hovering off her seat.

Yvonne choked out the words, 'You know when you think it can't get any worse?'

21

Evie

EVIE COULDN'T MAKE HEAD NOR TAIL OF WHAT WAS HAPPENING to Rosie's app. One minute she'd been on top of the world, parading the buttons and widgets on the phone, and then she blinked and the whole thing had shut down and the guards had been called in. The guards! Evie had had a few brushes with the guards in the past, a few misunderstandings and one understanding around race fixing, which she'd just thankfully never managed to get into any real trouble about. She knew if the guards meant business you were in trouble, especially in Dublin. In Ballyhay, it was easier to bend the rules if you needed to, sometimes, but Dublin was for the hardliners. She didn't like it one bit that Rosie seemed to be getting mixed up in something illegal. Although the girls had insisted that it wasn't Rosie at all, it was that fella she'd been doing a line with, Simon something or other. It didn't matter as far as Evie was concerned, the guards could tar you all with the same brush. Rosie could be guilty by association, and that would be enough if they wanted to press charges. You wouldn't be well, with all the toing and froing.

Thankfully, Molly's friend, Anna, was there surrounded by paperwork in the kitchen. She was a solicitor, a very well-dressed one in a nice, silky blue shirt with a high neck, very smart. You felt you could breathe easy around her. Evie had only caught the end of her conversation with Rosie, but she had sounded very thorough indeed, talking about EU law and fraud. Rosie was in good hands, but Lord bless us and save us, it was a lot to take in. Evie was on her third cup of tea of the morning, sitting quietly at the end of the kitchen table, watching the scene unfold around her. She'd been expecting trouble, she had known something was coming down the line, the cards had told her after all, but never had she thought it would involve the guards. Those tarot cards were just not descriptive enough, they were terribly frustrating.

Rosie looked like she hadn't slept a wink. She was wearing a black t-shirt, her hair scraped back off her pale, tired face, stooped over a computer at the kitchen table, pointing things out to Anna who was furiously scribbling notes onto a pad. The table was strewn with pages and photographs. Evie had no idea what was going on at all. She would love to help but didn't know where to start. Anything with computers was beyond her. She picked up and put down some of the pages in front of her, trying to scan them for information. She was a matchmaker after all, maybe she could help with that part of it, although it did seem very different to what she did in her snug. The page in front of her looked a little like a passport page, a picture of a young handsome man, bright smile and underneath a list of information about him: likes Mexican food, five foot ten, keen cyclist. But it was his eyes that Evie focused on, the sadness that flickered at the corners. There was a trace of history; he may look young but he had lived a long life already and experienced grief and loss. She placed her hand over the picture and closed her eyes, breathing slowly, waiting to see if anything came to her. He deserved happiness, she could feel that, he needed it. She opened her eyes and looked at the disarray on the table, pages and pages of text, and some photographs, some that looked the same as the one in her hand.

'Rosie, love, sorry to interrupt, what's this?' She waved the young man's page at her.

'Profiles, Gran.' She looked down to the table. 'Sorry, I should clean them up. I thought if I printed them off I might get a better understanding of what to do. I don't know, it really hasn't helped.' She rubbed her weary eyes. 'They're all the early subscribers to DeLuvGuru, like my friend Catriona, the people who really want to find love, you know, the genuine searchers.' She sniffed a little, and dropped her head forward to her chest in despair. 'I just have to figure this out in some way.'

'You will, darling, you will. Go easy on yourself now.' Evie shushed her, hating to see her this way, so twisted and upset. Her anger was palpable just below her grief, but it was directed at herself and not, it seemed, at that Simon character. Hanging would be too good for him, Evie had thought multiple times. She drained her teacup and started to tidy up the pages in front of her, maybe she could help order things a little. So many people looking for love, so many smiling, optimistic faces beaming up at her. She could understand why Rosie wanted to help them. Her hand fell across another young man's picture, she held it down and peered into his eyes. He was as light as a feather, this man would flit on the wind, he shrugged it all off, clicked his heels and danced through the day. He was carefree and beautiful. She could feel it, an invisible cord was pulling that page towards the previous man's picture. She placed a hand on each photograph, closed her eyes and felt the draw, a hot flash whizzed up one arm, shot across her chest and down to her other hand. She opened her eyes with clear certainty—they were a match.

'Gran, I thought I'd bring the boys down to the playground at the end of the road, if you wanted to come with us? It's only a short walk and it's a lovely day,' Molly interrupted, bending down and speaking quietly to her. Molly's face was pinched and washed-out.

'Yes, yes, I'd love that. It'll clear my head.' Evie rose to her feet. Her hands still firmly pressed on the pages.

Molly looked concerned. 'Do you still have that headache?'

'Not at all, I can do with the exercise is what I mean.' She lied. Her head had been throbbing hard and fast all morning, but her limbs were moving, which was better than the previous morning, and so she would use what she could, while she could.

Molly brightened. 'Wait until you see Rory on the climbing frame, he's part-chimp. I'll get their coats on.'

Evie put the two pages on top of each other and slid them onto Rosie's keyboard. She started to speak, 'Sorry to interrupt again, but these two young men are matched. I don't know if that's any help to you.'

Rosie looked up confused and then swung her attention back to the pages. 'Really, Gran? Are you . . . ? Can you even do that with pictures?'

'Well, I just did, yes. They're definitely a match.' Evie nodded her head with absolute certainty.

'How did that happen?' Rosie sounded very unsure and more than a little sceptical.

'Sometimes The Knowing works in strange ways, when two people have to find each other, the universe will make it happen.'

Rosie was silent, dumbfounded.

'I'm going for a walk now.' And with that Evie walked into the hallway to find her black cashmere coat with the good leather trim.

It was a beautiful, sunny morning. They strolled past the rows of houses with neatly clipped front gardens and freshly painted doors.

'It is a nice neighbourhood, isn't it?' Evie breathed in the fresh air, already feeling lighter and brighter.

'Good schools, too. Yes, it's great.' Molly paused. 'It comes at a price. The mortgage repayments are horrendous and let's not forget my favourite neighbour.'

'Oh yes, although I thought your mother-in-law was very pleasant at your lovely dinner the other evening, even though things went a bit off at the end.' She squeezed Molly's arm supportively. 'Which house is hers?'

'It's behind us. You won't see a blade of grass out of place there. If a leaf accidentally dropped onto the lawn she'd have a heart attack.' Molly looped her granny's arm and pushed the stroller with her other hand. 'Ah, she's fine, I shouldn't go on.'

'You're two sides of a coin, the two of you.'

'Maybe.'

'She can't make head nor tail of you. She doesn't see being a mam the way you do.'

Molly looked at her perplexed.

'Angela's more my generation, the way she thinks: you know, the children should be fed and watered and thrown out to pasture. She values work and not in the home.'

Molly sighed. 'You could be onto something. She says she wants to help, and then I ask her, and she's always busy and I feel like I'm asking this massive favour, every time.'

'Maybe don't ask her for a while.'

'Sometimes I need help, though.'

'So, you pay the price.'

Molly grumbled.

'You can't have it every way, Molly.' Evie knew she sounded stern. 'You borrowed money from her and now you're taking her for free babysitting. Isn't it possible that she feels a bit used?'

'But we're family?'

'And maybe you're taking advantage of that.'

'Am I?'

Evie cocked an eyebrow at her.

'But she can be so nasty.' Molly was getting fired up.

'Focus on the good things. She loves her grandsons and she's been very generous to you. But that has come at a price.'

'We can't pay her back.'

'Well, you're going to have to work something out. Remember, you're not entitled to a free babysitter.' Evie patted her granddaughter's arm. She was enjoying this little stroll, feeling the sun on her face, walking along the street with the warmth of Molly's arm on hers, hearing the chatter of her great-grandsons, one shouting at the parked cars as they passed them, the other plucking leaves from bushes in wonder and awe. The sheer pleasure in being alive for these little moments. How lucky she was.

'I forget you have all the heebie-jeebies, Gran. Could you see all that stuff? Was it signposted?' Molly sounded excited.

'Nothing like that, love. I had a little chat with Angela and I could just tell.' Evie wondered if now was the right time. Well, she'd have to take it as she didn't know how much time she'd have left, so she couldn't miss the opportunity. 'Like you, darling. I can see that things aren't right between you and Dommo. I know it's not my place to say anything, but I think too often in this family we don't speak our minds enough, we go round in circles with our chat and it's not helpful.'

'Is it that obvious?' Evie felt Molly's body stiffen.

'You know I always tell my couples to talk to each other. To be honest with themselves and with one another.'

'We don't even see each other to talk. We're . . . I don't know . . . lost to each other.' Molly sounded terribly sad.

'You're a good match. A great match, in fact. You have sparks and smiles in your hearts for each other. So, they've dimmed a little—that's alright.'

'I know, I know, Granny and her matchmaking. Please, don't worry about us. We don't need to visit you in the snug just yet. We'll figure something out,' Molly spoke into the air, trying to bring the conversation to an end.

Evie stopped dead in her tracks. She placed her two hands on Molly's shoulders and looked deep into her eyes. 'Molly, listen to me, you have everything you need in that man, in this family. This is love. This is it. If you've lost it, find it. And don't go looking in other places.'

Molly raised her eyebrows.

'You know who I mean. That male sleep nanny you've been making eyes at. He's bad news. You have it all. Don't you go losing it.' Evie hoped she didn't sound preachy, like some priest from the pulpit, but Molly needed to hear her this. She couldn't throw away her marriage.

'Charlie! Gran, I would never.' She frowned, and then with a wry smile said, 'I can look, can't I?'

'We can all look. He's a very handsome man. Like Omar Sharif in *Dr Zhivago* without the moustache.'

Molly sighed heavily, her eyes fell to the ground. 'I think Dommo might be looking around, too, you know. I think there could be someone at his work.'

'Nonsense. He adores you. I can see it plain as day.' Evie had wondered that as well, he had seemed so disconnected to the family unit—not that she'd say a word of that to Molly. But it was true, Dommo was distant.

'I hope you're right. I'm not sure anymore. I just—' Molly blinked back tears '—I married my best friend, Gran, I really did, but I don't know where he's gone. I don't know where *we've* gone.'

'Find it. Find him.' Evie leaned in for a hug. 'The hard work only starts when you say *I do*. All the time before that is the easy part.'

'Can you put some heebie-jeebie spell on us for our marriage to work?' Molly laughed to hide the sob in her voice.

'It doesn't work like that, you goose. Make your own magic and it will work. It was working for a long time before this.'

'I know and then the kids came, and they are our sunshine, but it's just been hard, you know?'

'Of course it's hard. I remember what it's like to have small children. I had your mother and her brother running rings around me for years. Life can be hard.' Evie could sense that Molly was standing on a precipice ready to jump, and Evie wanted to make sure it wasn't into the arms of another man.

She linked her arm with Molly's again and gave it a squeeze as they turned into the playground. Together they watched with delight as Rory sped off to the climbing frame. Little moments, Evie reminded herself. Breathe in the little moments and try not to think about the black crows circling.

22

Rosie

IT WAS THE WORST KIND OF BLIND DATE ROSIE HAD EVER been on. Her stomach was cramping with anxiety and her breath caught each time someone opened the door. She watched in amazement, her coffee in front of her, as people bustled around the city centre café, padded jackets swinging off the back of chairs, the rain draining in rivulets down the glass and pooling on the window sill and fresh daisies poking their heads out of jam pots on tables. How was everyone so normal? Just an average Tuesday, and yet, nothing was normal.

A small attractive, blonde woman, wrapped in a pink coat, with a dazzling tan and sparkling blue eyes, swung the door open, scanning the café. There was no photo of her on Facebook, but Rosie knew immediately it was her. They locked eyes and nodded at one another.

'Rosie?' She was unbuttoning her coat preparing to sit.

'You're English?' Rosie had caught a hint of an accent. 'He told me you were Irish, that's why he was in Dublin.'

'No, from Essex originally. We came here to run away from the debt collectors who were chasing John down in London.' She positioned the shoulders of her coat on the back of the chair and took a long hard look at Rosie. 'You're so young. Too young to be mixed up in his mess. He's shameless choosing you.'

Rosie still couldn't get it out of her head that it was all a misunderstanding, that Simon would call her with an explanation—he'd lost his phone, had the flu and had been knee-deep in work. He'd assure her that of course DeLuvGuru was the real deal and of course their relationship was, too. That he hadn't just vanished into thin air. That it wasn't all a lie. Even as she was sitting in the police station staring at the cement walls, hearing the metallic screech of her chair across the floor, even then she kept thinking this is a mistake, a terrible mistake. Simon wouldn't do this to her. But it was when Garda Aidan Lalor with the red hair and the pink cheeks started looking at her sympathetically that she knew she was in trouble. His questions had dried up and he'd started offering her tea and ginger nut biscuits, referring to Simon as a romance scammer. Rosie was horrified.

It had been Fergal Byrnes's idea to track down Simon's ex-wife. Fergal was Rosie's new, terrifying solicitor. Anna didn't do criminal law but, Fergal, an ex-fling of hers (which she pleaded not to be judged on because it was centuries ago when she was going through an experimental phase) owed her a favour and he just happened to be the top criminal lawyer in Dublin. Rosie had felt her spirit buckle at the word criminal. Anna shrugged her shoulders and said something about it being time to face the facts, which was horrible but it was true. Fergal Byrne wanted to gather victim statements to help Rosie's case. And so reluctantly, Rosie had tracked down Anita, Simon's ex-wife online. She was easy to find and responded immediately.

Rosie pushed away the bitter-tasting coffee and said, 'Thanks for meeting with me. I didn't know if you'd want to.' Rosie heard the shake in her voice; she felt unprepared for a meeting like this and she really didn't want to cry. She'd cried a lot over the last few days—angry, hurt tears that never dried up.

'It's okay. I've met a few of his women over the years. You're not the only one, you know that, don't you? He's a serial offender. A lying scumbag. I'm just raging the police haven't caught him yet. How hard can it be?' She seemed so blasé about it all, so matter of fact. She could just call him a scumbag and order a coffee with a finger gesture in the same breath. 'Where are the police up to?'

'I was questioned by them,' Rosie managed to stammer out, 'and I made a statement.' Pre-Fergal Byrne, Anna had held her hand while she made the statement down at the station, patting her and shushing her with encouraging words. Rosie had just been blurting things out, and Anna would stop her and rephrase it, saying, 'What my client means to say is . . .'

Anita shook her head. 'They're just so slow. He's been at this for six years, since me, and I wasn't even his first. He goes between London and Dublin, he's got women everywhere. I've met quite a few of them.'

Rosie pressed her lips together, trying not to cry.

'I'm sorry, it's raw for you.' Anita threw her a sympathetic look. 'At least you didn't marry him, hey? Did he propose? He's had quite a few engagements.'

Rosie shook her head, feeling her heart twist.

Anita paused and took a deep breath. 'Look, it'll get better. This feeling will end. I've had bucketloads of counselling to get me over this. You should look into it. You're a victim here. You need to look after yourself, don't let this define you. I've completely moved on.' She took a sip of her coffee and glanced around the café. 'He scammed sixteen thousand euro from me, I'd an inheritance. You?'

'Um . . .' Rosie felt so embarrassed. 'There was seven thousand euro I invested in the company. I thought . . .'

'Travel?' Anita squinted at her. 'Was it an online travel company? The last girl—I only had a few emails with her—he took two thousand euro off her on a travel company.'

Rosie was struggling to get the words out. 'No, dating. My gran is a matchmaker and I thought we were going to revolutionise dating.' The tears started rolling down her cheeks. 'I just can't believe this. I can't believe how stupid I've been.'

Anita passed her a paper napkin. 'Hopefully, the police will catch him this time. Honestly, how he gets away with it.' She tapped the edge of her coffee cup with a manicured nail. 'It's him, you know, it's not you. You're not stupid, he's horrible. He moves fast, he's like a whirlwind. Before you know what's happened he's giving you beautiful gifts, telling you he loves you and you marry him, in my case; in yours you opened a business with him. It's okay. We all make mistakes. Move on from this. Do you have family?'

Rosie nodded.

'Lean on them. Get some support, this is a bad time.'

Rosie desperately wanted to ask someone if any of it, anything about her and Simon, had been true. She knew the guards had told her, his ex-wife was telling her, her sister had practically slapped her across the face telling her, but still she couldn't believe it. Rationally, gathering the evidence, she could hear the facts that none of it was true. His apartment was an Airbnb, his name wasn't Simon, he had stolen her money, DeLuvGuru didn't exist, he had never loved her. But she just couldn't believe it. If it was all a lie then what was she? An idiot. A hapless, witless victim of a scoundrel. A fool. A complete and utter fool.

'It's just . . . I'm devastated by it all.' Rosie sniffed.

Anita nodded knowingly. 'Fight it somehow. Don't let him win. Six years ago, after this—' she splayed her hands out on the table '—my weight rocketed, I couldn't walk up the stairs without stopping for a breath, I was depressed and, well, just you know . . . desperately sad that this had happened to me.' She paused and Rosie watched as Anita's jaw set in a firm show of defiance. 'I decided not to let him win. I decided to live my best life, and I am, Rosie, I am. I've never been better. I've just opened my own women's only gym in Clontarf. I work with women on their bodies and their minds. I teach them to build up that female power that's inside all of us.' She clenched her fist and raised it in the air. 'That's why I meet his victims, although I hope to God you're the last one. But just know that you can and will rise up from this.'

Rosie heard her words. She knew they were kind and probably inspirational, but she just wasn't ready to be a woman who ran with wolves and howled at the moon.

'I'll make a statement, of course I will. We'll put it with the other statements I've made before, and hopefully they'll get him this time.'

Rosie sniffed out a thank you. Great, she thought, great. It's something. Fergal Byrne will be happy at least. Meeting with him had been what she imagined taking an ice bath might feel like—horrific, terrifying, mood-altering and maybe, ultimately, a little bit tingly. Fergal Byrne, two names, never one, wore a three-piece pinstripe suit with a gold chain running from a waistcoat pocket to a button latch, which Rosie assumed held a golden, engraved pocket watch he used to tell the time and not count steps.

Tall, imposing, permanently stuck in middle age, sporting a floppy hair-do straight from the 1990s. He was everything *Law & Order* had told Rosie to expect from a criminal lawyer. She had squirmed uncomfortably in the chair, in a windowless office surrounded by folders and cardboard boxes that looked one coughing fit away from tumbling. She immediately regretted not bringing Molly or her mam for moral support, but she hadn't wanted them to know just how much trouble she might be in until she understood it herself. She was wildly intimidated.

'We're renovating. Excuse the . . .' He twirled his finger in the air. 'I've reviewed your case.' He thumbed through a pile of papers on his desk, his voice booming.

'I didn't know any of this was fraud, or data collection—'

He held up a hand and she clamped her mouth shut. 'Let's deal with the facts, shall we, Rose? You invested in DeLuvGuru. You recruited hundreds of people to join. You took their money. You actively promoted the website. You are heavily involved in this company that is running a fraudulent service—'

She interrupted. 'As a matchmaker not as the fraud . . . I didn't even know that was happening.'

The hand rose again. 'Ignorance does not mean innocence, Rose.'

He paused to let that statement settle. Rosie tasted bile in her mouth.

'The registration was forty euro?'

Rosie nodded. 'It all went into Simon's bank account. I never saw that money.'

'I'll need to see your bank accounts and transactions to prove that.'

'You make it sound like I'm guilty already.'

'You're innocent until proven guilty. Let's work on that assumption.'

'It's not an assumption.' Rosie was up off her seat, outraged.

'This is a serious criminal matter, Rose: theft, fraud, deception.'

She sat back down with the sudden weight of reality crushing her.

'If found guilty you could face prison, or at a minimum you would never be able to serve as a director of a company again.'

Rosie pulled at her collar, which suddenly felt way too tight. 'Prison!'

'Now, that said, there is a case for defence. You have no prior record, you're an upstanding citizen, you are employed. If we can show the judge that you are a victim of a serial offender and that you have taken steps to rectify the misconduct we may find favour.'

'Steps?'

'You need to pay the pre-registered people back for starters.'

Rosie nodded, numbers flashing in front of her, including the balance of her depleted bank account. 'That makes sense, that seems like the right thing to do.'

'We'll keep gathering information to position you as a victim.' He nodded abruptly. 'I've agreed to waive my fee as a favour to Anna, but if this does go to court, or even in the preparation of a settlement, the barrister's fees will be exceptionally large.'

'Large as in . . . ?'

He stared at her blankly, and nodded. 'Large.'

She swallowed.

'It would help if the police could find Simon, but he seems to have a record of disappearing. We need to assume he's gone. This makes you the sole focus of this case which, if it goes to court, will be a public one because it is of public interest, so newspaper coverage et cetera.'

Public interest. Oh no, it was going to be everywhere, everyone would know. She'd never be able to hold her head up again. She was spinning. Rosie felt as if she'd fallen deep down into a well, and there was no ladder to help her to safety.

The next day Rosie found herself back at work, looking at the faces around the room—all of them nodding, agreeing, taking notes, murmuring 'so exciting' and other exclaimers under their breath. There were fifteen of them squished into the smaller boardroom, the one in which they never see a pastry or a custard cream. The poorer relation that only got still and never sparkling water. Sinead from marketing was chairing, her mouth opening and closing. Noise, just noise, Rosie thought.

She couldn't concentrate on CRUSH's Christmas plans. Her brain was officially melted. She felt exhausted, defeated and so unbearably scared she didn't know if she could sit in her own skin for the day. Prison was a possibility. How did that word even exist in her life? Prison circled around her head on an exhausting loop. It was terrifying. How had she not seen Simon for what he was? She had spent so much of her time with him, and the sex . . . eugh. She felt so horrible about the whole thing. Had there been signs? Maybe. His reluctance to be the face of DeLuvGuru made sense now, the second he showed his mug anywhere he could be recognised by one of his previous victims. Oh God, she was a victim. Rosie had no tech knowledge, and he had known that from the get-go—was that appealing to him? She didn't know her java from her html. Is that why he'd chosen her? Or was it the matchmaking spiel? Or once again, should she stop wasting precious seconds thinking about the why, when it was possible there was no why?

She was too tired to focus on this meeting. She sipped her tea and nodded a bit to something Sinead was saying about 'jingles'. The meeting disbanded, they all filed out. Rosie was sure she'd been given a task but couldn't quite recall what it was. She'd have to send an email out. Serious Steve sidled up to her, she could smell his aftershave.

'Rosie, can we have a word in my office?' He didn't make eye contact. This was not going to be good. She followed him in, reluctantly noting how her head was filling up with white noise. He gestured to an uncomfortable looking chair and sat himself down. That was when she noticed the looming presence of human resources in the room—the curly haired Saoirse.

'How are you doing?' Serious started off.

'Fine,' she rapid-fire responded.

'Look, we think it's best if you take some leave.'

'Excuse me?'

'Some leave from CRUSH, sort out everything with the police and . . .' He shifted in his seat, looking slightly uneasy.

'And if I don't want to?'

He looked over to HR, Saoirse leaned forward on the couch. 'Rosie, this isn't a request. We're not asking you.'

'Are you firing me?' Rosie's heart was racing.

'No, absolutely not. You need to take this opportunity to regroup and come back when this emotionally stressful period is over.' Saoirse's head clicked backwards, agreeing with herself.

Rosie felt her eyes narrow as she viewed them both with great suspicion. 'You don't want to be touched by a scandal, do you? If there's a fallout here from DeLuvGuru, from any of it, you don't want any part of it?' Rosie felt herself harden. 'You're supposed to be supportive when an employee is having a shitty time, not chuck them out on the street.'

'You'll be fully paid. We want you to take this time to regroup. We want you to see this as us supporting you,' Saoirse interrupted.

'You don't understand. I love it here. I race in every morning . . . I don't know what I'd do with myself . . .' Rosie watched Serious sit further back into his seat.

'Take some time for yourself, we have company counsellors who we can put you in touch with . . .'

Rosie didn't hear the rest. Leave, she heard that. Go. Come back when and if this has all blown over. Rosie clutched her notebook to her chest and exited the room. She didn't know how much more she could take. She scurried over to her desk and started to pack her lip gloss and pens into her bag. She didn't even throw a glance in Mark's direction, not wanting to catch his eyes.

She should have known Catriona would pick up on something; she raced over like a greyhound out of the traps. Her face creased with concern. 'You okay?'

Rosie shook her head. 'I'm on leave, effective immediately.'

Catriona's hand flew to her mouth. 'What? I'm so sorry.'

'Hey, Rosie,' Mark piped up from his desk, immune to the current drama unfolding.

'Not a good time, Mark,' Catriona rallied defensively.

He gestured to his phone. 'I just got matched with DeLuvGuru. Is that still a thing?'

'Oh no.' Rosie's chest officially caved in. She stared at the screen, her eyes unblinking. A million thoughts raced through her brain, the one taking up the most space was . . . prison.

Catriona looked confused. 'It's still matching people? I thought the app was shut down. Rosie, what are you going to do?'

23

Molly

MOLLY WAS LIKE A BANSHEE FUELLED ON CAFFEINE. SHE WAS tearing their bedroom apart. Drawers had been upended. Every one of Dommo's shirts were lying crumpled on the carpet, his shoes flung from one side of the room to the other. The bedsheets were strewn, bedside lockers pulled out from the walls. His jackets were inside out and every pocket on his pants was swinging outwards. She felt wild. She had vaguely heard herself panting and grunting as her frenzied attack continued, but the adrenalin coursing through her would not allow her to stop. She was a woman on a mission. If only she knew exactly what that mission was.

This morning, just before Dommo had left for work while he was gathering his bits upstairs and while she was spooning Weetabix and chopped fruit into her boys in the kitchen, his phone had buzzed on the work top beside her. She glanced over as innocent as you like, and there it was screaming at her.

All ready for our BIG meeting? Xxx

Time stood still. Shock circled her like a freezing hurricane, spinning round and round, until Molly was so dizzy she couldn't see anymore. Little dark shadows clouded her vision. She dropped a Weetabix-laden spoon that landed on the ground with a clatter.

'See ya, babe.' Dommo kissed the top of her head and grabbed his phone in one swift gesture. Ramming it into his pocket as he ruffled the boys' hair. 'I'll probably be a bit late this evening,' he shouted over his shoulder as he sauntered out the door. 'There's a big meeting this afternoon.'

The hall door clicked. The radio continued to play, her boys mushed the Weetabix between their fingers. And slowly her breath returned. She was surprised with how calm she felt. A sudden clarity washed over her, almost a robotic sense of what must be done kicked into operation. Without pausing to blink she turned the cartoons on, asked her gran to keep an eye on the boys and leapt up the stairs, taking two at a time. And then she released her inner banshee.

Molly knew it. Dommo was having an affair. Listen to your gut—every bit of relationship advice she'd ever heard preached that. If you suspect something, you're probably right. Your stomach knows things your brain fights you on. Where had she read that? Probably at the doctor's waiting room. Well, she suspected something, alright. And she had seen it, a big fat kiss on the end of a text. He could probably explain that away, twist it so she looked mad for suspecting him After all, an x on the end of a text doesn't necessarily mean twenty-four-hour hot and sweaty sex sessions? It could mean even more than that, though, couldn't it? It could mean love. Oh, that was way worse than mind-blowing sex. Love. Love would kill her altogether. She'd prefer it if Dommo was having chandelier sex with someone rather than holding hands and laughing with them. Oh no, she couldn't cope with him sharing his little sideways laugh, when one of his eyes winked shut. That was hers. She emptied out his socks and jocks drawer, unfurling the balls of socks. What was she looking for? What would Dommo possibly keep in his socks? She ran her hand along the back of the drawers, she must have seen it in a film once, in case he taped something there. What? What was she looking for? Love letters? Pictures of naked women? Dommo had never been into porn, he was more a fan of the wholesome, good-housekeeping type of woman than the sweaty, leather-clad ones that he professed would put the fear of God in him. No, this wasn't a 1980s movie, she wasn't going to find receipts with lipstick marks on them (did people actually do that—kiss receipts? Or was she confusing real life with a Russian spy novel again?) or shirts sprayed with some other woman's perfume. But there would be a trail somewhere. Breadcrumbs. She knew it, he wouldn't be capable of hiding his tracks. Dommo could never ever guess the murderer in Cluedo. You could be standing in the dining room with the bloodied candlestick and a corpse at your feet with a perfect candlestick shape in its skull and he'd ask you who did it?

She wished Anna were here. She missed her friend so much. She'd tried to befriend Anna's French au pair but she really was skinny and young, and it was very difficult to find something in common with someone who didn't look up from their phone. She knew Anna would either talk her down or help her rip Dommo apart. One or the other.

Molly grabbed her laptop and sprawled on top of their unmade bed. Dommo used this computer as much as his own, his gmail account should be an automatic log in. Within seconds she was scrolling through his inbox. Subscriptions to various parenting sites, technology forums—did he not get any personal emails? She searched Tansey, with her breath held—*no messages matched your search*. And exhaled.

Where had that conference been a few weeks back at which he had to stay overnight? Her brain ricocheted around her skull. Cavan? Yes, it was Cavan, because they had joked about the Ballyjamesduff pork festival, and whether or not he'd be able to swing into it after the conference and take some pictures of good-looking pigs for the boys. She started to type into the search, Hotel Cavan, but gmail suggestions started popping up on the screen, including a confirmation number for a hotel called The Red Cow Inn, which was five minutes from Dommo's office. Those dark spots dimmed her vision again, but mouth dry and fingers trembling, she clicked in. Three weeks ago, a booking confirmed for a Thursday night, and a follow up: *Did you enjoy your stay?* No. He was having an affair.

How fucking dare he?

She wanted to scream at him. How could he? What an absolute top-level lying scumbag he was. And an affair, it was just so low-rent. So predictable. So bored middle class. Eugh. Anyone could have an affair. She'd just read a typically salacious article in *The Mail* about how one in four people—not just men, women, too—had affairs. It was everywhere, everyone was at it. She could have had literally thousands of affairs by now if she wanted. There was that guy she bumped into multiple times a week in the aisles of Tesco's who'd made that joke, 'Do you come here often?' over the frozen chips. She would definitely be having an affair with him if life was anything like a TV show. That odd dad who went to Rhyme Time at the library who always clapped out of time, the one who stood on her bag, and squished the banana into the nappies. Surely it would be easy to start flirting over lattes and baby buggies with him? There was that DM she got from some random guy: *Heeeeey hot stuff.* Maybe she could start an online affair? He seemed perfectly . . . fine. And there was Charlie. Charlie. The hot nanny. Hadn't he said her hair was lovely? Didn't he call her a wonderful mother? And she was ninety-nine per cent sure she caught him looking at her maternity yoga pants in a leering fashion. And he was hot. He was shirts-off, Instagram-no-filter hot. Wouldn't that really shake Dommo's boat—Dommo shirts on, lights off, no cameras please Dommo—if she started to get her flirt on with Charlie? Oh, but she couldn't have an affair, she wasn't depraved. But she could flirt, and she could let Dommo find out, couldn't she?

Or was this the type of game-playing that she'd left at the school yard along with her braids, now that she was a grown woman with children? It was hard to know, because surely something like cheating was childish. Only a child would break something as deeply precious as a marriage because they didn't understand what it meant. She loved being married to Dommo, and yes, in equal parts she disliked it intensely, too—the sameness, the boring everyday routine, the certainty of it. But it was also what she loved—the sameness, the boring everyday routine, the certainty of it. It was comforting and safe and secure. He was home to her. She had always thought it was the same for him. She knew they'd hit a rough spot, but that was marriage. That's why it was a lifetime commitment and not an annual one. She knew she would still choose Dommo, that she would marry him again if life handed out do-overs with winning lottery tickets. Why wasn't it the same for him? Why was he choosing to run? And why didn't he talk to her about it? Although, how would she have liked that form of honesty—*Molly, I've got the hots for Tansey in the office*. She can't imagine she'd have used her listening ears during that conversation; she'd have thrown her bucket out of the sandpit, that much she knew.

Why was being a grown up so complicated?

And what was she going to do? Her husband, her Dommo, was having an affair. She'd assumed they were in this marriage for the long haul, together through thick and thin. Was she supposed to leave him now? She didn't want to. Or did she? What about the boys? She felt her stomach lurch. This would hurt them. She could never hurt them. Since they'd all been sleeping, she could see flashes of improvement. Andy wasn't so quick to fly into a temper when his toast wasn't cut into triangles and Rory had used the loo himself. No drama, no fuss, just a lovely little boy dominating the toilet. Molly even saw moments of triumph in herself. *Look*, she wanted to scream, *she was in here all along, the good mum I want to be*. She didn't snap when Rory pulled a bag of flour over himself and the kitchen, she sung nursery rhymes with Andy, she built a den that overtook the sitting room for four days. Things were picking up, she was sure of it, but now this.

Would the boys think Dommo was a bad man? He *was* a bad man. What a mess. How could he do this? It felt so unlike him. He was no saint, but he was always good and honest. She'd never known him to lie in all their years together; no, she was sure he'd never lied to her.

Molly closed the laptop. She didn't want to know anymore. She didn't want to know about hotels and Tansey and nights out at Brogan's. She didn't want to know about his secret life. She pushed it away and buried her head in the bedsheets, knowing that her entire world had just collapsed.

24

Yvonne

YVONNE WAS CONFIDENT THAT THE YOUNG WOMAN ON THE makeshift stage at McCarthy's gyrating furiously was no Beyoncé, despite her leotard. You had to admire her confidence. She was practically parading her innards in that outfit, and what with the hip-flicking and hair-shaking there was every chance that people would be too distracted to notice that her voice was on a sliding scale somewhere between woeful and shockingly bad. The two guitarists and one drummer all gazed at her with puppy-dog eyes as they played their instruments in various stages of rhythm, none of which complemented each other.

The locals were enjoying the show. The regular bar-flies were sitting front and centre admiring the wares on display. The band were from the college in Waterford, available at short notice and they performed for free. True to form, Maria Manifold had plastered the leisure centre with posters and handed out flyers on the main street, blatantly ignoring the litter laws. There was no charge on the door and Yvonne promised a free basket of chips for every table. One group of students had ordered tap water and huddled around their chips like a flock of seagulls. The rest of the pub was halfway full. There were a lot of student types who, Yvonne was fairly confident, had small bottles of vodka stashed in their handbags, especially the ones who ordered diet cokes all night but whose cheeks were getting redder and eyes glassier. Ah well. She wasn't going to worry about them tonight. Most of the pub were happily ordering drinks, eating snacks and looking for more food.

Yvonne hastily threw together a chalkboard menu— homemade burgers and a chicken and mushroom pie. Two meals that she could produce blindfolded and were delicious and wholesome. She'd bought the ingredients earlier. She'd loved thinking about the menu and figuring out what to buy, and what was going to taste really good. She knew she should be sad about the ruined frozen food but she was quietly delighted that that terrible menu wasn't hanging over her anymore. She could cook. And how she loved to cook. She'd splurged on an onion and fig chutney for the burger that probably meant she'd be selling the meal at a loss, but she had always been a perfectionist about any food she prepared. It was about taste. Incredible tasting meals. And they were selling and people were buying accompanying drinks so things were looking good. They weren't looking twenty-three grand good, but the place was busy, the chat was lively and the beer was flowing. It was something, Yvonne decided, and something was an awful lot better than the whole lot of nothing with which she'd been tormenting herself over these last few months.

You'd have to love Maria Manifold; she couldn't be a better supporter to Yvonne. She was up near the stage in a tight, black leather skirt and a sparkly black top with batwing sleeves trying to dance, or at least that's what Yvonne thought Maria was doing. She was swinging her arms a little, shuffling from side to side and making various waving gestures trying to get other people out of their chairs. It wasn't working. Yvonne had a nice chablis put to one side to enjoy a glass with her later in the evening to say thank you. It was really marvellous and surprising to have found such a great friend again.

The noise out of that band would make anyone's ears explode. They'd have to wrap it up soon, she thought.

'Any more of those burgers left, missus?' A shout came at her from across the bar, a young guy with his hair in his eyes.

She nodded. 'Will I put you down for one?'

'Please, with chips. I'm making a pig of meself. I've already had one and I'm going again, they're so good.'

'Ah, stop now. That can't be good for you eating two dinners in a night.' Yvonne gave him a motherly stare.

He grinned back at her, propping his elbows on the bar. 'Sure, I'll probably have three, then I'll go for a kebab on the way home from the pub. Mam says I eat her out of house and home and there isn't a pick on me.'

Yvonne had to laugh. She shook her head and took his money. 'I'll drop it over to you.'

That was the end of the burgers. Sold out. That felt good.

Lukas was working with her tonight too, hopping back and forth, working the taps at pace. A true barman, his happiest place was behind the bar on a busy night. He'd never find this kind of buzz as an accountant. At least he was smiling now, he'd been in tears earlier that morning when he'd called to her house.

'Lukas? Is everything okay with the pub?' It was so unusual for Lukas to appear at her house, in fact she couldn't remember ever having opened the door to him before. Something wasn't right. His face was pale, and his eyes were bloodshot.

He crossed his arms against his chest, covering his black leather jacket, somehow making himself look smaller and more vulnerable. His hand moved to his head to smooth out his blond hair, nervously, and he stammered, 'Hi, Yvonne. I wanted to talk with you.'

Yvonne flung the door open. 'Of course, of course, Lukas, come in.'

He walked stiffly, his body rigid with whatever it was that was bothering him.

Sensing his discomfort, Yvonne again asked, 'Is everything alright?' Quickly followed by, 'The pot's brewed, I'll pour you a cup and maybe we'll go to the sitting room.'

With the tea poured, they went into the next room and Yvonne gestured towards an armchair and shut the door to the kitchen. 'Well . . .' she started.

Lukas reached around to his back pocket and produced a brown envelope, slapping it onto the coffee table.

Yvonne didn't need to see the harp winking at her to know exactly what it was. Immediately she went on the defensive, shouting at him, 'How did you get that? What, are you going through my letters now? That's an offence, Lukas. I should call the guards.'

He glared back at her. 'I know. It was an accident. I was doing the invoices. It was just another brown envelope, I didn't even look.'

'Well, you should look. That's what I pay you for, to look.' Yvonne's eyes were popping out of her head, her lips twisted in anger. She walked to the table, snatched the envelope and crumpled it into her pocket. 'It's none of your business.'

Lukas slapped his hands to his hips. 'Of course it's my business. I work at McCarthy's, I love that pub. You and Mrs McCarthy are like my Irish family here. And I'm . . . I'm hurt, Yvonne, that you wouldn't share your trouble with me.'

Yvonne perched on the arm of the couch, staring wide-eyed at Lukas. She put her hand up to her cheek and shook her head, as she said, 'Lukas, I haven't shared this "trouble", as you call it, with anyone. Well, except for Maria Manifold, but that was just—'

'You told Maria, but you didn't tell me?' Lukas was clearly taking a personal affront to the entire in-debt-might-lose-the-pub situation. Tears glistened in his eyes, this man Yvonne had always found prone to dramatic emotions was really showcasing his talents now.

'It's really not about you, Lukas.'

Excitedly, Lukas raced towards her. 'It is. I am accountant.'

'*An accountant.* It's an indefinite article like 'A', we spoke about this before.'

'You see, you teach me, I teach you.' He smiled weakly.

'Well, you're not actually an accountant, Lukas, and this is not really an accountancy problem.' Yvonne felt like she was placating a child. She wanted this conversation to be over. She was terrified that he might start asking her real in-depth questions. Lukas needed to shut up. Yvonne could feel her pulse racing and knew her heart was speeding. 'Thank you for your concern but it really is none of your business.'

Much to her alarm Lukas did not leave, but made himself comfortable on the couch. 'How did this happen, Yvonne?'

'Well, when you run a business, matters can be complicated.' She felt her jaw tighten as she looked away.

He wagged a finger at her. 'You spend and you don't pay. I see it. My brother-in-law in Warsaw, the same thing happened to him, his business went under. He lost his house, he kept hiding envelopes and keeping secrets. He threw away his credit card bills without even opening them, can you believe it?'

Yvonne said nothing, fully aware that that was her own monthly ritual.

'Spend, spend, spend, shop, shop, shop. Until what? You're out on the street? I've seen it, Yvonne. Pieter had to move back with his parents. His mother is a terrible cook, you wouldn't want that.'

'Look, Lukas, I appreciate your concern, but it's all under control. That bill will be paid and your job will be safe.' She stood up hoping he would take it as a prompt to leave.

'It's not about my job. You're my Irish family. Tell me, where will this money come from? How will you pay?'

Yvonne raised her palms to the ceiling and shrugged. 'I'm not sure, I might put the pub on the market.'

'No, no, no. It is a bad idea, a very bad one.' He jumped up and started to pace wildly. 'There will be another solution, but

I need everything. You must give me everything. Your bank statements, too. All of it.'

'I don't know.' Yvonne couldn't imagine showing her full finances to anyone. She didn't even know what they looked like. Dire, she imagined. Excessive spending, impulse shopping, credit cards with ridiculously high interest rates, she was just too embarrassed to be put under the spotlight. She felt herself weaken, the shame was too much, the exhaustion of the pretence crippling her. 'No, no, Lukas. Please, no.'

'Do you want to end up back with your mother eating fish stew?'

She shook her head. 'Let me think about it. I mean, I don't want to sell the place, but I don't want you to see my finances either.' Oh, how the truth hurt.

Lukas came to a stop and snapped into a soldier-straight position. 'I will call you tomorrow morning and we will start to fix this. You will bring all your papers, and we will find a way out.'

Yvonne sighed deeply. 'I'll think about it. Please, please, don't say anything to anyone.'

Lukas grabbed her by the shoulders and pulled her into a chest-crushing hug. He squeezed her gloriously tight, broke away and said, 'We're family. Your problem is my problems.'

Tight-lipped, Yvonne nodded. 'Problem, not problems.'

He grinned, and Yvonne took a moment to quietly calm herself. She took a deep breath, painfully aware of just how much trouble she was in. Somehow the sheets were slipping off the bed and her secrets were being revealed, and by Lukas of all people. He wasn't supposed to know or care or interfere. No one was. This was her burden to carry, her mistakes to rectify. She had made this mess and now she wasn't even capable of fixing it. It was very possible that there wasn't a solution. Lukas looked wide-eyed and optimistic, but he had no idea of the extent of her debt. She couldn't see a way out.

25

Evie

EVIE NURSED A CUP OF TEA AND A SLICE OF LEMON MERINGUE
pie as she and Rosie perched at the window in a small café
that played background jazz on George's Street, in Dublin's
city centre. Rosie was on her third coffee of the day. Her eyes
carrying equal weighted baggage beneath them. She wore her
collar up and slunk into her chair like a fugitive.

'Darling, they don't know who we are.' Evie had enjoyed
watching the Dubliners racing past. People were always in
such a rush here, even the groups of tourists in sensible jackets
buttoned up to protect them from the rain that was spitting
in every direction, waving their phones in the air (so careless,
waiting to be robbed) were in a state of frenzy. Where were
they all going? Surely, they were already at their destinations.
Here was where they needed to be, and yet for some reason
it wasn't.

'I know, I just feel like we're doing something illegal. My stomach is cramping and that's always a sign I'm doing something I shouldn't be doing.'

'Or don't you think it means that you're drinking too much coffee?'

Rosie laughed and pushed her mug away.

'If I'm right about these two, they'll only have eyes for each other. They won't even see us here.'

'How can you be so sure?' Rosie eyed her curiously.

'Experience, I suppose. I know when it works. I feel it. Although I hadn't done that before just with the profiles on paper. That was new.' Evie took a sip of tea and gazed out the window. 'Nice to still find new and surprising things at my age, isn't it?'

'If this works, Granny, do you think that you might be able to match all the others, too?'

Her little face looked so optimistic. Evie was reminded of Rosie as a baby, her round cheeks, big trusting eyes, fat fingers reaching out for her special teddy. Evie had no hesitation, she would do anything for her. 'I'll do my best. We'll work together.' Evie felt it was ambitious and highly unlikely that she'd be able to match more than one or two couples. But Rosie was in such a state of distress that she didn't want to add to it. She had been lucky with those two young men in Molly's kitchen, they'd been reaching out for each other.

Rosie had sent them a private message explaining briefly what had happened with DeLuvGuru (very top line stuff) and how a professional matchmaker had spotted and matched their profiles. In the interests of science, Rosie and Evie had come to spy on them when they first met.

Evie took a sip of her tea and peered at Rosie. 'You know you could try it, too?'

Rosie shook her head. 'I don't know how to do that stuff.'

'Maybe give it time. Remember, you were the caul baby.' Evie had spoken quietly, aware that she had raised this issue many, many times with Rosie.

'Twenty-four years ago, Gran. A lot has happened since then, and hasn't happened if you know what I mean—there are no crystal balls in my life.' Rosie sat up high in her seat but immediately dropped low again. Her eyes clearly focused on a tall, skinny man in a navy jumper with a forest green scarf tied around his neck.

'Good, he's early.' Evie beamed, contentedly. 'Poor darling, he's nervous. He doesn't need to be. I'd love to tell him it's going to be fine. This is the day it all begins for him.' They watched as he ordered a coffee and a chocolate slice, and both noticed a slight tremor in his hands as he sat himself down, eyes fixed on the door. He began to remove his scarf and then decided against it.

'I hate spying,' Rosie reached across the table and spooned some of her granny's pie into her mouth, 'but if this works there's hope for the people who pre-registered for DeLuvGuru, and all that work and all that slimey-Simon mess I ballsed up might just end up okay.'

'It wasn't your fault.' Evie eyeballed her.

'Except it was.'

'No, I won't hear a word of it.'

'It's not just me who thinks I'm stupid, it's the internet.' She flashed her screen and Evie watched her chin quiver. 'I'm being trolled.'

'Just turn your phone off. You don't need to read what those nasty people are saying.' Even Evie knew what trolling was.

Rosie looked broken, like an army of trolls had stomped all over her in hobnailed boots. 'They're so horrible, look at this guy who calls himself Richard92, *DeLuvGuru another scam, another lie taking our money.* And then he hashtags it with *#Rosieshouldrot.*'

'Oh no.'

She tried to shrug it off. 'I mean I get it. I see why he's angry, but seriously, this is upsetting. He's just mean.'

'Block him? Can't you do that? Can't you just turn him off?'

'What's the point? There'll just be another one after him, and maybe I need to hear what people are really thinking about me. Maybe I need to hear the mean things, maybe I deserve them. I just wish I hadn't been so naïve and gullible and trusting, and happy that even an old, short man might want to be my boyfriend. I thought he was completely into me, but it was all a lie. What does that say about me, Gran?'

'Be careful, that's my granddaughter you're talking about. I won't hear a bad word against her.'

Rosie sighed. 'You know where I'm coming from.'

'I know you made a mistake of the heart. You're in your twenties, it can be a confusing time. We all make mistakes.'

'I bet you never did anything this stupid when you were my age.'

Evie paused for a moment. She had made so many mistakes at that age, so many missteps it was hard to calculate just how different her life might have been with a few different decisions. Michael hadn't been a mistake. She knew that. But what might have happened if it had been Karl. She had waited for him to propose that summer. But he never did. He wanted to establish himself first, finish college in Dublin, start working, make money. He was always so sensible. But she was in a rush to start her life. To live. And along came Michael, with his shirt sleeves rolled up and a mischievous glint in his eye. He didn't want to wait, not one minute, and he was scared he'd lose her. Michael was so certain about Evie and their life together. And so was she, but now she wonders if life had played out differently and Karl hadn't been as cautious back then would he have been her choice? She chose him now, but as what? It was so different meeting at this stage in life. There was an urgency that was also a practicality; all that nonsense, the power struggles and foot stamping of younger years' dating couldn't happen because there wasn't time. There was only time for the good stuff. Just this morning, Evie had received a bunch of flowers. A beautiful array of golden and red-hued petals with a note, *Evelyn, I can't stop thinking about you. Come back soon. Karl.*

The house had buzzed with excitement. Molly had rinsed out four vases and positioned them on the countertop for her to choose. 'He's the real deal, Gran. A true gentleman.'

Evie had buried her face in the flowers and posed for many photos for Rosie to send to Yvonne. She called Karl.

'Absence makes the heart grow fonder, and I am very fond, Evelyn.'

'You're making me blush, Karl.'

'Good, that's what I want to do.'

'I'll be back soon.'

'I'm counting the days.'

Rosie ducked even lower in her seat and nodded towards the door. They watched as a tall confident man, wearing a flat cap and a bright smile bounded into the café. He scanned the room until his eyes rested on Green Scarf who was staring into his coffee cup, rubbing his hands anxiously. In two steps he was at the table, and as Green Scarf rose to greet him Flat Cap pulled him in for a shoulder hug, causing a bump to the table and spilled coffee. With a clatter and a bang deserving of a much larger crockery disaster, the entire café turned to look at the twosome who threw their hands up in the air and exploded in mutual laughter. There was a flurry of dishcloths and dustpans, wide smiles and another two coffees ordered. They sat opposite each other grinning, and Evie and Rosie watched, no longer trying to be invisible in the corner, knowing that those two men would never see them now anyway, that they only had eyes for each other.

'Can you see it?' Evie was trying to read Rosie. She was desperate to understand if Rosie could see the light. Clear as day, there was a glow; a vibrating, warm, orange light danced between them.

'I can see true love happening right at that table over there,' Rosie said, delighted, hiding a pointed finger behind her coffee cup.

'That's . . . you don't?' Evie could never quite articulate what she saw, and also what she felt. A small sliver of their connection, their future happiness seeped into her. She knew how lucky she was to witness these miracles, to be in the shadow of the warmth of true love. She wanted to share this with Rosie. But if it wasn't there, it wasn't there. Rosie couldn't see it.

'You know what this means, Gran? It works.'

Of course, I know it works, Evie thought, I've been a match-maker my whole life. I match people, but somehow this was news to Rosie.

'We're on, we are really on. Thank you. We can make this work. All those people looking for love, you can match them, Granny, you can do it.' Rosie's eyes filled up with tears. The emotions of the past few days catching up with her, Evie supposed.

'I'll help, you know I will. But that's a lot of people. We can't even be sure that their match is in that group. You have to be prepared for that, Rosie. In truth, it's unlikely. That table over there, that might be the only match. And believe me, Rosie, that's enough. One match is a lot.'

Rosie's face creased with worry again, she looked down-trodden. 'Okay, but maybe. Maybe it's a maybe?'

Evie nodded in agreement. 'Let's settle on maybe.'

'I've started paying back the money. It'll take me a while, but I'll do it. But if I could find them love . . .' Rosie's eyes sparkled. 'If I could help them, then all of this would have been worth it.'

Evie's heart twisted at her optimism. She was sure a mess of this scale couldn't be repaired at rapid speed. It took time to find love, for many people it took a lifetime. And time was the one thing that Evie was short of.

26

Rosie

'Be a woman scorned.' Molly dug her fist into Rosie's thigh. 'Hell hath no fury, Rosie.' Another dig. This time much harder than the first.

'Leave me alone.' Rosie slapped her hand away. 'I'm serious, let me be.'

Rosie didn't know where to start or how to move forward. She wanted to match these people, but how? Granny had made one match, but what if the other matches weren't even in there yet? Was she on a wild goose chase? She was trying very hard not to beat herself up over Simon, but all the time there was the spine-chilling threat of jail looming over her, reminding Rosie of Rosie's bad choices. It was a lot. Rosie had lost count of how many days she had been wallowing like this. She found she'd get a burst of energy, a fire in her belly over something, and be wildly productive for a time before she collapsed in a heap. She'd cleaned out her bathroom cupboards, Marie Kondo-ed her wardrobe and now had slumped onto Molly's couch, and Molly was having none of it.

'You're just letting him win, Rosie. Your phone hasn't stopped buzzing. You have friends and a life out there in the real world and you're just ignoring everyone. Cop on, would you.' Molly had her hands on her hips in full mammy mode. 'You promised these people you'd find them love.'

Rosie pulled a cushion over her ears. 'That was before, when I thought the site actually worked, but now it's just a sham, it's all a farce.' She swung up dramatically from the couch, her hair flying, wielding her phone like a sword at Molly. 'And these trolls, eugh, Richard92—he's bad enough on his own but there are a lot of them—they're calling for me to rot in jail. In *jail*, Molly? It's a possibility you know? People out there who don't even know me have already judged me guilty.'

Molly paled and her voice lowered. 'Anna says it's unlikely.'

'Anna is not Fergal Byrne, Dublin's most experienced and straight-talking criminal lawyer, who says it *is* possible, especially if we get the judge on an off day. An off day?' Rosie collapsed again onto the couch cushions. 'He's allowed to have an off day. The trolls can have an off day, but I can't. It's all so unfair,' she wailed.

'I don't think the law . . . I don't think a judge . . .'

'You don't know. And I'm learning fast that not only is it very expensive to deal with the law, but often innocent people go to jail because they've been idiots. Fergal Byrne has a giant file of people just like me, who didn't know what they were getting into, and some of them have ended up in jail. As he's told me again and again, in the eyes of the law ignorance does not mean innocence.'

Her phone buzzed. She looked down. 'Yeah, thanks Richard92, you've made it very clear to me and to the internet that I'm a liar and a romance scam artist.'

'I hate that guy. Anyway, it's not true.' Molly grabbed one of the couch cushions from Rosie and hit her over the head with it. 'Romance is possible, Granny matched those two. Who knows what else she could do? Maybe these people all just need to meet and maybe you need to apologise to them in some way. Stand up for yourself, don't keep being a bloody victim, Rosie.' Rosie felt the soft force of the cushion on her face as Molly hit her again. 'Stop hiding.'

Rosie sat up on the couch and crossed her arms sulkily. 'Stop abusing me. I'm going to find some sister helpline to call. I'll just go back to my own flat.'

'And hide there. Brilliant. That's a great plan.' Molly held the cushion out, threatening to hit her again.

Rosie threw her hands up in the air. 'Seriously? What can I do? How can I possibly fix this other than by paying people back their money? I'm not technical, I can't magic that website into being, I can't match people. I can't do anything.' Rosie knew she sounded pathetic, but actually she felt a bit pathetic, and she also knew she should snap out of this. She was in a real spiral. Sometimes life was unexpectedly hard, she sighed to herself.

'Okay. Let's figure this out. We've all got problems, you know, some of us . . . Well, it doesn't matter now, but anyway, I've been thinking . . . I think you should throw a party, down in Mam's pub. She'd love to be a part of this to help you. Invite all these people and call it a matchmaking party, like they used to do in the old days, when they'd bring all the singles in town together for a dance. See if Granny can get some matches happening in the snug and just let everyone else have a good time, and you Little Miss Hiding, use the party to make your apologies.'

'How could that possibly work?' Rosie placed her palms over her eyes, defeatedly. There were so many pluses to having an older sister, advice and support, being able to nick her expensive conditioner in the shower, but the fact that she always became some preachy, moral voice who held Rosie accountable for her mistakes was not one.

'At least you'd be trying. So, what if only five people turn up, so what! At least you'd have got off your arse, you'd be making a public statement and you'd be taking charge of your future. You are not going to let him win.'

Rosie eyed Molly. 'The ex-wife looked like a body builder, have I told you that? Said she used to be really unfit and then after the mess with Simon, or John as he was to her, she seized the day and turned her life around.'

'You see. Black clouds into rainbows. Doesn't Mam have that cross-stitched on a cushion?'

'Probably.'

'You haven't posted on Instagram in days. You'll have an identity crisis soon if you're not online. And when's the last time you watched a re-run of *Dancing with the Stars*, it's just sitting there waiting for you. All that glitter, all that tan. Come on, Rosie, I know you're in there.' Molly plonked herself down beside her sister, eyes shining. 'Think about it. A matchmaking festival.'

Rosie could see her fake eyelashes from the corner of her eyes. They definitely weren't fluttering, more like heavy sails she could fly away on. She looked good, though. They made such a difference, her eyes danced. She'd insisted that herself and her granny visit a make-up artist before appearing on *Sonya's Sofa*. All manner of potions had been applied to them, filling in Granny's wrinkles and contouring and shining parts of Rosie's face she'd never have bothered with. Her cheekbones were high and she had a very angled jaw line. Rosie had done her hair herself in loose waves, and Granny was wearing her Lucille Ball blunt bob with fringe. Really quite modern, and it shaved at least ten years off her. Rosie had taken selfies of the two of them and posted them to her Instagram.

> Hot granny alert. Watch out Dublin. #sonyassofa #rightingwrongs #grannylove #matchmakingfestival

Rosie had had to beg and plead with Sonya to get another spot on her sofa. Sonya had not been pleased at all that she had promoted a sham site. She was going into politics next year and was sure being associated with a romance scam wouldn't sit well with voters.

'But I'm not the scammer,' Rosie had pleaded. 'I'm trying to rise from the ashes of victimhood by hosting a matchmaking festival. *Sonya's Sofa* is the ideal platform for me to launch it from, and your viewers will love my story. Be part of the sisterhood, Sonya.'

Rosie was surprised at how strong she sounded when she didn't feel remotely battle-ready. But yet, her old self was still there, the words were streaming out of her. She sounded like a warrior woman. There had been an excruciatingly long pause, where Rosie could practically hear the cogs turning in Sonya's brain down the line.

'Okay. But only if you bring your granny with you. I'm curious to meet her, and she's involved in the festival. Yes, bring her too.'

And so, they found themselves in a backroom of a small TV studio on the outskirts of west Dublin. Sonia had upgraded since they'd last met. They disembarked at the very last tram stop, just the two of them and an old man hugging a ham sandwich in a plastic bag were brave enough to tackle Dublin's wild west. Rosie's phone had directed them in a calm but authoritative voice to *Turn back now, turn back now.* But they traipsed on defiant in the face of technology.

Sonya hadn't held back, and Rosie surprisingly was up for her. With her granny at her elbow she felt empowered.

'He took advantage of you, he manipulated you.' Sonya practically levitated in delight at the evilness of this man who was rapidly turning into a Marvel comic villain in her eyes.

'No, no. I mean yes, but no.' Rosie was clear as mud. 'I didn't question him. I'm so embarrassed, Sonya.' And she was, she knew her cheeks had blushed red all the way through the forty-seven layers of make-up she was wearing. 'I was so charmed and delighted to have his interest and I thought I was in love and . . . I just went along with what he wanted. I allowed myself to be led by him—'

'We all make mistakes in our lives,' her granny interrupted.

'The victims here are the people who put their faith in DeLuvGuru because of what I genuinely believed to be true, because I trusted Simon. I wanted to believe in this so badly. I'm not the victim, they are.'

'You are the victim.' Sonya reached across and patted the back of her hand sympathetically.

'I'm not.'

'You are.'

'Not.' Rosie mumbled to herself and looked to her granny for support.

Evie piped up, edging herself slightly forward onto the sofa, she cleared her throat, and uttered a statement that caught all three of them by surprise. 'Our family still believe in true love, we've been matchmakers for generations, and there isn't a person I haven't met that I can't match.'

'Really?' Sonya turned her full attention to Evie. 'Not one person?'

Rosie stared at her granny. She knew a blatant lie when she heard one. How many times had she heard her granny call some people unmatchable or say something off the wall like: *They're not going to be ready in this life or their next one. That person has other lessons to learn this time around without dragging someone else into it.*

Evie shook her head slowly and continued to lie. 'Not one. Everyone has the ability to fall in love. Now, they might need to make some changes, here and here.' She touched her hand to her head and her heart, her pink coral nail polish reflecting the studio lights. 'But we all have the capacity for great love, overwhelming love. Even you, Sonya.'

Rosie had watched as Sonya shrivelled slightly. Her head shrunk back into her shoulders, hesitant like a turtle waking to sunlight after a long sleep. She'd seen people crumble in front of her granny before. It's not like she'd said anything particularly poignant or insightful to Sonya, but she'd clearly disarmed her. Her granny had that ability—she'd once shouted at a milkman who'd forgotten to leave her full cream milk, 'I see you,' and that was it. He collapsed, middle of the road in his milk van, and confessed to pocketing ten per cent of the dairy's takings. 'I see you.' That was all she'd said.

Sonya twisted a strand of her hair around her finger, and wriggled slightly in her chair, displaying a level of anxiety. She was a consummate professional, a cool, in-control TV host, and now she looked a little lost and off-balance. She regained her composure but not before a single tear had trickled down her cheek. 'Thank you, Evie.' Sonya took a deep breath and said, 'I may take you up on that offer.'

Rosie hadn't known what was going on. Was it possible her granny was playing Sonya in some way? But why? The interview had spun on its head and now her granny was in charge? Evie was going to matchmake Sonya, a former Miss Ireland and runner-up Miss World, who literally must beat men away with a stick. People were crazy, Rosie had always suspected and now truly believed it.

'So, it seems as if you're throwing a party?'

Rosie leaned across the couch and said, 'Yes, a matchmaking festival. If you pre-registered for DeLuvGuru, you'll get an email from us in a few days with an invitation to the festival in two weeks' time. This is my way of apologising. I promised all of these people I could find them love, and I really hope that we still can, but we're going back to the old-fashioned way. A good old party.'

'Details to follow, I've been told.' Sonya nodded happily.

Rosie blurted, 'It looks like we are throwing Ireland's Greatest Matchmaking Festival.'

'About time we had something like that. I'd imagine it'd be great fun with all the singles there. I might even go myself,' Sonya said.

The interview had gone pretty well. Afterwards, while Rosie was getting changed out of her dress and back into her jeans behind a flimsy screen, she noticed her granny and Sonya talking. Heads down, whispering. Then she saw Sonya handing her some money, it looked like quite a few fifties. Rosie watched as her granny deposited the cash into her handbag and quickly zipped it shut. Rosie asked her about it later, of course she did, and Evie said it was none of her business . . . but it was her business that brought them there. Rosie had to smile and think that while other grannies knit and make cakes—well, surely some of them do?—hers is pocketing fifties from a TV host. She should probably be outraged, but she was more proud of her than anything.

Rosie planned on channelling some of Evie's fearlessness into this matchmaking festival. Fergal Byrne had said a judge would look favourably on her trying to make amends. *Favourably* was one of his favourite words. Rosie felt he overused it, but he was definitely not someone you'd point that out to. It wasn't just about a judge—well, it was a bit she supposed—it was also about saying sorry for making a giant mistake, and really and truly hoping and praying that people might fall in love. And if they did, if the festival could be a success, there was a chance it might all have been worth it.

27

Molly

IT WAS SURPRISINGLY EASY TO AVOID SOMEONE IN YOUR OWN house. It had been five days now since Molly had discovered Dommo's affair, and three days since she'd kissed the sleep nanny. Oh yes, that.

There was very little time to dwell on the issue of adulthood and expectations once she discovered her husband was having an affair, because just two days later in came Charlie breaking her stream of misery. He had called by to check how the program was going and they found themselves sitting on the couch with steaming mugs of tea in their hands. She had practically fallen into him on the porch, with shrieks of *I was just thinking about you*. Affair, affair, affair. The words swirled around her brain with a furious intensity.

She had flicked a glance at Charlie, and yes, he was still handsome: dark, thick, luxurious hair, olive skin, dark eyes, a good nose, a dimple. We're talking full dreamboat package wrapped up in scrubs as he'd just finished the night shift, helping sick children. It was too much for poor Molly to bear, she was only human after all and her husband was a philanderer. Now confirmed.

'How's the little scamp Rory?' Charlie asked with what seemed like genuine interest.

Molly didn't want to talk about her children, now that she was thinking about becoming a seductress—well, maybe not a seductress but at least a flirt. A flirt didn't have to bother with the stockings and heels, a flirt could just flick their hair, laugh, occasionally rub a knee and wear lipstick. She started to giggle, to kick the game off and test the waters; she threw her head back and heard a hard cackle release from her.

'Oh, sorry, I was just thinking of something funny I heard the other day.' She leaned across the couch and patted his knee. Maybe she'd be good at this flirting lark.

'Well, share the joke please.' Charlie grinned at her. Oh, those teeth were magnificent, and was she imagining it, had he inched slightly closer to her on the sofa? And what was all this calling in to check on the program? It was malarkey, that's what it was. He had been paid for his three visits and now what was this, number five? No. Something else was up.

'It was one of those you-had-to-be-there things. Do you make regular stop-offs to check on all your clients?' Was that flirty? She wasn't sure, so threw in a huge, expectant smile at the end.

'Only my favourites.' Flirt. Definite flirt sign. 'And I knew your husband wasn't around and you may be having a bit of a struggle.'

Molly felt a lump in her throat that just might have been pure rage. She leaned forward to the coffee table and offered Charlie the biscuits. 'Chocolate covered wafer?'

'Well, rude not to. I hope you didn't bring out the posh biscuits on my account?'

Oh Jesus, he was flirting with her. It was on. She wasn't imagining it. He went for a biscuit and did a totally unnecessary brush of his hand against hers. Totally unnecessary. Definite flirting. With physical contact. She stared at her hand, the plate of chocolate biscuits, Charlie—all laughter vacuumed up out of the room. He placed his mug on the table, beside his biscuit. Dommo is having an affair she reminded herself. He is knee-deep in some other woman's business and whatnots. Charlie swung his arm to the back of the couch. A definite invitation to close the gap she thought. Will she do it? Should she? Dommo stayed in a hotel with another woman. He broke this, not her.

Here he comes, those dark eyes are at half mast, she's not imagining it. He's waiting for her to smooch in. A quick flash of a school yard appeared in her mind's eye.

Here goes nothing. She flew in. Definite lip touching, some mouth opening and then the sudden smell of him, the taste of him felt so foreign to her. She felt a hand on her shoulder, pushing her away. Charlie rose to his feet.

'Oh no, oh no.' He was shaking his head, his mouth open in what could only be described as shock.

Molly felt her stomach hurl and instinctively put her hand to her mouth and looked away. 'I thought, oh God, I thought . . .'

'No!' He literally jumped back a few feet, his hands ran through his hair and he scanned the room, possibly looking for back-up. Maybe he was going to grab the poker from the fireplace to fight off her unwanted advances.

'Oh no, I'm so embarrassed, I thought . . .' That sinking crushing feeling, that need to hide. 'All that stuff you said about my hair and you said I'm a great mum . . .'

'You are. I don't know what I said about your hair. You obviously misinterpreted me.' His arms were crossed against his chest protectively.

'But you're here. You keep calling in.' She heard the pleading in her voice.

'You pay for me to be here.'

'No, there was only three sessions paid for.' She shook her head furiously, weirdly delighted to have tripped him up somehow.

He spoke slowly. 'No. I am paid to be here.'

'But it was only supposed to be three.'

He pulled out his phone and prodded the screen. 'Look,' he turned it to her like a shield defending his honour. 'I am paid to be here.'

Molly squinted at the screen and saw the words *rolling contract*. Her mam. She must have paid for the full service, the deluxe package. That was so typical of her to go the full hog. But she never told Molly. All this time he's been knocking on the door and she thought . . . she thought . . . oh, the absolute shame of it.

'I'm so sorry.' She desperately wanted the ground to open up and swallow her, so she could just lie there under the earth until everyone, the world and his wife, disappeared.

Cautiously, he took a step towards her and crouched down to her eye level, still maintaining a distance in case she couldn't control herself and hopped him. 'Molly, I don't know what's going on with you and your marriage, but this isn't the solution.'

'Don't talk to me about my marriage.' She sniffed and suddenly felt all high and mighty, her crippling embarrass-ment being replaced by bolshie bravado. 'I think you should leave.' She said rudely, as if she had been the one to be kissed and not the kisser.

'That's a good idea.' Charlie started for the door, then turned back and said, 'I'm sorry about everything.'

'Just go.' Molly pointed dramatically at the door.

'I don't think I'll be back. The agency can send someone else.'

'Well, maybe they'll kiss me.' What was wrong with her? Why would she say that? Was she making a joke? Now? How inappropriate could she be?

He opened the door to leave, then turned and said, 'I'll recommend they send a female. Good luck with all of it, Molly.'

Why did he have to be so bloody nice? If she was a man he would have hit her, and she would have deserved it.

She got a text a few hours later.

> Maybe you should think about getting some
> professional help.

Molly had thrown her phone to the bottom of her bag and hadn't looked at it for days. The shame still surrounded her like a deep fog. The scene was on constant playback in her mind: *What had she been thinking? Why would she do that?* Meanwhile, she tried to outrun the embarrassment and her husband. She was lurking and shirking around her own house. Hiding out in the bathroom, taking extra-long showers and deeply conditioning her very short hair. She had started weeding the back garden, pulling at green shrubs that may have been flowers, she was never sure. She was to be found furiously cleaning out the playroom with her head buried in Lego baskets, far too busy to peep up and say hello to her husband. He was equally meek. Moving through shadows, microwaving God only knows what, opening and closing the fridge door, going to bed at 8.30 p.m. straight after he'd put the boys down. His eyebrows seemed to have shifted a few inches lower, his mouth drooped in a permanent sigh, his shoulders stooped. He stood in door frames, with a tightness to his chest, breathing heavily, and tried to talk to her.

'Can't hear you, I've got to get this oven cleaned,' she said, attacking it with a toothbrush and a lemon, because the internet told her that it would take twice the amount of time to do it this old-fashioned way.

'Are you mad at me?'

'I'm mad at this oven.' Molly gritted her teeth and scrubbed the bristles away.

And so, they'd managed to avoid each other in their two up semi-detached house in the suburbs. They looked at the TV, their phones, slid into different rooms and went to bed at different times, and drifted away from each other exactly how many married couples before them had and will continue to do for years to come.

But now the weekend loomed large, and Molly had a crippling anxiety that had started in her stomach and stretched to her shoulders. She found herself kissing her boys far too much, not releasing them from hugs until they'd actually pushed her away. She was clingy mummy, needy mummy, unhappy mummy. She knew she should talk to Dommo. But say what? She loved him. She didn't want her marriage to end. She didn't want to finger click, toss her hair and walk out the door, in the defiant stance of all betrayed women. She wanted him to tell her it was a mistake and that he wanted to go back to the way things were, or maybe not how they were but better. Was that even possible?

But now to more pressing issues, how to avoid your husband for two long days and two nights? It was Rosie who came up with a solution—well, not a solution, she wasn't to know just how badly Molly had been dreading the weekend—with a suggestion to visit Mam in Ballyhay.

'I just got off the phone with her, and you know, she sounded funny. I shouldn't have said that, Molly, I know you have more than enough going on. Sorry.'

'Funny? What do you mean funny?' Molly dropped the paint-brush she had been cleaning in methylated spirits, the stench coming off it was eye-watering.

'Really distant. Like I told her all about DeLuvGuru updates and the matchmaking with Gran, and she was just like, *Oh okay, right so.*'

'She didn't try and fix you?'

'No. That's my point.'

'That does sound strange.'

'So, I said you'd come visit. I threw the boys in, too. You can give Gran a lift back. I also wondered if Gran's matchmaking might go better on her home turf. I can't go, I've got to meet Fergal Byrne, he wants to discuss barristers for a court date. Court? It makes me feel sick.'

'Rosie . . .'

Ignoring her sister, she continued, 'I think Gran's having withdrawal symptoms, she's been in Dublin so long.'

'Well, for a woman who says she hates the city, she's been doing pretty well. She took the bus to the harbour at Dun Laoghaire today and walked the pier, sent me a selfie of her having an ice-cream by the waterfront.'

'Yeah, she's really struggling.'

'Anyway, I'm game. I'll pack the car up tonight and leave first thing.' The relief was huge.

'How's Dommo?' Rosie's voice sounded wary.

'Dunno, haven't spoken to him. Exactly why this is a perfect time to get away and sort my head out. Or Mam's head. I don't know. Maybe all of our heads.' She laughed, and heard the hint of crazy edging in.

This was Molly's plan. To pile the boys into the car, and stuff them with crisps and ice-creams on the way, bring her gran home and go see Mam. It was glorious. Away. She would get away. Run from Dommo and his affair in the Red Cow Inn, take her boys to hug and kiss, talk and talk, and best of all, eat her mother's cooking. Perfect. It was perhaps the most perfect plan her sister had ever come up with.

But then, on Saturday morning, Dommo wanted to talk.

'Evie's going to watch the boys. You and I are going for a walk.' His voice was stern.

'No.' Molly was caught off guard, she was downloading cartoons onto the iPad for the journey. 'I've too much to do. We have to beat the traffic.'

'There's no traffic on a Saturday morning. Come on. We're walking. The drive can wait a few minutes.' He didn't look angry, he looked determined, his jaw was set, and his gaze focused.

I won't be able to handle it if he decides to tell me about the affair now, if he tells me he's in love with Tansey, I won't handle it. Molly was spinning.

'Here.' He handed her a pink hoody with a sheepskin lining. Molly looked at it as a thing of mystery. It really wasn't very nice, but definitely felt cosy as she slipped it on. She wrapped her arms around herself and dutifully did what she was told and walked to the hall door. She turned her head back towards the kitchen and to the noise of the boys playing with their cars there.

'You're sure they're . . . ?'

'They're fine. Come on. We won't be long.'

It won't take long for you to end this marriage is that what you're saying? To break my heart, to leave this family. It won't take long.

The door clicked behind them and they set off down the street, walking as far apart as the narrow pavement would allow, dodging parked cars and lampposts. Dommo's strides were strong and purposeful, his arms swinging; she shuffled along, feeling as if every footstep were bringing her closer to the ending.

He broke the silence. 'I think it's good you're going to Ballyhay.'

'You're happy to see the back of me?' She spat the words at him. 'Be nice for you to have some free time.' She could be vicious; she was surprised at just how angry her voice sounded.

'Please, Molly, don't . . . I think it's good for you to get away, to have a change of scenery. I think you need a break.

I don't know what's been going on with you, I don't know why you're so sad and mad.'

'Oh well . . .' Molly couldn't find the words she wanted.

Dommo had quickened the pace and taken a left down another housing estate; he was marching fast now, the house fronts were blurring. 'I want you to know that everything I'm doing, I'm doing for us. I think sometimes you don't have any idea of what kind of stress and pressure I'm under. My job is—' he threw a look back at her, his face was pained '—it's terrible, Molly. I feel like I'll explode, and then I come home and it's terrible at home, too. You're so angry with me.'

'Your job. This is about your job?' Molly thought she might laugh.

'Of course you want me home more, I understand, to help out, but if I don't put in the time there . . . you know they promoted two people in my department this month and neither of them was me. When I leave early to do the baths or what-ever they're all still there, the office is full, and I look like I'm skiving.'

'You can leave to go to the pub, can't you?' she whispered under her breath, but he caught it.

'Twice. I've been to the pub twice, and honestly, it's poor form, they're there regularly on a Friday. It's part of the office buzz going for a few drinks to wind down after a stressful week. I don't go. I'm not one of the gang.'

'So, what's this all about, you want to go to the pub? I don't understand, Dommo.'

'No, I don't want to go to the pub. I want to come home to a happy house. I want to be bloody promoted and make more money so we can pay off my mother and get on top of this mortgage and I want my wife back.' He stopped dramatically on the street, looked into her eyes and said, 'Molly, I want my life back.'

'Your life? This is your life. This is the life you chose. You chose me, remember?'

He started walking again, shaking his head. 'I just wish you'd understand the pressure I'm under. You just don't understand.'

'No, no, no.' The rage inside her was slowly unfurling, she stomped her feet like Andy having a tantrum. 'Stop this now. Stop it.' She had stopped walking, her body felt rigid.

He spun back to look at his furious wife, her face red, her hands clenched into fists beating at her thighs.

'You better start telling the truth, Dommo. I already know. I fucking know. I know all of it. I know about you and the Red Cow Inn.'

'You do?' Dommo lurched towards her. 'How? Oh, I felt so guilty about that?'

'Guilty, you felt guilty. Oh, you poor thing. Poor Dommo.' She felt wild, the wind whipped around her, and some raindrops fell silently to the pavement. 'You don't even deny it. You don't even try and deny it. You fuck.' She screamed at him, jabbing her finger in the air, the rage engulfed her. She stepped towards him and felt her two hands find his shoulders, blinded by anger she pushed, hard, fast and mad. She shoved him and he tripped and fell to the ground. She turned on her heel, shouting into the wind, 'I'm gone! I'm taking the boys and I'm going to my Mam's. You and Tansey can have the house to yourselves.' Molly ran. And the rain picked up and started to fall, and by the time she got to her house, it was pouring in sheets, hiding her tears that were flooding down her cheeks. She flung the front door open and cried, 'Come on, let's go, let's go! Come on everyone!'

And they appeared one by one, and she loaded them into the car. Belts buckled, engine revving and she sped off out of suburbia and away from Dommo.

28

Yvonne

Yvonne had spent another night whirling under her bed sheets. Fretting and worrying was exhausting and that was the reason she finally picked up her phone and called Lukas. And how well he knew her, and how smart he was. She didn't have to utter a word; he spoke for her. And a few hours later she was knocking on his front door, in one of the newer estates in Ballyhay built on a windy hill with a view of the river from the chimney tops. She clutched her top-of-the-range laptop, and a folder stuffed with envelopes some opened and many unopened. She was swept into his pristine home and offered tea and biscuits by Esmerelda, and once again Yvonne marvelled at her lovely shapely bottom, well worth whatever money it had cost her. Lukas burst into the kitchen beaming, clearly feeling like he was in the role of accountant saviour. Well, Yvonne would have to knock that out of him quick sharp. She waited for Esmerelda to leave the room.

'Look Lukas, we just need to do a little bit of light accountancy, move a little from column A to B, focus on the pub.' Yvonne flipped open her laptop and switched it on, matter-of-factly.

Lukas did not respond.

'I'll just pull up the Excel sheets and we can put in some numbers, you'd like that?' she joked. 'And maybe some forecasts for next year, things might take off.'

Lukas stood up, his chair squeaked across the kitchen floor. 'No, I'm not doing this. Yvonne you need to leave.'

'Sorry, what?' She peeped over her screen and spied his pale face.

'I'm not moving some numbers around on the pub and pretending that there isn't a bigger problem here.'

She gritted her jaw. 'Maybe this wasn't such a good idea.' Maybe this was a terrible idea, maybe she should just forget about all of this and go back to her own idea: *Sell everything, run away.* No! That wasn't going to work either. She couldn't run. Run, to where?

'It was a good idea, of course it was, for the important stuff. Come on, Yvonne, get real.'

She exhaled and looked around the neat-as-a-pin kitchen, refusing to meet Lukas's gaze. She was mortified. How could she get real? How could she show this Polish man what she had done, and hadn't done, when she couldn't even get real with herself? She pushed away from the table and stood up. 'I want to go.'

'Fine. Go.' Lukas eyeballed her.

Small in stature but with fierce staring abilities, Yvonne felt irked. She closed down her laptop and clasped it to her chest.

'Please, Yvonne,' Lukas pleaded with her, a more conciliatory voice. 'Please. I can help you. Let's do this together.'

'But then you'll see . . .' She felt a hot burning sensation at the back of her throat. 'You'll see what I've done, and what I am, and . . .' She sat back down. 'I'm so embarrassed, Lukas.'

'I know what you are, Yvonne. A good, kind woman, who runs that pub with warmth and grace, and makes it the happiest place in the world to visit and work in. I know who you are, Yvonne.'

She stared at him open-mouthed. Quite shocked at his proclamation. She raised her hand to her hair and smoothed it down. 'Thank you, Lukas. I'm really quite taken aback. But no, I mean the other stuff.'

'You think I haven't seen the online shopping packages that arrive every day? I also answer the phone to the suppliers who haven't been paid, you know? I do the invoicing for you. And I've seen the bill from the revenue. I know about the other stuff.'

Yvonne had a sudden realisation that perhaps her secret hadn't been a secret all along. 'I hadn't thought about it like that. I didn't realise you would have seen that.'

'You can't be embarrassed, Yvonne. We all make mistakes, but it would be an even bigger mistake to leave here and not deal with it. We'll find an answer.'

He sounded so strong and determined, and she knew he was kind. She knew he meant what he said. *Oh, for crying out loud,* she told herself, *you couldn't be in a bigger mess. It's time to trust someone to help you.* 'Just promise me you won't call me a silly old bat?' She was only half joking.

'I promise. Let's get the tea on and take a look at what we've got.'

'You should know, Lukas,' she paused searching for the words, 'and I'd appreciate it if you would keep it to yourself, Warren Estates have made some preliminary inquiries. It seems that there is an American couple who've always wanted to own an Irish pub and they think McCarthy's looks perfect.' The words caught in her throat. Was it really possible that this is what she was considering? That it had come to this. The work of three generations falling away in three years because of her? The property agent at Warren Estates said the pub would sell well, she may even make a small profit. They'd taken photos and crouched and bent into odd angles to capture the rooms *just so*. It took every fibre in her being to stop herself from shouting, *NO! I've changed my mind*. She couldn't. 'I don't want to sell, you know that. But I'm worried that I won't be able to come back from all this debt.' It was her turn to cry now. She blinked back the tears stinging her eyes. She knew she might be panicking, that there might be another way out, but right now she couldn't handle more sleepless nights. She was in a constant state of anxiety, sometimes she couldn't catch her breath and the thoughts in her head were dark. She knew she had to watch herself from falling deep into the blackness. The voices were there pounding away at her, telling her how useless she was.

Lukas looked at her sternly. 'Let's get all the information together and see how much trouble we're really in.'

Yvonne sniffed. 'Thank you. Thank you for everything, and thanks for saying *we*. I know it's really *me*, but I appreciate the gesture.'

❖

Yvonne had lunch ready. She'd had it ready yesterday, it was just a matter of reheating it when the girls arrived. She made a lasagne with homemade fresh pasta sheets, which she'd rolled out the night before, garlic bread and a green salad with a vinaigrette that had just a little kick to it. She'd made a few sausage rolls for the boys, too; it was easy to whip them up and she knew they'd devour them drenched in ketchup. She couldn't be as confident with the lasagne. The house was spotless, and she smiled to herself knowing it wouldn't stay that way for long once the boys arrived. They always had an entourage of toys of all sizes and shapes. She had fresh roses from the garden in a vase on the table, but in spite of looking magnificent, the roses were severely lacking on the scent front. All talk, no trousers. However, there was a light scent of vanilla in the air from a burning candle. Yvonne looked fondly at her neat and ordered kitchen, her pristine white floors, her throw cushions and fluffy rugs. The first home that had been truly hers, just how she wanted it.

She smoothed out the curtains and ran her hand along the mantelpiece with a heavy sigh. She had felt a moment of hope that night with Maria when they spoke about her opening a restaurant in the pub. There was a spark, a split second where all roads lead to success and were paved with parmesan shavings, seared prawns and truffle oil. The reviews—all positive, of course—would be framed in the bathrooms, and you'd have to book weeks in advance to get a table. They'd drive out from Dublin for a night in Ballyhay. She wouldn't just be a publican; she'd be a restaurateur. Her imagination soared, and then popped and dutifully deflated as the prickly voices got louder. How could she start something else when she was failing so badly already? If she couldn't keep a pub alive, what hope would she have in getting a new restaurant off the ground. She wasn't a defeatist she was a realist.

The thing was, she did have ideas. She had always hoped that when her freezer full of food and the pre-paid long-standing orders finally ran out she'd start cooking her own meals, but by that point, in her head, the pub would have been doing well. So, for three years, in the depths of her subconscious she had been plotting, concocting menus, sniffing out fresh vegetables at the farmers' market and leafing through cookery books on a mission. When she'd try a new recipe, she'd catch herself wondering how that might work in the pub. But it was one thing to think about it, it was entirely different to do it. How much food would she buy? How would she cost it up? What would she do with all the leftovers? And what would she do when that failed and she lost even more money? Then she'd definitely have to sell the pub.

Anyway, she was too old. People didn't start businesses in their fifties. They retired and went to live in Spain to eat chorizo.

She heard a car pulling into the drive and felt her heart leap. She threw the door open and laughed at the packed Ford creaking under the weight of its heavy load. Cooing her hellos she gave a double-handed wave and started peering into the windows. The boys were red-cheeked and fast asleep, her mother looked comfortable up the front and Molly looked exhausted behind the wheel. There was a flurry of *Shush, don't wake the boys*, who inevitably woke within thirty seconds of the car stopping. Bags were unloaded, kisses exchanged, the kettle flicked on and off, coats strewn, shoes thrown and within minutes, Yvonne's house had been invaded.

Later, the house quietened when the boys had finished their lunch and were playing on the floor together, the lasagne dish had been scraped clean and the adults were picking the remains of the rocket salad from their plates. Molly filled Yvonne in on what looked to her to be Rosie's half-cocked plan for matchmaking all of Dublin involving her granny, who was bizarrely complying with a serene smile on her face that was vaguely familiar to Yvonne. It was also obvious that Molly was very troubled about something. She had feigned yawning and rubbed her eyes repeatedly.

'I'm just tired, Mam.'

'But you're as pale. Here, eat. There are some sausage rolls left.' Yvonne placed two on her plate and watched as Molly pushed it away. 'I thought you were sleeping, did the sleep nanny not work?'

She saw her swallow hard. 'No, it's fine. He did. The boys sleep, it's incredible, but I'm just tired.'

Unless Yvonne was going completely mad she could have sworn she saw glances fly across the table. What was going on?

'Is it okay, Mam, if I go for a shower and a lie down? I think the drive took it out of me.' Molly stood up from the table, her shoulders stooped, her head hanging low. She stepped over the boys and heaved herself up the stairs.

Yvonne turned to her mother, and whispering as quietly as she could, asked, 'What is going on? Nobody looks that depressed after a two-hour drive. The traffic wasn't that bad.'

And so, Evie filled her in. She recounted everything she knew, which Molly had released fully during their long tear-soaked journey when the boys had fallen asleep in the back.

Yvonne immediately felt guilty. Was that the natural state for a mother to feel when their child was upset? Guilty that she hadn't been there for her or asked her how she was. Guilty that she'd been so caught up in her own life that she wasn't able to reach out to her eldest daughter.

'She's a married woman, dear.' Her own mother, seeing her upset, reached across the table and stroked her hand. 'Molly needs to figure this one out herself.'

'I'm just so sorry for her. How could he do that?'

'We don't know what he did or didn't do. We know Molly's side of the story.' Evie tapped at the table with her fingertips, Yvonne could sense she was unsure of something. 'How's everything been here? How's the pub?'

Yvonne plastered on a smile and quickly poured her mother another cup of tea from the pot. 'All's well, Mam.' Another daughter lying to her mother, she thought. Papering over cracks on a crumbling wall.

29

Evie

Evie was sick of it. She was sick of looking over her shoulder like a mad woman. Waiting, waiting, waiting for some horrible disease to catch her, for a car to run her over or a piano to drop on her head. Waiting to die was no way to live. The truth was she felt better than fine. Her stay in Dublin had left her full of energy. Yes, she occasionally took an afternoon nap, but that had been a habit of a lifetime from working late nights in the pub. She always took an afternoon nap, so she could have her dancing legs on for the evening shenanigans. She was mystified as to where her death was going to come from. Those damn cards had her second guessing herself. The truth of the matter was that she was in great health and felt as good as she had forty years ago. Besides, she'd started to put some appointments into her calendar, events for next year that she wanted to go to. There was a New Year's Eve ball that she had the perfect outfit for: green sparkles and a fur stole. She thought she might rent a caravan on the seaside in Courtown during the summer for a week to let the boys run around. They could all go to the amusements and sit on the harbour wall and eat ice-creams, watching the boats sail by. She had so much to live for, so much to look forward to, it seemed outrageous that she would just bow out now. That she would gracefully dip to her knee and give in to the blackness.

And then there was Karl. What a surprise his reacquaintance had been. The cards had never painted him walking back into her life, had they? See, they didn't know everything. And yet there he was. A new friend, and yet the oldest of friends. Two days after her return, they had taken a stroll along the river and had lunch at the hotel. He wore a smart, grey-wool coat with shiny buttons, his hair slicked back and a bright red scarf tied around his neck. She had taken his arm and it felt nice and comfortable, walking casually on a sunny afternoon, admiring the rippling water and shimmering leaves blowing in the trees. He was excitable. He squeezed her arm and stopped occasionally to gesticulate.

'Well, I don't mind saying it, in fact I will—I missed you, Evelyn McCarthy.' His declaration made her smile, but she didn't stop him, oh no, she let him go on. 'Now I know you might have been hitting the nightclubs up there in Dublin and turning down men left right and centre, but I'll tell you right now I'm delighted you're back here with me.' He grinned happily. 'Isn't life something else that we find ourselves here?'

'Well, to be fair, Karl, I've always been here.' Evie wasn't sure where he was going, but she would play hard to get. It was always wise to hold your cards close to your chest.

'Yes, that's true, but leading a different life, I suppose, is what I mean. And so have I. But now look at us. You make me happy, Evie.'

And she laughed like nineteen-year-old Evie would have done.

His smile broadened. 'There's my girl. But Evie, I feel good, and I know you do, too. The housing project is up and going. It's running itself at this stage, I'm not needed there anymore. I want to live life. I want to wrap my arms around it and squeeze the living daylights out of what's left.'

They paused as a woman pushing a buggy flew past them, jogging in bright lycra with ferocious intensity. The tinny sound from her headphones lingering in the air behind her.

'You're so full of life, Karl.' Evie smiled at him with genuine affection.

'Why wouldn't I be? I'm one of the lucky ones. There's so much I want to do. I've always worked and I feel I've missed a lot of experiences. I want to see the northern lights, I want to dance with the Little Mermaid in Copenhagen, go on safari in Africa, eat sushi in Japan.'

Evie was dizzy just listening to him. But it was infectious. His happiness, the skip in his step and the glint in his eye.

'It sounds marvellous, Karl, it really does. But let's just enjoy our walk for now.'

His face fell, his shoulders dropped a few inches in disappointment. 'I've gone too fast, haven't I? I'm sorry, I just, I don't want to wait around. There's a clock ticking.' He left a lot unsaid in that sentence. Evie felt it hang between them.

'Let's just walk and chat for today.' Evie smiled encouragingly.

'Well, how about tomorrow? Can we walk again tomorrow? And the next day?'

'I don't see why not.'

'You can see where I'm going with this, Evie, can't you?'

'You're fond of walking?' She looked at him mischievously as he grinned into his chest.

'There's more Evie . . .' he crinkled his brow and looked unsure of himself. 'I . . . well, before, I didn't know I'd meet you again, but a few months back I booked a six-month cruise, it leaves from Dublin and takes in the Mediterranean, northern Europe, the Middle East, places I've only dreamed of. It leaves at the end of October.'

'Oh.' Evie's feet came to a full stop. He'd be leaving. He'd be gone. Oh no. 'Karl, I would miss you terribly.'

He faced into her, his eyes looking straight into hers. 'The thing is I took the liberty . . . that is . . . what I mean to say is . . . I've provisionally booked another ticket for you to join me.'

Evie took a step back in shock.

'Now I know this is too fast, I know it is. But would you at least consider it?' He reached forward to hold her hands in his.

Yes, yes, yes. 'No. I couldn't possibly, the girls, the pub, my matchmaking . . .' She shook her head, ignoring her inner voice that was shouting loudly.

He let go of her hands and retreated. 'I'm sorry, I've rushed you.'

'I can't just up and run, I can't.' *You could. You could go.*

'Of course, of course, I understand.' Karl looked crestfallen. 'You have a busy life here, I know that. I couldn't possibly ask you to abandon everything.'

Why not? You've nothing to lose. 'No . . . no. Six months is such a long time, and I . . . no.'

'I'll tell you what, I'll park the Little Mermaid.' He smiled back defeatedly. 'Just for now, though, just so you know. The cruise isn't until October, six weeks away, so there's still time for you to think about it. I wouldn't want you to feel pressurised by me being so impetuous.'

'Well, it is very unexpected.' They resumed their walk, Evie's head spinning slightly.

'I suppose it is.'

She couldn't bear to see him looking so downtrodden, so she retreated and said, 'I could give it some thought, what about that?'

'Fantastic Evelyn.' A jolly hop returned to his step. 'And until then, we'll walk every day.' Karl's smile stretched across his face.

And she nodded. She understood that, somehow, this was life, and she'd seen enough of it to know that this life may be giving her a second chance at something she could never have dreamed of, just before she was supposed to leave it. It was bittersweet.

She had been feeling Michael's absence like a presence recently. He was eighteen years gone, and now and again she still found her hand reaching for his. Just that morning she had sat at her kitchen table with a cup of tea in front of her and had felt him in the room. She'd closed her eyes and let the feeling of him pass into her. Evie wouldn't dare open them for fear the spell would break. It was like all the days of their love pouring into her, and it was calm and warm and lovely. It was the absoluteness of him. She had been loved by a great man. It gave her an abundance of happiness, all those memories saved safely in her mind. She'd love to rest her head on his shoulder, to breathe him in, to be a part of the two of them again. She sighed. She'd see him soon, she was sure of that. She had a feeling about it. He was nearby. Watching them all. 'Look after our girls, Michael,' she'd whispered in a prayer. And she knew that he was, and what will be will be.

30

Rosie

ROSIE COULDN'T BE SURE HER MAM FULLY UNDERSTOOD WHAT she was agreeing to. Rosie didn't even properly understand it. The phone line had gone quiet, she decided to switch to FaceTime to get her attention and pushed the video button.

'There you are, you look well—all those spin classes are paying off.' She smiled at her screen. 'It'll be in the pub, Mam, the festival.'

'So you said. We can open up the doors to the beer garden, and I'll give the smoking section an airing.'

'It's not like my twenty-first birthday party, Mam. It's going to be bigger than that.'

'Right.' She saw her Mam glance around at her nephews playing behind her.

'Or not, you know there's a definite possibility that the people who are saying they'll come and are tweeting about it, won't.'

'That's fine, we can hold three hundred in the pub and probably another hundred in the beer garden, so you'll be all set.'

She wasn't getting it. Hosting Ireland's greatest Matchmaking Festival at McCarthy's was a good idea; a drive from Dublin, a licensed premise, delicious food, an outdoor area and a built-in matchmaker. It was also available in two-weeks' time, which ninety-nine per cent of venues in the country were not, or more likely were not willing to hold a last-minute festival. And so, McCarthy's it was.

'The field behind the pub, Mam, who owns that? And would they give it to us for the day?'

'Mickey Kelly. He probably would. He owes your gran a favour—she matched him and his wife years ago. No woman in three counties would touch him. He'll have to move his bull.'

'Will you ask him? We can set up a campground and a stage there, maybe some entertainment tents?'

'I'll ask. His brother might be able to help with the stage, he's a carpenter.'

'Lock him in, Mam.'

'I know you don't want to talk about it, but any updates from Fergal Byrne?'

'No, Mam, nothing new.'

'You'll tell me, won't you?'

'Of course.' Rosie lied. She'd been deliberately light on information with her mam, never once mentioning jail. She'd deal with that when and if she had to. She just knew her mam would be beside herself and what was the point in bringing even more worry into her life over something she could do nothing about.

The good news was that ninety per cent of DeLuvGuru early registrants had responded positively to the festival news, especially as they had all been issued with VIP passes. Rosie wasn't quite sure what that was going to mean, but at the very least free entry and a sausage roll. This was going to be about finding love, real kick-your-shoes-off-at-the-door-get-into-your-PJs-and-order-takeaway-together love, she hoped.

Her next call to Mark, her desk mate at CRUSH, didn't go quite so well. 'It's not bloody state secrets, Mark. It's an Excel sheet for a gaming party four years from now.' Rosie wanted to throw her phone across her flat and smash it into smithereens. Mark was not playing ball, no amount of pleading or cajoling was working. 'I could really use your help here, would you please just email it to me.'

There was a long pause. Long enough for Rosie to stew in her frustration.

'Rosie, emails get hacked. You know it and I know it.' He sounded clipped and short, and equally annoyed with Rosie.

'Mark, no Russian cybergeeks want access to your party-planner documents.' Rosie realised that she should be trying to smooth-talk Mark and not shouting abuse at him, but it was surprisingly hard. She really did want his Excel sheet and knew how truly magnificent his party planning document was—it would wipe out six months of work for her. The matchmaking festival would be a much smaller event than the gaming Olympics he was planning in four years' time. It would be so easy for her to transfer the information, if only he would hand it over.

'It's a lot more than a party planner, you know that, and for your information, it's not just the Russians.'

'Chinese? Do the Chinese need to know who the best portaloo stockists in Louth are? Do they?' Rosie needed to hold her tongue. She was being way too lippy. She exhaled, desperately trying to control herself. 'What can I do, Mark? How can I persuade you to just press send?'

'Can I come?' He suddenly sounded small, positively meek.

She was caught off guard. 'Come where?'

'To the party, the matchmaking thing.'

Sometimes Rosie was such an idiot. Mark was single, like most of the employees at CRUSH, which in theory should have been a hotbed of hot-bed activity literally, but it wasn't. Everyone seemed to be practising abstinence there, willingly or unwillingly she wasn't sure. But Mark was single and looking to mingle.

She practically jumped down the line at him. 'Of course. Great idea. Oh, I never even asked how your DeLuvGuru date went, it was obviously bad. So sorry, Mark. I'll get Granny to meet with you. That's great, fantastic.' She was bubbling with enthusiasm now. 'The only thing is that I'll need the spreadsheet before the matchmaking thing, you know? In order to organise it all. It's just a bit of an idea now, I need to put the wheels in motion and kickstart the engine.'

'I really don't want to email it.'

Teeth gritted, Rosie didn't know how to manoeuvre this one.

'Let me have a think about it,' continued the keeper of the nuclear codes.

Rosie had just eaten her third meal of cheese and toast that day, lying on her bed, laptop on her knees, TV blaring some music video in the background. She'd order Uber Eats later, her fridge was a sea of almost-finished rice containers mocking her inability to whip them into a stir-fry. She also needed to tackle the laundry which was dangerously close to toppling over, suffocating her and blocking her one and only exit. Rosie did not want to end up as a headline in *The Mail*: WOMAN KILLED BY DIRTY WASHING. WHO COULD LIVE LIKE THAT? She was equal measures overwhelmed and excited by the festival. She had a bubbling feeling that she might pull it all together, and success would be such an almighty, two-fingered salute to Simon and everything he'd put her through. She couldn't quantify just how glorious it might feel.

Her phone buzzed and she braced herself for a devil-shaped emoji from Mark. But no, it was a text from Garda Aidan Lalor.

Are you at home? Are you free for an hour?

Her heart sank. This was going to be about Simon—something else, some other company that he'd forged her signature on, some old lady he'd stolen from. All of it a reminder of how stupid she'd been. Thumbs up had hardly left her screen before the doorbell buzzed, sending a jolt through her.

'You're here?' She pressed the speaker button.

'Yeah, I was passing when I sent the text, are you right?'

Rosie looked down at her tracksuit pants, oversized grey hoodie and Ugg boots. She quickly ran her fingers under her eyes to catch any stray mascara and redid her hair in a loose ponytail. Well, if he was going to throw her into jail at least she'd be comfortable. She stuffed her keys and her phone into her pocket and opened the door. There, in a neon yellow vest with an equally bright smile, a cap freshly tucked under his arm, his red hair recently smoothed down and looking somehow mischievous was Garda Aidan Lalor.

'Am I in trouble?' Rosie found herself mirroring his grin.

'The opposite—well, not the opposite, that doesn't make sense—but I'm about to finish my shift,' he stepped to one side so the Garda car was in clear view, 'and I wondered if you . . . ? Well, I thought maybe you could do with a bit of cheering up, after all that nasty business with that fella . . .' He blushed now, so deep that his freckles disappeared.

For once, Rosie didn't know what to say.

'So, if you wanted to hang out for a bit, there's . . . something that the lads in the station do . . . well, we all do it for a bit of a laugh or if someone's had a hard time. It's just a bit of fun.' He was shifting uneasily from side to side.

Rosie wondered if he was reconsidering his call-in. 'Okay,' she responded slowly. 'I'm caught off guard, Guard. Get it?' And much to her own embarrassment she leaned across the threshold and shoulder-punched him, regretting it immediately. 'Sorry, I didn't mean to do that or make that bad joke.'

His grin turned into a wide smile. 'I've heard it before, you messer. Come on, would ya?' He turned and started to walk towards the car, opening the passenger door, he said, 'Your chariot, me lady.'

She clapped her hands together and whooped. 'I've always wanted to have a go in one of these. Will you play the sirens?'

'If you're good. There's a spare cap in the back, too, if you want to look the part.'

Rosie decided Aidan Lalor didn't just look mischievous, he was, and she felt distinctly giddy. She threw herself onto the passenger seat and cocked the cap over one eye. 'Garda Rosie O'Shea. Nice ring to it.'

He'd sat in the driving seat beside her and turned the engine on. 'They'd never let you into the guards.' That got him another shoulder punch. 'I'll have to report some police brutality?' He glanced at her, smiling. 'Right so, Operation Let's Go Cheer Up Rosie O'Shea.'

He flicked the sirens and Rosie felt her heart leap out of her chest. The noise was ear-shattering and blood-curdlingly exciting. She gripped her hands on her seat belt. 'Sweet Jesus!' was about all she could manage as the car sped off at an alarming rate and just as rapidly halted at a red light.

'You don't run those?'

'This isn't the wild west, Rosie, come on.'

They settled into the drive with Rosie being a model of restraint and not pushing the many, many interesting buttons on the dashboard that were screaming 'do it' at her. They swung down into the docklands where the River Liffey met the Irish sea, surrounded by empty-looking office blocks and vast concrete carparks that stretched for miles. The car came to an abrupt stop in front of a large warehouse, a nondescript oversized shed.

Rosie grinned, feeling excited. 'Is this a drugs bust or something? I've already been in trouble with the guards, you know? I don't want any more drama. Well, maybe a little bit, probably not drugs, though—some light espionage, could you arrange that?' She was laughing at her own jokes, thankfully so was Aidan.

'No drugs, we only do drug busts on a Tuesday.' He popped his seatbelt and opened the car door, waiting for her to do likewise.

Aidan unlocked the main door and flicked on the lights. The air inside was so dusty that Rosie immediately began to sneeze. The warehouse had corridors of shipping containers piled up on top of each other forming neat lines. Aidan led the way, walking quickly, and she followed behind, marvelling at the size and breadth of the boxes that seemed to go on forever.

Her voice echoed. 'What is this place?'

'Lost and found. Some of these have fallen off tankers in the sea, there's no registration for them, so when they're retrieved they come here until we can find a home or sell the contents at auction. Down here, come on—' he turned around with a giant smile, and signalled to a corridor that snaked to the left '—we have lost luggage, which mainly comes off cruise ships.'

Piled in front of them were suitcases upon suitcases, a brick wall of travel luggage that must have been fifty cases deep and wide.

Rosie stood in awe at all these unclaimed bags 'What? Just lost? This is where they end up?'

Aidan was busy fiddling with a lock and a crowbar at one of the red containers, jemmying it apart. 'We call it limbo luggage. There she goes.' And with that the door swung open, revealing a packed honeycomb of cardboard boxes. Aidan pointed to one at the front which looked exactly like all the others, and shouted across to Rosie. 'What's in it?'

'How am I supposed to know?' She peered at it and at him. His eyes were shining and the expression on his face was set for fun, Rosie realised that this was the game. 'Ahhh, there are no clues, it's just a box. It could be anything.'

'Guess.'

'Mobile phones.'

His brow furrowed. 'Mobile phones? No way, I'm going with t-shirts.'

Rosie jumped towards the box, the anticipation bubbling inside her. She watched as Aidan took a paper cutter and sliced across the masking tape. Suddenly feeling worried, she placed her hand across his, stopping the action. 'You're allowed do this?'

His face settled into a look of calm authority as he nodded and said, 'All the lads at the station do it; we're all supposed to go through the contents and mark them into the log book in the office. Take a registration. It's okay, honestly, Rosie, I wouldn't do anything that would get you into trouble.' The look of sincerity that flashed across his face in that moment caused Rosie to trust him implicitly. The box flipped open and they both stared inside. Squeaky dog toys.

Aidan grabbed some chairs from the office and positioned them in front of the container; he also boiled the kettle, made some tea and found some chocolate biscuits. Within an hour, Rosie was wearing a fur coat from a five-star cruise liner, new tennis shoes that were three sizes too big, and had a silk kimono draped across her knees. Aidan, wearing a lab coat and a top hat, had taken on the role of a magician, pointing a tent pole at the boxes magicking their contents. They had both lost million-euro bets to one another, and a lifetime of washing-up vouchers had been exchanged. Twenty-eight boxes later, they hadn't guessed one correctly. He'd been right, Rosie hadn't thought about terrible Simon, Fergal Byrne, prison, DeLuvGuru, or the matchmaking festival for one second. She'd been wholly consumed by the surprise boxes, and the laughing magician twirling rubber chickens over a sealed cardboard box, shouting 'Superman comic books' over and over again. She felt so much happier and better about life. What a marvel the Irish guards were.

Aidan fell into the deck chair beside her, sipping his tea which, Rosie thought, must be cold by now.

'By my calculations you're four million in debt to me now, but on the flip side, I'm four-and-a-half million in debt to you.' Rosie totted up an imaginary calculator in the palm of her hand.

'You might just buy me dinner so, and we'll call it quits.' Aidan leaned over towards her, his long arms spilling out of the chair, a large smile and hopeful eyes.

Everything about him was lovely. Pure lovely. But she hadn't thought of that, like *dinner* that. Was it possible that he quite fancied her? But she made such bad decisions. There was something wrong with her decision-making process that led her to snakes and swindlers. She couldn't trust herself for one second. Rosie felt herself shrink into her chair and saw his smile falter.

'I'm sorry, Rosie, I didn't mean . . .' His voice trailed off. She watched him sit up straighter, he put his cup down on the ground with a clink. He stared at her. 'You've gone awful pale, Rosie. I'm sorry.'

Rosie's mouth was dry as she tried to explain what she knew she couldn't articulate. 'I just . . . I . . .'

Aidan shook his head and spoke softly. 'What happened to you—we see that kind of thing a lot, in different ways, but it's the same thing—men taking advantage of women. There are guys who spend all their days on dating sites taking money off women. They're the lowest of the low, and what happened to you was no different, Rosie. And if I ever meet that Simon I'd like to punch him in the nose for upsetting you.'

Rosie felt a shiver run through her. She suddenly felt small and fragile and exposed, and she didn't want to feel any of those things, or to be seen in that way at all.

'And I know we don't know each other very well, but I'd hate to think what he did to you could change you at all, because I think you're deadly, you know, just the way you are. You're dead sound, and you're easy to look at.' His eyes were fixed on his knees, his hands awkwardly clasped as he struggled for words that weren't a natural fit for him. 'So, whenever you're ready, like whenever, and if you want to of course, I'll buy you dinner.'

'Somewhere fancy?' she practically sobbed, half-laughing half-crying, touched at the honesty of this most unexpected declaration.

'Wherever you want.'

'I won't want fancy.' She took a deep breath. 'And it's not you . . . That sounds like a line, doesn't it? But how can I trust myself after letting someone like him into my life?' Rosie could practically hear her granny's voice in her head, *We all make mistakes, don't let one mistake define your life.* She smiled at Aidan. 'Thank you for bringing me here, and thank you for saying that, and I would very much like to go for dinner with you one day. Does that sound okay?'

He whooped loudly and solidly, and it bounced around the concrete floor of the warehouse. 'Rosie O'Shea, you've made me a very happy man. I'm bloody delighted, and I'll wait as long as you need.'

'Would you visit me in prison?' Rosie watched as the air slowly leaked out of Aidan. 'Sorry, that was a bad joke.'

She bit into a chocolate biscuit, thinking how she had ruined the moment, but it was really only half a joke.

31

Molly

MOLLY APPEARED, SWAMPED IN A DRESSING GOWN, HER EYES red and face puffy. Six days into her now prolonged stay at Ballyhay, and if anything, she felt worse than before. She flicked the kettle and through a series of sighs made a mug of tea and some toast. She plonked herself at the kitchen table and started to scroll through some news sites on her mam's tablet.

Rosie's face appeared and vibrated with a Skype call-in.

'It's you? You look awful. Maybe it's the reception. No. It's you.'

'Thank you, sister dearest. Seriously?'

Molly unfolded herself over the tablet and slurped her tea loudly.

'Seriously?' Rosie eyed her with disdain through the screen.

'My husband's having an affair!' Molly wailed.

'I know.' Rosie issued a curt response. 'And he's been calling me, by the way. I don't know what to say to him. I said I hadn't spoken to you, but he knew I was lying.'

'He's been sleeping with another woman. Did he mention that?'

Rosie ignored her. 'Is Mam there?'

'She's out with the boys. What time is your meeting with Fergal Byrne?'

'This afternoon.' And then as if an idea suddenly occurred to her, Rosie's voice rose in excitement. 'Hey, what are you up to today?'

'Well, you know my husband is having an affair so . . .'

'You said that.'

'Can you even imagine how that feels? Tansey. What kind of a name is Tansey? She's not even that attractive, I found her on Instagram. She's all motivational quotes and food pics; she did that celery juice fad last year, like so old school.' Molly picked up her mug of tea in both hands and stifled a sob.

'Come on.'

'An affair, Rosie.'

'So what. That doesn't suddenly give you the right to drink your tea with that disgusting slurp. We all have our problems, Molly, but we maintain basic human decency, it's all that separates us from the animals, our ability to sip tea nicely. Just watch.' She positioned a mug to her lip, raised her little finger all hoity-toity and sipped in an exaggerated ladylike fashion. 'See. Not an animal.'

'You're not being very sympathetic.' Molly crossed her arms and raised her chin ready for a duel.

'Of course I am. It's terrible, but I have an ex on the run from the police, a company folding due to fraud, which I may or may not be liable for, and there's prison looming over me. I owe a shitload of money to people who trusted me and I think the only way to get out of this hellhole I'm in is to organise some kind of giant party to make amends, which was your idea by the way. And on that, you need to bear in mind the only thing I've ever organised before was a skipathon in sixth class that ended up owing the school two-hundred-and-fifty euro when Rachel Brady threw her skipping rope through a window and broke it. And then I'm hoping with the help of my granny, who is great but is an old lady, to match all of these people and watch them fall in love. Because if they don't fall in love, I really, really think I'm going to lose it altogether, because all of this, and all of that—whatever that was with Simon—will have been for nothing. And I will be the biggest idiot God ever put on this planet and I won't have it, I won't, I won't.' Rosie would not cry, nope, she would not.

Molly sat up tall in her seat. 'Oh, right so. You've got some stuff going on.'

'You could say that, yes.'

Molly pouted in a self-mocking way and smoothed her hair down. 'Your husband's not having an affair, right?'

'No, you've got that extra-marital stuff all sown up.' She smiled at her sister and said, 'I was sleeping with a man who was actually a Jason Bourne, so that's nice for me.'

'Hmm, he wasn't actually Jason Bourne, though. I mean Jason Bourne would have been cool. You would like to sleep with Jason Bourne. We all would. Simon was more like a low-rent, petty criminal with two passports. More of a pickpocket Oliver Twist Fagin-type than an international man of mystery.'

'Not even like an interesting magician pickpocket who would slip your watch off your wrist without you knowing?'

'No, more like those gypsies who throw a baby at you to catch and then steal your wallet.'

They started to laugh.

'That was my kind of boyfriend for a few months, a baby-thrower pickpocket. I win the dating stories.'

'I'm so proud of you, Rosie.'

'And I'm proud of you, cheated-on mother of two.' She grinned from ear to ear. 'So, what are you up to because, Molly, I really need help?'

'I'm mainly moping around the house and drinking tea, and after lunch I'll eat caramel swirl ice-cream.'

'Right. That's sorted then, you're going to help me. I need someone on the ground. Mam is all over the place whenever I try to get her to lend a hand. Do you think she's okay?'

'I don't know. Honestly, I haven't been watching out for her much. She does seem distracted, but nothing I can put my finger on. I'll try to keep a better eye on her.'

'Cool, maybe it's nothing, I'm not sure.' Molly watched Rosie's eyes narrow, contemplating something. 'Okay, do you think you can help me?'

'How can I help you? All I do is push a buggy and wipe up snot all day.'

'You're hired. Seriously, Mols, there're eight days to go. I'm going to email you a to-do list that I got from a guy at work, Mark, who finally sent me his party-planner spreadsheet, dropped it off to my flat himself on a memory stick—blood from a stone, know what I mean?'

'No. I don't know what you're talking about.'

'Just start scratching items off, work through it. Top of the list, though, is an appointment in the council's office in town at 11 a.m. today. We have to get a temporary party permit for Mickey Kelly's field, it's the one next to McCarthy's. I've scheduled a meeting with some planner, Roisin somebody, and a councillor.'

Molly was suddenly paying attention, the beads of perspiration visible on her brow. 'Are you crazy? I can't do that.'

'Of course, you can. The form has already been lodged, someone just needs to be the festival's representative.'

Molly folded her arms across her chest. 'No way.'

'Just do it. I have to go. Look at that, I'm losing reception, the screen's frozen. No. No. You're gone. C'mon, Molly, I need your help. Come on. Email coming through. Byeeeeeeee.'

Molly didn't have a chance to say no again. But she wanted to. Sweet Lord, she wanted to. She couldn't just go to a meeting with people. She hadn't spoken to *people* about non-child related things since well before she'd had actual children. Which was around the time she lost her *actual* brain. No! She couldn't do it. Plain and simple. She hit the Skype button, calling Rosie back. How dare she anyway? Not only was she grieving her marriage, but she just wasn't capable. Didn't Rosie know that? Molly wasn't capable of doing anything except being a mum. Oh God, that seemed depressing. Surely she could do more than that?

She looked at the clock, she had forty minutes to shake herself together. To be useful. She quickly hopped into a hot shower. Praying the magic of steam would blitz her puffy eyes into some semblance of normal. After her shower, Molly flew to her mam's wardrobe, flinging the doors open and rifling through the dresses like she was on that TV game show, *Supermarket Sweep*, with only moments to go before check-out. So many of the dresses were brand new with their tags still swinging off them. They hadn't been worn, but then, she wondered, as a long, red-velvet evening dress flew by with a tag still in place, where would her mother be going in that? Molly found a neat, black dress, long-sleeved, and knee-length with a thin, leather belt at the waist. She paused before putting on make-up, unsure what people wore to meetings, but given her patchy, dry skin that had been through the wringer in recent days, she decided to go wedding-level: two layers of foundation, highlighter, a strong eye, lipliner and a bold lip colour. Her mam had enough make-up to rival a department store. Next, she examined her mam's shoe collection, many still in their boxes. Molly hadn't worn heels in so long she was one wobble away from a fracture, and she shouty-argued with herself over not sliding into a pair of runners.

'You are bloody useful, and you are not useful in runners, even though they are so comfortable!' she screamed at herself in the mirror, amazed to see this heavily made-up professional blinking back at her. With her short, pixie, blonde hair and Mam's sharp dress, she looked, well, even she had to admit it, she looked fantastic. If she didn't know she was a fake, she'd be fooled. Molly looked like she meant business, that she knew what business was. The uniform is half the battle she reminded herself, and it somehow made her feel powerful. Was that possible? No, maybe not powerful but just a little bit confident. She texted her mam, jumped into her car and fired Rosie off a quick text.

I hate you.

An hour later, Molly had swapped numbers with Roisin, the council planner, promising free VIP passes to the festival for her two sisters and had secured a permit in record-breaking time. It was easy. People were just people. And a meeting was just people in a meeting. She didn't know why this was a revelation to her, but it was. She hadn't mentioned her kids once, or exhaustion, or rice crackers and baby wipes. Molly couldn't hide her smile. She was delighted. She had done it. And there was more to do. As the adrenaline raced through her, she walked straight across the road to Elizabeth's Café, ordered a double espresso and sat down with a pen, paper and her phone. She opened up Rosie's email and scanned the attached spreadsheet through to point number two which had something to do with portaloos. Molly could feel her head start to bubble. She had ideas. She rang Rosie.

'We need to paint the place, jazz it up—it's so tired looking. It wouldn't take much. That bloody oak-coloured furniture, if I painted those stools white they'd look ten times better.'

'We've eight days and no money.'

'I'm fierce handy at making pompoms. You'd be amazed what they can do to a room.'

'Let's pompom the shit out of it.'

By two o'clock, she'd ordered paint and brushes to be delivered to the pub and was sketching out a design for a poster to go up around town. Her artistic eye was still a well-trained one from university, and she decided to steer clear from the green accent colours of DeLuvGuru's brand. Better to not remind people she thought, so she went for bright yellows and red.

The community had to get on board with Rosie's festival for it to work. It had to become *their* festival, Ballyhay's festival. *Their* festival she caught herself saying—she was really part of it now, too. She texted Rosie: *It should be called The Ballyhay Matchmaking Festival*, knowing that DeLuvGuru now seemed very tainted. On the poster Molly promised: *Lots of love, happy dancing, music to sing along to and fun with like-minded people.* She wasn't quite sure if it sounded a little like a kids' party, but the clock was ticking so perfection could wait. She did add the tagline—*Matchmaking included by the incredible Evie McCarthy: 'I've never met a person I couldn't match.'*

And then decided to put in small print, because she knew that claim wasn't true; there were plenty of people her granny couldn't match: *We can't guarantee you'll find love, because that's life, but we're sure that the odds are with you here.* Which was maybe a bit too much gladiator style, fighting to the death in the Colosseum, but it would have to do.

She put in a quick call to her mam to check on the boys and to ask if she could paint the furniture and repaint the front of the pub. Yvonne was all-in and said yes to everything. A few hours later, Molly decamped to the pub to use the computer in the office and stop working off her phone, which was hopping. She'd had to switch to hands-free because the phone was burning the side of her face. She'd even loved all that radiation seeping into her. It meant she was busy. She was making decisions that were not snack or nap-related and it felt marvellous.

Molly hired a local painter for the pub. She'd given him clear instructions and a fistful of stencils she'd fashioned herself to do the job on the outside. She'd forgotten she had a talent for creating beautiful spaces and art. But there it was, still alive. She knew instinctively how to make things look cosier, cleaner and more attractive.

Down to number six on the list—entertainment, music? And so Molly trawled the internet and found three bands who were willing to play in a field in Ballyhay with a week's notice. They weren't going to be world class acts; no, Bono's throne was safe. There was a group who had played in the pub recently with a lead singer who danced in leotards and had fifty-thousand listeners on Spotify, a local band 'The Ballyhay Trad Band' that was worryingly geriatric and didn't look strong enough to lift a fiddle let alone play it, but had been beside themselves with excitement at the prospect of playing at McCarthy's. So, there you go, Glastonbury it ain't. But they all agreed to play for pints not cash, so that was good enough for Molly.

Sitting in the back office of the pub, which was actually a cloakroom lined with cardboard boxes balancing on cardboard boxes, working off a miniature desk, her Mam brought in a cup of tea.

'Thanks Mam. Boys okay?'

'They're watching those pigs on TV out the front. We've an hour until we open, so you might want to start finishing up whatever you're working on to bring them back home? If that's okay? Is there anything I can do?' Yvonne surveyed the busy workstation. 'My dress looks well on you, by the way.'

'Thanks. No, it's fine, I'm just ticking off the list, I've got this.' Molly looked up smiling, she jabbed her pen in the air. 'You know, you've loads of clothes in your wardrobe with the tags still on.'

'They're from eBay,' Yvonne offered smoothly, and then a more worried tone crept into her voice. 'How are you paying for all of this, darling? The painting, the bands, the portaloos . . . it's just I can't—'

Molly cut her off. 'Credit card. Dommo and I have an emergency card for if the kids get sick. I mean, I probably shouldn't use it, but I guess this is an emergency, and the pub can pay me back after the event.'

Molly watched her mam stumble backwards and hold onto the wall of cardboard boxes for support.

'You can't be doing that. No.'

'It's okay, Mam. It's just a credit card.'

'No, it's not. There's no such thing as just a credit card. There's no such thing as just a little bit of debt.'

'You okay, Mam?'

'I haven't taught you girls anything, have I?'

'Ah, Mam, would you stop? You're great and you've done so well for yourself on your own since you and dad split. The pub is going great.'

Yvonne made a groaning noise in response and ran her fingers through her hair. 'I don't want you to make the same mistakes I've made.'

'What do you mean?' Molly was only half listening, racing through the unchecked list in her head.

'Just stay away from credit cards. They have very high interest rates.' Yvonne scratched the back of her neck anxiously.

'I mean it, they're bad news.' Distractedly she left the office, leaving the door swinging wide open behind her.

Rosie is right, Mam is all over the place, Molly thought. But she didn't have time to think about her right now, she had to find someone to build a stage in a field, distribute posters and build a marquee. Easy. She was pumped and she was fine. She wasn't thinking about Dommo and the twenty-four missed calls and messages from him on her phone. Nope. She wasn't thinking about him one bit.

32

Yvonne

YVONNE COULDN'T BELIEVE THE PUB. THE PAINT WAS STILL wet out front. It was now a bright yellow, with a scattering of love hearts shooting off from the front door, *like it's blowing a kiss* is how Molly described it. Maybe, she thought, maybe, or it just looks like red hearts on yellow paint. It was definitely fresh and different for the town. Her flower boxes, full of riotously coloured dahlias and begonias, really came to life against the yellow, too. There were flags out the front. Where had they even found flag poles? Flags with McCarthy's emblazoned on them and more love hearts blowing kisses or whatever it was they were doing. The McCarthy Matchmakers. The girls had renamed the pub. Yvonne wasn't quite sure if you were legally allowed to just put up a new name on a whim. She didn't think so, but it was only for a few nights, so what odds. They could always paint over it if anyone objected, but she doubted they would. There was a notable buzz around the town about the matchmaking festival. Word had got around, and everyone had an opinion—it was either great for the town or a money-making scam for those McCarthy's and their witch-craft, depending on which side of the river you stood. And then something surprising happened. Molly was out the back furiously sweeping the patio, Evie was in the snug poring over some of Rosie's DeLuvGuru photos of people ready for matching and Yvonne was straightening out the bar when a McCarthy's regular, John Henderson aka Gianni Versace sauntered in belly first, hitching up his jeans as he walked.

'We understand you may be needing some help.'

Yvonne stepped away from cleaning a table, a spray bottle in her hand.

He gestured with his head to the door. 'Me and some of the lads were thinking with the big festival coming up you might need some help around the place?'

'Well, yes, there're all kinds of things going on. But are you sure? Would you like to help?' Yvonne felt more confused by John's gesture than anything else. It felt out of character.

'Yes, we would. You and your mother have been nothing but good to the lot of us, we know your doors are always open, and if we didn't have a penny in our pocket you'd still feed and water us all. That's just who you are. So, we agreed we'd like to do what we can. It mightn't be much now, we're all ancient, but Ted Feeley's with us and he was a window cleaner, so he'll be good for that, and sure I can use a sweeping brush and Anne Maloney is good in the kitchen, though for washing up not cooking, mind.'

Yvonne's hand went to her chest and landed on her heart. 'Are they here?'

She followed him out the door, and there gracing the foot-path in front of the pub were the happy smiling faces of maybe a dozen Ballyhay folks, with sleeves rolled up and sporting good work shoes, and they erupted into a spontaneous roar of 'cheers' as she appeared.

'Told ya.' John's shoulder nudged hers. 'So, what'll we do?'

Yvonne swallowed hard. She was deeply touched by the generousity of her community. 'What are you all doing here?'

'We're here to help—she's an awful idiot!' John bellowed at the group to rapturous laughter.

'Thank you so much. Thank you.' Yvonne scanned the faces and said, 'Molly's out the back and she's got a to-do list as long as your arm.' She felt the air being sucked out of her. 'I can't quite believe this.'

And one by one, they filed past her, heading for the beer garden and to Molly who doled out tasks to the volunteers to make certain that Ballyhay's one and only matchmaking festival was going to be wonderful. As they passed Yvonne, some squeezed her arm or embraced her fully and whispered words into her ears.

'I'd never have met my husband if it wasn't for your mother. This is the least I can do.'

'I knew your dad, a great man.'

'About time someone did something like this for our town.'

'This town owes you McCarthys a great deal. It's an honour.'

Yvonne could scarcely catch her breath. Their kindness was overwhelmingly beautiful. The simplicity of helping each other was startling, and she was deeply moved. How truly lucky she was to have found her way back to Ballyhay and how she was going to miss this life.

The American couple had put an offer down on the table earlier that day. Herself and Lukas had agreed it was good. Yvonne had tried very hard to hide her emotions. Her debts were insurmountable. It wasn't just the revenue, it was the credit cards, the bank loans, the outstanding bills. Lukas had run every possible scenario, but the numbers didn't lie. Her only option was to sell the pub or her house, which would leave her homeless and with a business that was spiralling into debt. Yvonne had run the place into the ground; there was no way out. She felt hollow. Her stupid mistakes one after the other had piled up. For the first time in her life she was fully responsible for herself. She was fifty-five years of age, and she had nowhere to run; no husband to cushion the blow or bail her out. She had messed up all by herself. Oh regrets, they zoomed around her head: she should have listened, she should have taken that financial responsibility course Brandon had asked her to take, she should have stopped shopping for things she didn't need.

The previous night, while smearing on her cleanser, she stared at the expensive tub, remembering the promises the sales girl had whispered when she'd bought it: plump, revitalised skin. She'd bought two, four hundred euro they'd cost her. Even though she had a tax bill, and her first credit card had been declined, she'd persisted. She watched in the mirror as her fingers moved the creamy lotion around her face and reached for a cotton ball.

'What were you thinking, Yvonne? You've made a right mess of everything.' Her hand trembled as she started to remove the cleanser. 'You've thrown it all away, Yvonne, for what?' And then the tears started to fall, hot and angry at first as she swiped vigorously at her cheeks, and then she was over-whelmed by helpless sobs. Her body shook and her legs felt too weak to support her weight any longer. She slid to the floor, the bathroom mat curling into her side. All of it flashed in front of her: her ache for the pub. She would miss the life that belonged to McCarthy's: the echoes of her dad, the memories of her childhood. Lying on the hard tiles curled into the foetal position, she rocked and sobbed and wailed. She hated herself. Devastated. She was devastated. Not to mention scared of how she would tell her mother.

Molly was clearly not as taken aback as Yvonne, in fact it was as if she had been waiting for an army of willing people to appear and was fully prepared to administer tasks with mili-tary precision. Within moments, what seemed like half the village of Ballyhay were brandishing tools scrubbing, sawing, cleaning and polishing. Molly flitted between them offering words of encouragement and frighteningly clear instructions.

Amazed, Yvonne decided to take herself to the kitchen. Working people were hungry people. She would cook some snacks and insist everyone take a break in a while. The kitchen was stuffed to the gills with food. Yvonne had been delighted to be asked by her daughters to do the catering for the festival. When she'd asked exactly what they meant by *do the catering*, in that bossy tone they both seemed to have adopted recently, they'd shrugged and said, 'You figure it out, Mam.'

'How many people are we?'

Molly had blown air out of her cheeks. 'We can fit three hundred in the pub and then there's the beer garden . . . Don't forget we have Mickey's field, too.'

'So, what am I supposed to do? Five hundred sausage rolls? Just click my fingers like that?'

'Sounds perfect, Mam, and some of that chicken and mushroom pie, I love that. Sorry, can't stop, the portaloos are arriving.' Flit, flit, run, run, Molly was gone, and Yvonne had found herself boiling the kettle once again, stewing the tea bags and scanning through cookbooks. The internet told her she needed hold-in-the-hand party food when catering for a festival crowd. Food like chips wrapped in paper cones, Mexican tortillas, mini burgers, pulled pork sliders, ribs. The list of possibilities were endless and the clock was ticking, but the evil voices in her head loved nothing more than when she tried to embark on something new. *Remember, Yvonne, you're no good at this. Just setting yourself up to fail once again. Digging yourself an even bigger hole.*

It was crippling.

But right now, she had to shush them, she had a test audience, a hungry crowd of wonderful volunteers that she could try her festival food ideas on. She would whip up some Caesar salad pots, haloumi and veggie BBQ skewers, chicken and mango bite-sized sandwiches and chips—of course there would be chips—and maybe something with falafels. Yvonne took a deep breath, trying very hard not to think about anything except food, then straightened her apron and got to work. This would be her swansong, like on the *Titanic* when the musicians kept playing as the boat sank, or at least they had in the movie. She'd go down cooking.

33

Evie

THE BUSES STARTED ARRIVING AT MIDDAY. THE FIRST TWO were empty—well, except for a few locals back from Dublin shopping sprees. Evie had watched as Yvonne's face paled and she'd retreated to the pub kitchen to glaze the pastry on mini-vegetarian pies.

By two o'clock, in spite of the locals milling around the lounge, the pub felt cavernous. The flags flapping in the wind, the yellow walls, the bunting draped around the beer garden, the insane amount of pom poms hanging from anything that drooped slightly, the pristine scent of furniture polish all seemed to be mocking them. Not to mention the five hundred sausage rolls.

Rosie had arrived in Ballyhay two days before the festival, herself and Molly had stomped around the pub arm-in-arm shouting congratulations. Hip-bumping and slapping each other on the backside, snapping photos and squealing in delight.

Their celebrations had felt premature even then, and now as they gazed around the empty pub, their boastful cries seemed pitiful.

'They'll come.' Molly was pacing, checking and rechecking her phone. She'd left the boys with Lukas's wife Esmeralda for the day, who was planning to teach them to count to ten in Portuguese, overload them with sugar and spoil them rotten. 'I mean, it's still all over Twitter. They'll come.'

Pacing in the opposite direction, Rosie seemed even more worried. 'Am I too young to have a heart attack? Am I? Eugh, that Richard92 is still in my Insta feed. *One pathetic festival won't make up for empty promises. Rosie should rot.* Get lost Richard92!' she screamed at her phone.

'What a horrible man,' Molly agreed.

'He's as persistent as Dommo.' Rosie eyed her sister and said, 'Would you call him for God's sake? I can't go on ignoring him. Four times already this morning.' Her phone buzzed and jumped in her hand. 'Richard92, get a life would you? As if I haven't been through enough already.'

'Come on, come with me for a walk around, Rosie.' Sensing her despair, Evie offered her an elbow, which she dutifully looped. They headed out and into the back field.

'We're blessed with the weather.' Evie held her face to the sunshine, a September Saturday that felt like June. Blue skies reigned above them, and fluffy white clouds danced accordingly. Mickey Kelly's field had been transformed. A large stage, built by Mickey's carpenter brother with the help of YouTube, stood proudly on top of the upward slanting field. A band were setting up, cables and instruments flying every which way. A marquee tent anchored the space, and food and drinks would be served here along with, Evie had been informed, a chillout zone, with chill music. The Ballyhay locals were wearing high vis vests with *Need Help?* written across them. An ice-cream van was parked up at the gate. Some small market stalls were dotted around the perimeter of the field; there was a balloon artist, a face painter, a make-your-own floral headband stand and someone selling soy candles and leather key rings. An eclectic mix that Molly had managed to bundle together at the last minute. The proprietors dusted down the dust-free surfaces and drummed their fingers impatiently, wondering if anyone was going to turn up to a matchmaking festival in Ballyhay, or if they should shut up shop and go home.

'What a marvellous job you and Molly have done.' Evie was genuinely amazed at their ingenuity. The place was sorely lacking in customers, no doubt about that, but it was early still and Evie had learned one thing, having been in the pub trade for so many years: Irish people never wanted to be the first to arrive at a party or the first to leave. Things needed to warm up slightly before they'd show their faces. 'It'll be a great day.'

'If anyone turns up.' Rosie chewed on her fingernails. 'I mean some people will show—they have to, don't they? Gran, what if they don't?'

'They'll show. And some people will fall in love.'

Rosie squeezed her granny's arm tighter. 'Oh, I hope so, I really, really do. I hope there's a gorgeous man for me, too. I think I'm ready for my next relationship, it's been long enough now. Aidan's coming. Remember the guard, Gran, the one who came to the house? He's very nice. A really sound guy, not at all like Simon. He asked me out for dinner, but I said I was taking my time, but maybe I've taken enough time now?'

Evie sealed her lips closed with restraint, but somehow couldn't stop her head from shaking from side to side.

'What? You don't like him?' Rosie sounded puzzled.

'Of course, I do. He seems a lovely lad.'

'Are we a match, do you think? I like him. I think we could have potential. And he's so nice—he'd never try and steal my money. Did you see all the whizzy lights and stars for us?' Her voice peaked with excitement.

Evie sighed. What could she say? *The Truth*. The words popped into her mind's eye, whispered by someone, Michael probably, he did that sometimes. Kept her on track. 'He's not for you, love.'

'What?' Rosie squeaked in surprise. 'No. Wow, that's surprising. Are you sure? Really?'

'Really.'

She paused and looked straight into her granny's eyes. 'Well, if it's not him, who is it then? Who else is coming for me?'

'No one, not for you. Darling, you need to be on your own for a while.' *A long while*, Evie thought. Rosie needed to grow. She needed to experience life on her own and discover her own strength. She might find someone later, after she'd found herself. But right now, she was only a fraction of the person she could be and emptying herself into another relationship wouldn't allow her to blossom. And she would blossom, Evie could see that a rich tapestry lay in front of her with experiences she couldn't even imagine just yet. There would be highs and more lows, but Rosie would find her true character, and she would know herself. And then, maybe, she would be ready to share herself.

'Like a few weeks?' Rosie sounded crestfallen.

'Trust me, there are a lot of other excitements in life for you. They don't all come in a boyfriend package. Look what you've done here.' Evie stretched her arms out. 'Just see what you can achieve. You and Molly did this. No boyfriend helped you. You're more than capable on your own. You don't need anyone to back you up. You're brilliant the way you are.' Evie hoped she was instilling enough confidence in Rosie, she lacked so much in that area.

'We have done a good job, haven't we? Maybe I don't need to get tangled up in anything right now? Maybe you're right, Gran.' She squeezed her granny's arm and Evie exhaled a sigh of relief. It seemed Rosie had listened.

Evie spied a woman perched at one of the market stalls—a blonde woman with red fingernails and red lipstick sitting at a table decorated with headscarfs with a makeshift sign overhead: *Fortune Teller.* She started to walk in her direction until Rosie pulled her back, staring at her screen.

She shouted, 'Isabelle Love just Insta storied!'

'I don't know what that is?'

'It's huge! She's on her way. She tagged us in a post—she has one hundred thousand followers. She's coming, and I quote, *to find love.*' Rosie's eyes were on stalks. 'We're on.' She started jumping up and down. Her phone buzzed again. 'It's the bus driver, he's got a full bus. They're coming, it's on.'

'Go tell Yvonne and Molly. Put them out of their misery. Run, child, run.'

Rosie didn't need to be told twice, she took off like a hare.

Before she knew how she got there, Evie found herself sitting on a red plastic chair opposite the fortune teller, studying her face and watching as the breeze caught wisps of her hair and blew it like a moving crown of Medusa's snakes. She beamed, clearly delighted to have some company.

She spoke with a thick Dublin accent, lyrical and fast. 'I didn't think anyone was going to turn up here all day. I was going to go in for a drink, see if I'd any luck at the bar, shut down shop and see if there's any good-looking fellas inside.' She winked at Evie. 'Sure, you never know. That's what I was thinking, maybe no one's out here, they're all at the bar.'

She took some tarot cards into her hands and started to shuffle them. Evie never said a word. 'It'll be a great party, though, won't it? And in Ballyhay of all places. It's really put it on the map.' She smiled happily, handing the cards to Evie, and as she did their hands gently brushed and there was a jolt between them. She centred herself on her seat and narrowed her eyes on Evie. 'Oh, you don't want your fortune told. You already know it. You've a question for me.'

Evie nodded and felt the cards in her hands that were so like her own cards, heavy with the weight of the hands that had come before. *Was she going to die?* She didn't want to. She wasn't ready. With a heavy sigh she pulled the first card off the top of the pack and laid it on the table. The fortune teller waited a moment, her hand hovering over it before flipping the card. And there he was. He never failed to appear. Death.

Evie tapped the card, her pink coral nail clicking loudly. She raised her eyebrows and looked at the fortune teller who nodded at her in agreement.

'I know what you think that is.' She wagged her finger at her. 'I think you're wrong. That card doesn't have to mean death. It can. But it's a card that can also signify great change in a person's life. It's literally saying goodbye to the way things were, their old life has died, and there's a new one awaiting them. After death, comes a birth. The circle of life.'

Evie drank it in. Was this possible? Had she been wrong? Could she have misinterpreted the cards so completely? It wasn't a science, she knew that. 'I've had this card again and again,' she explained, 'and there've been other signs, coming at me, messages. I see them all the time.'

'What this card is saying to you, what the messages are letting you know, is that great change is coming, in fact your life is going to be unrecognisable a year from now.'

Evie read her face. She was telling the truth, or at least what she believed to be true.

'I got this card just before I got pregnant with my son. I definitely said goodbye to my old life then. Something big and new might be just around the corner for you.' She smiled happily. 'Maybe there's a nice fella here for you today.'

Evie felt confused. 'I never thought of it like that, I thought it was the end.'

'It can be, but it can also be a beginning.'

Evie laughed. She felt lighter. She'd have to think about this interpretation, but she had to wonder if she'd put a shadow over herself that didn't need to be there. Even at her age, life continued to be a mystery.

And the crowd arrived and they kept coming. A few hours later there was a queue out the door of Evie's snug. Molly had told her it was snaking around the front of the pub, but not to rush, there was *craic* to be had in the queue—it was a social event in itself, with everyone chatting to each other as they waited. A few people had actually coupled off and gone to the bar together. Evie wouldn't rush anyway; everyone needed the right amount of time.

There was a beautiful energy to the pub and to the young people she was meeting. Most of them were in their twenties. Their lives stretched out in front of them, they were doing their best to find their paths, to make sense of what was being asked of them, and they wanted to hold someone's hand and take them along. They deserved it, of course they did. Each and every soul deserved to be recognised.

Rosie had been right, the original DeLuvGuru people who had to show her their invitation before they sat in the snug were the genuine article. They were searching. Their urge for love was real and pressing. Like the tongue-tied young girl in pink, who blushed and giggled in front of her and couldn't get a word out. She'd placed her hands over the book and inhaled deeply. Evie directed her to the far corner of the pub and told her to wait there. She knew there was someone coming for her. And sure enough, three people later, an equally bashful young man, rubbed his eyes and picked his nails and she was able to send him to the girl at the bar in the pink dress.

Others were trickier. Some weren't ready or they'd drunk too much and it was too difficult to see them with the mask the alcohol had put on. There were too many people. Evie knew she wouldn't be able to match them all this way; she'd made a few matches maybe, it was hard to tell, but that might be it. She called Molly in.

'I need a break. Come with me for a walk around.'

Molly agreed and sent away the queue to quite a few grumbles.

The pub thronged with single people. It was electric. There was chemistry firing everywhere. The boys were peacocking and the girls were preening. Glances darted in all directions, smiles widened, everyone jostled for attention. The bar doors were open and people had spilled out into the beer garden and to the back field. The weather was glorious, it was a sunny September afternoon, a rare last bite of summer in autumn. The Ballyhay Trad Band had started up on the stage and a makeshift *ceili* was happening, dancers were being hastily put together with whoops of excitement and laughter. Back and forth they went, sliding up and down with a jig and a whirl to the sound of the fiddle, which was, considering the band was collectively a thousand years old, surprisingly lively. The lady in the ice-cream van was handing over vanilla, chocolate and strawberry ice-creams at a great rate, and the face-painting tent had a longer queue than the snug.

They strolled through the party. Evie admired the girls' fashionable dresses, their skirts twirling in the sun under the gaze of the boys. They didn't look so different to the girls who had spun in the gardens sixty-something years ago at the Bog dance.

The two women made their way back into the pub. Evie and Molly positioned themselves on high chairs with their backs to the bar, surveying the crowd. Watching the heads bob up and down, the laughs catching and trickling through the space, the chat was loud and boisterous. The mood heavy with excitement. Evie watched the door swing open and Karl, wearing a Panama straw hat and light pink shirt, enter. She saw him fill the room with his smile as his gaze landed on her.

He seemed to dance his way through the crowd, shuffling and side stepping playfully until he planted a kiss on her cheek.

'What a success!' He loudly congratulated Molly. 'You and Rosie must be so proud.'

'It's going so well, we can't believe it.' Molly glowed.

'This calls for a drink to celebrate, I'm sure there's champagne behind this bar somewhere. Give me a moment, ladies, to catch up with my good man Lukas and I'll be back with the bubbles.' Karl turned and headed towards the far end of the bar, trying to catch Lukas's eye.

'Oh Gran, he's one in a million.' Molly reached across and patted Evie's knee.

'There's no two ways about it, he's a very special man.' Evie couldn't hide her smile if she'd wanted to, she was always so happy to see him, so happy to be near him. She sighed contentedly, and then, after surveying the room, leaned across to Molly and whispered in her ear, 'You see the man with the red face, he's Paul the pig farmer. I'm delighted to see he's scrubbed up well. He looks very smart don't you think? Introduce him to Sonya. The *Sonya's Sofa* one.'

'The Miss Ireland one?' Molly cocked her head in the direction of a dark corner where Sonya was sitting alone, looking ethereally beautiful in an all-white summer dress, scrolling through her phone. 'I don't think a Miss Ireland would go for a pig farmer, Gran.'

'She will. Trust me. Those two are polar opposites; they've so much to learn from each other. They'll thrive under the other's spotlight. They'll fall headfirst and over heels. You'll see. They're a match clear as day. Go on now, go.'

Molly hopped off the stool and Evie watched as she approached Paul. He smoothed down the front of his trousers, his eyes flitting around the room nervously, and swiftly drained his drink as Molly spoke, smiling. He rose from the chair, looking puzzled and followed her as she weaved across the room. Evie saw how he practically turned around and retreated when Molly came to a stop at Sonya's table. Ever gracious, Molly made introductions and somehow Paul managed to pull himself together to sit opposite Sonya. She was smiling, and her face shifted and she looked natural, like all that junk she'd pumped into her face wasn't there anymore. She looked like the person she was, not the person she was trying to be. Molly walked away, and Evie could see Paul's shoulders shaking with laughter as Sonya put a hand to her mouth and giggled. The lights were there. They were a match.

Molly eased herself back onto her stool. 'I think you're right, Gran. I'd never have picked it in a million years but they both just lit up.' The biggest smile in the room now belonged to Molly, she was radiating joy, loving her new assistant match-maker role. She sipped happily on a diet coke. 'Rosie must have changed the lighting in here?'

'What's that?'

'The spotlights, Gran. Look at them. Sonya and Paul, it was like being on a stage at a concert. I could hardly see. I was blinded by it. She never told me she was going to do that. I'll have to get my sunglasses out.'

Evie took a deep breath, trying to calm herself. 'Is that so? What else do you see?'

'It's a bit of a laser-light show, Gran, do you need your glasses on to see it? The lights are just pinging around the room. I'm going to have to get behind the bar and fix that up.' She swung back to the bar and shouted, 'Lukas, can you dim the lights a bit? We'll all be blinded.'

Lukas looked up from the Guinness tap, where he was holding four glasses in one hand, beads of sweat streaming off his brow and smiled politely.

'Molly?' asked Evie. 'How do you feel?'

'Great. No, better than great. I feel so happy, Gran. I can see all these people here. I can feel the love and I can see it. I'm all warm and fuzzy about it.'

'If I asked you to pick out a couple here, who would you pick?'

'Ah, I don't know. I'm not the matchmaker, Gran, that's your job. But if we're playing a game, right—' she scanned the pub '—those two, him in the black, the handsome brooding type of guy beside the fella with the bad tan in the Wexford jersey. I'd put him with the girl with the pint of Guinness in front of her.' The young man in the Wexford top had come home from Australia two days before (their flight had been delayed twenty-four hours), bringing his Aussie mate with him for a holiday road tripping around Ireland. They spotted the signs for the festival as they were driving through Ballyhay on their way to Galway and decided to stick their heads in and see if there was any *craic* to be had. The Australian had no idea that the universe had been working hard since the day he'd met his Irish friend eighteen months before, while working on a building site in Sydney. Every morning, the Aussie had called into the local café for his breakfast and slowly a friendship had developed with the Irish barista. All the while, the universe had been laying out the paving stones for him to walk across McCarthy's bar towards the shy young girl from Ballyhay and begin a beautiful life-lasting love affair. Meanwhile, his friend in the Wexford top was blissfully unaware of the important role he was playing in his friend's life. Years from now, the Australian, on counting his blessings, will wonder how different his life might have been if he hadn't made friends with the Irish guy? If he hadn't agreed to visit Ireland, his first overseas trip? If his flight hadn't been delayed and they'd started their journey a day earlier? If they hadn't seen posters pinned to lampposts around this tiny town? If they hadn't randomly stumbled into a bright yellow pub?

'Go on. Introduce them. Don't waste a moment.' Evie nudged Molly.

Molly looked at her gran quizzically, but did what she was told. She hopped off the seat and marched up to them. Smiles, handshakes and she backed away.

Resuming her place on her stool, she grabbed Evie's hand. 'I felt it, Gran. That was . . . is that what you feel? Am I seeing what you see?'

Evie nodded. 'I never thought it was you. I thought it would be Rosie.'

'The caul baby. Not me.'

'You're going to love it, Molly. You're going to love it.' Evie could hardly believe it, all these years later, it was Molly who'd inherited the gift. It was Molly who'd get to feel the joy and hear the messages. Evie felt strangely peaceful about it all. She'd have to tell her how to block out the other voices, it had taken Evie years to work that out. It was right. It was the natural order of things. It wouldn't die with her. The matchmaking would live on in the McCarthy girls.

34

Rosie

ROSIE WAS FLAT OUT. THE INFLATABLE WRESTLING SUIT WAS deflating fast and Mickey Kelly blowing into the tube instead of using the stepper was only making matters worse. The face painter had gone off with the body glitter woman, leaving a slimy, glittery trail into the neighbour's field where one of the hay bales was rocking from side to side, and there wasn't a puff of wind out. The ice-cream van had run out of all the popular flavours and was now only selling coffee and pistachio flavoured cones.

Everything seemed to be going great. Rosie was glad she'd left her heels at home and had chosen sensible runners, because she was racing from one end of the place to the other, her phone glued to her ear.

The CRUSH mini-bus pulled up and out streamed forty of her fellow employees, blinking in the glare, possibly due to underexposure to direct sunlight as a result of working right through solar cycles. She couldn't help herself, she screamed in delight at their pale faces and hurled herself into the centre of them, hugging and kissing with wild abandon whatever cheek came near her. She even tousled Mark's curly head with affection.

'It's great to be out of the office on a Saturday.' Serious Steve looked a little nervous in the wild. His smile was a twitch and he kept crossing and recrossing his arms. 'We wanted to support you, Rosie, after how everything turned out. We felt it was the right thing to do. Asking you to take some leave—it was never personal. We wanted you to have a breather from CRUSH, to take a short break.'

Rosie felt a lump in her throat and nodded in agreement, genuinely touched. 'I know that now. I get it, I needed a break.'

Catriona swung herself around Rosie's neck laughing. 'I can't believe you did this. You? You are amazing. This is incredible.' And then whispered into her ear, 'Are you saying all these guys are single?'

'And looking for love.'

Catriona swallowed audibly. 'There's so many of them, and they look . . . I dunno, normal.'

'Some of them are so nice, too. I've been chatting away. Honestly, Catriona, you're going to have a great time. And get the waffles, they're incredible.' Her phone buzzed again, she made an apologetic face and answered it as she watched them spin off to different parts of the party. She knew her CRUSH family would be documenting the day, firing it off on their devices, but she hoped that they might look up now and again, have a go on the helter-skelter slide, eat one of her mam's sausage rolls and take a turn at making love-heart ice sculptures.

She saw his hair first, bright red catching the sunlight, standing on edge. Then she heard his laugh: loud and full bodied. He was with two other young guys with tight haircuts, flushed cheeks, dark, carefully ironed denim jeans and off-duty guard stamped on their foreheads. They were clutching pints of beer and laughing and jostling each other like they were on a school tour. Rosie watched, feeling the smile stretch across her face. He spotted her, and grinned from here to Christmas, crossing the field in half a second with two long strides. She ran to meet him, grabbed him for a hug, kissing his cheek hello.

'You got here early. I thought you had work.'

'I got one of the lads to cover my shift. I was mad keen to see it. Rosie, look what you've done, it's incredible. This is some party.' Aidan's eyes glistened.

She agreed, 'I think we might have pulled it off, it's yeah . . . I think we are hosting a festival.'

He pointed to the sky and said, 'Great weather, too.'

'Well, I'd nothing to do with that, maybe Molly did. She is running this place like a machine. She's amazing, I'm so surprised, I've never seen her like this. It suits her.'

'The trad band sound really good.'

'The auld fellas, they all drink in the pub, The Ballyhay Trad Band. I swear this is the best day of their lives. They're so happy that they won't ever leave the stage, which is grand because I think people are loving the *ceili*.' She looked down at her buzzing phone. 'Ahhh, I'm going to have to run, there's a problem in the car park at the front. Right.' She caught his blue eyes, sensing his disappointment at her running away, and said, 'I'll see you later when things have calmed down a bit. We might get a drink at the bar.'

'No bother, you're busy, I'm with the lads. We're having a great day.'

'Well, maybe I'll see you for that drink.' What a pity he wasn't going to be her next boyfriend. Maybe they could be friends; Rosie didn't have any male friends. And maybe later, Rosie wondered, maybe they'd meet years from now when they were ready. Rosie gestured towards the car park, Aidan towards his friends, and with huge smiles they waved goodbye.

She hurried towards the car park only to be interrupted by her phone buzzing once again. She should probably stick a siren on her head given the number of fires she was putting out. She didn't check the caller ID.

'Where am I needed?'

'Rose, Fergal Byrne here. I've good news. The judge has agreed to settle out of court pending some conditions, mainly that you repay the registrants' fees in full, and agree not to form another company for at least five years.'

She froze. 'It's . . . no prison, no record.'

'No, the slate will be wiped clean and you can resume your normal life.'

Liquid cement slipped through her limbs, heavy and slowly turning to a solid. 'It's over?'

'My office will be in touch to discuss a payment plan for barrister fees, because we never went to court they're consultation fees only, and we will need to sight that the registrants fees are being repaid, but yes, it's over.'

Exhale. Slowly she exhaled. 'And if Simon ever turns up?'

'There are a number of charges waiting for him. It's unlikely that he would avoid prison time. However, his whereabouts remains unknown so . . .'

Rosie felt waves of relief. 'It's really over.' She felt strangely dog tired and light as a feather in equal parts. She hadn't realised how delicately she'd been holding herself together all this time, and now she had permission to let go of it all and breathe. Just breathe. It was over.

She heard her name being called from the car park and spied a man in a high-vis vest, waving. Light-headed and feeling a little giddy she spoke, hearing a wobble in her voice, 'I'd better go. Thank you, Fergal Byrne, for everything.'

She moved towards the car-park attendant, every movement whispering to her: *It's over, you're free, it's really over.* Just like that it had ended. It was finished. Everything looked like a surreal version of itself, as if she were staring through a filter. It was over.

She found a minibus attempting a three-point turn, three centimetres away from a number of bumpers. Back and forth, moving a millimetre at a time, it was painful, like watching a beached whale trying to flap into the ocean. Quite a few lads in high-vis vests were shouting directions at the driver who was hanging out the side window, drenched in sweat. Rosie shimmied around to the front, really not sure what she could do to help this situation, her driving skills were limited to Xbox. She supposed she could stop any other cars entering the car park while the minibus driver figured it out. So, she did all the hand-signals, waving her arms in the air, insisting to the annoyed drivers behind their rolled-down windows that the carpark was closed and occasionally slapping a bonnet in affirmation.

Her phone buzzed again. Richard92, even her good news didn't stop this tormenting jerk. Well that's it, she would finally block him, it was over after all, the festival was a success and she wasn't going to jail. She didn't need to give this idiot the time of day. She clicked, there was an image attached. A photo of her with the caption, *Working the streets now.* Rosie spun around. The photo was her in this car park. He was here! She stared at her screen and walked backwards, retracing the exact angle the picture was taken from. 'Come out, come out, wherever you are.' She banged against a parked car. Slowly she turned and eyeballed the driver. He could have denied it, he could have played it cool and she'd have been none the wiser. His profile pic was an avatar, she'd never have been able to track him down. But no, coming face-to-face with his prey, Richard92 shrivelled. Brazen and confident and brandishing her screen like a weapon, Rosie tapped the driver's window. A pasty-faced teenager with ears sinking into the collar of his t-shirt reluctantly dropped it down.

'Borrow your dad's car did you, Richard92?'

A high-pitched quavering voice responded. 'I don't know what you mean?'

'Do you know how nasty that stuff is you're writing? I'm a grown-ass woman and you've made me cry.'

'I don't . . . I don't . . .' The panic was clearly washing across his face.

'There are guards here. I should call the guards. See what they can do with you.'

'Um, I just . . .' His breathing was becoming laboured.

Out of the corner of her eye, at the far side of the car park, Rosie viewed a streak of peroxide. Molly. She shouted over to her.

'It's Richard92, the troll. He's here.'

Molly threw herself across the concrete, leaping like a gazelle. 'How dare you show your face! You have been so mean to my sister.'

Richard92 started up his car engine with a splutter. Molly looked outraged. 'No, no, no. You don't get to run away.' She rammed her hand into the window just as it was rolling up. 'Ouch!' she yelped as her fingers got caught in between the window and the door. Rosie hammered on the car and yelled, 'Let down the window, you coward!' Ashen-faced and terrified, Richard92 released Molly's fingers and quickly sped off, narrowly avoiding a collision with the back of the mini bus edging out of the carpark, and burned rubber down the road.

'Good riddance!' they shouted after him.

'I got his picture. I can name and shame him.'

'My fingers hurt.' Molly cradled them in her good hand.

'Will I troll him? The hunted become the hunter.'

'Let him go. He's pathetic. Don't let him turn you into a troll.'

'You're right. I'm so much better than playing stupid games with loser boys.'

'Amen sister.'

35

Molly

MOLLY WAS SITTING IN THE PUB'S BACK OFFICE WITH HER hand in a bucket of ice. Who knew getting your fingers caught in a car window could hurt so much? Lukas had given her a brandy, a McCarthy favourite he'd called it. Good for shock. She couldn't disagree. She needed something to take the edge off, she could barely stop shaking. It had been pure instinct to protect her sister. The fury within her was wild. What a day, she mused, plunging her hand further into the bucket.

There was a gentle knock on the door. And if she hadn't already been in a state of shock she would have found her way there at the sight of Dommo and his pained face. He was frowning, his hair scraggy, he hadn't shaved, his eyes were red. He sucked his lips together, clearly not trusting himself to speak. Neither could she, she hadn't ever seen him looking so bad.

'What's wrong? Has someone died?' She jumped off the seat, leaned across the doorway and grabbed hold of him. Pushing her body into his, wrapping her arms tight around him and feeling him shudder, knowing that he was crying, shaking and sobbing in her arms. Dommo pulled her to him and leaned his face onto her neck. She shushed him and lovingly patted the back of his head, gently manoeuvring him into the titchy office. 'What's wrong? Is it your mam? Who's dead?'

He broke away from her, his face on hers, noses almost touching. 'No one's dead. Why are you saying that?' he sniffed.

'You're in Ballyhay, crying in my arms. Someone must be dead.'

'No.' He shook his head.

Molly took his hand and led him to the one and only twirly office chair, sitting him down. 'What's happened?'

'You left me. Molly, I can't, I can't even . . .' And he started crying again, deep heaving sobs.

She found a box of tissues on the bookcase and put them straight on his lap.

'I can't go to work,' he cried. 'I've just been walking around the house trying to figure out what I did wrong. Rory forgot his Paw Patrol teddy, I kept thinking he'd be so sad without it. I have it in the car, and you forgot your Clarins soap, I know you love it. I have it with me, too. I'll do anything, Molly, please. It's us, it's just the four of us. I'll do whatever you want me to do. I can't have you leave me. I can't be without you.'

Molly had not been expecting this. She'd assumed they'd fight. That they'd almost kill each other fighting, as soon as she had her energy back she'd planned to go in swinging punches. But now, here he was lying broken in her arms, begging her.

This was not her plan. This was a lot harder to tackle than windmill punches. She felt herself stiffen.

'And I know I fucked up, I know the Red Cow Inn was an almighty mistake. I know that. And the trips to the pub, like what the hell was I thinking?'

'An almighty mistake?' Molly stood up and felt herself stiffen, she could feel her hands forming fists and wondered if she'd be able to clobber him with injured fingers.

'Of course it was. A bloody huge mistake.'

She took a deep breath. 'Well, how does Tansey feel about being your almighty mistake?'

'Tansey? From work?'

Dommo looked genuinely mystified. He was shaking his head. 'What's she got to do with anything?'

'Come on, I'm no idiot, Dommo. I know you went to the Red Cow Inn with Tansey when you were supposed to be on that work conference in Cavan.' Her hands flew to her hips in defiance. Her ace card was played. He had nowhere to go.

'I did not.' He shot to his feet, the twirly seat left spinning wildly. 'Are you mad? I never went there with Tansey. Jesus, is that what you thought?'

'Of course. Why in the hell else would you go to the Red Cow Inn?'

He hung his head in shame. 'To sleep.'

Molly couldn't find the words.

Dommo rubbed his eyes. 'Remember Andy had been teething, and it had gone on for weeks, I hadn't . . . we hadn't slept. I couldn't function and I felt like a bloody liability even driving my car. I couldn't work. I made so many mistakes—I completely forgot to turn up for a presentation on network support that I was giving. I sent a company-wide email about this broadband partnership we're looking at that's completely confidential. I went live with a project that was still in test phase. That one was really bad. They're still reeling from it. Apparently it's a PR nightmare that they may never recover from. I thought I'd get fired. I deserve to. I got two warnings, Molly, in one month.'

'Why didn't you tell me?'

'You'd enough going on. How could I add incompetent-husband-soon-to-be-fired to your list.' He ran his hands through his hair. 'I was a complete mess, so I took what I thought was the easy way out. I told you there was a conference on and I booked into the Red Cow Inn for two nights, and I slept, went to work and I slept again.'

'Alone?'

'Of course, alone.'

'Did you get room service?'

'Steak and chips.'

'Bastard.'

'I'm so sorry. I'm so ashamed of myself.' Dommo had started to cry again, collapsing into the seat and burying his face in his hands.

'I'm the one who needed that. Not you. Not you.' Molly felt herself beginning to cry. She slumped against the wall. 'So, Tansey . . . ?'

'No, of course not. God, I would never. Are you insane?'

Had she concocted the whole thing in her head? Was it a misunderstanding of sorts? He had lied to her, though.

'You never had sex with Tansey?'

He shook his head. 'It wouldn't even occur to me.'

'There was a text. I saw a text on your phone, with a kiss on the end. Was that from her?' She was up again, eyeing him suspiciously.

'I don't know.' Dommo's eyes shifted, sensing that he was losing her again. 'Here take my phone, go through it. Tell me, what it is?' He rummaged in his pocket and she snatched it out of his hand, realising instantly that she knew his passcodes and it would be pretty hard to conduct an affair when your wife could just use your phone whenever she wanted. Still, though, she scrolled through.

'Aha!' Like Poirot the great detective, she found it. 'There it is, a big kiss. Explain that?'

'That's from Mary, the office manager. Her grandkids taught her all about emojis and kisses, she puts them on all her texts. She thinks she's gas.' He scrolled on. 'Here, look, the previous one has seventeen smiley faces. This is what she does. And look before that, it's all animals, it's like a farm. I don't know what that's about with the pig and the sheep.' He stared at his screen, his eyebrows wrinkled.

She believed him. That was the man she knew, not the one who had appeared in her head having weekend flings with office tramps.

'What happened to us?' Molly heard the despair in her voice.

Dommo shrugged. 'I think we stopped talking.'

'That's what Gran would say, once you stop talking it's all over.' She paused and looked at him. 'Are we over?'

'I hope not.' He fell to his knees before her. 'I'll do anything! Whatever you want. Please, let's not be done.'

'I don't want us to be over either. When I thought you were having an affair, it made sense kind of, why we were so off with each other.'

'I should have told you about work. I was just embarrassed to be such a failure.'

'Don't be embarrassed in front of me. I'm the bloody failure. I hate being a stay-at-home mum. I hate it. I don't know who I am in that role. And I'm no good at it. I'd fire me.'

'I think you're great at everything.'

'No, I'm not: the house is in shite, there's mess everywhere, paint on the walls—'

He interrupted her. 'Yeah, there's paint on the walls but it means you were painting with them, like how brilliant is that? And they're the two happiest boys because they have you as a mammy. Like, come on, they won the lotto with you and they don't even know they're the luckiest boys in the whole world.'

'Thanks,' she sniffed. 'I want to work, though, Dommo, I've realised this week. I love it. I do love the boys but I want to be away from them, too. I really do.'

'That's a great idea.' He looked up from her lap, his face now cradled in her hands.

'There's more—I don't want to live beside Angela anymore. We thought it would be a good idea, but it hasn't been. Gran said something to me and it made me think. It's all wrong. We're off balance with her because we owe her that money. She has ownership of us.'

'Ah, I don't think it's like that.'

'Don't, Dommo. I'm going to try to clear things up with her. I'm going to say sorry for using her as a babysitter. I think she does want to be a granny, she loves the boys, but she doesn't want to be a childminder. She wants the fun stuff, I get that. But we'll never pay her back like this. So—' she held a dramatic pause, not sure how the next bit would be received '—I want to sell our house.' She stared at Dommo, waiting for a reaction. 'We'll pay her back and we'll still have some money.'

He didn't say anything.

They had to get out from under their debt, they'd never have a chance to bloom otherwise. It was suffocating them.

'Let's do it, and I think you working is a great idea, because there's a good chance I'm going to get fired.'

'Seriously?'

He nodded. 'I hate IT. I only work there to pay the mortgage.'

'Let's get rid of the mortgage then, sell the house live somewhere cheaper.'

'Okay.' He shifted upwards and they found themselves in an embrace, an all-encompassing embrace of forgiveness and love and a few snuffles. 'Ballyhay is nice.'

'It is. Practically a commuter town,' she said between kisses.

'Let's talk more. Let's talk all the time.' They nodded in agreement.

'What happened to your hand?'

'It's a long story. But look, can you do a few jobs with the festival? I've only one hand now so I'm half useless.'

And before Dommo had time to wipe his eyes he was given six jobs to do, starting with refilling the cheese and onion crisp boxes.

36

Yvonne

YVONNE WAVED OFF THE LAST OF THE BUSES FOR DUBLIN from the doorway. She noticed an ache in her lower back for the first time, probably from stooping over the oven all day. What a success it had been. What a glorious day for the McCarthys. She was positively swelling with pride for her family, her girls had surprised her: industrious, hardworking, self-sufficient, wonderful daughters. They did something right, herself and Brandon, maybe they did the most important thing they could have done right. She should call him. She will call him. Now. She will call him now. Her hand slid into her pocket and she watched her fingers trace the screen. She knew that there was a long overdue conversation that she needed to have with him. She heard her breathing quicken, as the dial tone rung in her ear, willing him to pick up and not pick up at the same time.

'Yvonne? Are the girls okay?'

Her mouth was dry. 'Brandon they're glorious. I . . . I . . . wanted to tell you they . . . the festival was a great success, because of them.'

'Well, that's marvellous news.' He sounded stiff.

'We reared them well, Brandon. I want you to know that we did that right. I feel very proud of them.'

There was a long pause. Yvonne drew in a short snap of air and tried to steady herself, before saying, 'I'm sorry.'

She could hear him breathing.

'I realise now how much you tried to protect me in our marriage and I never gave you credit for it.'

'Oh, Yvonne.' There was a catch in his voice.

'I felt trapped, but you were just trying to keep me from making mistakes.'

Another pause that felt like an eternity.

'Well, you know, I . . . I regret that, too . . . I should have let you make mistakes. We could have figured things out together.'

'Probably . . . maybe . . . I don't know.'

'I'm sorry as well, Yvonne, so terribly sorry. My counsellor told me I was too controlling. I was unfair to you, I thought I was doing my best, but I wasn't.'

A beat passed between them.

'Neither was I, Brandon. We didn't do our best by each other at all, or by ourselves.' Yvonne wasn't crying. She felt strangely elated and clear-headed.

'I think we did great for a long time, and then we didn't.' There was a smile in his voice.

'I was happy. You should know that, for years, many, many years, I was happy.'

'So was I, Yvonne. We had good times.'

'We had lots of good times. And just look at those girls.'

'Our pride and joy.' Brandon's voice rose.

'I'm sorry it's taken me a long time to say this, I hope it's not too late and you can forgive me.'

'Of course, of course, and I hope you can forgive me, too,' Brandon gushed.

'Of course.' Yvonne felt calm and peaceful. She put her phone back into her pocket and smiled. That was good. Forgiveness tasted sweet. She placed her hands down onto her hips and wiggled a little trying to free up the twinge in her back.

The pub was still hopping, mainly locals now, and she checked her watch, only half an hour until closing time. Lukas had the bar under control, flicking taps and processing orders, he was happily dancing back there. The Ballyhay Trad Band removed themselves from the stage outside after a standing ovation and set themselves up indoors. Yvonne had to admit they were good; they'd great enthusiasm, although all their songs did sound remarkably similar, but then so did a lot of Irish trad music. She was no judge.

It seemed that there was no time like the present, if Brandon could forgive her, so might her mam. She steeled herself. Evie was in the snug enjoying some quiet time after such a demanding day but Yvonne knew she had to tell her now. She felt her stomach lurch. *Go, go, go,* she told herself. And *breathe, breathe, breathe.*

'Mam?' Her mother was nestled into some cushions, nursing a drink, her auburn hair curling neatly around her face, the golden light of the bar framing her beautifully. She looked positively majestic as Yvonne nervously approached her.

True to form, Evie smiled regally at her, her bright-red lips parting. 'Sit love. What a day, my dear.'

Yvonne scooted up the bench, her feet glad of the rest. 'Wasn't it? How did you go? Did you make any matches?'

Evie shook her shoulders slightly. 'Three definitely. The rest I'm not so sure of.'

'Rosie?'

'Had the time of her life. She's a born party girl that one. They all had a great time. She put her mistakes to bed.' She lifted her hand to her eye and rubbed it, sounding suddenly tired.

Yvonne mumbled, 'A new start for all of us.'

'What's that, darling?'

'Mam . . . I . . .' What are the words, Yvonne wondered? How can words explain what she had done? How she had destroyed the family business? 'I . . . I've been wanting to tell you something.' Empty, empty words.

Her mam patted the table encouragingly.

'I . . . I'm in difficulty . . . with money.' She swallowed hard, swimming now, falling into the words. Why hadn't she told her earlier? Eased her into it a bit. 'I messed up, Mam. I'm in a lot of debt, a lot. I can't run the pub. It can't run. I've messed it up. I've lost it.' Her head had found itself in her hands.

'What are you saying?'

She looked up, her mam's face creased into confusion.

'I've never been good with money, never, it just spills out of my hands, I don't know what happens to it. It should be here and it's not.'

'What?'

'I have to sell the pub, Mam.'

She watched as her mam shook her head slightly. Evie leaned forward heavily across the table. 'What are you talking about?'

'I'm so sorry, so sorry.'

'But . . . Michael . . .'

Yvonne watched as Evie rose to her feet. 'The pub . . . maybe the cards . . .' The colour drained from her face, she started to sway slightly. She lifted her hand to her forehead, trembling now.

'Mam, are you okay?' Yvonne, suddenly concerned, jumped up and pushed the table back moving closer to her. As she did Evie's legs went from under her and she collapsed onto Yvonne.

'Mam, Mam!' Yvonne shouted, crumbling under the weight of her mother, who had fallen heavily into her. Yvonne held her, watching in panic as Evie's eyes flickered and rolled back, her body shaking into a spasm—ten, fifteen, twenty seconds of tremors and then gone. The weight of a thousand bricks falling on top of her. Crushing her. Her mam lay still in her arms. 'Mam, shhh, Mam,' she whispered. And then from the top of her lungs, she yelled, 'Help, help, somebody help!'

Yvonne didn't know who called the ambulance or how much later it was until they arrived. Evie had been pried from her arms, laid out on the bench of the snug, swaddled in blankets and a cushion propped under her head. She was breathing. Someone, she doesn't know who, said it repeatedly to her, *She's breathing, she has a pulse, she's breathing.* The paramedics, a man and a woman, swooped in in bulky uniforms with efficient movements. Yvonne noticed their shoes, sturdy, walking boots. Great for going up mountains, she'd say. They used words she wasn't familiar with, clunky hard words, bending over her mam, talking to her, using soothing tones. She noticed the woman stroke her hair. She wanted to tell her to stop, her mam would hate that. It would upset the curls, but she didn't say anything, the words were strangled in her throat. They slid her onto a stretcher, it didn't look one bit comfortable. The man told her to come with them. She was her daughter. She should come. She should go in the ambulance. And then she was there, sitting in the back, holding her mam's hand, a wall of machinery and white boxes neatly labelled in front of her. The paramedic hovering, stethoscope in hand, blood pressure pump on her mam's arm.

'You can talk to her, you know. She can hear you.' The paramedic smiled kindly at her.

Yvonne didn't have breath, let alone words.

'We'll find out what happened when we get to the hospital, they'll run tests. She's stable now.' The paramedic squeezed Yvonne's shoulder.

'Will she be okay?' There they were, the words she needed answers to.

The paramedic shook her head gently and said, 'I can't say, but right now she's stable. That's good.'

'I was just talking to her. She was having a brandy, we'd had a big day, maybe too big. Too much. I forget. And then I told her some bad news ... oh Mam, I'm so sorry, I gave you such a shock.'

The ambulance came to a sudden stop, the doors were flung open, and Yvonne was guided out into the cold, dark night air as an army of people attended to her mam. She stood back and waited, and waited, and waited. A young doctor with bloodshot eyes and a fuzzy blonde ponytail that belonged to a schoolgirl asked to speak with her.

'Her heart's not returning to its natural rhythm. We need to stop it and restart it. Give it an electric jolt so it will resume normal functioning.'

'Her heart?'

'As I've explained, she's had a heart attack, but her body is not responding to the medication. We need to stop her heart and re-engage it.'

Yvonne nodded.

Her daughters were here. And Dommo. Where had they all arrived from, looking so pale and anxious? They hugged, and she melted into them, finally finding her tears. Warm, comforting arms. They sat on red plastic chairs, the four of them in a line and holding hands. Staring down the bright, white corridor with closed doors, knowing that in one of those rooms, Evie's heart was being stopped. The woman who was nothing but heart. Who had made her life about love and full hearts. Who had given her heart to her family time and time again. Was it even possible to stop a heart like that? Could a heart that full of life be put on pause?

'The boys, Molly, where are the boys?' It was as if something had snapped in Yvonne.

Dommo piped up, 'My mam flew down the motorway to watch them and bring them home from Lukas's house, they're tucked up in bed.'

'Angela, she's very kind.' Yvonne nodded. 'This is my fault, you know.'

'You gave gran a heart attack?' Molly asked confused.

'If it's anyone's fault it's mine. I asked gran to matchmake all those people,' Rosie sobbed.

'No, no, darling. It's me. If she dies, I'll never forgive myself.' Yvonne gazed sadly down the long corridor, wishing for a doctor to appear, praying for a smile. 'I've lost the pub, I need to sell it. I'd just told her and she collapsed. It's all my fault.'

Her two hands were squeezed, and shushing noises made. Molly stood up, tucking her shirt into her waistband and leaving her hands to rest on her hips.

'Enough of this, Mam, you did not cause a heart attack. I'm going to go get some tea for everyone, Gran is going to be fine, and she won't want to see you in a state when she comes through. Pull yourself together.' She spun on her heel and marched off down the corridor, following a sign for the canteen.

'She's so bossy.' Rosie shook her head miserably. 'Do you see what I've had to put up with all my life?'

'That's my wife.' Dommo smiled proudly.

'Lucky you.' Rosie eyerolled, and gently shoulder nudged him.

They froze, watching as the young doctor in green scrubs appeared with her ponytail swinging and walked towards them up the corridor. Her face was unreadable on her approach. They stood and clung to each other, monitoring her steps as she approached.

'. . . the procedure was successful . . . resting . . . moved her onto a ward . . . third floor . . . responding well . . . come visit tomorrow, 34A.'

They collapsed. Falling, with unspeakable relief, back onto the red plastic chairs. She was okay, she would be okay.

'Told you, I told you!' Rosie was almost shouting. 'I knew she'd be fine.'

The colour had returned to Dommo's cheeks as he said, 'Evie's made of strong stuff, giving us all a fright like that, I'll kill her.' His eyes glistened, and realising what he'd said, he started to laugh. The release was glorious and it was contagious. Yvonne and Rosie joined in.

Molly reappeared around a corner. 'I can't find the canteen.' She looked at their cheerful faces. 'Oh thank God, it's good news.' She squashed herself on top of them all in an elongated group hug. 'Of course, she's okay. She was always going to be okay.'

'Come on, let's go peep in the door of the ward.' Rosie bounced up, full of mischief.

'We're not supposed to.'

'Oh, come on, we're here now, we'll just peep. Five seconds.'

And so off they scrambled, not waiting another moment to be dissuaded, hurrying towards the lift and excitedly pushing the button to the third floor.

'If the matron catches us, we're dead. This is outside visiting hours. They take things like this very seriously in hospitals.' Dommo was wringing his hands.

Rosie laughed at him. 'Oooh, matron.'

'So mature, Rosie,' Molly scolded.

The lift door slid open, and instinctively they shuffled to the wall and moved as stealthily as any good spy film had taught them to. Collars up, head down. The corridor was eerily empty. Ward 34A was on their left, they pushed the door open and quietly stood just inside. There she was sleeping. Her eyes closed and a slight pink hue to her cheeks, white blanket tucked up under her chin, she looked peaceful. The relief was beautiful. Yvonne smiled and quickly linked arms with her daughters, squeezing them tightly.

'No, no, no.' A small, round woman in a white uniform with a severely shaped nose and bright red cheeks appeared hissing at them, 'No, absolutely not. Get out of here. You must respect visiting hours.' She flicked a pointed finger at the door. 'Out.'

'Sorry, sorry, sorry.' Apologetically, they shifted outside into the corridor.

She closed the door behind them and stood with hands on hips firmly in front of them. 'Let me guess, Evie McCarthy?'

'Yes, we just wanted—'

'No. She needs her rest.' She looked down her nose at them, which should have seemed difficult from her small stature. 'Her husband was here earlier, sitting at her bed, if you can believe it? I said the same thing to him. She needs her rest.'

'Her husband?'

'Mick was it? Michael? Nice man, shirt sleeves rolled up and braces. I told him to leave, same as I said to you. She's had a serious procedure and she needs her rest.' The nurse didn't notice the shocked faces on the family in front of her. 'Now, go. I have a full ward, I have better things to be doing with my time than dealing with visitors.'

Nobody moved.

'Will I call security?'

Dommo shook the others into action, whispering, 'Sorry, sorry, sorry.'

As they walked through the lobby of the hospital, Rosie turned to them and said, 'Did she say . . . ? Wasn't that . . . ? Michael?'

Somehow, they nodded and shook their heads at the same time and slowly made their way through the electric doors.

37

Evie

What a lot of fuss they were all making. Evie was fine. She felt fine. She'd be a lot better if she could just go home. She'd finished her tea ages ago and no one had come to collect the tray. The half-eaten toast and pool of milky tea in the bottom of the mug was annoying her. If she was in her own house, she could have washed the cup and cleaned it all away. Now, she had to wait for someone to collect it like she was Lady Muck. She couldn't possibly ring the bell, she didn't think it was the nurses' job to do things like move the trays anyway. They were run off their feet, poor things. They did everything, she barely saw a doctor, the nurses were fabulous altogether, so industrious and kind to all and sundry. No, she was a nuisance here to everyone, including herself, it was time she was released and sent on her way.

She'd had to hide a smile when the serious-faced young doctor with the ponytail had told her she'd had a heart attack.

She'd have had her committed if she'd noticed, the mad old woman laughing at her heart stopping. But it felt great to be proven right. She knew it, she knew it. She'd said it all along, it would be her heart that got the better of her, and she was right. Well, sort of. They'd stopped it and restarted it apparently.

'So, did I die?' Evie had wanted to know.

'Well, technically your heart stopped beating, and we had to shock the heart to restore its natural rhythm.'

Evie didn't hear the rest. *I died,* that was all she knew, *but somehow I survived. The cards had been right all along.*

Yvonne had been her first visitor, her eyes red from crying and skin blotchy.

Evie had wanted to give her the bed to crawl into, Yvonne looked worse than she was.

'I'm so sorry, Mam, I'm so sorry.' She'd hardly been able to speak for the sobs. Bundled up in her black puffa jacket, her head leaning against the bed, Yvonne finally managed to say, 'It's all my fault, I should never . . . I'm so sorry.'

'Your fault? You caused me to have a heart attack? Don't be ridiculous.' Evie took Yvonne's hand and said, 'My heart broke years ago when Michael died. Broke in two. It's been hanging by a thread since then, it was only a matter of time. And maybe now, in a way, it's been fixed.'

'But the pub, Mam, the pub . . .'

'Would you stop? I'm the one in the hospital bed, I'm the one who should be crying. It's a blessing, it's all a blessing. The pub is just bricks and mortar, that's all it is. It was great when it was great, but it's been dwindling and dying out for a long time. It should have only been a stopgap for you; you'd never have been able to make something of it, the business isn't there like it used to be. It isn't your fault, but you wanted it so badly, you were so determined.' She took a deep breath. 'You had it in your head that it was going to save you somehow, coming out of the marriage. It was never going to do that. It was just a job.'

Yvonne looked at Evie, confused. 'But it's more than a job, Mam, it's part of Dad, it's in my blood.'

'What? No. It's a pub. It was a means of making money and now it's not. Don't romanticise it, Yvonne. I used to resent the place so much for taking Michael away from me, he worked day and night, the place killed him in the end, I'm sure of it. I'll be happy to see it gone.'

'But I . . .'

'What's in your blood is totally different to your dad, he wanted to make money, he liked being the publican, the big man in charge. You, you want to keep that place open so the auld fellas have somewhere to go, so they're not lonely, so I have somewhere to be, you want to feed everyone and see smiles on their faces. You care about people, you're a good, kind woman, a marvellous daughter and a loving mother. So what if you can't run a pub? Sure, neither could I.'

Yvonne was sitting upright now, her eyes wide and startled looking. 'Mam, I've never heard you speak like this.'

Evie paused and thought for a moment. 'I should have said it a long time ago. I've been keeping my own secrets, too, haven't I?'

'And, if I sell?'

'Sell it, burn it to the ground and take off to Tahiti. Do what you want to do, not what you think you should do.'

Yvonne had nodded, caught the mascara smudges from under her eyes with her fingertips and wiped her cheeks. She smiled and said, 'I suppose I should take my jacket off, it's as hot as Tahiti in here.' She unzipped, and visibly relaxed, her shoulders loosening, colour returning to her cheeks. 'So, how are you feeling, Mam?'

'Never better. I'm eighty this year and I've been given a second chance. Life is good.'

Evie had been given a second chance. She didn't have a moment to waste. And yet here she was, three days trapped in a hospital bed, staring at a dirty mug. She could explode with the frustration. She'd so much to do. She was well rested and ready to go. Her blood pressure was normal, heart rate fine, the doctor had told her because of her age they didn't want to take any chances so would monitor her closely. But this was it, she'd been monitored long enough. She had some living to do, someone to see; she'd been given a second chance, and by God she was going to use it.

Rosie had brought her in a bag of good clothes. Her nice, green silk dress with the gold buttons, her wig with the blunt fringe that took years off her face and an absurd amount of toiletries and make-up. She'd even slipped in some false eyelashes. Evie would need to find a YouTube video on her phone showing her how to get them on right. Nothing more embarrassing than false eyelashes sliding off your eyelids and down your cheeks. Rosie was coming to pick her up in an hour, so whether or not the doctors liked it, Evie was on her way.

As soon as this tray was gone, she was going to have a shower using that nice vanilla soap wash, and pretty herself up. They would drive straight to Karl's house. And she would say yes. She would say yes to walking the next path with him, wherever that would lead them. She was not too old for love, and she was not too old to go on a six-month worldwide cruise with him. The truth was she'd go anywhere with him. As she always said to her couples; love was either there or it wasn't, and it was there with Karl. There was an abundance of it, she had just needed to listen to her heart. And her girls would be fine, they were an indomitable force. They had lived and loved and learned. They were a family, and they would always support and love each other. Now she could go. The pyramids awaited her, and hot Mediterranean sun, and Greek islands and French baguettes smothered in Camembert cheese. She would hold Karl's hand in hers, and together they would take what life put in front of them.

Epilogue

Six months later

YVONNE, ROSIE, MOLLY AND DOMMO SAT SHOULDER TO shoulder and hand in hand, occasionally giving a gentle squeeze or nudge of encouragement to each other. The bride was beautiful. Her cream dress was simple and elegant, nothing over the top, which suited a second wedding. She beamed happily, madly in love with her groom. Brandon and Patricia had chosen a small hotel for the ceremony and the reception, just sixty guests, one of which had only sent her RSVP at the very last minute. Yvonne looked beautiful, as always, wearing a bright lip colour, a muted green dress, with her hair in an elegant updo. But what was different about her today was her calmness. She was peaceful, and although she wasn't sure if she was supposed to feel this way on the marriage of her ex-husband, she felt happy.

The last six months had been tumultuous. She had sold the pub quickly, the American couple had taken over, and in a flash, McCarthy's was gone. O'Riardon's they called it, a throwback to some long-lost ancestor. They'd friendly, big toothy grins on them, and they kept Lukas on, which was nice. She's called in once or twice to wish them well, to run her hand lovingly along the bar one more time, and to say goodbye. *Closure*, her counsellor calls it. Yvonne thinks that's a very American word and couldn't they just say, *Getting on with it*? Was it rock bottom for her when she lost the pub? Maybe. It felt terrible, she knew that, but there are worse things, she also knew that. It did make her recognise that she needed help, particularly around money. Very early on, the counsellor recommended she attend an out-patient program in Dublin for addiction. Yvonne had fought every step of the way, until she couldn't fight anymore. And it had been difficult, horrible even. But she recognised the high they spoke about that she got from shopping and how she used it to chase away her feelings of loneliness or boredom. She was textbook apparently. And so, she decided she would have a textbook recovery. She was determined to get on top of her life once and for all. She hadn't shopped or reached for a credit card or browsed eBay for twelve weeks now. And with all that counselling and talking, she'd learned so much about herself. She was fifty-five years of age, and this was just the beginning.

She'd tell the girls and Dommo at the reception that she'd taken a job running the kitchen at Elizabeth's Café. Yvonne was going to create her own menu and give the venue a new feel, and maybe after a while, she would open in the evenings, too. She was taking a salary, and a cut of the profits. The

Ballyhay Trad Band had agreed to play there on a Thursday evening, and she'd agreed to feed them. She was excited.

'How's Mam doing?' Molly whispered a little too loudly to Rosie.

Yvonne reached across and tapped her on the knee. 'I'm great,' she whispered back. 'I'm happy for him, for them.'

Molly grinned and settled back into her seat, thinking that her mam, she did seem happy. It was so gracious of her to come. It must be difficult. Molly couldn't even imagine seeing Dommo marrying someone else. She linked her arm with his, and put her head on his shoulder, cuddling into him. He kissed the top of her forehead. He'd lost his job a few months back. Well, *lost it* was a bit rich really; it was still there, just someone else was doing it. He'd missed one deadline too many. He and Molly had been ready for it. They were so prepared that if it hadn't happened they might have been weirdly disappointed. They swung into action with their master plan. Their house was put on the market the next day. Dommo's payout was better than they'd expected and they were able to repay Angela. The relief was overwhelming and things started improving immediately. Angela had been thrilled to be paid back. Herself and Molly were never going to be arms-linking, dress-swapping besties, but Molly was optimistic that they would get to a better place.

They put a deposit down and bought one of the new houses off the plan in Karl's development just outside Ballyhay. It was half the price of their Dublin house. Finally, they had money in the bank. They rented a cottage outside the town and the boys were revelling in all the outdoor space: they couldn't tear Andy away from the swing set and Rory was learning to ride a bike. Molly didn't miss her Dublin life at all. She missed Anna, but she was working so much, she'd never have seen her anyway. Instead, they scheduled weekend nights out or trips away. She'd also taken a job. The hotel in the town had advertised for a wedding planner. It was a part-time job initially, but they were all hoping the role would expand into something full-time soon. She loved it. She met the couples and toured the venue with them, sampled meals, recommended music acts. She was organised and efficient. And yes, sometimes she saw it, sometimes the light of love shone between them, and sometimes it didn't. Her granny had told her it might take her some time to hone her skills.

Right now, she could see it. Her dad and Patricia, the light was circling them. There was love, there was happiness, there was a second chance for everyone.

'You can't see it?' she whispered to Dommo. 'Like, I'm literally blinded by the light off the two of them.'

'No, love, just you.' Dommo slyly checked his phone in the palm of his hand. The boys were with Angela, she'd sent a pic of them all painting, smiling. She seemed to enjoy being a visiting granny. She swooped in for day visits, bringing treats and lunches for everyone from a Dublin gourmet deli. It was grandparenting on her terms and she seemed happier. He'd found himself explaining the new norm quite a few times to her: *No, he wasn't going to work for a while; anyway, Molly was working. He was a house-husband now. He loved it. He couldn't be happier.* His mother couldn't understand, not really, but that was okay, she didn't need to. It was his family—messy, and disorganised and maybe a little bit dysfunctional, but God they were great at it.

'Can you see the light, Rosie?' Molly whispered.

'No. For the millionth time, I can't see it. I don't have your voodoo.' Rosie's dark hair was spilling over her shoulders, carefully curled loosely. She'd trawled the second-hand shops to find her dress, blue check, off the shoulder, to the knee. If it had come from CRUSH she might have called it The Adele. She had been promoted. Three months ago, she'd jumped some hurdles, cleared some hoops and tunnelled through to the light. And she got a pay rise—cha-ching! Well, truthfully she wasn't seeing any of the financial benefits; no upscaling her apartment, no weekends in Rome or Reiki massages. Instead she was on a strict (oh, so strict!) finance plan, implemented by Lukas from McCarthy's, now O'Riardon's, and overseen with razor-sharp focus by her mam. She had apps and calculators and banks and spreadsheets, and she was paying back DeLuvGuru registration fees and legal fees step-by-painful step. She'd be free of it all in eighteen months apparently. 'And you'll have learned so much from this experience.'

Her mam had seemed borderline happy that Rosie was having a financial awakening, full of backslaps and independent woman mantras. 'You'll learn what I wish I'd learned at your age, Rosie. Financial independence means you'll never have to rely on any man. It's the number one life skill to have.' Rosie had been seeing a counsellor, too. Herself and her mam put on American accents and joked about *their therapists*, but actually it had been great. She wanted to feel good after Simon, and not to make the same mistake again. She felt stronger somehow now, more equipped to make good decisions. She was single for the first time in her adult life, and it felt right. Just like Gran had said it would. She had stayed in touch with Aidan for a while, but their date never eventualised.

Last she heard he was seeing a teacher from Louth. Catriona was dating his friend, another guard. They'd met in Ballyhay, and she was uncharacteristically coy about him, but her smile spoke volumes.

'I now pronounce you husband and wife.'

Molly and Rosie quickly flashed a look at Yvonne, who was smiling happily. They relaxed and whooped and cheered with the rest of the room.

'It's a pity Gran isn't here to see this.' Rosie squeezed her mother's arm. 'She loves Dad.'

'She's happy for him, but there was no way she was going to leave the Caribbean early, wedding or no wedding.' Evie and Karl had prolonged their cruise by another six months, she'd texted that morning to say:

> I'm having the time of my life, I think you should all
> go do the same. Xx

Acknowledgements

I HAD THE STRANGEST FEELING WHEN I WAS WRITING THIS book that it was 'for someone'. That there was something written on the pages that someone needed to read. If that's you, and you are that someone, I hope I did you justice and you uncovered whatever was needed. It's also possible that I spent far too much time in Evie's shoes wondering about second sight and the otherness of it all! But there you go . . .

Many thanks to the wonderful team at Allen & Unwin: Courtney Lick, Christa Munns, Lisa White, Isabelle O'Brien, Sarah Barrett and particularly Annette Barlow for exceptionally sound editorial advice.

Thanks to Jacinta di Mase my fantastic agent. Thanks to my writing crew, Alli Sinclair, Lisa Ireland, Delwyn Jenkins, Nicki Edwards and my wonderful friend Elizabeth English.

The four main characters are named after members of my family—all incredible, awe-inspiring females—which I thought was appropriate in a book about the importance of family, sisterhood and motherhood. Thanks to Niamh and Cathy, my first readers and my favourite sisters. I don't believe I'd have ever written a book without you two and your straight-up advice. Same goes for my mum with her unwavering support and claims that I am the best writer in the entire world! And to the greatest of men, my dad and brother, Bren and Shane with much love.

When Joe and I got married, one of his wedding vows was to support me through book writing and deadlines, and, yeah, I think we managed to really work those vows as I wrote this during Covid, so: thank you Joe! Home schooling stretched all of us, but thank you to my two favourite humans, Cian and Hughie, for occasionally telling me I wasn't the worst teacher in the world.

If you are interested in attending an Irish matchmaking festival, look up matchmakerireland.com; there's one held every September in County Clare.